SWORD and SONNET

EDITED BY
AIDAN DOYLE, RACHAEL K. JONES,
& E. CATHERINE TOBLER

Cover Illustration by Vlada Monakhova

Cover Design by Holly Heisey

First Published in July 2018 by Ate Bit Bear

v 1.02

CONTENTS

Introduction   v

Words in an Unfinished Poem by A.C. Wise   1

A Subtle Fire Beneath the Skin by Hayley Stone   23

As For Peace, Call It Murder by C. S. E. Cooney   37

She Calls Down the Future in the Footprints Left Behind by Setsu Uzumé   49

Candied Sweets, Cornbread, and Black-eyed Peas by Malon Edwards   63

El Cantar de la Reina Bruja by Victoria Sandbrook   79

The Other Foot by Margo Lanagan   95

Eight-Step Kōan by Anya Ow   103

The Firefly Beast by Tony Pi   115

Her Poems Are Inked in Fears and Blood by Kira Lees   125

The Words of Our Enemies, The Words Of Our Hearts by A. Merc Rustad   133

Labyrinth, Sanctuary by A.E. Prevost   149

Heartwood, Sapwood, Spring by Suzanne J. Willis   161

The Bone Poet and God by Matt Dovey   173

And The Ghosts Sang With Her: A Tale of The Lyrist by Spencer Ellsworth   187

Dulce et Decorum by S. L. Huang   203

The Fiddler at the Heart of the World by Samantha Henderson   215

She Searches for God in the Storm Within by Khaalidah Muhammad-Ali   231

A Voice in Many Different Forms by Osahon Ize-Iyamu   245

Recite Her the Names of Pain by Cassandra Khaw   261

Siren by Alex Acks   269

This Lexicon of Bone and Feathers by Carlie St. George   287

Dark Clouds & Silver Linings by Ingrid Garcia   305

About the Editors   317
Acknowledgements   319

INTRODUCTION

Sword and Sonnet contains twenty-three fantasy and science fiction stories featuring women or non-binary battle poets. Throughout history, poems have been used as weapons in powerful and creative ways. Sappho writing in exile. Federico García Lorca and the Spanish Civil War. Langston Hughes and the Harlem Renaissance. Pablo Neruda. Maya Angelou's *Still I Rise*. The pioneers of hip hop. All the people in history whose pen was their sword, especially those from marginalized genders whose work has been lost or forgotten.

Before poet Christina Rossetti was old enough to write she had composed her first verse: "Cecilia never went to school without her gladiator." Emma Lazarus' *New Colossus* adorns the Statue of Liberty and is best known for the phrase "your tired, your poor, your huddled masses." Less commonly referenced are words from the same poem: "A mighty woman with a torch, whose flame is the imprisoned lightning." Our hope is that this anthology gathers part of that spirit.

One of the reasons poets are so often associated with revolution is that they help define how a country sees itself. Australian Dorothea Mackellar's *My Country* ("I love a sunburnt country/A land of sweeping plains,/Of ragged mountain ranges,/Of droughts and flooding rains.") José Martí's revolutionary writings were quoted by both pro and anti-Castro Cubans. C. S. E. Cooney's story in this collection is inspired by the events of Chile's military coup.

Poets have critiqued each other, as well as society. Roman poet Horace wrote *Dulce et decorum est pro patria mori*—it is sweet and fitting to die for one's country. Almost 2000 years later, British World War One soldier Wilfred Owen wrote an anti-war poem in response, a scathing critique of Horace's "old lie." S.L. Huang's *Sword and Sonnet* story references the title and ruminates on what it means to wield a weapon.

Emily Wilson became the first woman to translate Homer's *Odyssey* into English and commented that "female translators often stand at a critical distance when approaching authors who are not only male, but also deeply embedded in a canon that has for many centuries been imagined as belonging to men...Earlier translators are not as uncomfortable with the text as I am and I like that I'm uncomfortable." Cassandra Khaw's *Sword and Sonnet* story plays with the idea of modern sirens inspired by Wilson's translation. Alex Acks' future siren story includes a spaceship-devouring poet.

In his book *Venice Incognito*, James H. Johnson details the complaints of 18th century Venetian poet Carlo Gozzi, who bemoaned that modern women were emboldened by French philosophies, "filling their heads with 'fashions, frivolous inventions, rivalries in games, amusements, loves, coquetries, and all sorts of nonsense.' They have bolted from their houses, he continued, 'storming like Bacchantes, screaming out Liberty! Liberty!' while neglecting their children, servants, and household duties." Even in the 21st century, many men are intimidated by the idea of educated and free women. Suzanne J. Willis' story looks at a city where women's words are suppressed.

Kira Lees' story is set in Heian-era Japan and includes an assassin who feeds off the words of poets. Heian-era writer Sei Shōnagon was renowned for intimidating the men of court with her knowledge of poetry. Shōnagon was the author of *The Pillow Book*, one of the classics of Japanese literature. In her introduction to *The Pillow Book*, Meredith McKinney says:

"Anyone who hoped to be admired and accepted had to be deeply knowledgeable about the poetic canon, particularly the poems contained in the classic poetry collections such as *Kokinshu*, and able to weave apposite allusions to them into her or his own occasional poetry. Wittily nuanced messages, generally containing a poem, flew constantly between members of the court and some-times beyond; these in turn required a suitable extempore poem in response, written in an elegant hand on paper carefully chosen for appropriateness of color and quality, in every aspect of which one's sensibility and character would be displayed for intense scrutiny.

Although such exchanges of poetry were common throughout the court, by long tradition it was the romantic relationship that quintessentially embodied the essence of poetic exchange. A man could fall in love with a woman on the evidence of little more than her poems; a woman could decide to sever relations with a man if he demonstrated poetic obtuseness, as Sei Shōnagon several times describes herself doing in *The Pillow Book*...[She] was a masterful practitioner of the art of witty repartee and poetic exchange...and *The Pillow Book* abounds in tales of various hapless gentleman's defeat at her hands. She evidently had an astonishingly quick mind, and could cap any allusion that came her way."

Aidan once received a rejection for a story featuring a battle poet with the comment that "unsympathetic protagonists were a difficult sell" and mentioned this to S. L. Huang who remarked that she would love to read a story about a badass battle poet. The story later sold to *PodCastle*, but Aidan had the idea for an anthology of battle poet stories. Elise and Rachael joined the project and we invited a number of authors to contribute. After running a successful crowdfunding campaign, we held an open submission period. We were thrilled with the range of stories we received and hope you'll enjoy reading them as much as we did.

- Aidan, Rachael and Elise

WORDS IN AN UNFINISHED POEM

A.C. Wise

Rust-colored dirt blown in under the door coats the saloon's floor. The gunslinger occupies a corner where the amber light slanting through the tinted glass doesn't quite reach. When the door swings open, the gunslinger is the only one who doesn't raise their head. Spurs jingle on the man's boots as he crunches through the grit covering the planks. He wears a hat slouched low, greasy strands of gray-brown hair the shade of an owl's wing trailing beneath it. A belt slung around his hips holds a six shooter.

The gunslinger watches him move. There's a scrape to his step, even though he strives to keep his stance wide. The way he holds himself guards against some pain, but more than that there's something broken in him, like the jagged edge of bone against bone, but nothing so clean that it can be splinted.

As he approaches the gunslinger's table, there's a moment when the man turns his head as though he'll spit.

But instead he mumbles "Buy you a round?" his words scratching. Nothing so elegant as gin or bourbon; corn mash rough, matched by the crimson threading his eyes.

A half empty bottle already sits at the gunslinger's elbow, no glass in sight. The man fumbles his search for more words, and the barest ghost of a smile touches the gunslinger's lips.

The gunslinger watches as the man suppresses the urge to spit again, a visible thing, before he drops a clinking pouch onto the table between them. The gunslinger doesn't move—no tilt of head or hand. The man's shoulders rise, his posture a spooked cat's, bristling against something wrong.

The gunslinger is used to such. The man doesn't like them, but few people do on first meeting. This man is unsettled by what he can see—the subtle gold of their eyes, the angle of their hat, tipped low as his own. And he is unsettled more by what he cannot see, but

I

feels—an aura akin to ghosts clinging to the gunslinger. If the gunslinger were to move, the man, whose name is Emmett Tremaine, would hear the faint chime of secret metal sewn within their clothing. He wouldn't like that either. But the hurt in him runs deep enough to make him swallow his pride and take the seat across from the gunslinger.

"I hear you can kill a man with a single word," Emmett says.

There's a click in Emmett's throat, a sound of fear. He licks his lips, glancing to the bottle at the gunslinger's elbow. The gunslinger nudges it forward. Unasked, the bartender materializes with a glass then silently returns to the bar.

"Not only men," the gunslinger says. Emmett flinches, spilling whiskey as the mouth of the bottle skips across the rim of the glass. "And not just a word."

The gunslinger reaches into their pocket. Emmett's chair jumps back until he sees the movement hasn't resulted in a drawn gun. The gunslinger sets a single bullet casing in the center of the table.

All the hair on Emmett's arms, the back of his neck, and even his thighs, stands on end. There's a word etched onto the casing, the lettering scarce thicker than a spider's web. Before he can read the word, the gunslinger covers the shell with their hand, disappears it into their pocket, and smiles. It is the most unsettling expression Emmett has ever seen.

"I'm writing a poem," the gunslinger says. An explanation that sounds like a warning, a confession, and tastes of sorrow. To Emmett, it means nothing.

He shakes himself then reaches into his own pocket, hand trembling as he sets a daguerreotype on the table. It shows a seated man, a woman standing behind him with her hand on his shoulder. Her hair is braided into a crown around her head; her lips and eyes unsmiling. The man's chin and cheeks are clean-shaven, but he sports a mustache, and his hair is carefully parted and oiled. He looks nothing like the man sitting opposite the gunslinger, yet he is one and the same.

"She—" Emmett's voice breaks. He touches the photograph with one finger, nail rimed with dirt. The slouch of his hat almost hides his tears.

Emmett stands, a jerky motion. He yanks at the belt around his waist, nearly tears his trousers as he tugs them down. The tail of his shirt hides all but the end of the scar, still angry red where it streaks across Emmett's thigh. The gunslinger can guess where the scar begins. An inch to the left, and Emmett would have been unmanned in more than just spirit.

"I need her dead." Emmett speaks with his head turned, fumbling his trousers back into place, his humiliation complete. Not just want, but *need*. The gunslinger sees it, raw and ugly as Emmett's scar as he sits again and meets the gunslinger's eyes.

"Where?" the gunslinger asks.

"Foster's Creek." Emmett's shoulders hitch.

The gunslinger looks at Emmett a moment longer, their head tipped subtly as though listening to a sound only they can hear. Then the bag of coins is no longer on the table, and the gunslinger is on their feet. It is done.

The gunslinger's soft leather boots make no sound as they cross the room to place coins on the bar. The daguerreotype is no longer on the table either, but the bottle of whiskey remains. Emmett takes a slug as he watches the gunslinger walk to the door. There's a soft chime, the ringing of metal against metal. It is the sound of a thousand bullet casings sewn together beneath the gunslinger's clothes, the words carved on each forming an unfinished poem. Emmett upends the bottle, leaking whiskey into the stubble on his chin. When the bottle is empty, he slams it back onto the table, wondering what in name of hell and all its demons he has done.

Emily Tremaine, born Emily Wilks, and going by another name entirely now—Caroline Pitkin—lives in a narrow house at the end of a row of houses. The house isn't hers; she rents a room, taking in mending and washing for coin. Wind chimes made from flattened scraps of tin clatter as the gunslinger approaches. There's a side yard where freshly-washed shirts flap in the breeze and the shoots of something green struggle to grow. A handwritten sign in Emily's window advertises her services—one rate for mending, another for washing, both reasonable.

"Come in," Emily calls when the gunslinger knocks.

The gunslinger opens the door onto a room running straight back to the rear of the house. At the far end, there's a bed, in the mid-ground, a table with two chairs, and near where the gunslinger stands, a small pot-bellied stove. Emily looks up from running a hot iron over a pair of trousers, startling at the sight of the gunslinger as if expecting someone else. Her grip tightens on the iron's handle. The gunslinger shows open palms, arms held away from their body.

Strands of hair escape the loose braid trailing down Emily's back. Some of them are gray. Lines of care gather around her eyes. She is thicker at the waist than the girl in Emmett's photograph, but the gunslinger does not mistake her.

With exaggerated slowness, so she can track the movement, the gunslinger opens the satchel hung at their side and pulls out three shirts.

"Washing, mending, or both?" Emily relaxes a fraction, but the wariness doesn't disappear.

And at the same time, she lifts her chin—a touch of defiance armoring over the fear in her hazel eyes. Afraid or no, Emily Wilks won't be running anymore.

"Both."

The gunslinger lets Emily come to them and take the shirts from their hand. She shakes them out, and her eyebrow goes up at the holes marked in powder burns, bordered by the tell-tale ghosts of scrubbed-out blood stains.

"Sure you wouldn't rather I burn them?"

"No, ma'am."

"I was joking." Emily sets the shirts aside, assessing the gunslinger as if she's trying to read all the roads they've traveled to get to here and guess at the secrets beneath their skin.

"Get shot at a lot, do you?" The corner of Emily's mouth quirks upward.

"From time to time." The gunslinger allows themself a smile.

Despite being indoors, they haven't removed their hat, but they tip their head up enough for the light to catch their eyes. If there's a

4

hiss of inhaled breath at their color, Emily hides it well. She retrieves a scrap of paper and a stub of pencil.

"Want me to write you a receipt?"

"No need, ma'am."

For just a moment, the bones of Emily's spine stiffen, like an animal scenting something dangerous on the breeze. She smoothes her expression as she sets the paper down, moving back toward the iron.

"You can pick the shirts up at the end of the week, or I can have them delivered."

"The end of the week is fine, ma'am, and thank you."

The gunslinger almost asks whether they can call on her again. It works, sometimes. Some folks are hungry enough in their fear that the gunslinger saying how they're new in town and wanting a friendly face gets a smile, an invitation to dine. Sometimes they suggest a game of cards, or a drink. But every line of Emily's body speaks guardedness, so the gunslinger merely touches the brim of their hat and takes themself to the saloon down the way without a further word.

A sign hung from the eaves advertises rooms to rent and hot baths. The gunslinger pays two weeks up front, along with coin for a bottle of whiskey, a hot supper, and for a tub and water to be brought to their room. The bartender looks askance at the last until the gunslinger lays enough coins on the bar to shut the bartender's mouth and send him scurrying.

Soon enough, the gunslinger hears two men cursing as they wrestle a copper tub up the stairs. The gunslinger admits them, sweaty and irritated. He crosses their palms with gold for their trouble. The taller man moves his fingers in a quick sign to ward off evil and looks away, but he takes the coin just the same. Food, whiskey, and water arrive in short order. Once the gunslinger has everything they need, they lock the door and strip out of their clothes. Each piece rings with the sound of spent casings as it hits the floor.

In another time, the gunslinger might have run their hands over the shells, tracing the words with their fingertips, mouthing their poetry silently. Now, they simply hook the bottle and lower themself into the tub, closing their eyes before they can see the water swirl crimson around them. It doesn't matter how old their wounds are—whether shining pink, or old-white like a sun-bleached bone—they still bleed. Some wounds run so deep they never heal.

~

Two days pass before the gunslinger knocks on Emily Wilks' door a second time. Enough time for gossip and speculation to circle the town twice over. They carry a hamper of food from the saloon hooked over one arm. Emily opens the door, but holds her body in the gap to keep them outside.

"You." She looks the gunslinger up and down, gaze resting last on the hamper.

"I thought you might be kind enough to share a meal, seeing as I don't know anyone in town and I'm sick of my own company."

Emily presses her lips into a thin line, not fear, but anger. When she opens her mouth, the flint in her words strikes sparks.

"I'm not the sort of woman who can be bought. Not for food, or coin."

The gunslinger takes a step back, surprised to find themself doing so. Emily almost slams the door, but they keep their foot in place to stop it, bracing for pain that never comes. The gunslinger holds up their hands. They turn their hips, showing their guns and belts have been left behind in the rented room above the saloon.

"I meant no offense or harm," the gunslinger says. "If you say so, I'll turn right back around and won't bother you again. I'll send someone else to pick up my shirts and pay extra for the trouble."

Slowly, so Emily can't mistake it for a threat, the gunslinger removes their hat, letting Emily see the line of their jaw, the weird gold of their eyes, everything about them that can be read in their naked face. A heartbeat, consideration, Emily weighs them. The gunslinger wonders—do they want to cross her threshold? Another heartbeat. Yes. Even knowing what will happen.

This question, asked a thousand times, is always answered the same. For a moment the gunslinger tastes the ghost of whiskey on their tongue, feels stubble rasped against their chin, then they shudder the past free. Words murmur softly between the gunslinger's bones—a poem aching for completion. Quieter than it once was, but never silent.

And even so—yes. They still want to cross Emily Wilks' threshold and share a meal. They want company, and they want someone to see them truly. It is a hollow inside them, not like a bullet wound, but like the oldest of hurts, the weariness of winter's cold settled down inside them for good.

"All right, then." Emily steps back, and the gunslinger enters.

As their boot crosses the line of the door, their pulse beats high and hard. Fear, like they're the one to catch the predator scent this time, even though Emily stands with her arms crossed, frowning slightly. There is a tiredness in her. That same frost-ache, steadily icing her bones.

They hang their duster from the post of Emily's bed, revealing a jacket—the uniform of an ancient war—with brass buttons undone. The bars at the sleeves and the material itself are faded to the color of dust, the original shade lost. At times, the gunslinger barely even remembers which side they fought on.

Emily sits, and the gunslinger sits opposite her. The table is small enough that their knees knock together when they pull their chairs in close. The gunslinger removes two covered plates from the hamper, along with a bottle of whiskey. Emily pours for them both, using jars meant for winter preserves. She is the one to finally break the silence, startling the gunslinger with a laugh.

"Look at us," she says. "You'd think we were condemned criminals at our last meal."

She leans back, sipping from her jar, and her posture goes from rigid to loose, a look of challenge glittering in her eyes. Her legs are wide beneath her skirt, one cocked, the other stretched straight, weight resting on her heel. Surprising themself, the gunslinger blushes.

"Why did you really come here tonight?" Emily asks.

She doesn't look like a woman unused to drinking, but her cheeks are already flushed. There's a brightness to her gaze, as though she's willed the alcohol to affect her as quickly as possible. The challenge remains, electricity crackling the air between them, like the sky with lightning tucked inside its skin.

"To see you," the gunslinger says. It isn't a lie. Emily blinks, the words catching her off guard.

"Okay," she says it slowly. "And now that you've seen me, what happens?"

"Well." The gunslinger draws the word out, making it equally slow. "We finish our meals, and then with your permission, I'll take my leave and thank you for a lovely evening."

Emily blinks again. The gunslinger's words seem to undo her, making her cheeks flush in a different way. She is raw, open, and all at once she is all over need, her lips parted as she searches for something to say.

"Stay," is the word that emerges, a lightning-strike leaving them both stunned. The air sizzles with ozone, the waiting storm broken. Then Emily straightens, meeting the gunslinger's eyes, and her voice is firm this time. "Stay."

"Gladly."

The tension runs from the room. The gunslinger inclines their head, a smile not quite hidden. Emily pours another measure of whiskey for each, this time her blush is a young girl's, shamed at her boldness, embarrassed by her loneliness and admission of fear. She lights a candle; they eat and sip and the tension lessens. And they talk. Sometimes, Emily is animated, her hands describing the shape of words in the air. Others, she is sober, reserved. The gunslinger catalogs every one of her quicksilver moods, building a picture of her to sit alongside the real thing.

There is flame at her heart, but it burns in a hollow space. She contains both light and darkness, in concert and opposition. The longer she talks, the more clearly the gunslinger sees her. They see what Emmett loves, and they see why he wants her dead. Loving a woman like that, having her break your heart, that's one of those wounds the gunslinger knows well, the kind that never heal.

Candlelight softens Emily's features until she glows. The room blurs slightly, and in their mind's eye, the gunslinger sees Emily with a knife in her hand, a small thing meant for the kitchen, but its blade red and bloody. Emmett hollers as he staggers up from their bed, matted sheets tangled around him, the wound in his leg dripping crimson on the floor. Did she mean to kill him, or only hurt him? Did she mean to scar him, wound his pride, leave him with an ugly thing that any woman after her would be sure to see?

"Excuse me, could you point the way to the outhouse?" The gunslinger stands, unsteady on their feet in a way that makes Emily giggle. Or perhaps it's their words.

There's a door at the rear of the narrow house and Emily opens it, pointing along a foot-trodden path.

"Try not to get lost."

The gunslinger puts heel to toe, walking a tightrope, arms out to the side. Emily laughs again behind them. Overhead, the sky spreads a canopy of stars. The gunslinger tilts their head back. If they could, they would fall upward in this moment, with Emily's laughter in their ears, and keep falling forever.

When they return, Emily stands beside their duster holding the daguerreotype. The gunslinger freezes. She holds the picture out, a silent question.

She meets the gunslinger's eyes, her expression mixing hurt and anger, with the edge of violence tucked inside.

"I'll leave," the gunslinger says.

"No." Emily crosses the room, the daguerreotype drifting like a fallen leaf behind her.

She fists the gunslinger's shirt, and despite the difference in their heights, she hauls them forward, bringing their faces level.

"Tell me," she says.

The gunslinger shakes their head, looks down and away. A soldier, a warrior, broken now and unable to meet her eye. Emily seizes their chin, unrelenting, and turns their face back toward her. The color in her cheeks is all anger now. Then her lips crush theirs, hot and bruising. Her tongue tastes of whiskey. She bites down as she draws back, leaving her lips smeared with the gunslinger's blood.

"Then I'll tell you," she says.

She still holds their shirt, breathing hard. Strands of hair drift loose around her face; she is terrible, radiant, wild. The lines of her —the ones around her eyes, the ones that curve soft and heavy at her hips and waist—they are not the lines of a young woman. They are the lines of someone who knows pain more intimately than any lover, and the gunslinger longs to worship every one of them. They stand still, hypnotized, as Emily speaks.

"I never loved Emmett. He knew it, but he was proud, and he wanted to believe given time I would come around. He thought he could win me over, with kindness first, and then threats. There was another woman, not for him, for me. Emmett found out and swore he'd ruin us both if I didn't give in. He used my love to extort a child from me. He thought to chain me to his side by my womb, but our girl was born blue and still, the cord wrapped around her neck. He believed I was heartless simply because I couldn't love him, but I loved that little girl and it broke me. He had no idea. And then, Car—"

Emily's voice cracks, she shakes her head. A deep shuddering breath, then she looks up, wiping furiously at her eyes with the hand not holding the gunslinger's shirt.

"While I was giving birth to a dead babe, the woman I love was dying of the fever. We were both in our beds, screaming our torment mere houses apart, but by the time I was well enough to go to her it was too late. She died alone."

Her shoulders slump, the rage holding her together draining. Under the weight of grief, Emily's legs fold. She's still holding the gunslinger's shirt, so fabric tears, buttons and bullet casings scattering. Emily ends up sitting with her legs splayed, the gunslinger crouched in front of her. A shell rolls to a stop beside Emily's hand.

"What are they?" She picks up the nearest one and traces the word etched in its side.

The gunslinger shivers, feeling the letters under the whorl of Emily's fingertip. Just as they feel every word written on every shell littering the floor.

"A poem," the gunslinger says. They close their eyes, because it's easier this way, breathing shallowly. "But I don't know how to read it, because it isn't finished yet."

Emily picks up another casing, reads the word.

"Doll." And another. "Father." And another. "Silver."

The gunslinger mouths each word with her as she says it.

"What does it mean?"

The gunslinger feels her watching them, but doesn't open their eyes, their body shivering beyond their control.

"When I was a child, my grandmother taught me that there is a word at the heart of every person. A sin they can't forgive, a love that has undone them, a wound that will not heal. That word, spoken from the mouth of the right gun, will kill them. Not only that, it will unravel them completely, make it as though they never walked the earth at all."

The gunslinger opens their eyes, gold and rimed in tears.

"Oh." Emily's lips part, more a sound, a shuddering breath, than a word.

"My grandmother is a terrifying woman," the gunslinger says. The words turn into a broken laugh, a cough, and they taste tears.

In their mind's eye, their grandmother is putting a gun into their hand for the first time. A rattlesnake's fangs sink into their ankle, and their grandmother sucks out the venom. They are listening to rain on a tin roof, sweating and shivering under a blanket while shadows rage and dance on the walls. A gunshot echoes flatly off of empty, ghost-haunted mountains, and their grandmother takes their hand.

"Your mama couldn't be bothered to stick around long enough to love you, and your daddy was on a wicked path before you were ever born. You remember that, child. You're cursed, same as me. We're the ones who live."

They see their grandmother's face, skin bronzed from the sun, teeth stained brown as a beetle's shell, and eyes as blue and cold as ice in the heart of winter. It all happens at once, then and now, forever and always.

"I can fix it for you," Emily says, and the gunslinger's eyes jolt open.

Their breath snags, and for a moment they're certain she's talking about the poem. About their life. About everything gone wrong. Then her hand brushes the torn shirt still hanging from their shoulders.

"No charge." Emily shifts her hand from the fabric to their skin.

Scars meet her palm, each one a memory, a reminder sure as the words carved into the bullet casings around them of a life lost, a choice made to serve the poem rather than turn away. Emily's hand shifts again, resting over the gunslinger's heart. It beats like a trapped thing, begging to be unburied.

If they turned from the path now—could they?—what would it mean? Darkness howls behind them, a wind to flay the skin from their bones. A litany of the dead follows in their wake, and without the poem their deaths meaning nothing, only a series of words scattered and senseless.

The gunslinger meets Emily's eyes. She should be afraid. They want to tell her this. She should run as far as she can and never stop. But salt-tears prison their voice, holding it hostage.

Emily's mouth is gentler this time, but twice as hungry. She eases the gunslinger's jacket and shirt over their shoulders, letting them fall like shed skin. There are more bullet casings sewn inside of both pieces of clothing, ones that didn't rip free.

They rise together, Emily and the gunslinger, their hand in her hair, her hand at their waist. No more clothing tears. Each piece shivers free, like leaves in a storm. The back of the gunslinger's knees catch the edge of the bed and they tumble, pulling Emily with them.

They taste her shoulder, the hollow of her throat. Their fingers trace the faint, pale discolorations where once her belly stretched to hold a child that didn't live. Time slows. In the past, which is also the present and the future, the gunslinger dips their hands into a copper tub, cupping hot water to pour it in rivulets down their lover's back.

The skin under their hands is soft and scarred, young and old, it smells of gunpowder and honeyed soap, it is every color. They trace their thumb along a stubbled jaw, along a smooth one. They taste whiskey from a thousand lips—painted and chapped, bitten and smooth.

Above them and under them, Emily shudders again and again, but she never makes a sound. When the gunslinger touches her face, her cheeks are wet with tears.

∾

The gunslinger wakes to the moon peering through Emily's window, sharp and bright as a sickle. The bed is empty beside them. As their eyes adjust, they see Emily, still naked, in one of the chairs beside the table. The candle has long since burned out; the bottle of whiskey is near empty. Emily's head is bowed, her fist pressed to her lips, and her shoulders tremble.

Springs creak as the gunslinger rises. Emily turns, holding out her hand, uncurling her fingers. In the moonlight, the gunslinger sees red soil in her palm.

"When I ran away from Emmett, I couldn't take my baby with me."

The gunslinger kisses Emily's forehead, kisses the tip of her nose. They fold her fingers over the earth one at a time and kiss her knuckles. They pull her close, hold her with their hand against her hair, and sing her a lullaby.

~

The gunslinger is unstuck in time.

Their grandmother puts a revolver in their hand. She shows them how to square their stance, sight along the barrel, and shoot. They pull the trigger for the first time.

And they pull the trigger for the hundredth time in one day, breathing the scent of wet pine, churned mud, and black powder. Melting snow drips from the trees. All around them, the frozen crust is splashed red. Soldiers in uniforms of both colors stiffen and cool. Those who loathed the gunslinger, those who loved them, those they called brother, sister, sibling.

These bodies the gunslinger knows intimately; they have heard them groan in pain and pleasure, tasted the sweat from their skin, shared blankets on cold nights, broken bread with them. The gun smokes, hot in the gunslinger's hand. A howling fills the air, whipping past the gunslinger and rattling through the trees, even though there is no wind. Tears stream from the point of the gunslinger's chin.

They want to stop. More than anything, they want to lie down in the snow and the mud, soaking in the blood of their lovers and enemies. But if they stop now, the poem will never be finished, and all this death will be for nothing. So they keep walking. And all around them bullet casings shine—hundreds of them, each inscribed with a single word.

A gunshot echoes in their head, sharp as a crack of thunder, but today they have not fired their gun. The earth accepts a plain wooden casket. Within, their father lies cold and still. Dead of a bullet wound, dead of a heart split in two. Their grandmother rests a hand on their shoulder, wet with rain. "It's for the best," she says, throwing a handful of dirt onto the coffin holding her son. The gunslinger picks up a handful of dirt turning to mud between their fingers and does the same.

The gunslinger kneels in front of their grandmother's chair. She wears a bullet casing on a leather thong around her throat. It is inscribed with a word the gunslinger has never seen, never wants to see. They have never loved her more fiercely than in this moment; they have never hated her as much as they do right now.

Outside, a storm howls. Rain pelts the tin roof and the walls shudder. In the mountains all around them, the tunnels of empty mines grumble in the dark like open mouths, crowded with ghosts. Inside the gunslinger's skull, between their bones and their skin, the poem shrieks like a banshee, loud enough to drown out the wind.

"Unmake me." Their body shudders, the words leaving their throat bloody and raw. Their voice is the sound of a blade-tip etching words into countless bullets. "Unmake me, please."

The bullet drops. The chamber turns. Casings tumble to the ground. Their father is lowered into his grave. Their grandmother is placing the gun into their hand, and they have already walked a thousand miles with words scribed into spent shells chiming against their skin.

"I can't unmake what is still being written," their grandmother says, laying a gnarled hand on their head. The weight of it burns. "But if the poem is ever finished one day, perhaps you will end, too."

～

The gunslinger wakes, wrapping a sheet around their body, and staggers to Emily's back door, barely making it before they vomit up a thin, bitter stream of bile. Scents fill the room—Emily frying bread in bacon grease and cooking eggs. She holds out a plate, but the gunslinger shakes their head, stomach churning. Instead, she pours strong coffee, and the gunslinger gulps it down, relishing the heat and the almost-burnt flavor.

"I don't have a proper bath, but I keep a tub for cleaning up. It's too small to be any good for washing clothes." She nudges a small, wooden basin with one foot. "I got warm water on and a clean cloth ready to go."

The gunslinger realizes their jaw is clenched, teeth almost chattering, and gooseflesh covers their arms. Emily fills the tub, and the gunslinger closes one hand into a fist at their side. If she'd wanted to, their grandmother could have taken the memories from their head; they are certain of it. She could have stopped everything from happening, but she chose not to. The gunslinger has never met anyone with more witchy power than their grandmother, but as far as they can tell, she's never used it to do anyone a lick of good. Not even herself.

The gunslinger crouches beside the filled washtub, letting the sheet fall and dipping the cloth Emily hands them into the water. The surface tension breaks, ripples hiding their reflection. They run the cloth over one arm, then the other. When they dip it back into the tub, the water pinks. The gunslinger washes their legs, their face, their neck.

"I can do your back, if you like," Emily says.

She takes the cloth without noticing the pale red hue. The gunslinger closes their eyes. For a moment, it is their hands cupping water to drip down another's back, then the cloth traces over their skin. They feel the moment Emily tenses, catches her breath, and drops the cloth on the floor with a wet splat. She steps backward, staring when they turn to look at her. The blood is unmistakable this time.

"What are you?" Emily covers her mouth with her hand.

"Cursed."

The gunslinger straightens, retrieves their clothing, and pulls it on over still-wet skin. The scent of pine haunts their nose, stronger than fried bread, coffee, or eggs. Droplets of melting snow hit the ground. They take a step, and their boot breaks through a crust of ice. Juxtaposed over Emily's small, narrow house, a man runs ahead of them through the winter trees.

He clutches his right leg, limping, leaving a trail of crimson blood on the snow. The poem howls through the gunslinger, shaking them, a terrible thing of feathers, teeth, and claws. The man turns and fires wildly. The bullet catches the gunslinger in the shoulder. It knocks them back a step, but it doesn't stop them. They have fallen, heart-stopped, and risen again so many times already. They cannot rest. Not until every last soul on the battlefield—regardless of uniform, love, or loyalty—lies dead around them.

The gunslinger shakes themself, then sets their hat on their head, tugging the brim into place. Emily watches them, wide-eyed, her gaze following them all the way out the door.

At the blacksmith, they pay for the use of a horse. The journey back to Stillwater takes less than half a day. As they ride, the gunslinger considers that Emily could have run much farther, but she chose not to. They consider also that Emmett could have given them the word they need to end her without them having to make the journey back to his homestead, but only if he knew what it was. The gunslinger is not surprised; Emmett Tremaine never knew his wife's heart at all.

∾

The gunslinger leaves the horse tied to the fence outside Emmett's homestead. Rather than going to the door, they circle around to the back where the land slopes up and away from the house. There, just outside the fence line is the grave—small and covered in red earth. The wooden plaque holds a single date for both birth and death, and one name—Rose. Not Wilks, or Tremaine, as if the child Emily grudgingly made with her husband never belonged to either of them. Cornflowers grow in the house's shadow. The gunslinger picks a handful and drops them on the grave.

They make another stop before leaving Stillwater—the boneyard at the edge of town. So many died from the fever that took Emily's lover, but the gunslinger knows her grave by the name it bears—Caroline Pitkin. The name Emily took when she fled to Foster's Creek. And—if the gunslinger guesses right—the word that will undo Emmett's heart.

~

Instead of riding straight back to Stillwater, the gunslinger rides farther west, to a town that no longer has a name. When the mines dried up, so did the people, and now only one occupied house remains. There are ghosts in the hills, the same men and women who bled the mines dry of their silver. Their eyes watch the gunslinger as they ride toward the single house with smoke spooling from its chimney.

Their grandmother isn't home, but the door is unlocked and a plate of food waits for them on the table, still warm. Beside the plate there's a carved box. The gunslinger flips it open; there are three things inside—a spool of thread, a needle, and a box of bullets.

Rage builds inside them, and for an instant, it screams louder than the poem. They want to dash the box into the lit fire. They want to tear their grandmother's house apart, search the mattress, the walls, rip up the floorboards, desperate to find anything to give all of this meaning. Of course they know they won't. They can't. It is a paradox. The poem will not have meaning until it is complete. But if they refuse to complete the poem, it will never mean anything at all. Faith, it is an act of terrible bloody faith, and they must believe until the end.

They think of their grandmother sucking venom from their snake-bit wound. They think of her gnarled hand, worn as old leather, resting on their fevered brow. They think of the gun that struck their father down, and the bullet on its cord about their grandmother's throat. Does the poem howl for her too? Does she believe in its greater purpose, or is she simply too afraid to turn around, look at where she's been and see nothing but the dark, nothing but death and heartbreak behind her?

The gunslinger lifts one of the bullets from the box, turns it so it reflects the firelight. If they knew the word to stop their grandmother's heart, could they do it? Would she want them to? The gunslinger replaces the bullet, and slides the carved box into their pocket. Their grandmother is the one constant in their life. In the end, it probably doesn't matter whether they could kill her. She's too cussedly stubborn to die.

～

Emily stands outside her house, waiting for the gunslinger when they return. Her dress is new, the cloth matching the dusk sky overhead. The gunslinger's shirts hang neatly over the porch rail, stitched up and cleaned, sleeves and tails fluttering in the breeze.

"Walk with me," Emily says.

Bullet casings chime, metal against skin. Each one whispers as the gunslinger follows Emily through the center of town. Townsfolk out on their porches look on, marking them, then turn away. When the dusty road carved between wooden buildings gives way to scrub grass and scattered trees, Emily stops. There are cornflowers here too, their color deep as bruises in the fading light.

"You're not afraid of me," the gunslinger says.

Emily looks toward the horizon, then tilts her head up to the emerging stars.

"You're afraid enough for both of us."

"I left flowers." The gunslinger says it like an apology.

"She's up there waiting for me. Caroline, too." Emily gestures at the salt-scatter brightness overhead. Light so plentiful it almost hurts.

The gunslinger remembers wind-chapped lips pressed against their own. But there is no one waiting for them amongst the stars. Bullets and words murmur, softer than the breeze. The gunslinger wants to touch Emily's shoulder, but everything is heavy. Heaviest of all is the gun at their hip, loaded with a word that will stop Emily's heart.

"I saw the other grave, too," the gunslinger says.

"Then you know the word to unmake my husband." The gunslinger thinks she might be smiling, but it's too dark to see.

"Yes."

"Will you?"

"Do you want me to?"

Emily doesn't answer. It's also too dark to see if there are tears on her cheeks, but the gunslinger suspects not.

"Is there really a word at every person's heart?" she asks.

"Sometimes it's two," the gunslinger says.

Emily starts when they take her hand and press the other bullet they've been carrying into her palm. It's warm from their skin, but Emily still catches her breath as though it's cold. The metal is tarnished, the words faint. She squints to read them; the gunslinger sees them every time they close their eyes.

"Jericho Hill." She meets their coin-colored gaze. "What happened there?"

"A battle," the gunslinger says.

It is too simple a word. Massacre. Slaughter. They were a butcher then, their brothers and sisters, friends and lovers lambs falling to their gun. The screams of the dying echo in their ears.

"Take it." They un-holster their gun faster than a blink, holding it out to Emily handle first. "You have the words. Use them."

The gunslinger's cheeks are wet. The poem rattles the cage of their ribs. In answer, a thousand, thousand word-carved bullets sing. They have stood here so many times before. They've looked into eyes of every color, begging, but in the end, the answer is always the same. The poem keeps on writing itself, dragging the gunslinger in its wake.

Emily takes the gun, cracks it, and drops the bullet with her word into her palm. She snaps the chamber closed, and hands the gun back to them. There is a hardness in her eyes, and a little bit of cruelty. The hand holding out the gun is the same that dragged a knife through Emmett's flesh. She couldn't simply run from him. She had to wound him, to shame him, to make him burn badly enough to want to take her life.

"There's only enough mercy here for one of us, and I think I'm the more deserving." Emily's lips curve, a shape like irony, but her gaze doesn't waver.

The gunslinger accepts their empty gun. There's a sound like hard rain as Emily lets a bullet drop to the ground. The gunslinger doesn't have to look to know the words written on it.

There are more bullets in the box from their grandmother, one bearing a word, a name—*Caroline*. The gunslinger tries to take comfort in the idea of Emmett's death, knowing they could use the bullet any time. It is easy to picture Emmett's features twisted in surprise, the spray of blood arcing through the air. The comfort is a small, cold one.

"Your poem," Emily says, "when it's finished, I hope it's a good one."

She brings her hand up so swiftly there's no way the gunslinger could stop it. There's a faint click as the bullet glances past her teeth, then she swallows it, welcoming her daughter into her body once again.

The gunslinger closes their eyes. They are in the churned mud and snow of Jericho Hill, surrounded by the dead. Their lover's breath rattles, blood on his lips. The gunslinger holds his hand and watches the light drain from his eyes.

The gunslinger walks. The gun heavy at their side. They are riddled with bullets, but they cannot die. They could stop this at any time, but they are too afraid to turn around and face the dark, to find out that they are nothing but a butcher after all. Their grand-mother's hand rests on their head. The poem shrieks like a wind out of a lonely canyon, sorrow without end. They have to believe. The poem must be completed. It must mean something in the end.

A woman can survive swallowing a bullet. There is no reason for Emily to die. The gunslinger's cheeks shine wet in the starlight. The gunslinger tells themself this over and over again.

When they open their eyes, they are alone. A faint breeze blows through the scrub grass and shakes the stalks of the cornflowers. That color, that bruise-deep blue, it should mean something. The gunslinger cannot think what. So they turn back toward town, walking as they always have, alone.

About the Author

A.C.Wise's fiction has appeared in *Shimmer*, *Tor.com*, *Clarkesworld*, and *The Best Horror of the Year Volume 10*, among other places. She has two collections published with Lethe Press, and her novella, *Catfish Lullaby*, is forthcoming from Broken Eye Books. Her work has been a finalist for the Lambda Literary Award, and won the Sunburst Award for Excellence in Canadian Literature of the Fantastic. In addition to her fiction, she contributes a monthly review column to *Apex Magazine*, and the Women to Read and Non-Binary Authors to Read series to *The Book Smugglers*. Find her online at www.acwise.net and on twitter as @ac_wise.

Author's Notes

The first story I tried to write for *Sword and Sonnet* was very different from the one that ended up in the collection. I abandoned that one halfway through because something about this setting and these characters spoke to me and demanded to be written. At the core of both stories—the one that got written and the one that didn't—was the idea that words have power. They can be used to heal or destroy, and sometimes both. The other seed for both stories was the idea of faith and sacrifice, and the questions that come with believing (or not) in something larger than yourself, primarily—what you will give up for that cause? Even though the execution of the stories was very different, those themes were obviously ones I always wanted to explore for this anthology.

A SUBTLE FIRE BENEATH THE SKIN

Hayley Stone

The wall opens. It's been so long since anyone visited that Gennesee cannot recall the word for door; it's only the wall scraping off its body, taking apart the darkness with barely-recalled light.

Her chains rake the dusty floor as she crawls forward, muscles too atrophied to hold up her spine. Any sense of decorum has left her. She's close enough that the fresh blast of air goes down her throat like lake water, fleshy and cold, no different from the fingers of the chief archivist after she swallowed a page of his personal musings. A single page probably wouldn't have been enough for her to digest the shape of his mind, letting her pull the words she needed to command her release, but she'd had to try something.

That was more than two years ago.

She has not seen another soul in all that time, and has often wondered if maybe all of the archivists are dead. To aid that possibility, Gennesee used to paint epics of plague and war in her own blood on the walls. She tried strengthening the spells with heroic couplets, but the subject and form clashed. Had she succeeded, many innocents would have died along with her enemies, and there was nothing noble about drowning an entire ship to kill a few rats.

It wouldn't have mattered, anyway. The magic of the Library is too old, unmoved by pretty turns of phrase. Its walls have rejected her every attempt to escape, bouncing back syllables like arrows pinging off a shield. In the time since her arrest, Gennesee has forgotten most of the Library's history, and much of her own, but occasionally a dim memory surfaces, disturbing the stillness of her mind.

She is here because she tried to murder the wrong person—or failed to kill the right one. Words can be twisted to tell any story, as she well knows, having once strangled a foreign queen by manipulating a few trochees in a breathless poem about love.

The figure comes toward her. As Gennesee's eyes adjust to the glare, she finally sees that it's a woman, and not the man she was expecting. The question of why balances her on a knife's edge between disappointment and intrigue. She had hoped for another chance to turn the chief archivist's mind against him, building new verse off the disquiet magic of the Library itself to see if that made a difference.

"Will you take some water?" the woman asks gently.

Born between the ragged sighs of a dying god, Gennesee doesn't need food or water to survive, only breath and will, but she nods. As the woman leans down to help her drink, Gennesee narrows her eyes. "I know you," she whispers, voice husky from disuse. It isn't the woman she recognizes, so much as her thin leaves of pale hair, the curving spine, and that miserable blinking tic while she's waiting to speak.

"No," the woman says, "but you knew my father."

A child. The chief archivist has never said anything about a child. But then, their conversations over the years have mostly revolved around Gennesee, her past crimes, and all the knowledge she has accumulated over her long immortal life, rarely turning more personal than condemnations over her repeated attempts to escape.

"Why has he stayed away so long?" Gennesee asks, wiping her mouth. "I hope I didn't frighten him too badly the last time he visited."

"My father is dead. That isn't why I'm here." Gennesee wants to ask questions, unpacking all the delicious details of his death, but instead she keeps silent, allowing a brief caesura for the archivist's daughter to say what she has come to say. "Many believe you are a monster, but I don't share their conviction. I've dug up all the stories, read the firsthand reports. I know how you single-handedly beat back an invading army, and turned aside floodwaters during the Great Storm. You even saved the Library from burning back in the days of King Esthar, may his words last."

"So?"

"So our country is in danger. That same enemy you vanquished is once more at our gates, and you know their weak points."

Gennesee almost laughs. *That same enemy.* There have been many. The Misks, whose language swarmed with beautiful similes, and the Aranar with their grating tendency to overcrowd stories with narrative asides—but that was also a long time ago. By her estimates, at least forty years have passed while she has been here in the Library, with only the chief archivist's brief visits breaking up the monotony like the slow, ponderous blinks of a giant.

That same enemy. There is no such thing. The enemy of today will only be a thin, vestigial organ of opponents she faced in the past. People are as fluid as language, always streaming into new hatreds, new ways of killing each other. Nothing will be as Gennesee remembers, and for a moment that realization irks her, like a misplaced pause in the middle of a sentence. She will have to spend countless hours clearing away cobwebs, learning colloquialisms and slang, catching up to technology and culture, all so her words do not bear the moldering stain of her incarceration.

Otherwise her power will not work. But perhaps the woman is unaware of that fact.

"And in exchange for my help?" Gennesee replies, not bothering to correct her. She senses an offer coming. She can always tell when the turn is near, the same way an elder's bones ache before rain.

"It's not within my power to grant you permanent freedom, but I can give you something just as worthwhile," the woman says, and reaching into a satchel at her waist, she pulls out a loose collection of papers, each a decaying shade of yellow. "During his time as chief archivist, my father made copies of every letter ever sent to him. You might recognize some names among their authors. In exchange for your help, and your word that you will return to the Library after the war, I will give you these letters."

She must know what she's offering. Such detailed correspondence will mean almost certain death for those who imprisoned Gennesee as soon as she moves beyond these walls. More than any other Bespoken, Gennesee is the reason critics stopped referring to her kind by that name and started calling them death poets. She needs only a sample of a person's writing to know what poetic form their mind will accept, the words that will break or unmake them, putting them under her control. What is writing, after all, but one's heart and mind tattooed upon the skin of a page?

Reading is her preferred method, but there are other ways of acquiring the words. Touching a few strands of inky scrawl is usually enough for Gennesee to lift text from a page and settle it in her mind, like sealing butterflies between glass. Eating prose *can* work in a pinch, but too often her teeth trap articles and pronouns, gumming up the context. Only desperation moved her to try this with the chief archivist's note, knowing it would amount to nothing.

An entire letter—let alone a whole collection—is a feast compared to the scraps she relied on even before her imprisonment, when she had been forced to scour hastily-scribbled missives or badly printed pamphlets for weaknesses to exploit, killing in service to the crown. The situation must be dire for the woman to approach her with such a dangerous offer, or maybe she simply doesn't care about the lives of a few powerful men and women. Both are intriguing possibilities.

Gennesee creeps forward on stone-scraped knees. Her decision is not a difficult one. "You have a deal," she says.

She raises her hands, still shackled at the wrists, and reaches out to seize the letters. A hash of cuts on her palms show the journeys she has taken down the black aisles of her cell, following a ribbed path of spines, her long length of chain trailing behind her. The room had once been lit by rudimentary poems, sunlight filtering down from stanzas in the vaulted ceiling—poems one of her kind put into place back in ancient times—but the chief archivist had each of them scratched out before he left, punishing Gennesee with the presence of books she cannot read. All those words held hostage by the dark. Where better to store a culture's forbidden literature than alongside a monster? Gennesee has tried picking up the stories with her fingertips, but the magic of the Library is too strong, blinding even her powers of touch.

At the sight of Gennesee's palms, an expression of sympathy crosses the woman's face, but is quickly gone, like a bat losing its shadow beneath the overhang of evening. She pulls the letters away. "Half now," she says coolly, "and half when you return."

"What good will the latter do me if I am trapped here?" Gennesee demands, her voice tightened by frustration.

"You of all people should understand the value of knowledge," the woman answers, dangling the letters close again, adding in a seductive whisper, "the power of a few words."

She is right, of course. This conversation has proven the impermanence of Gennesee's situation, shaking her awake. One day in the future, after this bloody quest has ended, when another archivist makes the mistake of trusting her, or some foolish monarch finally pardons her, Gennesee will walk free from the Library a second time. She will serve the rest of the letters like knives to the throats of those who betrayed her, accused her, sealed her away. And she will start over, and she will be free.

"Very well," Gennesee says. "I agree to your terms."

"I hoped you would," the woman says, stuffing the letters back into her satchel. She helps Gennesee to stand, and there is steel beneath her touch, all the strength Gennesee never sensed from the chief archivist, her father. *Even more intriguing.*

Off come the shackles, and Gennesee rubs her wrists as the chains coil to the dusty floor. Her legs tremble beneath her after so long on her knees, but it is nothing a sestina cannot fix. "And to whom do I owe my release?" Gennesee asks, gaze drawn to the woman's satchel.

The woman gives a thin smile. "I am chief archivist of this library. That should suffice. Now, if you will please follow me…"

Door, Gennesee remembers suddenly, stumbling after the chief archivist, and passing through the great white wound in the wall.

～

None of the letters she is given mention Gennesee by name. Others are discussed in passing, but she cannot tell whether the names mentioned belong to Bespoken in other countries, or simply men and women of a certain rank here at home:

Kiwiri's attendance cannot be relied upon, they are too busy holding up the right flank… Monson left late this afternoon following a disagreement with Sariah over the decision to withdraw our forces from the Gate… Fallas traded

barbs with me over that shipment I was going to send you… The Bespoken may
be our single greatest asset now.

That last notation is of particular interest, as it suggests a new recognition of Gennesee's usefulness, rather than centering her inside a dialogue of fear as before. She wonders what offer these traitors would have made her today, as opposed to the one they had used to trap her: promising rich moral rewards to assassinate a royal envoy, making her believe their cause was just, their complaints worthy of an answer, only to stage a very public failure for her and then claim she built the framework for the whole scheme herself. All so they would have a clear route to power, to controlling the king. With her out of the way, only the archivists remained to advise him, and they were far more concerned with preserving the Library than defending the sovereignty of the kingdom as a whole.

Gennesee pours over the letters, memorizing their contents, and especially their authors. When she agreed to the treason that led to her imprisonment, she had not known the names of her patrons. They visited her through young messengers with good memories who delivered the missives orally, though that was not unusual. Even before she had committed any crimes, she was mistrusted. Blamed for every sudden suicide or disappearance, as if she had nothing better to do with her time than torture strangers. The only people who wrote to her were other Bespoken, immune to one another's forms, and her lover, who had died waiting for her freedom from the Library. Everyone else feared giving her an alley into their minds.

Perhaps they were right to do so, she thinks, watching as one of the authors spills his intestines onto his desk and begins organizing them for her pleasure, eyes growing blank as a clean page.

The man had pretended not to know who she was, feigning ignorance even as she introduced herself, even as her lips formed the poem that urged him to take up a letter opener and press it into his belly. The same themes had come up again and again in each of his letters, almost repeating himself, so Gennesee structured the spell around two repeating rhymes and two refrains. It was child's play. The spell easily cracked the soft shell of his mind, and afterward, nothing he said made any sense, including his denials.

And yet.

For one fleeting moment after his heart stops, she worries she has made a mistake. His death sits with her, an uneasy companion. She tries to reason her guilt away. The letter was attributed to him, after all, and her spell would not have worked if those had not been his words.

So what if he did not confess to being involved in the plot to imprison her? Given more time, she could have gotten answers out of him, but she is not after explanations or excuses. She hungers for the peace of vengeance, a way of laying all her anger to rest. There is a hole inside her as dark and vast as the one she had been thrown into. Something must be done to fill it.

∾

The frontline provides a decent distraction on the days she is not hunting for the authors of the other letters. The top brass aim her at the enemy, as if she is a weapon no more complicated than a club, and stand back watching her work. She drafts poems into the dirt that are felt behind enemy lines, as strong as an earthquake, toppling structures, and burying anyone alive inside them. Often she goes ahead of the vanguard during battle, moving enemy soldiers to madness inside of a breath, speaking in allusions and apostrophe, and commanding them to death.

On those days more than any other she feels the sharp truth of what she is: inhuman, more verse than body, syllables stretched into a flesh-shaped scream. Meter ripples beneath her brown skin, toned like muscle, and when she moves, the tight scrolls of her hair jostle each other like competing figures of speech.

She learns everything she needs to know about the enemy from the contraband smuggled into the army camps by their spies, mostly books but some propaganda material, too. Although they are designated eyes-only, often they find their way into the hands of bored soldiers. The two sides share a common tongue, give or take the odd turn of phrase and more flexible conjugation. In fact, Gennesee's dialect sounds closer to that of the enemies' than her allies. When she reads their words, it reminds her of home—not a place, but a time.

One evening she gets her hands on an enemy soldier's unfinished manuscript and stays up all night reading about star-crossed lovers, sword fights, and other lighthearted escapades, and she scarcely understands how someone in the middle of a war could write something so genuinely hopeful, without a trace of bitterness. Later, when the casualty reports come in, and Gennesee spots the author's name on the list, something fractures inside her. Something she had not known could break.

She does not know why, but she holds on to the pages of the story, carries them with her like a charm. When she visits death upon the next few letter-authors, the story is there with her, rolled up inside a hollow tube at her hip, and for every step toward vengeance she takes, the pages rasp softly like the hiss of a warning snake.

～

"You seem to have made good progress," the chief archivist says cheerfully during one of their rare meetings. Gennesee refuses to set foot inside the Library until she absolutely must, and the chief archivist is smart enough to know the Library is all that protects her, so they speak through the threshold, one on either side. "I confess, I thought it would take you longer to move through the list. How many remain?"

"I thought you asked me here to discuss the war," Gennesee says. "Whatever else I do does not concern you."

If she sounds defensive, it is because the topic rubs her the wrong way, going against the grain of her conscience. The murders have brought her no measure of peace, nothing close to the calm pleasure she found while reading that soldier's story. Nothing she has done has made the authors give up their doctored confusion. They react in the same predictable fashion when she arrives, good manners giving way to baffled horror. The last even accused the chief archivist of sending her, as if Gennesee were no more than a marionette twitching on strings.

"Yes," the chief archivist agrees, practiced formality sliding back over her features, erasing the gloat. "How is the war going? I hear reports you are a great asset in the field."

"It goes," Gennesee answers in a clipped voice. Her eyes slide toward the satchel the chief archivist wears each time they meet, a deliberate reminder of what she is working toward, though it feels like a taunt.

Silence lays bricks between them, a wall as comfortable as lies. "Would you like to come in?" the chief archivist finally asks, as she always does.

"You already know the answer to that."

"I have no reason to keep you here," the chief archivist reminds her. "We have some papers on loan from the Archive in Trent I thought you might like to read. The collection includes an inspired treatise on metonymy as poetic reductionism, penned in the hand of one of our country's first poets. Not Bespoken himself, but a man of humble origins."

Gennesee resists the temptation, but cannot keep herself from asking, "Indeed? And what is so reductive about metonymy?"

"He believes there is danger in shorthand, in favoring simplicity over complexity. By substituting a name for a mere attribute, you diminish the reader's capacity to empathize with the object or person in question."

"That is the point," Gennesee replies. "Not everything needs humanity."

"I think you mean not everyone has humanity," the chief archivist says, "and I would disagree, but such is a debate for another day. If you will not come in, perhaps I can have someone bring you something. Some refreshments, perhaps? You look weary."

She does not merely look weary; Gennesee *is* weary. The past few months have drained her. She doesn't like that the chief archivist sees it, and likes her decision to comment on it even less.

"Was there anything else?" Gennesee asks pointedly. She surprises herself by longing not for violence, but for some place quiet, far away from this forsaken place, where she can be alone with her favorite story, following its familiar twists and turns, jolting down the same path toward an ending that does not exist—a happy ending. She knows it would have been a happy ending.

"Nothing for now," the chief archivist says, sounding disappointed. "Good luck on your hunt," she adds as Gennesee is leaving, and though the words for the archivist's destruction spring to her mind in the form of a stinging sirventes, she fastens her lips and keeps walking.

~

While entering the sixth month of Gennesee's mission, during a brief interlude in the war, she gets the idea to complete the soldier's unfinished novel herself. She starts small, laying the groundwork for a finale that honors the original author's intent. Something grand and romantic, but without too many flourishes.

Gennesee has never written a book before. It takes time for her to learn how to stumble without reaching out to catch herself on poetry. How to curve a story without decapitating a line, and pull an emotion other than misery and pain through her words.

For a while, she forgets about the letters and their authors, the few who still live. This is more important. She has to believe that, to stave off the fear. Fear that she is wasting her precious moments of freedom, pointlessly fiddling with commas and periods and plot. Fear that when she finally finishes, nothing will have changed at all. Not the world with all its darkness, nor herself, a soulful poet monster-made.

Her desire for vengeance grows stale while she works, and as she nears completion, the fog of her grief begins to clear, and she begins to make out a single truth in place of her anger, like a plinth emerging from the mist; if she must return to the Library, she wants to leave something more behind than corpses.

Rather than waiting for the quartermaster to fill her request for more parchment, she begins writing over the faces of the remaining letters, over the words that mean nothing to her, and the names that mean even less. She scrawls the final scenes across the backs in one heady burst of inspiration, squinting against a stab of sunlight as morning comes, as it inevitably must.

The next day, she returns to the Library and when the chief archivist invites her inside, she accepts.

~

Gennesee follows in silence as the chief archivist leads her back to her cell. Around her the Library looks unchanged, with all the same antechambers and channels, reminding Gennesee of a heart more than a building. The walls glow, inscribed with poems too ancient to be read and too powerful to be understood, but as Gennesee passes, her body angles toward them of its own volition, like one magnet attracted to another.

"You surprise me," the chief archivist remarks over her shoulder as they reach Gennesee's room. She struggles to keep her hands from tightening into fists at her side as they speak, her nervousness plain. "I trusted the letters would be a powerful incentive, but I had no idea how deep the well of your hatred is, that you would return immediately for the rest... It is unexpected."

"I did not come back for the letters," Gennesee says.

At that, the chief archivist stops.

"Even more unexpected," she murmurs, facing her. "Tell me then—why?"

"You always offered me refreshments before," Gennesee says, some of her old spite returning. She smiles leanly. "Are we doing away with the formalities now?"

The chief archivist stalls, blinking rapidly. "The others *are* dead, aren't they?" she blurts after a moment, the question she has no doubt been dying to ask from the moment Gennesee entered the Library.

"Many," Gennesee says, "not all."

"Then you are not done."

"On the contrary." Gennesee glances down at the tube housing the completed manuscript. "I am quite finished."

"The war..." the chief archivist begins to say.

Gennesee cuts her off. "This has never been about the war. Neither for myself—or, I suspect, for you. *Amara*."

"How—"

33

Gennesee approaches the frozen archivist, close enough that her warm breath makes the woman turn away her face. "Did you think I would not figure it out? None of the letters had anything to do with me. But many had a great deal to say about *you*. And the men and women I killed—they were all far too young to have been involved with my imprisonment."

"Yet you killed them anyway," Amara points out.

"Metonymy," Gennesee says, feeling her throat tighten around the word, squeezed against her neck by guilt. "I confused myself for my poetry. Anger for right. Violence for justice. I have returned because it is what I owe them, not for any of your fake letters."

Amara is silent a long moment. "And my name? Where did you learn it?"

"Every author I visited had it written down somewhere. Did you think I would not go through their letters?" Gennesee gave her a pitying look. "Oh, Amara. That is sad, lazy planning."

Gennesee moves past the stunned archivist and into the room, running her gaze across the space. In the soft light of freshly-carved sonnets, the shelves shimmer and glow, as though she is looking at them from across a distance of hot stone. She approaches one shelf, running a hand across the embossed title, smiling to herself.

"Some even guessed you were responsible for unleashing me on them," Gennesee adds, turning back to Amara, "eliminating those who were voices for your removal as chief archivist. Those advocating for negotiation and peace. You neglected to mention that it was our side who began this war—on *your* counsel. I expect your successor will not behave so recklessly."

Amara opens her mouth to speak a denial, or perhaps defend herself with a confession, but Gennesee shakes her head. "Careful, Amara. You, of all people, should understand the power of a few words."

"You think you've won," Amara says in a shaky voice, sounding just like her father had that last time he and Gennesee spoke, when the old man was closer to death than either of them realized, the stress of his job slowly pulling him into an early grave. His fear had been palpable then, as his daughter's is now. "But you will never leave this room as long as I am alive. I will make sure of that. Here."

She yanks the remaining letters free from her satchel and pitches them at Gennesee. "Your reward."

The letters catch like wings in the air, before floating down to rest at Gennesee's feet. She selects one from the pile, picks it up, and turns it over.

Both sides are blank. There never were more letters, only the premise for a trap.

"Clever," Gennesee says, and nothing more. She knows Amara wants her rage, her hatred. But she will not have them. Gennesee will never give such priceless pieces of herself away again.

After the chief archivist is gone, and the wall sealed shut, Gennesee withdraws a quill and inkwell from a pocket in her dress. She sits beside the chains that once held her, and marrying pen to paper, opens a new door.

About the Author

Hayley Stone is a writer, editor, and poet from Northern California. She is the author of the sci-fi novel, *Machinations*, which was chosen as an Amazon Best Sci-fi & Fantasy Book of the Year for 2016. Her short fiction and poetry have appeared in *Fireside Magazine*, *New Myths Magazine*, and various anthologies, with new poetry coming out in *Wild Musette* and *Star*Line* later in the year. Find her at www.hnstoneauthor.com and on Twitter @hayley_stone.

Author's Notes

When I set out to write *A Subtle Fire Beneath the Skin*, I originally planned for it to be a revenge tale in which the main character, Gennesee, is punished at the end for all of her bloody transgressions. Very much a classic "set out for revenge, dig two graves" scenario. I always knew the letters the Archivist held back would be blank, and I thought that was the point of the story. I was wrong.

As I wrote, the story began to evolve alongside its main character, moving in an unexpected direction. It became about the role stories have in shaping us, for good or ill, and the life-saving power of escapism. The latter feels especially fitting, if not ironic, since one of Fire's major inspirations came from chained libraries. Ever since learning about chained libraries, I'd had an image in my head of a woman being held instead of a book. That seed of an idea finally sprouted into this story when I started to wonder how she would shed those chains—and why she was wearing them in the first place.

Good poetry, like great fiction, can be either a tool or a weapon—a way for a writer to reach out to a reader in solidarity, or bash them over the head with some uncomfortable truth. Sometimes even both at the same time! While I may have taken that idea to a literal extreme here with Gennesee's magic, I believe real poetry is no less affecting. The best poets—(some of my favorites include Warsan Shire, Audre Lorde, Ada Limón, and Margaret Atwood)—not only change you with their work, they make you feel seen.

There is a line in the story that asks: "What is writing, after all, but one's heart and mind tattooed upon the skin of a page?" The story I set out to write was not, ultimately, the story that emerged, but it was truly the story on my heart. One that ends in personal growth, instead of self-destruction; a character ultimately freed by love, not hate. And that is my wish for those who read it, too.

AS FOR PEACE, CALL IT MURDER

C. S. E. Cooney

for Brian Shaw

"Sing us your love songs now!" the soldiers said to the poet Quattromani. She was in no position to sing anything ever again. They had sliced off half her tongue, then seared the wound shut.

The others watched from the floor of the arena. Huddled masses, et cetera. Teachers, artists, journalists. Religious leaders of every stripe, collar, and headscarf, who each in their day had done equal amounts of good and damage. Union leaders. A few of the wrong sort of politicians—a motley crowd of liberals (left hands hacked off to mark their leanings) and ethical conservatives. Anyone who'd opposed the new supreme commander's spectacular coup.

Ordinary people, in other words. Like Quattromani. Some of the prisoners had even read her poetry—though not all had liked it.

"Sing us your love songs now," the soldiers taunted her, and Quattromani, who had only her life left to lose, stood up.

She was not very old. Looked older. Had never expected to live as long as she had—outgrowing the mute misery of her early years, surviving addiction, solitude, a life on the road exposed and exploited, hunched and frangible with cynicism. Had never expected to learn to love herself or what lay beyond herself, to enjoy that unimaginable ambition: maturity. Nevertheless, there she was.

I am of age, she thought. *I have lived long enough.*

But looking at the soldiers with luminous tenderness, with the bitter taste of blackened meat at the back of her throat, she knew it would never be enough. Even before she drew the tin whistle from her rags, smiling with broken teeth, before she set the plastic mouthpiece to her crusted lips, the soldiers and teachers and painters and politicians who watched the wonder of her realization dawn, beheld her last song on her face just before they heard it. Before it pierced them, and they bowed their heads and prayed.

The soldiers executed her the next day.

They were the same soldiers who had cut out her tongue and taunted her, the same who had wept and prayed when she played on her whistle. But with enough smokes and six-packs after their shift, with a night of hard sedated sleep between them and her song, their eyes were sufficiently dry for target practice the next morning. They took her to the usual place, the back wall of the arena, and shot her like they had the others.

∾

When Quattromani was still alive and touring, opening for bigger bands, playing bars, performing at house concerts and folk festivals, the song that later enshrined her in our memory wasn't her most popular. But after the soldiers executed her, a few people—the prisoners, the witnesses—recalled the original lyrics of that last melody. Or, at least, they took time to invent new lyrics just as good, attributing them to her. Many ordinary people are also poets.

The name of her song was *The Reeling Wall*. Anyway, that is how it came to be known after Quattromani's death, when the other prisoners took to singing it at their own fusillades.

"The soul is a song
And it ends like a song
When the last breath is drawn
At the paredón…"

∾

Do you know why we call Quattromani the War-Ender?

I will tell you.

But first I should tell you about the Warbirds.

∾

The Warbirds were relics of two wars before. The tech that had gone into them was lost—along with all the bright minds of a once-thriving international scientific community, committed to fostering the R&D of artificial intelligence. There used to be thousands of Warbirds, many makes and models, spying for different factions. The CorvAI Corps, so called. Intelligence agents. Spies of the sky. In time, these ur-birds fell, and from their scraps and circuitry new Warbirds were built, and when those fell, new Warbirds, like their fiery predecessor the phoenix, arose from their parts, and so on, and so forth.

The Warbirds today were feral: patchwork descendants of pure-brand ancestors, and hardier for it, unhackable. They had learned, over the last century or so, how to repair and rebuild themselves. (No, not learned: were *programmed*, lovingly, by the last of the Drone Crones—whom Quattromani had known, incidentally, when she was a child). The military, unable to access the troves of insight the Warbirds had to offer, didn't see the use in them anymore—but there were too many to destroy economically. From time to time, a war memorabilia hobbyist would still track down a group of them and study their activities from a pop-up blind for days, avid as any ornithologist. But mostly, the Warbirds were left to their own devices: gossiping, watching, gathering and storing information that nobody alive was able to decode.

Wild Warbirds spent much of their time scavenging for solar tiles, then hoarding them in out-of-the-way aerie arrays. These solar nests were more like nursing homes than nurseries: places a weary Warbird might alight to recharge its degrading batteries, meet with old friends, spread the good word, a favorite new tune, maybe pass on a pro-tip or two—such as how to find—in those rare situations when a Warbird might need a human hand or tool—the right sort of person to lend it, and the precise coordinates of where such a person might be found.

No one knows the limits of a Warbird's individual intellect. What we do know is that, as a collective entity, they are something of an uncanny library. Adventurers, opportunists, music-lovers, linguists. A sentient, if not precisely *alive*, bank of burgeoning memory on the wing.

Along the barbed-wire battlements ringing the old stadium, the Warbirds folded down like gloomy origami, and listened to the music. In the static silence of their busily-shared thoughts, they compiled and collated everything they knew about the stadium, every tidbit and factoidal oddment. Juicy as entrails. Shiny as eyeballs. The smorgasbord of data was the invisible carcass they feasted upon.

The stadium had stood for at least two centuries. It predated the coup, and the last war, and the war before that. It predated the Warbirds—so, naturally, it fascinated them. The stadium used to host an international tennis open and a flurry of summer music festivals. When there were no more tournaments or festivals, it fell to ruins. Later, when there were tennis and concerts again, there had been some jibber-jabber about turning the stadium into a park, or a cultural center. But national stability didn't last long enough to see any of those projects funded to fruition. After the coup, the supreme commander repurposed the ruins for an internment camp.

The night the Warbirds came was the same night the soldiers deposited Quattromani into the stadium's maw. This was no coincidence. Having known Quattromani since she was a filthy scrapkid—barely a tune in her!—the Warbirds had followed her musical career with proprietary interest. Over the course of her life, they had sought her out to solicit her aid more than once. She always gave it. They regarded her as a friend, perhaps even an honorary member of their raggle-taggle CorvAI Corps. But the the soldiers they saw as magicians with only one act: they could disappear just about anyone. And now they had Quattromani.

The Warbirds waited outside the stadium that night, and the night after, and for many nights. They watched and listened. They heard Quattromani play her tin whistle the evening before her execution. They knew the tune already. They remembered everything.

Even after Quattromani died, the Warbirds lingered on their thorny metal perches, unruffled as gargoyles. The soldiers, always superstitious, started taking potshots at them. But the shots were nothing the Warbirds couldn't easily deflect. It was not a matter of bullets, but of aim. The Warbirds had a few suggestions on that frontier. "Aim three inches to the left" had always been a popular projection. Or, "Isn't that cloud distracting?" Or, "There's something in your eye, pal."

The original programmer-mechanics had designed their Warbirds to be passive collectors of information, not destructive devices. But they had fitted out the flying forces of the CorvAI Corps with a few personal security measures, aimed at increasing their chances of survival in the field. Mostly these were in the area of deflection, distraction, and distortion—i.e., the ability, a very small one, to project a low-grade telepathic suggestion into the minds of potential adversaries. It was also how the Warbirds communicated with their Drone Crones during a live drop, transmitting brief surges of coded infodumps mind-to-mind until they'd gotten their point across.

∾

Like I said, after Quattromani's execution, the prisoners filled that old stadium with music again. A cappella, untrained. Always *The Reeling Wall*—though, as the months wore on, those that remained got through fewer and fewer verses. Then, only the refrain. Followed by a staccato burst of bullets.

From their sentinel stances, the Warbirds recorded everything. More Warbirds came to listen, the glow of their cameras winking like acid stars. They were, in a word, ear-wormed.

That was in the summer.

By autumn, the stadium finally fell quiet.

Finally, the Warbirds took wing. They rose like dark spores off the squat and rotting fruit of the stadium. Scattered skyward in all directions. Eerie on the wind above suburbs, cities, countryside—or perched on branches, windowsills, depot roofs, storefront awnings—or pacing the tops of tanks, the training fields outside the barracks, the satellite dishes crowning the supreme commander's palace—the Warbirds passed along their song.

They did not sing, exactly. But all their *thought* was music. Quattromani's music. And music was what the Warbirds, thoughtfully, suggested.

Inexorably. Persuasively. Day and night. Without succor. Without surcease.

The Warbirds spread *The Reeling Wall* from one end of the country to the other. An epidemic of auditory illusion worse than tinnitus: a high, wild, whistling thing that lanced the brain like a darning needle and left the taste of burnt meat and blood on the tongue. Citizens, soldiers, corporate lawyers, farmers, white-collar workers, blue-collar workers, artisans, artists, everyone heard the song equally. No one was spared.

For days, the supreme commander could not leave his bed. How he rocked and blubbered, pleaded, stormed. He lit candles and tipped the hot wax into his ears so that he would not hear the song anymore. But it was not his *ears* that heard it. And the Warbirds never stopped remembering, not for an instant, never let *him* stop remembering, never let *us* stop remembering, their long and shade-less summer of Quattromani's music, and the salvo that never failed to follow.

Had the song stuttered for even just one damned hour—a quarter of an hour—a handful of minutes—I'm sure the soldiers would have directed their counter-air defense missiles into the ether, and blown every last spy drone of the old CorvAI Corps right out of the sky. But they could not move for weeping. Instead, like their supreme commander, they clutched their heads. They laid down their arms. They wept. They wept like they had wept the first time they heard Quattromani's song, the night before they executed her.

Only this time, they could not stop.

∾

That, by the way, is why we call her the War-Ender.

But before any of this happened—long before—there were the mudflats, a child, and a broken crow. I want you to remember them. It's important to know where things come from.

∾

42

Imagine a Warbird, cracked almost in two. Dented, bent, limp, battered. Ragged wings, alas. It is helpless, and aware of its helplessness, though hardly what you'd call alive.

The child squats, pokes.

She's a scrapkid, and the metal man's always looking for some shardware to repurpose. If she brings him back a whole Warbird, he might just let her select from his bucket of glasscandy. Her favorites are those twists that taste clean and green and keep her up three, four, nights running, her thoughts as fast as code, the wind rhyming high above her.

Cleaved and flightless it may be, but the Warbird is far from stupid. It can still suggest. Come closer, kiddo, have I got a suggestion for you...

The child hears a single word, "Help."

The plea is so wraithlike and weak it might be coming from her own belly, whose complaints she has learned, over time, to ignore. She can ignore this too. Sore and swollen she may be, but she is also stubborn—or she would not have lived this long. (She has not lived so very long.) She is not open to persuasion. Not from this wretched piece of scrap with pallid eyes.

"Help."

The child has never been asked to choose between serving herself and serving something else. The first is hard enough; she has already failed her own body and its needs. She has caved to its gluttonies instead, and been eaten alive by them. She knows nothing of mercy. No one has ever shown her any.

Nevertheless, she lifts the Warbird into her arms, and strikes out —not for the metalman after all, but for the last Drone Crone in the world.

∼

The Drone Crone, hands stuffed in the pockets of her coveralls, watches the burdened child approach her hut.

The hut is scaled in solar paneling to give the equipment within their necessary boost, but on dark days, the elastomeric dynamo wheels can also generate a charge so long as the hut's rolling. The

Drone Crone has drawn the metal shutters closed against a brittle wind, but these may as well be lace for all their rustwork of holes. Through one of the sizable eyelets, she can see the child clearly. The hard stamp of suffering on her face. Her resignation. How the weight of the Warbird she carries bends and bows her.

The Drone Crown knows a Warbird is mostly air and wingspan. The child, she thinks, is weak.

Anemic? Malnourished? Yes, these. And by the cuts at the sides of her mouth, a glass-eater too. Lost cause then.

The Drone Crone sniffs. Dismisses her vestigial concern for the sticklike straw-girl that some withered, lizard-corner of her brain keeps trying to re-ignite. She doesn't have time for humans. She's the last of the old CorvAI Corps programmer-mechanics, those meteorologists of intelligence currents who keep intelligence current. Unemployed a while now. Years. Her superior officers, her colleagues, her kith, kin, and country—all dead and gone. But she loves her work. Lives for it. She rebuilds Warbirds out of the corpses of fallen Warbirds, teaches them, tinkers with them, tweaks their programming, treats them like friends. Pays no mind to the clankers and scrapkids who scavenge in her hut's wake for chips or wires or lenses that have outlived all their lives of usefulness, bringing them as barter for the metalman, for a sweet suck of his glasscandy.

Those scrapkids. Indiscreet appetites. They'll bargain for a twist but settle for a snort: glassdust being better, they figure, than nothing. Better, certainly, than a package of cheese-snot foraged from an ancient MRE—about as fine a meal as the little bastards will ever know. If only they knew. But calories are none of their concern.

Here's, however, a scrapkid scratching at her door.

Stunted, bloat-bellied, barely larger than the bird she cradles. Big eyes, green as glasscandy. Ropy hair crawling with vermin. Skin as black as a Warbird's wings.

The Drone Crone glances again at the scrapkid's stony old face. That forgotten feeling stirs again. Call it pity.

Again, she ignores it. Gently lifts the Warbird out of the kid's arms with hands as large and gnarled as the roots of a swamp oak. Settles it on her charging table. Immediately, those dim eyes brighten to pale, cunning coals. Otherwise, the Warbird does not move.

She gets right to work. Solders the cracked shell. Patches the wing membranes. Hammers out the worst dents. Polishes that blunt beak clean of unspeakable effluvia. As she works, she clears her throat. Once. Twice. Begins to talk. Her voice—like her hair, her mouth, her patience, the functional parts of her liver—is tripwire-thin.

"Did right to bring her here, scrapper. Thought she was downed for good. Wanton harriers, those goddamned GTAMs. Hey. You're shaking. Not much to you, is there?"

The child blinks at the question. Inquires urgently, "Candy?"

The Drone Crone shakes her head, muttering about rat poison and caffeine and psychotropic corn syrup, and tosses the child a handful of food-chews.

"Eat 'em," she advises. "They expand in the gut like sawdust. Sit there for days. Make you all warm and sodden. Nourishing too," she laughs, "though they taste like armpit. Name?" she asks suddenly. "Like to know what I'm feeding."

The child mumbles something.

"Eh?"

She says her name louder, sullenly.

"Well, Quattromani. Let's see what you saved today."

From a canvas pouch on her tactical belt, the Drone Crone takes a flight controller. The Warbird bucks awkwardly, turning on the table like the hands of a clock gone wrong. Rights itself. Flaps to the Drone Crone's shoulder. Cocks its scabrous head.

"Yes, yes. Welcome back. I see you're about bursting with news." The Drone Crone's head cocks, just like the Warbird's. She looks at the child. "Oh. You want to reward her, do you? Won't do any good. She's fiending for the one thing only. There's no great end for her."

"Candy?" asks Quattromani again, more hopefully. This time of the Warbird.

The Warbird vaults from the Drone Crone's shoulder to one of the shelves that line the metal hut. It sorts through a heap of tattered shine—washers, coins, charms on broken chains, gold teeth

—and pecks up a long, thin, tin cylinder. Hardly a gleam on it. On one end, a scratched plastic mouthpiece. Along the body, six holes.

"Wants you to have it," the Drone Crone translates, handing it down. "You *yourself*, mind. Not the metal man."

Quattromani takes the object, inspects it dubiously. "What is?"

The Warbird bright-eyes her with its twin cameras. A twinkling look, almost. It descends back down to the table, paces back and forth, back and forth. And as it paces, it looses into the child's mind such a, such a—*melody!*—as she has never heard before...except, perhaps, in the high rhyme of wind through wires, when she's riding the glass, flying fast, and nothing, but nothing, can touch her.

The child puts the tin whistle to her lips.

About the Author

C.S.E. Cooney lives and writes in the Borough of Queens, whose borders are water. She is an audiobook narrator, the singer/songwriter Brimstone Rhine, and author of World Fantasy Award-winning *Bone Swans: Stories* (Mythic Delirium 2015). Her work includes the *Dark Breakers* series, *Jack o' the Hills*, *The Witch in the Almond Tree*, and the poetry collection *How to Flirt in Faerieland and Other Wild Rhymes*, featuring her Rhysling Award-winning poem, *The Sea King's Second Bride*. Her short fiction can be found in Ellen Datlow's *Mad Hatters and March Hares: All-New Stories from the World of Lewis Carroll's Alice in Wonderland*, Jonathan Strahan's *Best Science Fiction and Fantasy of the Year Volume 12*, Rich Horton's *Year's Best Science Fiction and Fantasy*, Mike Allen's *Clockwork Phoenix* Anthology, *Lightspeed Magazine*, *Strange Horizons*, *Apex*, *Uncanny Magazine*, *Black Gate*, *Papaveria Press*, *GigaNotoSaurus*, *The Mammoth Book of Steampunk*, and elsewhere.

Author's Notes

At first I wanted to write a rousing fantasy story about a bard strumming up an army for some epic battle against EVIL. Something like *The Revenge of the Minstrel Boy, or, HIS HARP SHALL SOUND AGAIN!* But too many other thoughts started crowding in too quickly, nudging me to the next thought down. And down and down.

What really happens to poets during a battle? A war? Under a dictatorship? What happened to Osip Mandelstam, who wrote scathing poetry about Stalin? Well, Mandelstam was arrested twice, and died in the purge year of 1937 in a transit camp near Vladivostok. Where did I learn that? From another poet, Aram Saroyan, in his play *The Laws of Light: Pasternak, Akhmatova, and the Mandelstams under Stalin.* Poets have to keep each other alive somehow. I've known since childhood that Lorca "vanished" in 1936 during the Spanish Civil War. We recently learned that Neruda was probably poisoned. At Columbia College Chicago, in 2006, I took a class called Art and Revolution with Professor Carmelo Esterrich. He told us the story of Victor Jara—a Chilean poet, a singer-songwriter. A bard. When Augusto Pinochet staged his US-backed coup d'état, Jara was one of hundreds of prisoners herded into Estadio Chile. The way Carmelo told it, Pinochet's soldiers broke Jara's hands and mocked him, saying, "Now play for us. Now play us your guitar!" And then, though his hands were broken, Victor Jara opened his mouth and started singing. The soldiers shot him. Years later, that stadium— Estadio Chile—was renamed for Victor Jara. When Carmelo told us that story I started crying in class. So much for poets in a war.

Poets in a war are arrested, imprisoned, tortured, disappeared. Many are executed. Some survive—like my friend Amal's grandfather, Ajaj El-Mohtar. The poetry he wrote in prison on a bit of toilet tissue is now framed on the family mantelpiece. He was a poet who survived. His son Oussama became a poet. Oussama's daughter became a poet. Amal and I met because of poetry. "In my house," she told me once, "the word poetry always had a capital P." That's the kind of poet I wanted to write about. The kind of poet who could end the war that ended her.

SHE CALLS DOWN THE FUTURE
IN THE FOOTPRINTS LEFT BEHIND

Setsu Uzumé

There were seventy of us gathered in the ring of bonfires, and the world beyond was as black as death's belly. Warriors of spear, bone, and blade, wrapped in leather, mottled with clay all turned inward, as a woman with a drum marched toward a pile of blankets. Her trousers were long, and rippled like grasses as she walked. It smelled like mud and sweat and horses, oil, smoke, and meat.

"Naicto!" shouted our chief.

"Naicto! Naicto!" My voice rushed together with my kin.

Naicto, fate-namer, blood-crier, put up her hand. We cheered, the wind blew, and the flames roared. Her long black hair crinkled out behind her like unthreshed wheat planted by grain-eaters—those we traded meat with.

Until they refused. Now we will trade blows.

She pulled a folding stool from the side of the drum, opened it with the flick of her wrist, and sat. Her bare toes were red in the firelight. She spread her knees apart, tugged her trousers back with a flourish. Her thighs and calves were thick with muscle, red as the mud we painted ourselves with. I thought she could crush the world with those legs. The songs I sang of her under my breath to the rhythm of hooves could never do her justice.

And my songs would never carry fate.

She set the drum on the ground between her legs. Raised one hand high in the air.

The chief nodded.

"Join me now, where the earth breaks, where the sky cracks open," she shouted.

Shrieks echoed a response. Other drummers, seven of them, situated between the bonfires; but only Naicto could tell us the truth.

Naicto hit the drum, and the fires turned white.

She drummed with a fury to match our hearts, her fellows around the circle accenting and complementing the sound so it wasn't lost across distance. This was my third dance, and it had gotten better every time. We danced while she drummed. Elotei writhed around me, sinewy as their bow. Serag, whirling like her blades, dared new partners to join her with every glance.

Naicto's music overtook us. I began slipping between worlds. I fought the trance, knowing I would lose. The ecstatic dance took us, weaving us together like wool into felt for her use. I wanted to see her, to hear her, to remember her prophecies word for word.

But no one remembered, unless it was their fate she revealed.

"Rotha," Naicto sang. "You will return to your babes and your herd."

I did not know Rotha. I cheered for him anyway.

"Kartho," Naicto howled, her voice in our ears, rumbling in our throats. "Your horse will die saving your life."

Behind me, Kartho shouted her animal's name, rage and grief as immediate then as it would be during tomorrow's battle. Her fear rippled through the dancing warriors, sharpening the song, and driving us higher, stomping the ground with our dance as though we might kill the earth.

The bonfires were blinding. The rhythm didn't change, but the dance felt slower. Sweat rolled down my skin. I smelled Elotei's flesh and the cracking clay that stained them like sun-baked earth. Their hand dragged across my back as we danced, the creases and callouses of their palm sharpened into surreal detail. Then Naicto sang my name.

"Terag."

Elotei looked up at me, their eyes glazed. I straightened, wanting Naicto to see me in the spinning, thundering crowd. I've always wanted her eyes on me, my name in her mouth, my life in her song; but for the first time I understood what that might mean.

Tell me, I prayed.

"Fight, and your sword will slay the chief. Die, and you doom us all. Cast her out of the circle."

The drumming rolled like the splitting of a frozen lake, and my blood turned to ice. *Us*, she said. The whole tribe. This, they'd all remember.

I drew breath to deny it, to plead with her, but it was too late. The dancing continued. Elotei pushed away from me, and the irregular ripple through the crowd warned of the consequences of that prophecy as the chief and his two most loyal riders pushed through the dancers toward me.

Without losing rhythm, they pulled me from my place in the crowd and tossed me out of the circle into the black.

I hit the ground hard, rolled, and came to a stop face-up. Grass scratched and tickled my flesh. My side pulsed but didn't hurt. Nothing would hurt until tomorrow.

Exiled, I lay on the cold earth, too high to move. Denied the circle, I was no longer fueled by its song and fire.

There was no moon. I could not see if the sky's dome was a breath or an eternity away. Over the next ridge we would ride, and take what the Hathey refused to trade. Nonmoving tribes were numerous. They built huts, planted, and ploughed. Moving tribes were fewer in number and fewer in kin; but we were strong. Strong enough to live alongside our animals, not chain them in pens. Strong enough to hunt and capture and tame, not wait meekly for wealth to be willed to us. We traded flesh for tools and baubles; both meat of the hunt, and in marriage contracts. The arrangement was good, until a promise was broken.

Until a deal was not honored.

Spittle cooled the corner of my mouth. The thrum of music soured into the first warnings that my high was ending.

What had I done—would I do—to deserve this?

The muscles in my neck were as stiff as gnarled tree roots as I turned my head back to the warriors. I could not see Elotei from that distance. Did they remember me, my childhood love? Was Serag warming them on battle's eve as generously as she once warmed me?

I wondered if Naicto howled their fate, their life and death, sealing it with thunder and fire.

Her, I saw well. A black blot against orange firelight, her body jerking as she sang our outcomes, hands fast as bird's wings, and mighty legs tapping the beat at either side of her drum.

But I could no longer hear either.

I closed my eyes.

When I opened them again, the fires had been snuffed out. Long wisps of smoke rose up and the sky cast a hazy orange dawn across the plains in memorium of those who would meet their fate that day. I sat up, aching and creaking, caked orange mud itching the space between my breasts. I scratched the itch with bound hands —tied with my own bow string. More insult than injury. If I cut it to free myself, I'd be down to one spare.

I ran my tongue over the sourest spots of my mouth and spat.

My horse was nearby, grazing, his back legs were hobbled by a rope strung between them. My saddle, tack, and coat had been stacked on the pile of blankets that had served our fate-namer the night before. She must have ordered it moved when she ordered me tied and kept from the battle.

"Terag," said Elotei, riding up to me. "Take this."

Elotei's horse, Effa, nuzzled my face. I shied away from her, fixing my gaze on the white hairs of Effa's muddy hooves, the mud on Elotei's boot, a blend of earth and the red clay. I knew Elotei's eyes would be war-bright, still high from the clay, the dance, and the fate-namer's song; whether or not the words survived until dawn.

"Terag," they said again.

I loved them for coming to me, and hated them for seeing me like this. I hoped they'd forgive me and prayed they'd forget.

The chief's bellow was short and soft at this distance, and the answering trill of the riders was as high and cold as the wind that brings an avalanche.

Elotei dropped their drinking pouch, half-empty, then took their place in the column. The chief and his riders were at the center, flanked by Naicto and the drummers, along with the lightest archers meant to keep to the edges of the fighting. That's where Elotei belonged, the plumes on their leather helmets flashing green and violet in the ruddy light.

My skull pounded with every other breath. I couldn't tell if I was starving or nauseous.

And I had to piss.

I had to figure out how to piss with bound hands. Trousers kept saddle sores at bay, but they made squatting over a ditch a more careful process. I staggered over to the blanket stack despite the landscape's efforts to topple me with its spinning. I made sure my last bow string was still in my saddle bag, and then cut myself free.

I wish I had packed another head.

Without the clay and the song to heighten my senses, I had to clear my body of whatever remained. I made water, and, knowing it would feel better when it was over, took a whiff of the foulest mud in the camp. All the feasting and drinking I'd done before the dance came back up and scattered across the ground.

I donned my coat and helmet, strapped my sword to my belt, then tacked my horse. Rig was a slow, steady creature. He didn't need to be hobbled so far from the herd. When I led him to the blankets for an easier mount, he stood calmly. My last glimpse of the camp was not the churned earth from the dance, or the cold husks of bonfires, but the mud I'd left on the stacked blankets. My footprints, eclipsing the fate-namer's.

I wasn't a traitor. I would prove it. I sang to myself in rhythm with Rig's hooves.

They will see.
They will see.
They will see.

I rode across the expanse up to the ridge. When I caught up with the column, the assault was well under way. My third dance had not gone well. My third battle would. I was sure of it.

The village had built a wall of spiked poles facing outward. I had never seen anything like it. It channeled the riders to one entry point where the villagers mounted their defense. The rest of my kin rode around the village, picking off whoever they could see through the spikes. Many had dismounted, discovering they had more room to maneuver without our animals.

It was a mess.

Had Naicto seen this? Why didn't she warn the chief?

I rode into the battle. Rig hesitated, sensing my churning guts. I kicked him onward, imbuing each muscle with impulsion until he was as sure of my seat as his own galloping. From the waist down, I was a horsewoman. From the waist up, an archer. Last year I had fought with a wound in my side. Life ebbed from me, and I still rode, loosing arrows until my bowstring snapped. Today I was merely dizzy. I could survive this.

I couldn't hope to breach the walls. I knocked and loosed arrow after arrow, looking for easy targets. The backs of Hathey villagers that had left the safety of their wall. Rig shifted beneath me and I turned to look when I saw the unthinkable: Naicto riding toward me as fast as her horse would carry her. I caught a flash of grim certainty in her eyes, and the next thing I knew I was on the ground.

Blades clashed. Spears knocked. Enemies thrust violence upon each other and howled their horrible triumphs. I fought to recover the wind knocked from me, as Naicto pulled my sword from my belt.

I raised my hands against the killing blow.

"You should not be here, traitor," said Naicto, flinging my sword far beyond my reach. Her voice, already low, bore the rasp of last night's naming.

I backed away from her, scrabbling to my feet. "I'm not a traitor. I sobered up and rode as quickly—"

Her eyes frightened me. Naicto's lip curled and she put her hands on her chest, just under her collarbone, beating out a slow rhythm.

"Terag will betray the chief, riding against his will. Terag will die an old woman, knowing every storm long before it arrives."

Her voice penetrated my armor, my skin. My joints burned with a pain I had never imagined, forcing my body to curl into itself. The awe and desire I had felt for her shattered into icy terror. She needed no drum, no ritual. She could call fate at any time.

"Stop," I begged her.

"The song cannot be unsung." She stepped toward me, pain sharpening my senses so I could hear the mud squishing under her boots. The ragged edge of her voice. "Fate cannot be changed."

"I will not betray my people!" I wailed.

"And yet you're here, despite all." She knelt at my side. Took hold of my coat with one hand and dragged me up, still tapping a drumbeat against her own leather coat with the other.

"You are sober because I needed you sober. Listen well."

We were part of this world and not. Without the high of the mud protecting our minds, was this what the dance felt like? My skeleton burned, riddled with brittle needles, every movement an agony. Would I die like this now, or was this a taste of my future twenty years hence?

"You will not die today, traitor. And you will not fight." She held me by my coat, her breath tickling my face, her voice barely a whisper now, louder than any scream. She pointed her chin and I turned my eyes across the battlefield. "If you fight the Hathey, you will save the chief. He will keep killing. Bodies will poison the river and the whole region will die."

I watched the blood-spattered chief hammer the crude shield a Hathey villager had raised against him. The two were of nearly equal size, and the chief grinned through the gore and flaking red mud. Further down the wall, riders were pulling spikes from the ground to carve new paths through the wall.

He reveled in the chaos. We all did. High on blood and magic. We couldn't be beaten.

"He must die here. He, and all the singers. Men like him will never remember, and they will never rest. They cannot have the future."

Pain and betrayal thickened my tongue. "You're the traitor," I spat. "I curse you, I condemn your name forever!"

"Yes. You will."

"You could have stopped this. We're dying!" I cried.

"This massacre?" she said lightly. "It ends here. I've sang this song all my life, and something always fails. Each song, every dance —they all mix in this blood, under this sky. I cannot stop the chief, but I can stop you from saving him."

I balled rheumatic fingers into a fist. I had known pain, would know it again.

I punched her in the throat. She let go, choking.

I crawled away, my hands slipping in the mud. Then the world tilted again...

It was like a hangover; but worse. I had only known Naicto's power in the ritual. Never in this raw, unrefined form. I felt wiser and worse than ever in my life. The aftershocks of her song surrounded me, as though time were a circle—simultaneous—rather than a straight line from past to future. I saw the way time converged on our people, possessing and crushing us, while we thanked our fate-namer for healthy children, full bellies and easy winters. We were soaring like eagles with Naicto's song guiding us, but the flight was a fall. This village had been prepared for us. Warriors and drummers were dying. The rush of air felt like freedom, but today we'd hit the ground.

Naicto coughed, distorting her rhythm. She drew breath to sing again.

Eyes streaming, I launched myself at her. We wrestled, fighting and twisting, until my knees were on her biceps, my hands around her throat.

"No more songs, no more lies!" I shouted.

Her mud-red face swelled.

The air left in her lungs formed two words.

"Terag...remember."

All her fingers curled but one, which pointed. I watched a young girl leap onto the chief's back and bury a knife in his neck. The chief howled.

Another Hathey snatched my sword from the ground and ran at him, hacking and stabbing at the chief's face, gut, and his open hands with the clumsy brutality of one who'd never held a sword before.

We were done for. I had to find Elotei.

"Where is—"

Naicto's legs came up, her ankles crossed in front of my face, and she yanked me backwards into the mud. My head smacked the ground and my ears rang. She scrambled away, then vaulted to her feet, tapping out another rhythm on her chest.

I didn't hear the words, but they rolled toward me. Like the silence between lightning and thunder, or the weightless second after a horse throws you.

Impact, and darkness.

⁓

I woke up with a roof over my head. I couldn't feel the air. Betrayal clotted my throat worse than the muck still staining my clothes. The stuffy air reeked of sweat, blood, piss. Failure. Shame.

I was a prisoner.

I scratched my face, and red mud came off under my nails. I rubbed with my palms, flecking off more of it. I stripped to the waist, scouring the clay off every inch of my skin with a ferocity I couldn't deliver to my enemies. I had been kicked out of the dance for treachery I never committed. I barely fought in the battle where our chief died, and Elotei. Sarag. My horse Rig. My friends, my loves. I didn't know if they were alive, or if Naicto had seen fit to sacrifice them as well.

I was alone on a mat in a tiny hut. There was a hole in the roof and a cold fire pit. My weapons were nowhere to be seen.

Blood welled where I scraped too hard, washing the flakes from my skin. I wept. Not from pain, but because I had no one to save, and no one to kill.

Just memories of what I hadn't done.

The door opened. White light slashed my eyes.

Naicto stepped inside, long trousers rippling as they'd done the night of the dance. "The village repelled the attack," she said. "I asked them to see to you."

"Why am I still alive?" I grunted.

She embraced me, her fingers tapping my back. I stiffened, but couldn't bring myself to push her off.

"You did well," she said. The lilt in her voice wasn't quite song, but I felt stronger; the way I might in a few days.

"The chief is dead, we lost. How—"

"I told you. I have seen that battle, many other fates. The dance, the circle…The red clay binds your fate to me so I can see them in terms of each other but there's more to it. It becomes one blade of grass in a meadow. But the sky, the wind, the water…one fate is all fate. We can't keep pulling it one way and expect to survive. He had to die." She rubbed her hands together slowly, then opened them, the lines in her palms still stained red from the clay. "This power has to die."

I shook my head. "You didn't answer my question."

"You sing memory. The red clay doesn't work as well when you dance. I needed you sober, and alive, to remember this day. Understand it. Prevent it, if it comes again."

"You let the other drummers die before they completed their training. Why not just refuse to teach them? Lead the chief down a different path? There were dozens of other choices!"

She shook her head. "And for the Hathey? The Lokta? We drink the same water, breathe the same air." She put her hand to my chest. My heart beat like war drums and hoofbeats and Hathey hammers for walls and graves.

"We fight to eat. To win. To live. If there's any tool that would make that struggle easier, we would use it. We did use it. The balance has to be restored. The drummers knew enough of the song that they would find the recipe for red clay. It would all start again, until there was no water at all. Just blood."

I couldn't fathom the depth of this failure. That our greatest weapon, our connection to forces beyond us, would turn around and do this to us.

"What are you? Did you not marry us, live with us, eat with us? Ride with us? How could you lead us toward this horizon?"

"We fuck, we fight, we forget every time, and an ending you cannot conceive of creeps closer. Nothing changes." She pushed me away. "The future looks like a mountain, but it is mist. It flows in and out and cannot be captured. Those that ride into it without full understanding will fail. Remember this. This betrayal you feel. Only memory can save us. Your songs. Not mine."

"And if I let you go?"

"They will hunt me. The death of the other drummers, unforgivable. Kartho will become chief and she won't understand." She wiped mud and grime from her face. "You know, I can't sing my own future. Too many possibilities."

"Kartho is afraid of you. She wouldn't risk you as an enemy," I said.

She smiled. "Of course she will. She thinks the mist is a mountain. A dance, a fight, no difference." She retrieved my discarded vest, dressed me. I had never imagined I'd be so close to her. Talking with her as an equal. That I'd be angry enough to fight her, or trust her enough to agree. That we'd both be traitors in a Hathey hut.

She tied the stays of my vest. My scrapes and cuts had scabbed over.

Then she took my shoulders and held them steady.

"You must remember what happened here. Especially if they find another who can name fate. Remember how to see through it."

The calluses on the insides of her knuckles were like an archer's, but across all fingers rather than two or three. There was no difference between her drumming and her weapon, hunting flesh to fend off hunger, hunting fate to fend off disaster.

I remembered wanting her. Fearing and envying her. Being repulsed by her. But I couldn't deny her. What she had done was unforgivable, and necessary. I wondered how long she had known she must betray her people, and if that's why she didn't speak to us outside of ritual. I couldn't imagine what it was like to know someone's fate, their fears and desires—how they will end.

She clapped me on the shoulder again, and hobbled outside. I followed.

The village was a ruin. Some of the huts had huge holes in their walls. The animal pens were wrecked and empty. Villagers called for their herds in the far distance, while others disassembled the spike-wall to repair the pens. Some of the villagers had gathered bodies into a line, to search for familiar faces and perhaps redistribute tools that would be better suited to living hands.

I found the chief. His face was mostly intact, and had a pinched look I could only describe as hungry. The drummers too, were dead. My blood ran cold at the precision of Naicto's prophecy. She was as much to blame for the Hathey's deaths as my chief.

I did not find Elotei. Prayed they were well.

This was not my village. These were not my people. Watching

them die was easy. Watching them rebuild the damage we had done...less so.

I left on foot, following the horizon to where our next camping ground would be.

As I crested the rise that had separated us a day ago, I stopped. I could tell how far away some mountains were in terms of days, but not all of them. Depending on the light, and my own weariness, they seemed just within, or far beyond my reach. But when I looked back at the village, I knew how large the huts were. I would never choose their life, fixed to one place, but it broke up the land into pieces I could conceive of. I knew how close or far I was.

I walked on, singing to myself, my feet swishing a rhythm through the tall grass. Through my song I smelled Rig's fur and saddle. I heard the thump of Elotei's water skin hitting the mud. I tasted the feast before the battle and the bittersweet breath of mourning that I had been spared Naicto's scheming.

The village sang behind me, and the earth sang below me.

The mountains and mists sang the same.

About the Author

Setsu Uzumé grew up in a pagan household in New York. They are the host and assistant editor at *PodCastle*, as well as a member of Codex and SFWA. Setsu writes and occasionally narrates dark fantasy. Their work can be found at *PodCastle*, *StarShipSofa*, *Beneath Ceaseless Skies*, *Goodman Games*, and *Grimdark Magazine*. While they have dabbled in many arts, only writing and martial arts seem to have stuck. Find Setsu on Twitter @KatanaPen, because @Sword-VsPen was taken.

Author's Notes

This story took seven years to brainstorm. It draws on a number of elements, including some material from the weirdest humanities class I took in college. Three lessons stood out:

1. The best poems can be read 500 years later, in a different language, and still make you feel.

2. Shamans (and their equivalents) were the first artists because their role involved storytelling, music, costume, stage direction, dance, mythic teaching, and a bunch of other forms before they were forms.

3. If it's cold enough, you can shit into your hand and make a knife.

Time and language came up again with another professor at a different school, who described Aquinas's take on divine omniscience as "present to all time," or perceiving cause, event, and consequence simultaneously. In this story, the seer sees all time, but she's limited by her context and can't possibly convey the full scope of what she knows. She knows she won't survive, that her way of life won't survive; but people will remember if they feel something. Keeping memory alive is a poet's job.

And the best poets use the tools at hand.

This story is about prophecy, time, and why we have oral traditions. It was written in less than a day, while listening to Piotr Musial's "For Honor! For Toussaint!" on repeat. Side note, it's been fun to see if people think Naicto saw ahead 500 years, or 5,000. We do keep forgetting and repeating.

CANDIED SWEETS, CORNBREAD, AND BLACK-EYED PEAS

Malon Edwards

No one wanted to come out of their houses. Not at first.

They could see my father's blood soaking the cobblestones. They could see it dripping from the machete in my hand. They didn't want to come bab pou bab—face-to-face—with Gran Dyab La, the wicked little girl who had just disemboweled her own father.

I wouldn't either, if I were them.

(Vrèman vre, I'm not really the Great Devil Child. Se pou tout bon wi. If I'm lyin', I'm dyin'. I just swing my machete like her.)

These people knew that. I had lived on Oglesby Avenue next to them for the last three years, since I was eight years old. Since Papa and I followed Manmi here to La Petite de Haïti in Chicago. Since Papa and I no longer called La Petite de Haïti in Miami home.

I had been nothing but kind to them. I had been nothing but polite to them. I had been nothing but respectful to them. My mama raised me right.

But even that didn't make them come out of their houses.

I could understand if Papa had been out there. Wearing the softening shadows of the fading half dark. Long, sharp, hungry teeth slobbering all over the place.

I could even understand if Papa was still lying in the street. Me standing over him. Guts steaming on the cobblestones. Blood searching for the gutters.

But the half dark had lifted. The Sack Man, papa mwen, my wonderful and horrible father—Eater of Children—was gone.

All that was left was me. All that was left was efreyan.

(I saw what I did. I was there when I did it. I'd be afraid of me, too.)

I was scarier than the Shadow Man. Even though he had stalked timoun yo in the half dark on the way home from school.

I was scarier than the Sack Man. Even though he had snatched timoun yo into his gunny sack just steps from their front doors.

I would replace the nightmares of all the timoun yo on this street. Instead of having terrible dreams about the Sack Man or the Shadow Man stalking and eating them, they would have terrible dreams of me. Standing over my father. Tonton Macoute in hand.

They would tell their friends on Yates Avenue about their terrible dreams. And those friends would tell their friends on Bensley. And those friends would tell their friends on Calhoun. And those friends would tell their friends on Hoxie.

And I would become a lougawou. The boogeyman. The monster in the closet hiding behind the clothes. The monster under the bed ready to grab feet and ankles.

I didn't like that. I had to change that.

~

The first person who came out of their house was a little girl. She didn't see me as a lougawou. She didn't see me as the boogeyman. She didn't see me as the monster in the closet or the monster under the bed. Annefè, she saw herself in me.

She was about three and a half years old. Maybe four. Ti fi te adorab. She had afro puffs, just like mine.

She walked over to me. She took my right hand. She looked up at me.

She had to crane her neck way back. I must have looked like a grown up to her, even though I was only eleven and three quarters years old. I was taller than all of the girls and most of the boys in my Covey Four class back then. I'm taller than all of the girls and all of the boys in my Covey Four class now.

"Ki non ou?" she had asked me.

"Michaëlle-Isabelle," I'd told her.

"Mwen te tande sou ou menm," she had told me. She had said this with a sing-song lilt in her voice and a lovely smile, as if what she'd heard about me was a secret.

With my left hand, I slipped Tonton Macoute, my machete, behind my head into its sheath sewn onto the outside of my backpack and crouched down. I wanted to look dirèkte-man into this little girl's big, beautiful dark brown eyes.

"What did you hear about me?" I asked her. I couldn't help but smile as I did. She was all kinds of precious.

"I heard you sent away the half dark. Fwa sa a li ale pou tout bon. Pou tout tan."

"Forever, hm?" I asked her. My tone was playful. It held a hint of a tease. But only a hint.

This little girl was shrewd. Perceptive. Discerning. She had to be.

She was out here all alone. With me. Without her parents. She would have known if I was talking down to her. She would have known if I was dismissing her tiny convictions.

"Wi," she had answered, and her smile was so lovely that I wanted to bite her baby-fat cheeks and eat her dimples.

(Maybe that was the Papa part of me. He was the Sack Man, alafen. And the Shadow Man, vrèman vre, but we're not talking about that lowdown, dirty, no-good sneak right now. Li ban m kè sote on my way home from school today. I thought I was going to die from fright. Right here. Right on this street. Right in the half dark. I won't forget that. I'm still mad at him for that.)

"Who told you that?" I asked her.

"Manman mwen ak papa mwen." The little girl pointed to her house two doors down. The curtains in the front window twitched.

"Y gen rezon. I calmed the half dark. I sent her away."

"Will she come back?" The little girl asked me.

I didn't answer her. That wasn't my answer to give.

∽

More people came out of their houses when they saw the little girl's manman ak papa sweep her up in their arms and plant kisses on her baby-fat cheeks. I supposed her manman ak papa were relieved I didn't slice their little girl in half with Tonton Macoute.

They knew I could. My father's blood was still on the cobblestones. Trickling into the gutter. It was awkward.

I gave them some space to let them have their moment. As they cuddled and kissed and smushed their adorab little girl, I just stood there, shifting from foot to foot. Their display of love and joy and kè kontan went on for some time. They were heart happy. I didn't want to interrupt that. I didn't want to spoil that.

But I had to go. I had to find manman mwen. She had taken papa mwen somewhere. To hide him. To heal him. To let him start again in another part of this city where the pickings were ripe for the Eater of Children. It was what he did. It was what she did.

I didn't know where they were. But I knew he was still alive. I could feel it. I had to do something about it.

As I turned to leave, the little girl's mother pulled me to her. Her arms were muscular. Her embrace was warm. Her words were needed.

"Mèsi," she told me. I could feel her tears on my cheek. "Mèsi anpil."

"Padekwa," I whispered.

The little girl's mother could feel my tears on her cheek. I couldn't remember the last time my mother hugged me. I couldn't remember the last time any mother hugged me. I couldn't remember the last time any woman hugged me.

The little girl shifted on her mother's hip, leaned across her, and hugged my neck with her skinny little arms.

"Mèsi! Mèsi!" she told me. She could feel my tears on her baby-fat cheek. It was so soft. It was so pliant. It was so close. I really did want to eat her dimples.

But instead, I laughed. I couldn't remember the last time I laughed.

"Ki non ou, ti boubou?" I asked her.

"Mwen rele Michaëlle-Annabelle," she told me, chin raised.

I wanted to tell her that was a beautiful name for a beautiful little girl, but more people had come out of their houses. They came over to us. Some of the women gave me hugs. They could see I needed them. They could see I wanted them.

Some of the women pressed sweetmeats wrapped in wax paper into my hands. They could see I needed them. They could see I wanted them. Sugar plums. Sugar-coated almonds. Peanut brittle. Pain patate.

Some of the men pressed my hands with both of theirs; large, gnarled knuckles ashy but gentle. They introduced me to their daughters and the heirloom machetes they had just given their ti fi cheri yo until they could commission new, shiny custom-made ones from the blacksmith. Their names were Carmelite and La Verite, Nadège and Nadiyo, Tiya and Tifiyèt, Zette and Timizè.

None of those machetes was as special as Tonton Macoute. Except for maybe Timizè. There is nothing wrong with giving a Little Misery by blade to the Shadow Man, the Sack Man, the Pogo, or whatever else is lurking in the dark on the streets of Chicago.

～

I didn't notice the food. Not at first.

There were so many people who wanted to thank me and tell me how I inspired their daughters that five of the wooden picnic tables had already been set up in the middle of the street before I realized what was going on. They were having an impromptu block party.

I wasn't all that surprised. I had just banished the half dark from the South Side of Chicago. People wanted to celebrate. People wanted to eat. People wanted to dance to music in the street under the night sky as the gas lamps kept the full dark at bay and our fears in check.

We hadn't done that since Ol' Heck was a pup and now he's a grown dog, as manman mwen would say.

"Chile, you sound more and more like your mama every day."

I hadn't realized I said that out loud.

"You shole is right, Ms. Elaine. An' she look jus' like her daddy, with them Duverneau eyes. All his people got them."

"You ain't never lied, Ms. Irene. An' look how tall she is now. She got that height from her mama."

"An' her daddy, Ms. Savannah Mae. Don't fo'get 'bout that tall drink of dark water."

Ms. Irene shook her smooth, dark, bald head. "Girl, you better shut yo' mouth talkin' like that in front of chirren."

Ms. Savannah Mae kissed her teeth. *Tchuip.* "Listen to Ms. Elaine talkin' 'bout this chile's daddy like she jus' came to town, thirsty as all get out, 'cause it's a ten-mile walk on a dusty dirt road 'tween here an' the next town over where them nice Christians ran her out wit only a church lady hat an' a burlap suitcase to her name."

Ms. Elaine kissed her teeth back at Ms. Savannah Mae. *Tchuip.* "It ain't like you both wasn't thinkin' the same thing."

Ms. Savannah Mae leaned over to Ms. Irene and stage whispered: "That fast skirt over there need to get back to church an' get right wit God."

Ms. Irene raised her hand, closed her eyes, and bowed her head as if she were in church and the Sunday morning service was just getting good. "Preach, Sister Reverend! Save this heathen heifer!"

"Now, Ms. Savannah Mae," Ms. Elaine began, "we three know the moment any of us walk into a church—"

"—God gon' strike us down dead on the spot for our sins of gossip an' lust!" Ms. Irene finished, and all three women cackled like that was the funniest joke in the world.

I looked at all three women for a moment each, with their smooth, dark beautiful skin and their smooth, dark beautiful bald heads. I frowned. "Who are you?" I asked them.

"Who do you think we are?" Ms. Irene asked me, wiping her tears from laughing so hard.

My brow furrowed. My frown deepened. "You seem very familiar to me, but I can't place you. None of you."

"Chile, you better eat befo' this good food get cold," Ms. Elaine told me.

Ms. Savannah Mae took me by the elbow and led me over to six picnic tables pushed together end-to-end, covered with red and white checked tablecloths. "Look at this here spread: macaroni and cheese, glazed ham, coleslaw, collard greens (I eat mine's wit candied sweets, which over there), cornbread (I made it myself), black-eyed peas, chit'lins (the hot sauce over there), mashed potatoes an' gravy—"

"—an' then, chile," Ms. Elaine said, at my other elbow, "when you ready, you can have some dessert: peach cobbler, sweet potato pie—"

"I'm not a child."

Everything stopped. Everything except the music. No one moved. No one spoke. Everyone just looked at me. It was the longest ten seconds of my life.

"Let me fix you a plate, chouchou mwen," Ms. Irene said finally, and grabbed a heavy-duty paper plate that could withstand all of that koupe dwèt food. Everyone started eating and talking again.

"Listen," Ms. Irene said, as she scooped food onto the plate for me, "we know you ain't a child no mo'. Not after the way you sliced the Pogo's face an' that Bobby Brightsmith tentacle right off it, who we know you hidin' in yo' backpack right now so he won't scare all these nice people back into they houses—"

"—an'", Ms. Savannah Mae cut in, "we know you ain't a child no mo' after jus' seein' you slice yo' daddy's belly open so he wouldn't eat you, his beautiful baby girl."

"So, chouchou mwen," Ms. Elaine said to me, "we all the way there wit you on that. Like the Bible say, 'When I was a child, I spake as a child, I understood as a child, I thought as a child, but when I became a woman, I put away childish things.' We know you don't think like a child no mo'. An' we know you don't speak like a child no mo', either."

"An' that saddens us." Ms. Irene looked around at everyone enjoying the good food. "All of us."

As we sat down at a table with Michaëlle-Annabelle and her manman ak papa, I looked at Ms. Irene and said: "You still haven't told me who you are."

Michaëlle-Annabelle smiled at me. I still wanted to eat her dimples.

Ms. Savannah Mae frowned. Not a deep one. Not as a rebuke. Yon ti kras. Just a little bit. "We gon' tell you, chouchou mwen, but we ain't got time fo' no questions. You gotta eat. You need your strength."

I started with the macaroni and cheese. Se te koupe dwèt. Non, it was better than delicious. It was ambrosia.

Ms. Elaine started with the story. "We the Three Whispers. It's our business to know e'rybody's business."

"But don't take that the wrong way," Ms. Irene continued. "We nosy, but we ain't malicious. We ain't tryin' to do nobody bad. We jus' tell you what you need to know when you need to know it."

"An'," Ms. Savannah Mae added, "we tell you what you need to do when you need to do it."

Somehow, I knew Ms. Irene and Ms. Savannah Mae wasn't just talking about me, but the collective 'you.' Everyone on this block. Everyone on the South Side. Everyone in the Sovereign State of Chicago, even.

"But how do you know what you need to tell me and what I need to do?" I asked them.

Ms. Savannah Mae gave me the nicest cut-eye I had ever seen. "What we say 'bout askin' us questions, chouchou mwen?" Her tone was soft, but her eyes weren't playful. She had been serye.

Ms. Elaine tut-tutted Ms. Savannah Mae. "Leave her alone, Sister Whisper. Kaëlle jus' curious."

"Well, Kaëlle better keep eatin'," Ms. Savannah Mae said, and crossed her long, dark, lovely arms, "'cause she ain't got much time an' she gon' need her strength when they get here." She nodded at what little macaroni and cheese I had left.

My fork paused in front of my open mouth. "That's the second time one of you said that."

"An' it gon' be the last time you hear anybody say anything at all, if you keep talkin' an' stop eatin'," Ms. Elaine said. She watched me finish my macaroni and cheese, and then said, her voice soft and reverent: "Bèl Flè made us."

"Bèl Flè is a myth," I said, moving on to my greens and candied sweets.

Ms. Savannah Mae kissed her teeth again. *Tchuip.* "Girl, you better shut yo' mouth an' stop talkin' that blasphemy. Bèl Flè shaped us from her rich, dark pure soil."

Ms. Irene smiled at me. A kind one. A respectful one. "Bèl Flè is very real. She rebuilt Chicago after the war, layer by layer, all wit the purified soil from the coal dust boiler in her chest."

"She ain't tellin' no lies, chouchou mwen," Ms. Savannah Mae said. "Bèl Flè then spread that rich, dark soil on top of all the nuclear ash. An' when it settled, when it wasn't gon' blow away into Lake Michigan—or Iowa—she put a bit of copper an' uranium an' gold—an' even diamonds—an' e'ry other precious metal she could think of far beneath that life-givin' dirt surface."

"An' from those metals," Ms. Elaine said, her tone and her eyes bright, "she forged three steam clock hearts, very much like the one you have in your chest right now, an' put them in our chests."

Ms. Irene finished the tale. "But befo' she left Chicago to bring life back to the rest of this war-ravaged country, she shaped the Clockmaker, taught him how to build steam clock hearts an' clock-work machines, an' then told him to populate Chicago again."

I ate a forkful of black-eyed peas and a bite of Ms. Savannah Mae's cornbread. It was fluffy. It was delicious. "That's a fairy tale they told us in kindergarten."

Ms. Irene crossed her long, dark, lovely arms and rocked side-to-side. "That's 'cause fairy tales the only way you young'uns gon' remember y'all's cultural history."

"You ain't never lied," Ms. Elaine said, and also crossed her long, dark, lovely arms and rocked side-to-side.

Ms. Savannah Mae leaned over toward me, put her mouth behind the back of her hand, and pretended to say under her breath: "Unless Ms. Savannah Mae's lips are movin' or she compli-mentin' you."

All three women stopped talking. All three women looked at each other. No words were spoken. No cut-eye was given. And then, all three women cackled. Loud, long, and lusty.

"Are you like the Three Fates, or something?" I asked them.

"Them heifers cain't do what we do," Ms. Savannah Mae shot back, and they all cackled again.

Ms. Irene put a saucer of peach cobbler in front of me. "Eat up, baby girl. You almost finished, which is good. Them coyomorants gon' be here soon. An' they ain't no joke."

"You ain't said nothin' but a word," Ms. Elaine murmured.

I ate a forkful of peach cobbler. It was good. Sweet and tart. But I wanted some more candied sweets.

"What's a coyomorant?" I asked Ms. Elaine.

"The Devil on a Sunday mornin'," she answered.

Ms. Irene had given me an explanation that made more sense. "A sleek an' powerful clockwork machine that's a hybrid of a coyote an' a cormorant, built from some of those precious metals Bèl Flè put in the ground. It even got wings. Your brother, the Pogo, convinced the Clockmaker to build them."

"Convinced my ass." Ms. Savannah Mae kissed her teeth. *Tchuip.* "That awful so-an'-so brother of yours tol' the Clockmaker if he built those coyomorants, then he'd gift him the Sack Man, trussed up like a Thanksgiving turkey, to do wit whatever he wanted."

"An', of course, the Clockmaker agreed," Ms. Irene said, arms folded, rocking side-to-side again. "The Sack Man ate the Clockmaker's chirren, jus' like he ate most of the chirren in Chicago. Both of them beautiful l'l girls."

"See, that's how you know them coyomorants nasty," Ms. Savannah Mae said, her lip curled with loathing. "That's how you know they vile. A grievin' father made them wit revenge an' hatred an' anger in his heart. So you gotta be ready. You gotta be strong. Them coyomorants gon' strike as soon as you make a mistake. An' if you do, that's gon' be yo' last one."

Ms. Elaine nudged Ms. Savannah Mae with her elbow. "Now, why you gon' say somethin' like that? You wanna' scare this dear heart right befo' the biggest battle of her life?"

"M pa pè," I told Ms. Elaine.

"We know you ain't, chouchou mwen," Ms. Irene said, and patted my hand. "E'rything gon' be all right. That's why we here."

"But Ms. Savannah Mae really isn't scaring me," I said, my voice firm. Sometimes, when grown folk are talking, we young ones had to repeat ourselves to be heard.

I sho' hope not," Ms. Savannah Mae said, "'Cause they here."

❧

You didn't see them. Not at first. No one did. Not even me.

We didn't see them because they had stalked us from the dark spaces between the houses. We didn't hear them because the piano and the trombones and the trumpets the saxophones and the bass and the drums made their approach stealthy.

We should have seen the glint of the gas lamps on their midnight blue metal skin. We should have heard their claws sparking on the cobblestones. But even if we did, we wouldn't have had enough time to run.

You were the first person I thought of when I heard the screams. The musicians and the people dancing were the easiest targets. Joy had closed their eyes, spun their bodies, licked their fingers, and freed their souls.

Your manman snatched you up as I stood. Your papa flipped the picnic table as I slid Tonton Macoute out of its sheath. You were safe. For now. I had something between me and the coyomorants. For now.

But there were so many of them. They were sleek. They were powerful. They were fast. They were ruthless.

People were dying all around me. People were running in every direction all around me. Even the Three Whispers. Your manman ak papa ran straight to your house. I ran straight to the coyomorants.

Two of the coyomorants had just knocked down the trumpet players. Their beaks were bloody. Their claws were bloody.

I stepped into Form of the Iron Butterfly, just as Papa had taught me so long ago, and dropped four, quick vicious chops onto the backs of both coyomorants. Two sets of wings tinkled on to the cobblestones. They had looked too frail for flight, anyway.

The two coyomorants snarled and whipped around at me, quick as snakes, with a claw strike each. I was shocked by their speed, even though the Three Whispers had warned me. I parried one strike and spun away from the other. My footwork was clumsy. I gasped when the second claw scored my left shoulder blade. I could feel the blood flowing down my back.

Michaëlle-Annabelle gasps.

I tried to put some distance between me and the two coyomorants and moved back. I stumbled. The cobblestones were trè uneven there.

One of the coyomorants pounced to take advantage, and I parried its claw as I fell onto my back.

Michaëlle-Annabelle gasps again.

My breath was knocked out of me. The coyomorant went over the top of me.

Predispozisyon—trained instinct from hours upon hours of working with Papa—saved me. I deflected a rake of the coyomorant's claw with Tonton Macoute positioned to protect my face and my neck, and then kicked the machine off me with my Preacher boots. The ones I'm wearing right now.

Michaëlle-Annabelle looks down at my boots and then back up at my face. Her big, beautiful dark brown eyes are wide. Her mouth is open in a small silent O.

My kick sent the coyomorant flying into the other one. Jagged shards of midnight blue metal went flying end over end in every direction from the crash of metal bodies.

Both coyomorants struggled to move. Both coyomorants struggled to get up. Both coyomorants struggled come at me again.

They wanted to rip my throat out with the three long, sharp metal claws on their front paws. But they couldn't. Their sinuous, flexible spines, which gave them their speed and quickness, had been broken. The red lights in their eyes winked out.

Yo te mouri. Truly dead.

"Wi!" Michaëlle-Annabelle cheers.

That gave me some time to get my wind back. But not much. Six of the coyomorants had seen what happened to their sisters. Their head crests flared from the sides of their faces when they looked at me.

They were trying to entimide me. It didn't work. They wanted to avenge their sisters' deaths. I wasn't going to let them. I wanted to live.

I got back on my feet and took a deep breath before I stepped into Form of the Rising Butterfly. I wanted to be calm. I wanted to be swift. I wanted to match vitès avèk vitès.

The coyomorants sprinted toward me from across the street. I kept my form and calmly advanced, Tonton Macoute raised to strike. Just before they reached me, two broke off to flank me on each side. I slowed my advance. I stayed in form.

This wasn't going to be fasil.

I struck first. The four coyomorants in front of me were surprised. I smiled.

Three quick Rising Butterfly strikes separated three of the coyomorants' heads from their bodies. The coyomorants were built by the Clockmaker for speed and agility, not strength. Papa trained me for speed. But Papa also trained me for strength.

I stepped into Form of Queen Alexandra's Birdwing and unleashed brutal savagery on the last coyomorant in front of me. It didn't stand a chance. It didn't look like a coyomorant when I was finished with it.

In my peripheral vision, I could see the flanking coyomorants pounce. I stepped into Form of the Monarch. I needed the confidence from that form. This was going to hurt. And it did.

The two coyomorants swiped and slashed and raked and sliced. I parried and deflected most of their blows. But not all of them.

Their claws found my ribs and my forearms and my thighs and my lower back. But I did not fall. I did not drop Tonton Macoute.

But I was getting tired. I knew I couldn't last much longer.

Michaëlle-Annabelle's bottom lip quivers. Tears stand in her large, lovely dark brown eyes.

So I stepped into Form of the Viceroy. I feinted left and then right. Both coyomorants flinched back to avoid Tonton Macoute. Enpi, with a smooth spin that flowed into Form of the Rising Butterfly again, I sliced left and then right. Heads rolled.

I could hardly catch my breath. My chest was heaving. I wanted to collapse.

And when I saw that all of the adults had come back outside with their pipes and their hoes and their rakes and their machetes to help me fight the rest of the coyomorants, I did collapse. Mwen te fatige.

"And so are you," I say to Michaëlle-Annabelle, wiping the spilled tears from her baby-fat cheeks and tucking the covers under chin.

She yawns. "Tell me the story ankò, but this time all in Kreyòl." Her voice is sleepy.

"Aw, ti boubou, I have to go. I have to find manman mwen ak papa mwen."

"Silvouplè, Michaëlle-Isabelle," she begs.

"Dakò. But I will tell it in Kreyòl ak Anglais again because y manman ak y papa told me you need to practice your Anglais."

"Mèsi!" Michaëlle-Annabelle murmurs, and takes my hand into hers.

"No one wanted to come out of their houses. Not at first," I start all over again, but I don't get any further than that because Michaëlle-Annabelle is fast asleep.

About the Author

Malon Edwards was born and raised on the South Side of Chicago, but now lives in the Greater Toronto Area, where he was lured by his beautiful Canadian wife. Many of his short stories are set in an alternate Chicago and feature people of color. Malon serves as Grants Administrator for the Speculative Literature Foundation, which provides a number of grants for writers of speculative literature.

Author's Notes

Michaëlle-Isabelle, the heroine of my Half Dark series (*"The Half Dark Promise"*, *"Shadow Man, Sack Man, Half Dark, Half Light"*, this story, and more to come) is based on my daughter who is strong-willed, feisty, adventurous, keen on new experiences, and when confronted, will step up to the challenge and fight back until the confrontation has been resolved. (Her name is inspired by former Governor General of Canada, the Right Honorable Michaëlle Jean. I thought her first name was the perfect name for a young Haitian girl living in an alt-history Haitian-influenced Chicago founded by Haitian trader Jean Baptiste Point DuSable).

I see *Candied Sweets, Cornbread, and Black-eyed Peas* as the mid-point in Michaëlle-Isabelle's hero's journey, but not entirely in the Joseph Campbell sense of the concept. I used to play text-based MUDs back in the day (mostly solo-leveling), and after an intense battle where I'd nearly died, I'd go to an inn to rest up, eat, re-stock my food stores, and interact with some of the other players and their characters until the next battle.

But this story is more than just resting up for the next battle. It's about a black community overcoming the fear of one of their own to support her when she needs them most, it's about strong, black older women (based on my mother and her sisters) passing on love and knowledge to a young black girl who is quickly emerging as a leader, and it's about the camaraderie of sharing Southern black food in a blend of a block party/family reunion-like atmosphere. I wanted to draw a straight line from my alt-history Chicago to real-time Chicago and show how a dangerous Chicago still has positive elements within it.

EL CANTAR DE LA REINA BRUJA

Victoria Sandbrook

Mothers, hear me! I am alone but for your graces. My mistakes have bound me. My weaknesses have hobbled me. My pride has torn me from you.

A lejandra pricked her finger on her rough iron chains and whispered lilting iambs until all appearance of fatigue fell from her. When they came for her, she would look herself again.

Well. Not her true self. Not even the self she'd donned a decade ago to snare herself her king. What chaos there would be if her husband's guards—nay, the entire kingdom!—discovered that the bruja chained in the metal palanquin had been their queen these ten years. "I must hide you from the priests," Ciro had said, pallid with self-pity over his own deceit. "They would burn you for heresy." Thus, Alejandra discovered what husband-kings did with unwilling, powerful wives. Now he risked much by dragging her on this yet unblooded campaign. But he had a rival to conquer: a widowed queen he thought to wed. With his wife's help, of course.

The cabos—honored soldados, yes, but still babes with new chains of rank about their necks—held swords aloft when they opened her door. Unnecessary but flattering.

One motioned Alejandra forward, her voice as stern as a sargenta's. "You're to survey the battlefield, Doña Alejandra."

Doña! Alejandra locked her jaw against the reply that boomed in her head. *I was a goddess, wretch! I am your queen, dung-hurler. Avert your eyes and hold your tongue lest I find a better use for them.*

She—Alejandra Isabella Celia de Las Vientas, Reina Coronada, Daughter of the Wind Women, Rightful but Secret Queen of the Valle—rose with the power of her ethereal forbears at the tip of her tongue, ready to fell the insignificant caba with the thunderclap of a curse.

But her own enchantment stopped her. The same spell she'd originally used to slough off her gossamer goddess soul. The same spell that had given her the form to seduce the delicious young King Ciro she'd spied from above. The form he'd bedded after exchanging whispered vows that made her his queen. The form that could be chained as her windborne self could never have been. The form that could not bear enough magic to break the spell that made it.

So she—Alejandra Isabella Celia de Las Vientas, Reina Coron ada, Daughter of the Wind Women, Rightful but Humbled Queen of the Valle—demurred and did as she was bid.

~

I will suffer the great pain I have wrought. With a whim, I bought but tears and chains. With my words, I will buy freedom.

~

They skirted around the camp, parting dense, high grasses in silence. Birdsong, ever Alejandra's companion in the palanquin and in her tower-room in the palace, lilted and swirled on the breeze. The morning air was damp, cool against her wrinkled red gown. The stiff stalks tried to seed her hair with burrs and dry bits, but the chaff fell from her like dutiful supplicants. The insolent caba behind Alejandra would have no such luck.

A quarter-mile from camp they stopped at the still-bleeding stump of a newly-felled tree before a field thick with mist. There stood her husband-king, not yet in his mail, draped in a sapphire brocade cloak. Ciro looked younger than his fifty-two years, skin the firm tawny-tan of cypress thanks to the week-long march, gray-streaked hair masked in the haze, the set of his bearded jaw, eyes limned with desire. Just not for Alejandra.

Ciro signaled to the cabos to wait back in the grass.

Alejandra stared into the fog as their footsteps retreated. How far away was the enemy, she wondered. Were they waiting just beyond her sight, ready to pounce? Were they still abed, assured of victory?

Ciro began. "Wife."

"Your Majesty." She curtseyed.

He handed her the willow stationery box.

Alejandra's hands trembled as the wood breathed relief into her, its protection spells easing. "What do you ask of me today?"

He squinted, as if trying to conjure the future from the mist. "A dry field for our side. Muddy for the enemy. Fog to cover the vanguard. To drive them well toward the eastern mountains."

By way of reply, Alejandra whispered an old couplet to the tree stump. It transformed, offering her a lacquered desk and fine chair at which she could sit. The willow box went on top and slightly to her left. From it she drew a sheet of paper milled by lovers quarreling at midnight; a dark tincture-ink of mustard seed and sheep's birthing blood; her bone quill, carved from the crooked finger of the still-living but long-forgotten god that had forged her in her first-mother's womb.

Her quill kept time with the birdsong while Ciro's impatient coughing and throat-clearing cut in at ill-chosen intervals. Alejandra's lips mimed the words between breaths, ever cautious not to speak without intent. Before her, the cantar de gesta—the song of great deeds—formed in layers, as if each syllable, each line peeled back another length of mist-covered field toward the enemy.

Alejandra reached the end and spit on the paper. She rolled it tight and licked where the seal should have gone. The paper singed and fused. Then she handed it to the king.

"Tie it to a burning arrow," she said, "lit with a flint by a man on a gelding. Shoot it toward the enemy as you signal the charge."

His finger brushed the charmed seal and she clucked her tongue.

"You know what happened the last time you read one of my poems, my king."

Ciro ran the same finger along the line of her jaw. "Yes it took me long enough to break free of your thrall, didn't it?" The hem of his cloak brushed her hand. He was looking for something in her face. Alejandra did not blink.

"You have a great reward coming if we win this war." His voice was soft. He always was a fine seducer.

"Yes, Your Majesty." She hid her hope where she'd long ago buried it inside her. Her answer was rote.

Ciro seemed not to notice. "You've waited a long time, with more patience than I thought you had in you."

"Yes, Your Majesty." Steady breathing. Steady. Easy.

He dipped his head until his lips were against her ear. "I have missed you in our bed. What a shame that you never bore me an heir. At least we know Queen Émilie, mother already to a royal brood, will be more equal to the task."

Alejandra told herself to stay cold. Cold like a decade of nights in that tower room alone. Cold with fear, if that is what it took. Though it was fear of failure ahead, not of the past. Not of him. "Yes, Your Majesty."

He stepped away and called the cabos from the high grass. He looked toward the battlefield instead of to her. "Then it is a good agreement we have reached, bruja. Surely we will neither of us find fault with a positive outcome."

"Yes, Your Majesty."

≈

Carry my words, if you cannot carry me. Grace them with speed if you cannot grace me with hope. I will burn from this earth-bound life a new sky for myself.

≈

The battle was won under cover of an uncanny mist. Alejandra's relieved tears surprised her. After so many years with only the most quiet power within her grasp, she had doubted herself. But maybe her mothers were with her, just hidden on the subtle breeze.

The enemy retreated east, but settled camp with a wide, fast river between themselves and the Vallean ranks. Alejandra stared at the firefly-lights of their cookfires from her stone desk in the river shallows, water raging at her feet, loose hair blowing about her shoulders. Was Queen Émilie looking back at her?

By the light of Ciro's lantern, her bone quill etched lines in shell-blue ink, on thirsty linen paper that gulped the pigment. She kept her eyes on the opposite bank as she delivered the balada, folded and tied with a hair from her head.

"Ford the river at first light with this braided into your stallion's mane. Let no horse ahead of yours. After the army has crossed, push the paper into your wineskin and pour out a measure on the first man you kill."

Ciro smirked. "What if I kill a woman first?"

Alejandra kept her face a mask. "Then wait for a man. But drink no more. You must pour the rest into the river after the battle. When you return to camp, the skin will be full again."

The king shook his head and looked at the unalarming paper. "All that from a poem?"

"I know no other way to cross a river once the bridges have been burned, nor another means of tormenting our enemy's dreams after the battle." Alejandra turned back to him, eyebrows raised. "Unless you preferred to change your orders, Your Majesty."

Ciro chuckled. "The fresh air has given you some of your spunk back, hasn't it, Ale? This time next month, you might be free again."

"May our enemy fly swiftly before your sword, Your Majesty."

$\sim$

Six battles, six spells. Written beneath canvas canopies, astride fallen logs. Scrawled in mud-ink and saffron paste on papyrus and vellum and pressed-pulp. Blessed with tears and dandelion down. Offered on the battlefield by man and woman, by fire's heat and icy gale.

The camp bards wrote much of the blessed campaign of Ciro, King of the Valle. He hid his army in the thinnest morning mist. His horse crossed the raging Cillotar River in a single bound. A great cat prowled his fields of battle, granting swift deaths to all who fell. His foe fled in terror every time they met, ceding villages and towns and cities, bleeding soldados and civilians alike. In the fantastic revelry, only Alejandra understood where magic ceased and fear took hold.

The Vallean army did not press forward unscathed. Many in the ranks paid the cost of the king's requests for magnificent victories. Alejandra heard them first, crying in the dark, beneath the full moon. After a few weeks, she could smell them, even from her place on the furthest outskirts of camp. By then she was starting to ache in ways she never had before and she was out of spells to aid in her own comfort. But she could aid others.

"Please," she begged at the palanquin's window slits, hoping the cabo before it pitied the sick as she did. "Ask the king if I might help. I'll wear shackles if I must. I can disguise myself as a crone. I can work only at night, to relieve the healers—"

"Silence!" His hiss shocked her. She could only see the back of his head, hair cropped short beneath his livery cap, chain of rank tarnished where it touched his skin. And then, after a tense moment, he turned his chin toward the palanquin. "Can you save them?"

"Not all of them," Alejandra admitted. "But more of them than will live if I do nothing."

He nodded and said no more.

An hour after he was relieved from duty, a coronel-doña and her alféreces escorted Alejandra and her willow box to the healers tents. The sick and dying and dead lay next to each other on cots and pallets and horse blankets. The flies seemed to know where to find their easiest marks.

Alejandra rolled up the sleeves of her gown, once a pious red cotton now patchy with ochre spots of mud and sweat. She looked at the first poor soul before her, writhing with fever and delirium. "Get this man some water, alférez." Someone darted to the corner to comply, but the coronel grabbed Alejandra by the arm before she could kneel next to the patient.

"Come back to this one," she said between gritted teeth. Alejandra took the woman's measure: ten years her junior; a dark coronet braid unraveling beneath her bedraggled feather cap; her chain of rank boasted double links of gold and silver between the steel but was caked with mud and something darker. The coronel's hazelwood eyes dared Alejandra to countermand the order. Intrigued, Alejandra assented.

On the other side of the tent, the coronel's younger, sicker double lay atop a cot, bandages oozing above pale and graying skin. She still wore her battle-torn tunic though they had not seen action for days.

The colonel swallowed before pushing the willow box at Alejandra. "Her. First."

"Of course, doña." Alejandra lowered herself onto a stool next to the dying girl. "What is her name?"

"Rocío. My sister."

"And your name, doña?"

The coronel snapped. "What does it matter? She is dying, not me!" She stopped herself just short of a sob.

Alejandra kept her voice steady. "You lay your sacrifices at the feet of idols and icons. The stone and paint that give them form are languages spoken without a tongue. What others do with their hands to name the gods and their power, I do with words."

"You speak to the gods on our behalf? But you're no priestess, you're a bru—"

"All I need is your name, coronel. Your sister needs you now more than your piety."

The coronel's lips went white as they thinned. She brushed a thick curl of hair off her forehead. "Pilar."

Alejandra bowed her head. "Then I will work as quickly as I can."

"See that you do."

Alone with her patient, Alejandra chose a tincture of willow heart, ash from a priestess's funeral pyre, and petals of the rare, black-flowering cherries that blossomed in mournful clouds on the Vallean Mountains every thirtieth spring. She removed the largest bandage, shushing Rocío's whimpers. Then she dipped her bone quill first in tincture, then in blood, and began her work.

The spell wrapped first around the sword wound in Rocío's torso, its lines fracturing only with punctuation and rhyme, the iambs lining up just so as Alejandra worked in the round. The vial of tincture ran red then crimson as the nib mixed brew and blood.

After three circles about the wound, Alejandra's mester de brujería sprawled outward, tracing organs and infection. The confining meter of the cuaderna via was not her forte, but Alejandra fought through it. When the sword wound began to dry then close, Alejandra pressed the nib deeper to draw forth Rocío's blood: there was still a fever to fight. The text ran beneath and over the girl's bare breasts, across the fleshy skin over her pelvic bone, in eddies about her liver and kidneys.

Sweat had collected on Alejandra's brow and when the first drop fell on Rocío's healing body, the girl's eyes opened with true waking.

Alejandra smiled, licked her quill clean, and hailed a passing cabo. "Call the coronel-doña. Her sister will live."

The man's eyes were wide with horror at Rocio's naked and bloody form, but by the time Alejandra had turned back to the girl, the words that had saved her were already fading.

"Doña? Who are you?"

"Just a voice, child. Thank the Wind Women next time you pray."

~

Mothers! Hear me! Through these mortal hands I wear, your work has saved so many. Those hours I was your vessel will never be far from my mind, tantalizing and heartwrenching at once. But another hour nears and I will have rent my chains. Will you be with me in the end? Say you will be with me in the end.

~

Alejandra awoke before dawn the morning of what should be the last battle, in a real tent, her body comfortable beneath serviceable furs of dappled lynx and red fox. A cabo stood within, staring at the back wall and affording her no privacy, but what was privacy when it only came with metal walls and a chamber pot? She deserved better, but she had earned this much with her healing these last weeks. How many of Ciro's officers had she pulled back from the brink? How many cabos and coronels and generals, dons and doñas had been spared death or grief through Alejandra's words?

Enough that Ciro could not keep her a secret any longer. A decade ago, his decision to brave the priests' scorn might have warmed Alejandra's heart, reminded her of how much she'd loved him. But her years of forgiveness were behind her. Instead, she had thanked Ciro before his officers and nobles, and had enjoyed her tent while it lasted.

She dressed in a fresh gown sewn from recovered war banners, torn and battered. It threatened to be a maudlin choice, but she reminded herself that it was her only source of cloth and Ciro did love his heraldry. The trim silhouette flattered her, though she missed her fuller palace figure, soft with fine foods and little work. In the end, though, what she looked like would matter so very little.

Alejandra rode to the ridge from which Ciro surveyed the battle-field, still trailed by her cabos, but at a distance, as her newfound respect afforded her. Her willow box was strapped to her back, her hair braided and knotted by lilting couplet as was her custom in the palace. She'd conjured a diadem for herself, its gemstone blue and clear for her husband-king's honor. He could not object to overt signs of her power. Not now that she'd won the hearts of his people.

"My queen," Ciro said when her horse drew up beside his.

Her smile was genuine. "Your Majesty. What do you ask of me today?"

Ciro gestured to the vista before them. "Bring down the enemy." As if he asked no more than her favor before a fight.

The tall heights of the eastern mountains, just reaching their summer glory. At their foot, a stoic stronghold carved from the mountain's black heart. Impenetrable, it was said.

Well.

Alejandra dismounted and called a desk up from a grassy hillock. She ordered her things just so. From the box, she retrieved brilliant green ink pigmented with the vibrant yellow pollen of a wolf pine and the powder of a delicate mushroom that grew only beneath blood moons and turned blue when crushed. She pressed the nib of her quill into the soft flesh of her ring finger. Ten drops of Alejandra's blood turned the ink black.

She turned to her husband-king. "Your knife?"

"As if your quill couldn't do?" But he handed her the weapon.

Its heft was tempting. How much did the cabos love her now? Could she test them?

For the first time in three months, since that first morning before that first battle, her will tested the limits of the enchantment. It held. Alejandra could not carve her freedom from Ciro with a knife. She smiled at the weapon. Maybe she would not have anyway. Maybe.

She lifted her overskirts and tore her cambric shift with her dagger. The piece she removed was ragged about the edges but strong in the middle. It would do nicely.

Alejandra looked out at the fortress as she composed this last cantar de gesta, the bone quill never faltering in its task. She knew battles now, the careful choreography between great foes, the difference one brash soldado could make to a compañía, the difference an impassioned compañía could make to its tercio, the ways a tercio could grasp victory from the jaws of chance. In bodies she knew, in bodies she could name, the tide would rise and fall and rise as she saw fit.

But the final stanzas offered her the promise toward which she'd worked these long months. She wrote her own tack toward freedom in words she hadn't dared compose—even in her solitude —for fear she would sap their power too soon. She shed a few tears, laughed at her haughty pride over her craft, and set the quill down.

"It's done then?" Ciro asked, reaching for the fabric.

Alejandra stilled his hand with a soft touch to his wrist. Her eyes never left the field before them. "I must carry this one into battle, Your Majesty."

All he said was, "You'll need a different horse. Tell any coronel you see, and ask for whatever armor you would choose. We ride in an hour."

She'd expected him to deny her. But he did not. Was it trust? Willingness to risk her for his ends? Did it matter?

Luck or chance drew Coronel-Doña Pilar to the stables just as Alejandra arrived.

The coronel did not take her king's orders to heart. "You cannot risk yourself, dear doña! What would we do if you were killed? Captured?"

Alejandra smiled and looked the few free horses up and down. "There is work to be done on the field. No one can see through this task but me." Then, to distract Pilar as much as herself: "How is your sister?"

"Well." The coronel fell into step behind Alejandra. "She's still confined, but finds it hard to complain of spending every waking hour with her son. I would not be so easily kept abed."

"Nor I."

They shared a smile, then Alejandra stopped before a chestnut mare with a scar beneath one eye. The horse stopped prancing and took Alejandra's measure. "This one should do."

"There is no better horse in this army, doña." Pilar's voice was strained. "She has never led me wrong."

Too many coincidences. Alejandra's eyes stung and her chest constricted. Her mothers were with her.

Mothers! Hear me!

"Then it is to be," she said aloud. The coronel's jaw gaped. "Go back to your sister and nephew. Do not set foot on the battlefield this day—"

"But my compañia—"

"I will explain; the king will not gainsay me now. No eagle can ignore a changing wind."

"What?"

"Go, Pilar. By nightfall, the tale will be told and you'll be glad to be alive to hear it."

∾

Please do not forsake me.
Please do not forsake me.
Please do not forsake me.

∾

Alejandra was unarmed and unarmored when Ciro called the

charge. He insisted she keep away from the vanguard, that she had no place in the first lines. She instead led Pilar's compañia, which trailed a great siege engine. Boulders had been flying toward the fortress all morning, but every one had shattered against the walls. The enemy's army, bedecked in black as deep as their stronghold, flooded out of the gates to meet the charge, the debris bedamned.

When the first clash of swords rang back through the tercios, Alejandra stood in her stirrups. The king's bannermen were in the thick of it, which meant Ciro was, too. Her hand went to the spell tucked beneath her belt. It was time.

"Hold here," Alejandra shouted to the soldado behind her. A caba protested, but the queen ignored her and urged Pilar's war-mare into a gallop.

The clean, unbroken tercios formed alleys through which she rode toward the fray. A wind ran down from the heights behind the Valleans, as if to speed Alejandra on her way. She wanted to face it, to throw her arms wide in welcome, but she did not falter. Even as the sounds of death met her. Even as flying boulders whistled over-head and their horrifying pounding made her tremble. Even as she caught sight of Ciro, unhorsed, locked in battle, his banners drooping in the hands of dying cabos.

The mare pressed through the fighting. The bards would later argue whether it was chance or grace or the power of a beautiful woman riding like the Wind Women that kept horse and rider from harm. But Alejandra knew she was blessed. Ciro looked up as she caught a banner in her hand. He shouted at her, unintelligible over his battle-rage and the screams of good people dying on good swords. Alejandra unfurled the cambric spell, tied it to the banner pole, and raised it high above her head. She shouted one powerful word, both mundane and magical in the same breath.

"Yield!"

The field fell still in waves. Alejandra's voice carried on the wind to every soldado, cabo, coronel, general on both sides. To every ear in the fortress. To the sick and healing in the Vallean camp. A lone boulder flew and crashed, ignored. In the deepening silence, Alejandra could hear the newly formed pebbles raining down around the bodies and rubble.

Then one horse moved, a white blur across the field. A dark figure sat astride, taking the form of a woman in mail. Her horse and sword and face were spattered with blood. Her mahogany-brown coronet of braids was already flying loose. By her bearing if by nothing else, all knew her as Queen Émilie.

Even Ciro did not move as the woman approached. Though Alejandra did watch him try.

"You!" Queen Émilie shouted as she closed the distance between them. "Who are you?"

Alejandra bowed as best she could atop the mare. "I am the voice on the wind, Your Majesty. I sent the skylark to your tent each dawn. The fresh breeze for your fevered and fading. The courage to return to the field seven times in the face of certain defeat. Our enemy bore you my letters with every charge but this one. Now, I deliver him to you. And I bring you an army. And myself."

Émilie's hands were tight on her reins. "The poems...the love poems...they were real?"

"Do I look real?" Alejandra dared a smile.

"Yes!" She sobbed a laugh. "Yes, you do. Then I did not conjure your face in my loneliness."

"No, Your Majesty."

The queen urged her horse closer. "And you are not harmed by this Vallean scum."

"No, Your Majesty."

Closer now, the queen looked tired, road-weary, and she had every right to be. She removed a glove of mail and leather and touched Alejandra's cheek with trembling fingers. "And I have not lost everything."

"No, Your Majesty."

≈

Daughter! Hear us, beloved one!
We are here. We are here. We are here...

≈

The bards would have it that the Kingdom of Valle-Monts is ruled in deed by Queen Émilie and in word by Queen Alejandra. Many songs recall the romancero the Vallean queen wrote to woo her lover, a new cantar and ballado with every battle. They sing seldom of the royal dead, for what money is there in remembering Ciro the Captor? They sing memorials for the others, though, the hundreds or thousands who fell before the winds changed and bound the kingdoms in love.

There is, of course, some truth in their tales. The romancero would never be read or sung again if Alejandra would have it: she knew too much of battles to wish such a book of such spells to be left for Émilie's children. But she writes her consort-queen poems —*just* poems—to assuage the loss of those first, heartfelt pleas.

Alejandra, if no one else, thinks of Ciro often. Of his trial and death. Of his funeral pyre at which she stood vigil. Of the ashes she collected beneath the cloud-crowned full moon that now swirl in a vial of vinegar in her willow box. His usefulness has not yet waned.

The other dead plague her. On stormy nights, she walks the wind-battered battlements and sings into the moaning gale, naming them to their gods in every tongue she knows.

But she chooses to stay, to keep her mothers from gathering her up and crossing the earth over with joy. And if the bards knew this much, they would make a fortune. For what tales they could tell of the La Reina Bruja, Daughter of the Wind Women, who bound herself, saved herself, and named herself savior.

About the Author

Victoria Sandbrook is a speculative fiction writer, freelance editor, and Viable Paradise graduate. Her short fiction has appeared in *Shimmer*, *Cast of Wonders*, and the anthology *Sword & Steam Short Stories*. She is an avid hiker, sometimes knitter, long-form talker, and initiate baker. She often loiters around libraries, checking out anything from picture books to monographs. She spends most of her days attempting to wrangle a ferocious, destructive, jubilant tiny-but-growing human. Victoria, her husband, and their daughter live in Brockton, Massachusetts. She reviews books and shares writerly nonsense at victoriasandbrook.com and on Twitter at @vsandbrook.

Author's Notes

This story arrived in a moment of need. On the surface, that need was for a story that might be of interest for this anthology. I'd been working on something else that, well, wasn't working. I suggested this story in a message to a friend with a single line that got to the heart of both Alejandra's problem and the steps she takes to solve it, and my friend encouraged me in the strongest terms to write it. Which was good, because by the time she replied, I was already very much sold on writing it.

What I didn't realize at the time was how much I needed to put some attic-wife rage on the paper. Maybe I'd been feeling a lack of agency in my own life, or at odds with my chosen and ascribed social identities, because I wanted to tell a story where subversion and words had more than one purpose. Alejandra blew in and took over, seething beneath the surface and biding her time. As I explored the magic she used, I loved uncovering layers of its rebellion: a resource-driven art of the written-word that flaunted the establishments of (fictional) politics and religion. I layered in references to epic, heroic, and religious poetic forms from Spanish literature and it just felt right.

Another thing I love about Alejandra that sharpened in revisions is her faith—in her plan, in the gods that raised her, in possibilities of her own power, in the future. She's not unshakable—and she's willing to admit to the hubris that landed her where she is when the story starts—but she leaps into action trusting that her future is not set in stone, that not everyone is bad-hearted, that she can outlast her ordeal. So for all it's attic-wife rage, there's hope. And I think we can all use a dose of that.

THE OTHER FOOT

Margo Lanagan

C orporal Bell (Queen Mabel's Own, Copper Star) pushes the soil into the hole. With the first push, everything's covered but a bit of leather and one round eye of sawn bone. With the second, the hole is just a hole again, just earth into earth. Fill it up, to the brim and beyond.

"There, now," she says when it's done. "March all over that."

The booted feet hang back, of course. It's only rhymes they've ever jumped to.

So she spins up something, a child's verse playing soldiers, rumpety-tump. And up they hop and do the job, saving Bell's only foot a deal of stamping. What a sight, in the sunshine—really quite cheerful, for all that this is a kind of funeral. A funeral's bootlace. She sits on a stump and smokes a pipe and mutters them on when they flag.

And when they're done, rolls a stone on top. To match the others, all in a row, all rolled by Lochrie, only this last by her. And didn't she do just as fine a job alone.

She calls the boots back off the grave, seizes her crutches and stands priestly. "Sleep you well, then, my captain. I will tell your deeds abroad until I die, and send them on along the river or the road, wherever words are rhymed and rote-remembered." And salutes.

She pokes the sack open, hops the red-shod feet out and the brown and black ones in. "That's right, knock the dirt off your-selves. Why should I carry all that extra?"

Slings the sack by its loops across her back. Stands a moment in the sunshine, the pretties on the ground beside her waiting.

"Shall we, sweet things?" she says. "Because we can. It's head-chopping day in town today. There won't be a soul else around."

The cottage is just the same. Oh, but lace at the windows. My, my. Tickets on themselves now. Airs and graces.

Bell knows how to not be seen, around here of all places. Every covert and tree-root, just about every leaf. It hasn't been long. She knows how to be soundless, even on crutches, and with a sack. She was a wanderer and a thief between army and Lochrie, and now she is again. She dallied respectably here through three rounds of seasons, but that's all done and she cuts her shoes from roaming-leather now.

Oh, it's neat as a pin out front. And look, there, the girl herself comes sweeping to the doorway and puts out a little cloud of floor dust, bends and sweeps it off the step, bends farther—nice balance! —and sweeps it from the path, too, into the flower beds either side.

In Bell's shirt-front the dancing-shoes are straining. "I know," she murmurs. "You want to torture her too, yes? And very soon you shall. But for now?" She settles them with a lullaby, of sleeping sheep full of sweet milk and grass nibblings.

There is one corner of the pig-pen where she can't be seen from the house. She works her way up there, and whispers Pansy and Broadarse over, scratches their noses. "Ah," she says, "you remember me! Fed you all those slops, brought you up from hardly more than a hatful! Ye-es, you like that there under the chin, don't you? Does Little Miss Clackfoot know to do that for you? Oh, I think not!"

She would dearly love to take her sackload past the chicken house to the other hut, where she kept the boots since Lochrie couldn't abide them in the house. She'd chant them up a storm in there, as she used to sometimes on a moonlit night.

Instead she positions herself well back in the forest, with a good view of the yard-side door. She sends the shoes forward to skulk in the bushes at the forest edge. She waits. She'd like another pipe, but she's not stupid. She cracks and drinks a stolen egg.

The girl comes out with the bucket. Oh, it eats Bell up to see brooms and buckets in Karin's hands that once she herself handled just so unthinkingly! To see her easy stride across this territory, on the feet Lochrie carved, while his love moved from his old battle-mate across to prettier Karin, slenderer-waisted and bigger arsed-and-titted and unbesmirched by witchery or war. Tell her a verse and all you ever got was blank eyes and a shake of the head. Hymns, it was, and Bible verses, were the only things that spoke to that one. Tedious chit.

And Bell runs the shoes forth as the girl, the goodwife, turns from the well.

"Agh!" The bucket drops, the water leaps and slops. "Oh!"

Bell sets the shoes to a flurrying little dance.

Now the girl is supposed to burst into tears as she once so easily did. To run inside and slam the door and weep the after-noon away. Leaving all clear outside for Bell to make off in her own good time.

But Karin stands her ground. She watches the shod feet's madness, fists pressed together at her chest. She shudders—as you would, seeing your chopped-off parts having such a fine time without you.

And then she raises her pretty face, searches the forest with her big lovely gray eyes with their long inky lashes, and says, "Phoebe Bell, is this your doing?"

Well! Child has grown herself a brain, what do you know? Bell breathes silently in the undergrowth.

When she peers around the tree again, Karin is standing hands on hips, and it's clear, with the sun like that and the cloth caught against her, that the girl's expecting.

She blurs for an instant, and that egg requires re-swallowing. When it's down again, the shoes are bobbing red in the air at Karin's waist-height. Bell grabs them with a word, a sharp one that Karin can't fail to hear, even as the girl is swiping at them with a mop handle.

"Don't you dare!" Karin says in a voice Bell's never heard from her, and she sends a shoe thudding into a tree. Its partner dithers and drops. "Come out and show yourself," Karin cries at the forest wall. "You big brave soldier, you!"

"Gracious goodness me, haven't we got some spirit?" says Bell. "Now that we've taken all we want."

Leisurely she extracts herself from her hiding place and swings down the path to the sunny cottage.

"And plugged with a babby too! Or have you just been putting away the cream cakes and the jammy toast? How you used to fancy your jam. Why, we never could keep it up to you, though I ran you pot after pot from the market."

"You're no surprise to me, you sour old bitch," says Karin. "I knew you would come back here and try to make trouble. You've no life of your own worth living, so you must come messing up other people's again."

"Phaugh!" says Bell. "That's rich, from the girl fetching water from the well *I* dug, sweeping out the house *I* built. Begging on our doorstep all starven and weeping then eyeing up my man the minute we saved you."

"*Saved* me?" That's got her good and rattled. "What did I need saving from? Your damned muttering! Your foul magic, that had to be chopped away!" And she sweeps her skirts aside as if Bell has never known or seen, as if Bell wasn't right there holding the shoes as Lochrie's axe came down.

"Oh, woe is you. We have all lost a leg here and there. Those seem to be holding up well." She tilts her head, appraising the false feet and the figure above them. "Though they're carrying a lot more lately, aren't they? And more to come." She waggles her eyebrows.

Karin spits and kerfuffles a moment, then lets her shoulders drop. "Will you just be gone?" she says wearily. "With your nasty sack and your nasty mind and your…just go away from here."

She makes for the house, but not swiftly enough. Bell has a crutch in the door before she can close it.

"God *almighty*, Bell, will you—"

"Will I step in for a cool drink on this hot, hot day? Certainly I will. Since you ask." She still has some bulk to wield in overpowering the new plump Karin.

"And those smelly things—can't they stay outside?"

"They cannot—isn't it sad? They get so lonely without me. And without their wee red friends," she adds, holding the door and dancing the red shoes in. She drops the sack to the floor and loosens the mouth of it so that the boots can wander free. "There, my loves, my lambs. We're all together again now. My heavens, but haven't you *improved* this place!"

She swings herself into the middle of the room. Karin has skittered to the far side of the table and is glaring across like a peeved market wife.

"What's this?" Bell lifts the tip of a crutch to the mantel. "A china shepherdess? Well, I never did see such a thing." She moves it slightly, and smiles at glaring Karin.

"Do what you want," hisses Karin over the leather-squeak and buckle-clink of the moving boots, over the shuffle of them on the hard-packed floor. "Break everything in the place. Go ahead, do it!"

"Oh, but why? When I can just enjoy your anticipating, without lifting a finger? We get sick of it, you know, plunder and pillage. It's almost as dull as dancing. Did you make that quilt? Wouldn't *that* be a long, dull task!" She pokes it and the crutch-end leaves a dirty smudge. "Oh, dear. That's regrettable."

"Just *go*. And take these stinking—"

A halloo interrupts her, from down where the path meets the road into town. Cheerful cries, perhaps with a touch of liquor in them? Does this little miss keep him from his liquor, so that he must do his drinking in the town? Bell wouldn't be surprised. She crosses to where she can see him without being seen herself.

And Karin is gone, leaping over the boots for the back door, running around the house.

"There you are, my lovely!" he cries. And the face on him! He never showed Bell that face.

"Lochrie, she's here!" Karin drops her voice to tell more of the terrible news.

There is no point running. The man has two legs, and Bell is winded just from the sight of him. She never wanted this. All she wanted was to worry Karin as a dog worries sheep, shake her pins, such as she has, drag her through that time again, that winter they were cooped up here together, making each other suffer, Karin growing more beautiful by the day and Bell more curmudgeonly. Pick at the scab and make Karin watch it bleed. She didn't expect, didn't want—

But here he is, blocking the front door.

"The axeman himself," she says firmly.

"Get out of my house," he says. "And if you ever come back and threaten my wife again—"

She throws the crutch like a spear and it catches him in the middle of the forehead. For an instant it pushes his head back out into the sun, his face surprised, lit up and looking at her.

Then he recovers, and roars. Little Karin out there screams something at him. But in he comes, and they're fighting as they used to, him all noise and giant swiping, she spinning free and landing blows that would fell any other body but his.

She is perfectly happy. There is room for nothing but the fight—well, perhaps for enjoying Karin's screeching from the door. This is better even than sexing with him in front of the girl. Karin will *never* know him like this, never dance with him this way!

Bell lets Lochrie pin her just for the joy of breaking his hold. She whacks him so hard with a crutch that it cracks. All about them, tripping them up and struggling beneath and around them, the agitated boots spread wider and wilder—the hut is full now of the smell of them, leather and magicked flesh and bone. They love a good set-to—fisticuffs or cannon or swordplay, they aren't fussed which. The shepherdess is gone from the mantel; shards of some other glass thing glitter on the floor.

Lochrie is tiring, as he always does. But he's no less angry—this won't end as it once might have, in sex or laughter. She's not properly punished yet; she can see it in his eyes.

And he can see (because he knows her through and through—it cuts the heart out of her, this knowing) that she will never give in, never let him near her face or belly. But he keeps coming, the fool. Karin, this love of Karin, it has him by the nutsack, cutting off blood to his brain.

Well, Karin can have him, when this is done. With her next breath Bell starts yammering, one of the pitched-battle scenes from her *Ballad of the Three Queens*. On the strength of that, all the boots leap high and go at Lochrie's head. He tries to cover it but they kick his hands away. He falls among them as into a horde of running rats, and Bell stands above him, chanting, beating time, ruining his ugly beloved face.

Through it all, Karin's bird-skreeks sound, and all at once she is flung down over him and taking the blows to her back and body.

That's where it stops. Though Karin noises on, weeping over Lochrie's head.

Bell snatches up the sack, hoists herself around the upturned furniture to fetch her crutches, muttering the boots after herself.

"Not you," she says as the red shoes try to dance into the bag. Them she takes to the stove, and opens the door and throws them into the blaring gold inside.

All she can see of Lochrie is his bloodied paw bloodying Karin's sleeve. She chants the last boot into the sack.

"Well, I'm off," she says. "I shall go find me another war, I think. That's where I'm best used, marching soldiers to glory."

The little miss turns and spits fire over her shoulder: "I hope you die there, slowly and in great pain!"

Bell leans in the doorway. "And I wish *your* little family well, my sweet. May you have twenty children and all of them three-day labours."

She smiles upon the wreckage, listens awhile to the knocking inside the stove, then hops off the step and swings away down the hill.

About the Author

Margo Lanagan's novels include *Tender Morsels* and *Sea Hearts*. She has also published seven collections of short stories, and a picture book, *Tintinnabula*, illustrated by Rovina Cai. With Scott Westerfeld and Deborah Biancotti, she wrote the New-York-Times-bestselling YA fantasy trilogy ZEROES, about teens with socially based superpowers. She has won four World Fantasy Awards and been shortlisted for Nebula and Hugo awards, and twice honored in the Tiptree awards.

Author's Notes

In the last year I've been making runs at rewriting Hans Christian Andersen's story *The Red Shoes*—those shoes have always given me the horrors, and there's a lot of punitive Christian patriarchal rubbish in it that requires to be either unraveled or just burned to cinders. I've written at least three lengthy re-tellings in various directions, none of which quite caught the essence of the shoe-horror.

When the *Sword and Sonnet* editors asked for a soldier poet, they gave me a new slant on the story by foregrounding the almost incidental soldier in Andersen's original. This single compressed, violent incident coalesced around her. Writing it, I could feel all the other versions boiling themselves down to vital traces in this one, while Bell's duty as a poet made room for itself in her character and the plot. Having Bell paraphrase J. M. Coetzee's words, "after a certain age, we have all lost a leg, more or less," felt like tying the final thematic bow on top of the story.

EIGHT-STEP KŌAN

Anya Ow

When Shyenmu was aged magical eight her mother drove a dragon away with a seven-step quatrain. She had composed it in the seven steps she had taken from her terrified farstepper into the dragon's reach, a poem powerful enough to shame a dragon into leaving the lifeblood river. With the dragon gone for years, the villages prospered. Then, the fish began to die.

"You should've left this to me," Shyenmu's granddaughter Kaeyen said. Their farsteppers took them tirelessly through into the Bounding Sea, the vast steppes of grass bisected by the river. Her farstepper clacked its beak as though agreeing, the great flightless corvid fluffing its sleek black feathers.

"Why? I'm not so old yet that I can't ride." Shyenmu was aged magical eighty now, a prosperous age for dragon-seeking. Not that anyone else had seen it that way.

"You'll hurt your back. If you fall, you'll break something. Your bones are brittle and we're going to have to stop every half an hour so you can take a leak."

"Respect your elders," Shyenmu said, though she grinned, nearly toothless, and sucked her gums loudly as Kaeyen shook her head. Kaeyen was already in better spirits today than she had been for weeks. Their village was far behind them, slow-dying.

~

"Mama," Shyenmu dared to ask on her birthday, lucky at nine, "how did you shame a dragon?"

"Shame is not the right word for it," Mama said, smiling. They were seated at the kitchen table in their cottage, kneading dumplings for the Lunar New Year. "How do you shame a river?"

Shyenmu tried not to scowl. When Mama had returned from

103

shaming a dragon she had said nothing about what she had done. She had gone back to her sweet potatoes and her neat field of bok choy, her chicken coops and longbeans. Even Shyenmu had only known when the diviner from the Eternal City had come a week after, with a box of taels and an Imperial letter of commendation. The letter and the box remained sealed under Mama's bed, untouched.

"Why don't you want to tell anyone what you said to the dragon?" Shyenmu asked, not for the first time since the diviner's visit.

Mama creased a ball of chives and garlic paste within another dumpling, setting it aside. She smiled, tired. "Because I shouldn't have done it."

"What? Why not? The dragon went away. It was dangerous. It was making the water poisonous for people."

"But not for anything else. The fish prosper. And we can still eat the fish. The river rejected only *us*. Because we despoiled it. We shit and pee in the river. We throw our waste into it. Village after village. Downstream, where the river wends into the Eternal City, it dies."

"The water is clean now," Shyenmu said. The dragon had come to the river above the village when she had been unlucky four. She didn't remember much of life before that.

"And we've started our bad habits all over again. That's the problem with people. We don't learn. One day the river will start dying again. Then we'll miss the dragon."

Shyenmu didn't think so. She'd missed all the fuss because she'd been sick when Mama had gone to face the dragon. It had been raining, and while chasing a wayward chick near the river bank, Shyenmu had fallen in and taken a lungful of the dragon's saliva, which had eaten away her lungs, burned her skin. Papa said she had almost died. But for the dragon leaving, she would have.

"Do you wish you didn't do it?" Shyenmu asked when she had made four more dumplings. The question had crawled out of her, a malformed worm that had been growing slowly in her gut all year.

Mama grew a little pale. She looked directly at Shyenmu, meeting her eyes. "No. People are selfish creatures. Who am I to be different?"

It would take thirty years and a child of her own before Shyenmu understood.

~

"Dragon saliva," Shyenmu said, squatting by the stream.

"It's...beautiful." Kaeyen squatted beside her. The water that streamed past glittered in the early morning, full of trapped starlight. Their farsteppers drank from the stream with evident delight, cawing softly. Fish sat low and fat in the stream, pink and as long as Shyenmu's arm, their fins flicking.

"It'll kill you if you drink it."

"I know," Kaeyen said, frowning, trying to swallow her exasperation. "You've only told me a hundred times. Don't worry, Grandmother."

"Worry keeps me alive." Shyenmu got up creakily, rubbing her back. Her bones ached in the cold. "I'm going to put the kettle on. You should catch us some breakfast."

"I *love* this delegation of labor," Kaeyen said, though she was already heading to her farstepper for a net.

Shyenmu made tea, because it was easier to go through the motions than be reminded of the dead. Kaeyen had inherited her mother's sharp tongue and brash wit. Shyenmu's beloved daughter, Mirren, who had died a month and a day ago, drowning in pus. The dying river was poisoning more than its fish.

Shyenmu roasted what they could eat with sesame oil and chives, hanging the rest of Kaeyen's catch to dry on their saddles. The farsteppers caught their own fish, long-toed feet planted in the water, indifferent to the chill. Now that they'd found a dragon-touched river, they'd only need to follow it upstream. Shyenmu painstakingly drew a map in her diary as she ate. She'd made the paper herself with compressed stone, just before leaving.

"Do you know what you're going to say to the dragon?" Kaeyen asked. She was a good fisherwoman, far more adept with the net than her father. It was a dying profession. Most days, Kaeyen eked out a living by running a tea shop with her friends.

"Not at all."

Kaeyen looked disbelieving. "Grandmother."

"My mother didn't know what she was going to say either when she rode out to talk to the river."

"Did she tell you what she said? To the dragon?"

"She did." Shyenmu stared down at the map she was making, at the small mark she had made for her village. "It won't help."

"Was it beautiful?" Kaeyen asked, hopeful.

"It was. But not because of the words." Because of her grief, because anger and desperation had given her poem power, had burned the air when she had spoken it, enough to change the river. Shyenmu had no such poetry in her. She only had questions.

"And you can do that again, can't you? You're her daughter."

"You're her great-granddaughter," Shyenmu said, smiling for a moment before Kaeyen's frown stole that away.

"I was. And for most of my life I hated that. Everyone hated great-grandmother for killing the river. For driving away the dragon. I was glad that she gave that box of taels to the village."

"I was glad too," Shyenmu said, though for different reasons. The taels had been the price for silence, bought from the Eternal City. Whenever her mother remembered it was there, her face would tighten and grow pale. It was the source of many ills, the bringer of false friends, the cause of the rot that had set into her mother's marriage and driven her father to another village. When the mayor had called it blood money Shyenmu had agreed. It had bled away the light in her mother's life and made it joyless. A dragon's revenge was paid in gold. "Eat up quickly. We should ride upriver while the sun's still pleasant."

～

The taels bought a winter's worth of supplies for the village for everyone else. "That's people for you," Mama said, when Shyenmu complained.

"Why aren't you angry? You saved them once. Not just them, but the other villages. And the City. The Emperor paid you for that."

"I didn't save them. I saved *you*. It's only taken everyone this long to notice." Mama smiled, tired, spooning a dollop of sweet potato porridge into Shyenmu's bowl. "Eat up."

"I'm tired of sweet potato! I'm tired of just eating the same thing every day. We used to have fish. We used to have chickens. Eggs."

Mama didn't flinch. She waited instead, taking each blow until Shyenmu grew exhausted. They ate in silence. Mama had only a quarter of a bowl of porridge, as usual. "I'm not hungry," she said, when Shyenmu offered as usual to share, although today Shyenmu was mulish about it.

Normally, Shyenmu would nod and move on, swallowing her guilt with the rest of her meager dinner. Today, she set her bowl down. "Why do you always lie?"

"What do you mean?"

"You're obviously hungry. I can hear your stomach."

"You're listening to the wind," Mama said, smiling, and even that beautiful wry smile was a lie: it didn't touch her eyes.

"And you *did* save the village. People used to die from the river. They'd fall in, like me. Or people who don't know better drink from it when they're visiting. Or bathe in it. Or they don't let the fish dry off for long enough before they eat it."

"And now people still die from the river," Mama said, finishing her porridge slowly, "but there's no dragon to blame, so they'll create another dragon."

"They're blaming you. Us."

Mama nodded. She reached over, ruffling Shyenmu's hair, chuckling as Shyenmu reared away, scowling. "It will pass."

"You're lying again."

"Ah, and you're growing wiser." Mama set her spoon down in her bowl. "Yes. They'll blame me. And because you are here, you. If your father had stayed, he would have been blamed too."

"He's a coward. He ran away."

"He's human. It's human to be a coward. Eat up."

"You weren't a coward," Shyenmu muttered. She obeyed, and afterward, washed the bowls out the back with what water they could spare from the rainwater tank. Mama watched from the kitchen window. She was pickling vegetables, jars and jars of them, brining them in sugar and vinegar. Puzzled, Shyenmu asked, "I didn't know we had spare food."

"It was a present."

"A present? From who?" No one else in the village had surplus crops.

Mama smiled. There were smudges beneath her eyes. She wiped her hands, and came out of the kitchen, hugging Shyenmu tightly, breathing in the scent of Shyenmu's hair. "Ah, you've grown so tall now. Taller than me."

"Almost." Shyenmu straightened up carefully, holding the pots, unsettled. It was not the nature of the One People to show affection so openly. "Are you okay?"

"Why do you ask?"

"I'm sorry I said you were a liar," Shyenmu said. It was the nature of children to hurt their parents, but perhaps she'd gone too far.

"Well," Mama said, stroking her hair, "you're not wrong there."

～

"Great-Grandmother went looking for the dragon again, didn't she?" Kaeyen said, as they followed the river upstream, where the trapped starlight in the water grew slowly brighter.

"Why do you ask?"

"I always thought it was strange. How she disappeared when you were still so young. Especially since Great-Grandfather abandoned you both years before."

"Oh, it was a long time ago," Shyenmu said, and chuckled as Kaeyen scowled.

"Then you won't mind telling me what happened."

"Yes. She went away to look for the dragon. The others convinced her. Said they'd look after me, no matter what happened."

"Those bastards!"

"I wouldn't be so harsh on them. They were desperate. And even though Mama never came back, they kept their word. Some of them. I had help when I needed it for the garden. And they stopped treating me like an outcast." In the early days of her grief Shyenmu had swung between gratefulness for the new company and rage.

"Why didn't you move away?"

"And leave the garden? The house?"

"You thought Great-Grandmother would come back," Kaeyen guessed. "That's why you never left. Even during the lean times. And the plague. Grandfather used to argue with you. Said there were richer lands to the south. Jobs."

Shyenmu nodded. "So I told him to go, and he went."

"Another coward."

"I wouldn't be so harsh on him either."

Kaeyen sniffed. "You're not harsh on *anyone*. It drove Mom crazy."

"So it did."

"I miss her," Kaeyen said, subdued. Shyenmu nodded, her hands knotting over the reins. It wasn't right that a parent had to bury their child. Even if death would have been a relief. She looked away as her eyes stung.

"We'll be close to the mountains by evening. We can set up camp at the foot."

"What if the dragon comes upon us during the night? We should find someplace to hide while we sleep."

"It won't fly during the night."

Kaeyen looked at her oddly. "You received a package from the Eternal City by courier. Before you decided to go dragon hunting." Shyenmu nodded. The village was far enough away from a trade route that a visitor from the Eternal City, even a courier, drew notice from every villager. "What was that about? A book about dragons?"

"Not a book. An answer to a question. I wrote to the University of the Eternal. I didn't think anyone would write back. Let alone go to all the trouble of sending a couriered reply." Shyenmu smiled wryly. "My handwriting is very ugly and I didn't address it to anyone."

"What did you ask?"

"'What is a dragon?'"

Kaeyen blinked. "What? That's really what you asked? *Grandmother*. Everyone knows what a dragon is. It's the celestial spirit of a river, shaped like a great bearded serpent. The stones are its bones, the water is its blood; when it breathes life into a river it both purifies the water and curses it against people."

"Not against *all* people," Shyenmu said. She reined her farstepper to a halt, getting off heavily, ambling over to the river bank. Kaeyen gasped as Shyenmu bent and thrust her palm into the water. The dragon's bite was icy cold.

"Grandmother!" Kaeyen scrambled off her farstepper, hurrying over. Shyenmu waved her back, drawing out her palm, wiping it on the grass. The skin was clear, with none of the lesions of dragon poison. Kaeyen stared, open-mouthed for a long moment. "How?"

"I guessed as much."

"Because you were cured from it before?"

"Perhaps." Shyenmu said. She climbed laboriously back onto her farstepper.

"The University told you that?"

"After a fashion. Dragons aren't the only things that love riddles."

~

Another woman would have stolen away in the night, ashamed of abandoning her child, regardless of her best intentions, afraid of being talked into staying. That was not Mama's way. She had already determined to go: she made breakfast, though she did not eat. The bags were packed by the door, the farstepper saddled, and the breakfast was lavish: century eggs, fish congee, even fried youtiao. Shyenmu wished her mother's guilt didn't taste this good, but she was hungry and her mother had always been a good cook.

After Shyenmu washed the bowls and stacked them away, she sat back down at the table. "Why?"

"It's time."

"Because of the village?"

"Because of everyone," Mama said, and smiled her tired smile, "and because of me."

"You?" That was new. The women of the One People were expected to sacrifice themselves for their children. "You're going away for *yourself?*" Shyenmu flared. "You're just like Papa. You're running away."

"If I were," Mama said, folding her hands over the table, "I would take you with me."

"What are you going to do? Ask the dragon to come back? Even if that would work, it'll be the same as before. We can't touch the river anyway. We should get the village mayors to talk to each other. If we stop poisoning the river it won't poison us back."

"It's easier to ask a dragon to return than to ask everyone in the world to be less selfish. Besides, the dragon is gone because I was selfish. So I will go." Mama reached across the table, but Shyenmu flinched away from her palm. She flattened the fingers on the table instead, yearning. "I go before I become a burden."

"What if you don't come back?"

"Then it will be your turn." Mama rose from the table. "You'll know."

"How long will you be away?"

"I don't know. I'll have to look for the dragon first. I don't know where it might have gone."

"When…" Shyenmu swallowed her words. Changed her mind. "When will I know if I have to come after you?"

"The farstepper will return if I fail." Mama circled around the table, and Shyenmu was stiff as arms circled her shoulders. "I wish I'd been less strict with you in the time that I had," Mama said, and Shyenmu buried her face against Mama's ribs, stifling tears, "but what's done is done." She would not say that she loved Shyenmu, even at the end, nor did Shyenmu manage the words. The One People had no words then for filial love, only piety.

∽

They saw the dragon as they crested the mountain pass, and the dragon saw them. It had made of itself a necklace for the high peak known as the Steps to Heaven, curled around stone, its sinuous translucent form bright with starlight. Its bearded doglike head was open in the fast-flowing stream, tusks yawned wide. It did not move.

"Stay here," Shyenmu told Kaeyen. Their farsteppers were grumbling, shifting nervously.

"Not a chance."

"This is as close as you get. Stay here or I'll send you home."

"With what words?" Kaeyen said, though she was sheet pale, her hands shaky. Shyenmu clucked her tongue, nudging her reluctant farstepper forward, and was glad to see that Kaeyen didn't follow. Her mind was an open blank, her lungs burned from the cold. It was a long ride down the pass, threading through scree and stone, the dragon's great golden orbs tracking their every step. The farstepper beneath her warbled anxiously, and flinched as the dragon snorted. It was the last chick of her mother's farstepper, which had returned a month and a day after her mother had left the village for good. Perhaps it knew.

When the farstepper would go no further, Shyenmu dismounted. Her palms were damp, hands trembling so violently that she fisted them to hide the shivers. The eye of the dragon on its left flank was bigger than her head, set in a scaly head taller than her cottage. The dragon breathed out, a gust of chill wind and starlight. Within its gaping throat was the heart of the river.

Shyenmu walked a step. Then the next. She fought her fear, drew armor from eighty years of unlucky memories. A third step, her mind growing clear. At the fourth, she knew the truth of the University's riddle. At the fifth, she understood her mother's regret, at the sixth, she saw her own, which she had hidden deep. At the sixth she smiled, at the seventh she loved the dragon. At the eighth she took a breath, and at the ninth she stopped, and spoke a kōan for the spirit of the river.

The dragon is the spirit of the river,
The dragon is the water celestial,
The poisoner of children,
The eater of selfishness.
What can you do about the dragon?
Is it better to ask:
What do you call the dragon?

"Mother of regrets," Shyenmu said, holding up her arms, "my mother, I am here."

The dragon shuddered. It closed its jaws, heaving itself away from the river. The farstepper fled, speeding away to Kaeyen. Shyenmu did not watch it go. She was looking past great arching horns and the coils of endless scale, as the last of her mother let go of her regrets, and rose, upward and upward, taking the path of mothers before her, towards the vault of heaven.

By the time Kaeyen made it down to Shyenmu, her skin was growing translucent, her hair crowned in starlight, and as she smiled, her teeth were growing slowly into tusks. "Why?" Kaeyen said, her eyes bright with tears. "Did you know?"

"A dragon is a wish for a more fantastic world," Shyenmu said, kicking off her beaded sandals, stepping into the chill of the river. "It is every mother's wish for their children. Goodbye, grand-daughter."

"Will I have to come back?" Kaeyen asked, uncertain.

"Someday, if you are selfish." Shyenmu smiled, and reached over, hugging air over Kaeyen's shoulders. Her touch was now as poisonous as the river. "And that is not such a bad thing to be."

"I love you," Kaeyen said, because love was the language of the young, and blinked away her tears, getting back on her farstepper, leading Shyenmu's behind her. She looked back at the arch of the mountain pass, and then she was gone. Alone, Shyenmu sat in the river, waiting to fly.

About the Author

Anya Ow was born in Singapore and has Hainanese, Peranakan, and Hakka ancestry. She moved to Melbourne to practice law for a few years, and now works in an ad agency as a designer and as the chief briber of studio dogs. Her first novel, *The Firebird's Tale*, was published in 2016. Anya's short stories have appeared in venues such as *Strange Horizons*, *Daily Science Fiction*, and *Aurealis*. She can be found on twitter @anyasy.

Author's Notes

This story was inspired by a famous Chinese poem, 七步诗, the *Seven Steps Verse/Quatrain of the Seven Steps*, an allegorical poem attributed to Cao Zhi. It was published in 430 in *A New Account of the Tales of the World* and romanticised in *Romance of the Three Kingdoms*. It's one of my favourite poems of all time, a poem that many Chinese people would be familiar with. Cao Zhi's brother, Emperor Cao Pi, was jealous of his brother and suspected him of trying to usurp his rule. Cao Zhi was told to produce a poem in 7 strides to prove his innocence, which he does. Moved, Cao Pi spares his brother in the end.

There are a couple of versions of his poem, but the condensed version within *Romance of the Three Kingdoms* is better known:

煮豆燃豆萁 / Boiling the beans while charring the stalks,

豆在釜中泣 / The beans in the pot cry out,

本是同根生 / We are born of the selfsame root,

相煎何太急? / Why should we hound each other to death with such impatience?

I loved the concept of a poem having the power to change the mind of an Emperor–what about something more? Like the anecdote, this story is very much about family relationships and regret. It explores consequences, the repetition of sacrifice through generations, as well as the weaponization and de-weaponization of pain.

THE FIREFLY BEAST

Tony Pi

O n the third day, I found the swordsman with fireflies in his
eyes.

Mortals might dismiss the glow in his pupils for reflections of the
setting sun, but not I. The swordsman had been bedeviling a
fortune-teller on Hollyhock Flower Alley, upending the man's stall
with a laugh. The fortune-teller fell to his knees to gather his scattered wares, and the swordsman raised his foot, ready to stamp
down on his victim's back.

I couldn't allow him to harm the man. I sprang the distance
between us and thrust my iron flute below the swordsman's foot,
using tigress strength to stop dead his forceful stomp.

Our eyes locked, and the number of fireflies in his pupils
doubled. He kept his foot on the flute and raised the other to
balance one-legged upon my weapon. "What surprising strength
you have, meddler," he said.

"Glowing praise when it comes from you," I replied, though I
couldn't tell if he was possessed, mesmerized, or the Firefly Beast
himself. "May we speak?"

The fortune-teller crawled away as fast as he could.

"Or dance to flute and sword, bruise and blood. Which do you
choose?" With an unearthly lightness, the swordsman somersaulted
backwards atop the garden wall behind him. His golden *jian* was
drawn and ready.

I tucked the flute into my sash. "The matter of your exile is best
served with words."

"Ah. So the City God intends you to succeed me as guardian of
Chengdu? Follow." He took a step backward and fell out of sight
behind the wall, though he left a trail of fireflies in his wake.

I glanced around me. Those who had business in the alley were
fleeing, lest they be caught in the confrontation. I leapt onto the

garden wall but not where he had perched, wary of his insects and ambush.

The swordsman had anticipated me, and already sped alongside the wall to match my place. He grabbed for my leg but I side-spun to avoid his grip, and vaulted the distance to the roof of the leisure pavilion at the heart of the scholar's garden.

Beyond the wall, the sunset inked the stone-and-waterscape of the garden with shadow, but the hundredfold sparks of fireflies graced the islets and gossamer bridges. The pavilion beneath my feet was on the largest isle.

The Firefly Beast leveled his sword at me and crossed one bridge closer. "You're welcome in the Garden of Stars and Lightning, demoness. What do they call you, and what is your nature?"

"Call me the White-Gold Guest. As for my true nature, Firefly, if you fail to leave Chengdu of your own accord, you'll know." I bared my teeth. "It need not come to a duel. From what I've heard of your tenure as the City God's Firefly, you gave your foes a chance at a peaceable escape. I admire such honor, and will grant you the same courtesy."

He laughed. "Call me not Firefly but Beast, for of late that befits me better. Oath and honor are no more my concern, so leave me to sate my whims. He owes me that much for my centuries of service."

"I will not break *my* oath, Firefly." I refused to call him Beast. Perhaps if I called him Firefly, he would remember his duty to the City God. Like me, the Firefly Beast was a demon seeking atonement for past wrongs by defending the city. But he broke his oath two summers ago, allowing evil to pass through the four gates unchallenged while he himself toyed with the lives of Chengdu's citizens.

"This is an age of usurpers and rebels, white-gold sister. Generals and governors crave their own kingdoms, and break their oaths of loyalty to war over the country." His firefly eyes flared. "Look at what happened here in Chengdu. Meng Zhixiang refused to acknowledge the weakling prince as Emperor, and claimed these lands as his own, reborn Kingdom of Shu. Why should we not embrace that freedom as well?"

"Because there are consequences to abandoning our wardenship of the city," I said. "Chengdu will suffer if we do not quell its ghosts or keep demons at bay. If you do not leave of your own accord, then I will make you."

"You must make an example of me before you challenge the other *yaoguai*, I understand. I'd have done the same in your place, when I first took the post. But do you have the skill?"

Firefly leapt and sailed through the air, golden blade leading and aimed at my heart.

I parried the strike with the iron flute, but his sword burst into a cloud of fireflies and threw me off balance. The sudden light dazzled me, but not so much that I didn't see the swarm gather to rebuild his sword. I smashed down on the roof with the flute as strongly as I could, making waste of the pavilion roof we stood upon. The Firefly stumbled, and we each retreated to islets of our own amid the cloud of tile-shard dust.

He wiped a spot of blood from his cheek. "Such monstrous strength. I suppose it's a start."

"I'd still prefer to talk."

The Firefly crossed a bridge to close in on me. "You and I will always be demons. No matter how hard we try to repress our old, wicked appetites, they will devour us from within."

I leapt across wide water to put more distance between us. I didn't ask which appetites he meant, for I too struggled with temptations of my own. "Then let me help you quell those urges once more, but beyond these city walls. Leave the citizens be."

"Such devotion for a people you do not yet know."

"The city itself may be new to me, but I've known the lands around it and those who loved it," I revealed. "Over a century ago, I chanced upon the Flower Rinsing Creek outside Chengdu, where the poetess Xue Tao lived. I heard her recite of cicadas and moon, of willow catkins and partings, and it touched a stillness within me I knew not before."

The Firefly's eyes burned bright. "Ah, the courtesan-poet turned Daoist priestess. I remember her well. Such vivid poems she wrote! When gifts were sent to the circuit governor's palace, I'd steal inside as a lightning bug to hear her compose such masterful notes of thanks, even when she meant her words as a backhanded compliment."

I smiled, for his anecdote rang true. "With this face and voice I went to her, to hear more and learn, but also to protect her. It was that sage soul who told me of her love for Chengdu, and taught me the art of poetry."

"You, a demon poetess?" The Firefly laughed. "I don't believe it. Recite something you wrote."

One poem sprang to mind: "The White-Gold Guest". Though I had not appeared to Xue Tao as a pale tigress, it was she who named this guise, for the wanness of my skin. I'd taken the phrase and crafted a *yongwu* poem to hint at my true self.

The White-Gold Guest comes uninvited
In ribboned onyx coat, on soundless footing,
Through sky-tall grass and wraith-mount mist
To feed her old hungers with a poet's feast.

The Firefly's grin faded as he contemplated my words. "Well-crafted. Then you are a tigress demon?"

I nodded. "The path of my atonement began with her lessons on poetry at her cottage. *Yongwu*, *fu*, *yuefu* and even lantern riddle poems."

"Your path will end here as it did for me," the Firefly replied. "I did good deeds for a time, barring *mogui* from entering the city and sparring with hungry ghosts within. But all that virtue could not deaden my demon nature."

I knelt and trailed one end of my flute in pond water, rinsing it of dust. "I don't expect to be forgiven for my past atrocities. I won't deny that I battle my bloodthirst even now. But I will seek my better self."

The Firefly's sword shivered apart again into fireflies, forming a glowing swarm in demon-shape, four-armed and twin-horned. The fireflies inside the swordsman's eyes escaped and rejoined the swarm, leaving him to collapse in seizure.

"Have you ever entered the minds of men and lured them to

their darkest desires?" The glittering swarm spoke in chorus, a thousand voices merged into one.

"No."

"I used to promise myself, no more than a touch of my demon power. Burrow into a mind but only indulge in small temptations. This swordsman despises fortune-tellers for an old but false promise of riches. He wanted to hurt that man until he confessed to be a charlatan. I've tasted his shameful ecstasy, and that of others. That nectar's an addiction I cannot break. Nor will you conquer yours."

"Yet you had the strength to protect Chengdu despite your inner struggle. And still have, if the tales of the City God's Firefly are to be believed," I replied. "Lives saved, catastrophes averted. I only hope to be as vigilant a guardian as you."

The Firefly drifted on the breeze above the water. "Then let's put you to the test, tigress. A bloodless challenge to settle this. If you win, I will leave Chengdu and never return. Fail, and you will leave me be, now and forever."

A risky game. I didn't trust him fully, but perhaps a part of him still sought redemption. The City God only asked that I remove the Firefly from Chengdu, but had left the means to my choosing as a test of my method and mettle. If the Firefly and I could settle this bloodlessly, he might one day find his way back to the right path. "What are the rules?"

"A chase in Chengdu. Capture any part of me, unharmed, before the sun rises."

"What's the catch?"

"No changing shapes. I will remain fireflies, and you a woman."

While I kept some of my tiger nature in human form, I wouldn't be as fast or strong as I would be as tigress. A challenge, but not insurmountable. "I'll agree to that if you heed this rule: if even once of your fireflies leaves the bounds of Chengdu's gates and walls, it means you accept exile without question."

The Firefly flickered in thought. "Cunning trap in clever phrasing. If I fly higher than the height of the city walls, I'd be caught by that rule."

"You can't have all the advantages."

He agreed to my terms. "Shall we, my White-Gold Guest?"

I recalled an old saying. "If you don't fight, you won't make friends," I replied as I flung my flute at the Firefly. But my weapon sailed harmlessly through the heart of the swarm. The thousand fireflies fled over the garden wall like sparks from a crackling bonfire, borne on the wind.

Our chase across the city began. The Firefly Beast would split into smaller swarms then merge again as he sped through the evening streets. It must have been a startling sight for those who had not yet gone home for curfew, to see a woman clad in pale silk racing after the clouds of fleeing fireflies.

He led me through alleyways; back and forth across the Golden Water River; along the city walls where sweet hibiscuses were newly planted; but always beyond my reach.

The drums played a tattoo of six hundred beats, signaling the closing of the ward and city gates.

I was undaunted by my failure thus far to catch the Firefly, and he continued to taunt and test me. His fireflies scattered, forcing me to choose which ones to follow. I picked the slowest one and leapt to catch it, but it slipped sideways and led me on a mad dash through a minister's manor, where I startled servants like a fleeting ghost in white.

Chasing the firefly back onto the street, I ignored the warnings of the night guard, dodging those that tried to arrest me. To strange and secret places the Firefly led me, from demon gambling dens, to the hidden corridors of the Imperial Examination Hall; from the tomb grounds of Fugan Temple where ghosts roamed, to a snow-kissed garden that could not, should not be in summer heat. Many mortals and devils had seen me failing to catch any fireflies. The Firefly Beast meant to humiliate me.

More than half the night had gone. I needed another way. The Firefly Beast knew the city too well, and I was always a whisker away from being fast enough to capture him. I was tired, frustrated, and tempted to take my rage out on the next living thing. I only barely contained that impulse. If I failed to deal with the Firefly Beast tonight, I'd always live in his shadow, proof that I wasn't skilled enough to replace him as protector.

I needed to find stillness within me, again.

I stopped at a lotus pond that Xue Tao told me about, where she'd seen a pair of matched birds upon the water and composed a poem about them. What had she said about the healing power of poetry?

There was a grand *fu* poem written by Mei Sheng, called *Seven Stimuli*. In it, a prince suffered an illness brought on by his indulgences in sensual pleasures. A scholar offered vivid verses on activities that might cure the prince, from music to hunting, but only the seventh and last—the promise of words of sages—would heal the patient.

Perhaps I could lure the Firefly Beast with words as well. A poem on the firefly, if told as vividly as in *Seven Stimuli*, might snare him in thought long enough for me to catch him.

With dawn nearing, I didn't have much time to compose a poem. But Xue Tao was a master of weaving poetry on the spur of the moment. A guest would name a topic and she'd write a *yongwu* poem there and then. We had played that game together many times before.

I found a pavilion by the pond where someone had left a cup of tea. It was cold but quenched my thirst. I played with the cup as I meditated on the nature of fireflies.

Xue Tao's *yongwu* poems tended to take the form of four lines, seven characters each. I was never as good as she was, but I had to make it poignant enough to stir the Firefly's heart.

Some of the fireflies came to see what I was doing from a safe distance, curious but cautious.

"Have you given up, tigress?"

I let the question hang while I focused on my intent with the poem and its imagery. But I couldn't polish the verse. The skies were turning red, and I was running out of time.

I tensed, drew a deep breath, and spoke.

Behold the brocade of fire-stars on a summer's eve,
At twinkle and billow upon a godly breath.
Your flying lanterns toil to kindle your golden light
To guard us all against the darkness we fear.

On the last word I leapt with all my might towards the swarm, hoping my poem still entranced the Firefly Beast. Startled, the fireflies tried to scatter, but I trapped one of them between empty cup and open palm as I fell into the pond. I struggled and dragged myself out of the muddy water, but kept my firefly prisoner.

The remaining fireflies swarmed together and remade the Firefly Beast. He stayed silent until the rays of the morning sun touched us.

At last, I let his firefly go.

The Firefly bowed. "A thought-provoking gambit, one that gives the listener pause. I will keep my word and leave Chengdu to you, City God's Tiger."

I bowed in kind. "I meant what I said, City God's Firefly. I'll help you cope with your impulses outside the city."

"Then find me at Flower Rinsing Creek. Perhaps you could teach me how to add a verse to that poem."

The sun shone through the swarm from behind, blinding me to the City God's Firefly. I didn't see where or how he took leave of the city, but knew we'd meet again.

And so I succeeded the Firefly Beast as the Guardian of Chengdu, and began the formidable task of ridding the city of hauntings and devils.

About the Author

Originally from Taiwan, Tony Pi lives and writes in Toronto, Canada. His fantastic fiction covers many subgenres, but historical fantasy, particularly set in ancient China, is one of his favorites. He won an Aurora Award in 2015 in the category of Best Poem/Song for his poem, *A Hex, With Bees*, and several of his stories have also been nominated for Best Short Fiction (Aurora Awards) and Best Speculative Fiction Story: Small Cast (Short Form) (Parsec Awards). More about his fiction may be found at tonypi.com.

Author's Notes

One of the characters from my stories about Song Dynasty China is the mysterious Pale Tigress, and I wanted to explore her intriguing past. As she is long-lived, it opened up the possibility for a story set before the Song Dynasty. I began researching poets of Ancient China in the Chengdu area, originally intending to have her be an apprentice under the poet Du Fu, when I came across the biography of Xue Tao, a famous courtesan-poet of the Tang Dynasty who came to live in Du Fu's cottage. After that discovery, it could be no one else who befriended my character but her. From then on, Xue Tao's intriguing life and her poetry shaped how I conceived of the Pale Tigress' past, and the style of the ancient poetess inspired the poems in this story. Her poems are still around, so I highly recommend tracking them down if you'd like to get a taste of Tang Dynasty Chinese poetry.

HER POEMS ARE INKED IN FEARS AND BLOOD

Kira Lees

Not rotted away,
if these pillars in the river
did not remain,
how could we ever know
the traces of long ago?
-Sugawara no Takasue no Musume, *Sarashina Nikki*

Her sword is wet with the blood of dying words. As she pulls the knife from his throat, half-finished poems and flights of imagery flash and fly up into nothingness. The poet slumps to the ground, gurgling a dirge that is lost upon severed vocal chords.

She wipes the word-soaked blade across her tongue, his thoughts and poetry filling her, enhancing and shaping her own paltry ideas, and those ideas shaping into kana and kanji, and into poems. Under Minister Ushiwara was a phenomenal poet, one for the ages, but lacked the skill of sharpened blades. And so, his voice is hers now.

As she licks clean the blade, she notices that some of the blood-words have stained her sleeve. *Wrist. Kiss. Desire. Tongue. Palm. Secrets.* She quickly sheds her outermost uchigi, angry at herself for the uncharacteristic mess. Unnoticed, three small drops fall onto the lip of the robe underneath. *Step. Shatter. Undoing.*

She cannot read them.

The court ladies buzz like summer mayflies along the Tokaido Road. *Under Minister Ushiwara was killed in the night. He is the fifth courtier-poet to be killed in the night this year. What mononoke haunt the palace? What ill-fortune plagues the emperor?*

The buzzing stops as soon as her screen slides back, and she glides into the room. No introduction is needed. Everyone knows her. She has been affectionately (and unaffectionately) nicknamed Uguisu. Her poetry is renowned in court, not only for her knowledge and skill, but that she can best any male courtier's verse, even those long studied within the Morokoshi tradition.

"Ushiwara has died?" she asks, her voice as soft as spider's feet upon a web.

The senior-most lady nods, "In the night. His throat slit."

"What a loss to the court and his family," she replies.

"By a rival's assassins no doubt," a senior lady-in-waiting scoffs. "Who are these devils who do not have the skill or honor to challenge our poets in a duel but must stab a sleeping man? Be a man and show your face!"

"I think it's awfully romantic!" the youngest lady replies, head filled with bandit princes and monogatari.

"Maybe his face is not one you would wish to see," Uguisu states as she carefully flicks a dead leaf from her dress.

The poem she delivers in honor of Ushiwara fills the room, with language as clever and images as sharp as the deceased poet himself had often used, but she uses a much subtler hand, deftly calling upon the dead man's words while twisting them as slowly as a knife, turning them into her own. She spoke not only with Ushiwara's voice, but the voice of the poetry collections, calligraphed and bound. Each syllable a brushstroke upon the mind, that then fades as quickly as a thousand years. More than one lady is in tears when she finishes. Even the empress herself dabs her eyes with her sleeve.

"Most lovely and fitting," a man's voice sounds from upon the veranda. Even muffled behind a screen, it vibrates her to her core. The ladies titter and laugh, trying to catch a glimpse through the screens.

"Governor-Poet Oshi, you startled us," the empress smiles.

Oshi no Kyo is a man who looks as if he has walked straight out of a monogatari, eyes as black as ink, body as lithe and graceful as a stroke of calligraphy. He was used to a life in the provinces, far from court. His wife had long ago begun an affair with the bull hand, it was whispered, so he had come to the capital a broken-hearted man. His only desire was to observe the world and perfect his art.

"May I have the honor of responding to your poem?" he asks, and maybe it is the winter wind, but she swears she can feel the warmth of his breath on her neck.

He is next. Her bloodlust calls. He is next. Her heart warns.

Words leave her, and all she can provide is a simple, "You may."

He approaches the screen. Even through the rice paper, she can tell his form is fine. And when he opens his mouth, what comes forth floats along the air, rising the whole world up to meet the divinity of his words.

This is love. The air whispers. But no, a monster cannot love. A vampiress cannot love. Love is for those with the ability to be moved. For those with their own thoughts. Uguisu's mind has been crammed with so many other voices, that her own thoughts are empty and drowned out.

This exchange of poems is headier than any love-making. If only the words were her own. It is not her body he makes love to.

"I would like to include your eulogy and my response in the collection the emperor has commissioned me to make." The ladies gasp. Being part of an imperial collection is the greatest honor.

"Of course." The answer is heavy as a lie upon Uguisu's tongue.

"I'm sure there are more of your poems. If you could you send me some of your best?" He asks. It is a sly request for an invitation. Uguisu hides her face behind her sleeve to hide her conflicting emotions.

What poems his blood must hold! His collection would provide ample food for years. So many poems to feast upon! His mind the rich pulpy innards of fresh fruit.

She watches his footsteps as he leaves, his footsteps a poem across the parchment of freshly fallen snow.

~

They stole your voice when they did not teach you how to sing. Grandmother's voice floats over time, like a swan across a pond of years. The sound of swishing in the silent night, as Grandmother taught her the moves to fight, to kill, to drink, to become. *You are only taking back what is also yours.*

The low clink as their blades hit. A crane takes flight across the lake. And she awakes from her memory-dreams, to find herself looking across the sea of sleeping gentlewomen upon reed mats, surrounding like sharks, the ship-bed of the empress.

It is time.

She rises on noiseless feet and glides through the screens, past quiet lovers and out onto the veranda. She will never get used to that first chill of night air, uninhibited by screens. It is like slipping into another's skin, wearing a life you do not lead, do not possess.

His footprints lead her to his room, like blood drops to a wounded man. She slips past the screens and looks upon his face without the cover of sleeve or screen.

For the first time, words rise to her throat. They do not taste of blood or man but her own. The taste is so heady, so new; her hand stays. Her sword clatters to the floor.

At once, Oshi awakes. He unsheathes his own knife from beneath his pillow but freezes as he sees Uguisu.

"You," he whispers.

She could pretend this was a lover's tryst, as unorthodox as it was for her to go to him than he to her. But looking into his eyes, she only feels tired and no longer wants to pretend she is anything other than what she is.

She flees. Words fall from her. *Red. Chrysanthemum. Petals. Blood. Snow. Winter. Painted. Cheek.* Words she cannot read. She does not know where she runs, except *Away*.

And still he pursues her like a hunter, bounding through the snow, following her trail of dying words. He catches up to her at the spring that feeds the palace ponds, in the center of the garden. He dares not follow her out upon the thin ice.

"Why?" he asks—the greatest poet of the court, excepting maybe herself, and a single word is all he can spare.

"You, you who has a bed of words to sleep upon and will not share. My voice is not that of the men I silenced, but of the thousands of women who were silenced when their brushes were snatched from them, when their words were stolen as children, when they were removed from the womb."

"I would share my poems with you." There are tears in his eyes.

Whatever lover he had built from her words, he can only see the wretched creature before him. And yet…

Uguisu looks upon him. His earnest eyes. "I cannot kill you. And I will spare you the choice of killing me." The words flowing from her tears, warming the ice, thinning it, melting it. This was how women spoke poetry—not with blood, but tears.

The ice cracks beneath her feet, and she falls into the icy waters. He rushes after her, but there is nothing to see but his own reflection in the clear black water and a few koi, awakened from their winter sleep, and hungry.

～

"No blood? Not even a single word?" Left Minister asks.

"No, her body has completely disappeared," Right Minister replies.

"Let the fishes have her then, and let her ghost haunt her unblessed bones." Left.

"We did find Governor Oshi next to the pond. He was nearly frozen to death, but the doctors have brought him back. He's distraught." Right.

"Ugh, these poets and their moods. Sometimes these young politicians take their poetry too seriously. Find him a nice Eamon girl to marry and he'll forget all about that damned yokai."

Left.

Right.

Left.

Right.

The men continue down the veranda, words frozen in the air before they can travel far, voices contained by the quiet evening.

Left.

Right.

Left.

Alone, a young girl-child, hardly more than a violet root, listens as their voices fade away and watches koi flutter in a pond. Unseen to any but her, words rise to greet her like a friend. Since she cannot read, these words form their own alphabet. She reaches out a curious hand to touch one. It disappears into the air, but not from her mind.

⁂

About the Author

Kira Lees grew up among the shadows of deserted steel mills and abandoned coal mines. Always dreaming of another world—one that wasn't so gray nor so dull—she made up stories in her head and told them to anyone who would listen. Now that she's older, she recognizes those brownfields and decay have found a way into her writing. She graduated from William Smith college with a BA in English and currently lives on a hillside in Pittsburgh. Her work has also appeared in the *Rough Magick* anthology.

Author's Notes

Her Poems are Inked in Fears and Blood is inspired by the Heian period in Japan, and the many influential women writers that era produced. While women enjoyed more sexual autonomy and freedoms than one might expect, their talents were confined to women's roles and they were referred to by their father's or husband's court position. Sei Shōnagon, Sugawara no Takasue no Musume, Murasaki Shikibu, and others' real names are lost to time.

Chinese was the official court language, and much of men's poetry was written in Chinese. Women were usually excluded from studying the language (much as Greek and Latin were considered unnecessary for European women), but some women, including Shōnagon and Shikibu did learn. However, most of their writing was in native Japanese, and ironically their work lead to the development of the Japanese language. The parameters set in place by the men led to women laying the foundations for the Japanese literary canon.

Heian court life was very different from the more popular shogun and samurai vision of Japan. Career progression was determined not by military strength, but by one's political acumen, wit, and knowledge of Chinese classics and the strict etiquette observed by the court. Ivan Morris's informative, if dated, *The World of the Shining Prince* is a fascinating source, as is *The Tale of Genji* and various diaries written by the women mentioned above.

My fascination with Japan began when I learned about Murasaki Shikibu and a culture obsessed with beauty and poetry. I'd always wanted to set a story within a place and time that is beloved to me, and when I jotted down the first few lines of this story, I realized I suddenly had found my entrance into the deceptively peaceful and secretive world of Heian-Kyo.

I was inspired by those two tidbits—the development of Japanese literature through the exclusion of knowledge of the Chinese language, and the unknown names of some of Japan's greatest writers. I used no proper names for any of the female characters to underline this point. For all their brilliance, most of the women accepted their lot as the way of things. In some ways, the story echoes our present world that weeps at the loss of talented but immoral men—or worse defends them—but doesn't think of the women artists and actors and writers who we have lost due to these men's actions.

The title is morbidly inspired by Keats' *When I Have Fears That I May Cease to Be*. For those knowledgeable of Heian-era women, I slipped some subtle (and not-so-subtle) references to them into my story. I hope it inspires you to read the truly brilliant work of these women. The clever and funny Sei Shōnagon, the poetic and somber Sugawara no Takasue no Musume, or the thoughtful and observant Murasaki. Even if their real names are lost, their words are not.

THE WORDS OF OUR ENEMIES, THE WORDS OF OUR HEARTS

A. Merc Rustad

Prince Aretas, son of the Ever-Hungry Queen, had gone into the forest. Yarchuse knew the truth even before ae coaxed the story from the prince's boot prints bruising dry earth. Ae shivered, hand splayed above the trail. Dammit.

Ae heard the prince's naïve belief etched into his tracks: **I can end this war without more death. I will speak to the Heart of the Forest and find peace.**

You foolish child, Yarchuse thought, clenching aer jaw against a spurt of panic. The forest would never relent, just as the queen would never cease her war. Yarchuse was weary and yet ae would serve until death or an end found aer.

"He left before dawn," Yarchuse said, exhaling slow. "He would have reached the forest by now."

"Did no one witness my son?" the Ever-Hungry Queen said, her voice a crack of stone and air. "Why was he not stopped?"

Yarchuse stepped forward before the queen's wroth spilled across the soldiers and courtiers who waited in rigid silence along the poet wall. "Majesty," ae said, "the blame is mine. His Highness asked for his breath to be sung into the barricade." Ae tilted aer hand at the shimmering wall rising into the dawn-streaked sky around the camp. "I thought it was a precaution should he need to flee—"

The Ever-Hungry Queen's teeth flashed as her lips peeled back in rage. "Tomeslinger, I want my son back. Alive."

Yarchuse weathered the queen's fury easier than her soldiers would. Ae was not one she could kill in a moment's passion. Ae kept aer expression impassive. "We will get him back, Majesty."

Ae bowed, spinning a handful of soothing words—*ease be with you, let your blood calm, breathe free*—between aer fingers. Ae slipped the spell with careful precision around the Every-Hungry Queen's ankle, where the magic would spiral up her limb and seep unnoticed into her heart. It was a familiar habit for Yarchuse now, even if it had become more and more difficult in recent years. Since the princess's death, the queen had calcified herself, allowing only her rage to burn.

"You have until dusk, tomeslinger." The threat in her voice was expected and yet held far more weight and promise of retribution if ae failed.

Yarchuse straightened, uneasy and masking aer mood with a brush of words: *chill lake water untouched by wind*.

Kel, aer closest friend, was on the other side of the camp feeding. Yarchuse resisted calling on her for support. Ae would not appear weak before the queen's anger.

The Ever-Hungry Queen whirled in a blaze of armored silk and tomeslung shield-beads. She stalked through the gate, her entourage at her heels. The soldiers who had been on dark-sky duty exhaled and bowed to Yarchuse in gratitude. Ae waved them back to their posts. Everyone was exhausted from the long, unyielding campaign.

And the prince, though his mother was unaware, was skilled in earth-warding magic of his own. With the poet wall spun to allow him to pass unchallenged, Aretas could have lulled the moors to hide him as he crept down the sloping hill towards the great forest. Yarchuse silently berated aerself. When Aretas had asked for access to the wall, ae had not thought the prince would be such a fool.

"Attir," Yarchuse said to the chief earth-warden scout, who stood unmoved by the gate. "Take the raptors and see if you can discern where the prince is in the forest. Hurry."

The woman saluted.

Yarchuse believed the boy lived, for the forest was not subtle when it tasted victory. If Aretas was dead, all in the queen's camp would have heard the trees' triumph. How long would the prince survive was not a question Yarchuse could answer, and ae feared it would be too damningly short. If the prince died, so would ae—in her grief, the queen would turn her army against Yarchuse aerself, and even ae could not win such a battle.

Yarchuse D'Maatone, elite tomeslinger in the Tenth Regiment of Acumen Scrolls, Slayer of the White Sorrow, Champion of

Urantanadon, was not certain ae would have the courage to submit aerself to such a death. Aer cowardice would mean slaughtering aer own followers in self-defense, until ae were nevertheless over-whelmed and murdered. Ae prayed silently to the Unearthly Library: *Grant me courage and wisdom to fulfill my duty. Let this day not end in more blood.*

～

The Ever-Hungry Queen first began her insatiable war against the trees after her first-born daughter was crushed under a willow tree while hunting fox. It had been three years ago. Yarchuse had returned from cleansing the city of Urantanadon from the whisper-rot only to attend the heir apparent's funeral.

"It was an accident," the princess's bodyguard said before he was executed. "The tree moved to protect the fox and she wouldn't back down."

Yarchuse offered to read the place of the princess's death, but the queen refused. "There is nothing a plant can tell that will return my daughter's life. Burn it all," she ordered. "All the trees in all my lands will pay for what we have lost."

So Yarchuse had shouldered aer newest mantle and led the wardens and aer fellow tomeslingers on the Great Uprooting. The Worded City was razed of greenery; the gardens burned; the markets were allowed harvested vegetation only if it was on the edge of rotting. Yarchuse still tasted the acrid smoke in aer throat long after. The Queen did not listen to the protests of the gardeners and the alchemists who worried that the purge of flora would harm the people.

When the Worded City was stripped of plant life, the war boiled outward. Trees fled but were cut down and burned regardless. Yarchuse did not relish this work, but ae obeyed. The irony that aer tome's base elements were made from wood-pulp paper and vellum was not lost on Yarchuse. Ae hoped that when enough forests burned, the Ever-Hungry Queen would relent and turn her focus elsewhere.

But she had not.

135

And now, on the edge of the moors, the last bastion of the forests gathered in defense. Behind the trees lay the ocean, unwelcoming of earth-born flesh or root. It would end here, somehow.

~

Yarchuse shielded aer eyes with aer hand, squinting against the midday sun. Bone-speared birch warriors and hulking oak berserkers were just visible on the crest of the moor. A thousand thousand trees ready for war. Attir should be back by now.

Beside aer, the apex raptor Kel let out an impatient huff. She canted her head sideways and looked down with a slitted gray eye. *Wood burns whether alive or dead*, she signed. Her huge foreclaws flashed with silver scrolling. *We should attack now!*

"The fire wardens are still spent," Yarchuse said, sharper than ae meant.

Then we go without. The apex raptor stood nearly sixty hands tall at the peak of her skull, radiant with a turquoise and scarlet crest, the plumage about her neck undulating into spilled-oil shimmers. Sling-forged armor protected the contours of her sleek, powerfully muscled body. *You and I*, she said, *we are **death**.*

Ae forced a pinched smile. She would have smelled aer emotion if ae hadn't limed aer own body with a scentless mask. Kel's strength wasn't reading human facial expressions.

Together they had won a dozen battles at the behest of the Ever-Hungry Queen. Yarchuse had ridden with Kel into war, aer flesh arm raised in challenge, coiling and spinning destruction carved from syllables between aer fingers. The exhilaration had always been flush and wild in aer heart: the thrill of victory as enemy soldiers fell before aer and Kel. Ae felt invincible, commanding aer magic and bolstered by the great apex raptor.

Now, ae couldn't attack without risking Prince Aretas's life.

The prince was a fool, and to the Ever-Hungry Queen, that fool was worth more than the lives of her entire army. The prince's spelled armor would protect him for a time, but eventually words would crack under root and bough and thorn.

They stood on the edge of the slope rising to the camp, a

dozen paces outside the poet wall. The wall was a practical, unadorned barrier: spun from defensive words, solid and unremarkable, yet strong enough to withstand siege. It was nothing like the elegant arches and spires of the Worded City, the complex algorithmic weaves of architecture slung from Words of creation and strength. Ae missed home with a sudden, sharp pang.

Kel let out a low clicking sound, startling Yarchuse from aer anxious thought-spirals. Ae looked at the raptor.

The scouts are returning, she signed. *Look*.

The trio of earth wardens galloped across the dip of land between where the forest rose and the next great hill the camp was built upon. The human wardens rode tomeslung raptors—creatures little bigger than ponies, in the shape of Kel and crafted from her essence by Yarchuse's power, but spun from letters and words of stealth, speed, stamina.

Attir swung down from her spelled raptor and bowed, first to Yarchuse and then to Kel. "Tomeslinger. General."

Kel lowered her head, jaws wide, and Attir's mount placed its muzzle on her tongue. She licked the layer of ink from its constructed snout. Kel's chest rumbled as she swallowed the memory of what the smaller raptor had observed.

"His Highness' trail leads to the trees," Attir said. She wiped sweat from her face, still breathing hard. "From what I could feel through the soil, he's alive but he's deep. I..." She shuddered, a whole-body tremble that made Yarchuse flinch in sympathy. "There's something old in there, your Excellency. I don't know what it is."

Kel suddenly reared back, snapping her head up and clacking her jaws together. The tomeslung-raptors skittered away, silent.

"What's wrong?" Yarchuse asked, fear sharp under aer tongue. Ae rarely saw Kel in distress, and never outside battle.

She shook her head, her neck raised so she didn't swat Yarchuse or Attir flat with her might. *It wants you*, she signed, and her claws moved almost too quickly for Yarchuse to follow. *It calls you poison and it* ***wants***.

She stamped one hind foot and the ground trembled. Attir's eyes widened in panic. The other two wardens slid down from their raptors, heads bowed in wary submission.

"Calm yourselves," Yarchuse said, holding up aer hand. "Kel, show me."

The great apex raptor snarled but lowered her jaw again and Yarchuse touched aer palm against her heavy lip, the ridge of her teeth shap against aer skin. She unspooled the impressions she had swallowed in a breath and Yarchuse inhaled sight and weighted understanding.

*The residue spins images of burning forests, ax-felled groves, wood broken apart and left to rot unsanctified. Above the carnage looms an astral human figure wreathed in **death**: Yarchuse D'Maatone, a scion of un-mercy unleashed against nature. The vision is Yarchuse when in war: with radiant ceremonial armor and a flesh-wrapped tome hung from aer belt, words of malice curled between aer fingers. Yet as the forest sees ae, aer eyes are pitted hollows and aer teeth like saws. Ae breaks the boughs of fallen saplings under heel and rips foliage from branch with vicious spells.*

Ae yanked aer hand away from Kel's lip and shuddered.

Ancestral ballads, Yarchuse thought in horror. *Is that what the trees imagine me?*

"Inform Her Majesty the prince is alive," ae said, aer voice hoarse. With effort, ae straightened and infused aer tone with confidence and authority ae did not feel. "But do not reveal anything else as of yet."

"Excellency?" one of the scouts asked, her brows crinkled together in worry. "We can't lie—"

"I don't ask that," Yarchuse said. If it was ae the forest wanted, then it was ae the forest would receive. Ae just needed to buy aerself time to forge a rescue, somehow. "I will see the prince returned alive and unharmed, but Her Majesty *must* stay within the walls until then. Do you understand?"

The scouts couldn't, not with so vague a promise, but they were not about to defy Yarchuse's command. The wardens saluted; the raptors bobbed their heads.

Ae gestured the gate open with a quick-thrown word of parting, and the poet wall rippled open to let the wardens and their raptors through. "Attir, wait a moment."

Attir remained with her feet planted firm. "Your Excellency?"

Kel huffed in rage, her feathers smoothing down along her ruff as Yarchuse placed aer hand on her flank. Her plumage hid aer trembling fingers.

"Bring me my armor," ae said. "I am going into the forest."

∽

Yarchuse's mail coat hung heavier than ae liked, weighted with a construct-arm to give aer a symmetrical appearance. Ae tied in the delicately worded strings in the construct, then flexed aer second arm. It glimmered chiaroscuro and the fingers were equipped with retractable knives like claws.

The sunlight dazzled across Kel's armor and feathers. Her swaying gait devoured the distance between the Ever-Hungry Queen's camp and the edge of the forest. She'd argued with aer, but only briefly. By the time Attir had returned with Yarchuse's armor, informing ae that the wardens were on their way to report to the queen, Kel had accepted Yarchuse's plan.

"Send our demand, Attir," ae said, looking down from where they rose atop Kel's mighty back, aer legs on either side of her thick neck at the slope of shoulders.

Kel halted, the vibration of her unsettled growl shivering through Yarchuse's limbs. Ae gripped the thick feathers at the base of her neck for support.

The warden swung off her mount, knelt, and pressed her hands into the grass. Yarchuse's demand was simple: ae would offer aerself to the forest in exchange for Prince Aretas, alive and unharmed. The wind bowed the moorland grass and carried the scent of far-off rain. Time stretched unbearably slow.

Then Attir jerked to her feet, wincing. "It's agreed, your Excellency. The forest will give up His Highness if you surrender."

"Done."

The warden spread her arms and a low grumbling in the soil rippled outward, a new wave through the grass until it reached the trees.

Yarchuse slid down from Kel's back, steadying aerself with aer

139

hand on her side. Aer heartbeat tripped rapidly against aer breastbone.

You need not be alone, Kel signed.

"I know," Yarchuse murmured. "But I must. I need you to protect Aretas."

She snarled. *He is not worth your life.*

"My life is worth peace," ae said softly. Ae clung to this conviction, all ae had now. She lowered her muzzle and pressed the bridge of her nose against aer chest. Yarchuse wrapped aer arm around her head in a hug. "You give me strength, friend."

Kel purred, a rumble through her chest and into her teeth and Yarchuse shut aer eyes a moment as ae held her. Neither of them had ever been able to say farewells.

"General! Excellency!"

Yarchuse started and let aer arm drop to aer side. Kel straightened.

The prince stepped out of the forest, naked and glistening with dew. He trembled but didn't stumble as he walked. His body was whole: pale skin unbruised, hair tangled in golden curls, brown eyes wide and damp and unafraid. Even at this distance, Yarchuse saw no cause for alarm.

Kel huffed. Her ruff flared in anger. She tapped code with her hind toes so only Yarchuse would hear. *That's not the prince.*

"What?" Yarchuse pitched aer voice low, muting sudden panic.

Look closer. He smells of not-flesh.

Yarchuse kept aer flesh arm by aer side and inconspicuously wove a mirror between aer fingers. Ae looked into the spelled glass, tilted towards the naked prince, and saw she spoke true.

In the magic, the prince's bones were willow fonds, his veins sap, his heart a knot of tangled bloodwood. The illusion was unlike anything Yarchuse had ever witnessed. The magic in aer hand cracked, strobing between what was true and what was meant: wood, flesh, leaf, marrow. Ae would have bought into the false prince's illusion, and even now, ae still wanted to believe this was the Queen-Regent's son, alive and unharmed, offered in good faith for aer life. The magic in the construct was powerful indeed.

I will destroy this forest, Kel snarled, the thump of her claws nearly overwhelmed by her guttural rumble.

"No!" Yarchuse dissipated the mirror and laid aer hand on her flank. Ae didn't try to conceal aer own trembling. "Listen. This not-prince is meant as a decoy, but if we show we know it to be false, the boy will die. He must be alive still. Protect this construct and forestall the queen's wrath. Please, my friend. Buy me time to save His Highness."

For you, my heart, she said, with the slow, deliberateness of a death knell, *I will rip every plant from its roots until the world is naught but stone and kindling.*

Yarchuse smiled despite aer knotted stomach and the rapidity of aer heartbeat. "I know."

Attir pulled a robe from her raptor's saddle-bag and held it ready.

Yarchuse sent a silent prayer to the Unearthly Library, aer spiritual anchor. Ae had entered the ethereal place of wisdom when ae undertook aer tomeslinger trial to be admitted into the Tenth Regiment of Acumen Scrolls. It had been the most beautiful thing Yarchuse had ever beheld, for the Library contained all the souls of every book, and they shone with the incandescent radiance and power only words could display. When ae died, aer body would be composed into a book and aer soul shelved in the Library beside legends. But only if ae died with honor, unbroken, and aer remains returned to the Worded City. Yarchuse did not know what magic saturated the old forest, or how that would taint aer spirit in death.

Yarchuse stepped forward.

The rustle-creak of leaf and bough from the tree soldiers was too loud to ignore. Yarchuse swallowed, aer throat dry and raspy. For all aer power, ae was still human and fragile in comparison to the trees.

Huge birch warriors, white-barked and studded with thorns from their briar kin, shook spears of bone and rust-salvaged iron. The massive oak berserkers, crowned in bloody foliage, rumbled and thumped their roots like drums. The forest peeled aside to create a tunnel into the ranks, the ground flattened smoother than marble. It looked like a great maw opened into the belly of death.

Yarchuse glanced over aer shoulder just before ae was within reach of the trees. Kel stood unmoved, her great form a silhouette under the sun. The false prince bowed to the raptor, who inclined her head in return. Attir wrapped the robe about the boy's frame. Then the false prince pulled himself up onto Kel's back, unhesitant and familiar—so like Aretas had done countless times past. Kel didn't move.

Yarchuse looked forward and stepped into the forest.

The trees did not look at Yarchuse as ae marched deeper into their midst. Towering trunks and canopied foliage let in only the faintest slivers of light, enough for aer eyes to adjust. Deeper ae trod, and ae felt more than saw the trees closing rank behind aer. There would be no retreat.

The air weighed heavy against Yarchuse's senses. There was age here, wisdom and emotion so deep it was all but unknowable. Aer breath came with effort. There seemed to be no end to the forest. Would ae walk forever and never find what ae sought?

"I know your illusion," Yarchuse called. There was no echo to aer voice. "I know the prince is still here. Deliver him to me unharmed. We can come to a truce!"

The trees fanned out into a circular grove open to the sky, and Yarchuse stepped into the clearing. The movement of bough and trunk had been so smooth, so subtle, ae was momentarily dizzy at the sudden change in the woods. At once Yarchuse saw the lost prince: still in armor, lying in a bed of soft green moss. Aretas' chest rose and fell in easy sleep.

Standing to the side and towering over the prince was an ancient tree of no determinate species. Their bark was like the starless sky, their leaves as silver as moonlight, and their branches were limed with runes in the language of trees. The Heart of the Forest.

Deathsinger, the Heart said, their vibration-song felt in bone and soul alike.

Yarchuse gasped, the weight of the Heart's scrutiny buckling aer knees. Loam and shed bark bit into aer kneecaps. Ae struggled to keep aer construct arm raised, the tomeslung magic flaring out in a domed shield. The Heart of the Forest stood unmoved and unimpressed.

"You offered a falsehood," ae said. "I've seen through your illusion prince. Release His Highness and take me in his place."

No.

"Do not make me hurt you," Yarchuse said. Ae readied aer magic, spells of lightning and steel, heat and ice.

You have harmed all my kind enough, the Heart said, and fury thickened their voice until its power crashed upon Yarchuse in a moon-towed wave. Ae flinched and focused on aer shield, fear flaring bright in aer mind.

No more.

With a mighty crack like the shattering of the land's bones, the Heart's power rent Yarchuse's asunder. Ae was flung backwards into the moss-sheathed stones. Breath wooshed from aer lungs, and then pain filled aer ribs in place of air. Yarchuse gasped. White and silver bands flared across aer eyes.

The Heart snapped its woody vines like whips, and the flora wrapped about Yarchuse's arm and waist and throat, lifting aer off the ground. Pressure closed about aer neck and middle, and Yarchuse frantically redirected aer focus to aer armor under the vines' grip.

"Your illusioned prince will not last," Yarchuse said, panting. As hard as ae struggled, ae could not even loosen the vines' grip on aer body. "It is folly—"

Is it? The Heart lifted Yarchuse until ae was face-to-face before the ancient forest. **Long have I called to the sapling, and he came. We offered him rest and he accepted. He believes it is his duty to die here so this destruction will end.**

Shock jolted through Yarchuse. Ae sensed no lies from the Heart. Ae glanced once more at the sleeping prince, prone and peaceful in the loam. Ae had always thought Aretas idealistic but good-hearted, one who knew what his duty was and was unafraid to uphold it. He had grown bolder after the death of his sister. On his seventeenth year this spring, when he had come of age, he had gone to the fleshsingers, mages who specialized in healing, and requested they reshape his body to minimize his breasts and pronounce his genitals to better suit his chosen gender.

Yarchuse had accompanied Aretas, for ae had always been like an elder cousin to the queen's children. The joy in the prince's eyes when he woke from the surgical trance had made Yarchuse's heart swell in pride. Later, at dinner, Aretas spoke to Yarchuse alone. "I want this war to end," he declared. "I will accompany you until my mother relents."

And so he had, challenging the queen's orders and mingling with the soldiers and the raptors, pleading his views of a better world. It had not stopped the Ever-Hungry Queen's campaign. Even Yarchuse could not sway her, although ae had never tried—even when the prince begged aer to try.

If ae had used aer voice instead of aer magic, could ae have prevented this in the first place? Spared Aretas from believing he had to die to stop his mother's war?

"He is not responsible for this," Yarchuse said.

The Heart threw Yarchuse to the ground, and ae tumbled. A rock bashed aer shin, sending pain flaring up aer leg even through the armor. The padded spells absorbed most of the impact so ae didn't shatter aer spine on impact.

Who, then? You, deathsinger? Only your saplings seek peace, while your thick trunked elders remain unbending.

Yarchuse swallowed against panic. "Not all of us."

Your song is empty, singer-of-death. When your monarch embraces the illusion in her court, it will take her life, said the Heart. **As she has taken the lives of so many.**

"There's another answer," Yarchuse said, shakily pushing aerself to aer knees. "We can *stop* this slaughter."

When did your queen stop, even after we offered our sibling in sacrifice for what was lost? She burned innocents and younglings who had done no harm!

"I know," Yarchuse said, and the admission ripped at aer gut, all the guilt ae had repressed for so many years rising like bile. The fight fled aer body and ae slumped back on aer heels. Ae did not try to stop aer tears. "I was wrong. She's wrong. All of us who participated in this war, we were misguided and I can never atone for the life lost."

The Heart lashed their vines but did not strike Yarchuse this time. Their anger shook the ground. **Speak then, deathsinger.**

Yarchuse shut aer eyes and with effort, withdrew all aer magic. Aer armor faded into unfortified cloth. The tomeslung words flaked away like dead scales from aer skin, leaving aer mortal body exposed and vulnerable. Ae shivered as the damp, heavy air from the deep forest chilled the sweat on aer body.

"Keep the flesh prince here and do not kill the Ever-Hungry Queen," Yarchuse said, and ae felt the Heart's fury build, mingled with aer own deep guilt. Ae did not wish to leave the prince here, and yet, it had been his choice. Yarchuse could not steal that from him when ae had done nothing to support his cause. "Let your wooden prince be a proxy. So long as it lives, so does the flesh prince. You and the queen will each hold a piece of the other's heart. As long as there is peace between root and bone, neither prince will come to harm. The queen loves her son and she will relent her destruction rather than hold another funeral."

Slowly, Yarchuse opened aer eyes and looked up at the Heart. The great being's vines folded back against their darkened bark.

And how long do you believe such peace will last? Fleshroots do not have the years as the forest does.

"But you do remember, and humans can, too," Yarchuse said. Each breath ae took felt like a small victory. Ae lifted aer hand in supplication. "I will create mirror robes for your prince, which will show our Aretas, a constant reminder to my queen and my people. I cannot give you back the lives lost under fire and ax. I can pull the words sewn in the earth so that your roots may take hold again and not crumble. It will take time."

And when it is done, what have my woods gained but fear for our lives if we return to your lands, to your cities? The Heart stretched out a bough, branches tipped and shaped like fingers. Bark paused a breath from Yarchuse's chin. **We cleanse your air and give you sustenance. For ages past we sheltered and harbored your people. We asked for naught, yet you took and took, and when my kin defended our cousins of fur, you turned upon us all. What promise can you make that it will not happen again?**

"I have no answer," Yarchuse said. Ae bowed aer head. "I'm culpable in this destruction and I can't ask forgiveness for what I've done."

Ae breathed in slowly. The fear had faded into dull heartache. How many lives could have been spared if ae had not been a coward and had defied the Ever-Hungry Queen's war-lust from the onset? Ae was the most powerful tomeslinger in the land. Ae could have prevented so much carnage, and ae had not. It was a guilt ae would never undo or repay.

"If you require my death, so be it. I ask only that you give me time to unmake the ruined earth and I will return to you when finished and you may do unto me as you see fit." Yarchuse swallowed. "I give you my word."

The Heart's branch-palm lifted aer chin and ae stared up at the great tree. **I see truth in your words.**

Yarchuse held still, waiting. In all aer life, refusing to fight or defend aerself now was the hardest battle ae had ever fought.

A shallow gasp heralded the prince's awakening. He sat up slowly, blinking and gazing about in awe.

We will regrow, the Heart said, **and perhaps in the seasons that come, your people will as well.**

"I hope so," Yarchuse said.

Your prince will stay, and he will be treated with honor, as one of our kin.

Aretas inhaled and bowed his head. It was as if he had heard the entire exchange. "I accept."

Go, the Heart said, withdrawing their hand from Yarchuse's chin. **We will agree to this truce, an exchange of princes. Let carnage end. We wish the world to grow.**

Shakily, Yarchuse rose to aer feet. Ae looked at Aretas, who smiled brightly. "Thank you." Ae bowed low to the Heart in respect. "When my work is done, I will return to you—"

No, the Heart said. **I will not take your life the way your people have taken ours. Uphold your word and heal our shared lands. Show your saplings a better way.**

Yarchuse had no response, aer throat closed off in shock, relief, and overwhelming shame. Ae looked at the prince, who smiled brightly. "I will," ae said. "My word is yours."

The Heart spread their branches wide, and the grove parted into a sun-dappled tunnel.

～

Yarchuse stumbled through the woods, aer thoughts strewn afar as the full weight of what ae had promised, what the Heart had offered, settled into aer mind.

When ae returned to the Worded City, ae would erase from aer tome all spells of war. In their place ae would begin crafting words and incantations for healing, for peace. The prospect gave aer hope.

When ae stepped from the trees' shadows, ae saw the Ever-Hungry Queen's army repentant and battle-ready covering the moors.

Tension rippled through the front ranks. The bulwark guard lowered spears in preparation, the fresh-painted tomeslung words of defense glistening on armor and steel shields. Attir and her raptor waited halfway between the front line and the forest. And beside them towered Kel, the false-prince still on her back.

Yarchuse lifted aer arm. "Stand down," ae called. "There is no longer any need for war. The prince lives. Let the trees go in peace. They will not wage war any longer if we will not."

Behind aer, the forest began a slow, solemn retreat, fanning out as it migrated in majestic waves inland again, parting to either side of the army. The Ever-Hungry Queen stalked forward. The woodland prince slipped from Kel's back and approached her.

Yarchuse reached Kel's side, and the apex raptor kreed in relief and curled her neck around aer, her eye level with Yarchuse's. Ae smiled and pressed aer forehead against her cheek. "It's done," ae whispered.

Then ae turned as the Ever-Hungry Queen embraced the prince. He held onto her, and there was no death, no blood. Yarchuse sighed in aching relief.

"Let us return home," the prince said. "All of us." He looked over one shoulder and nodded to Yarchuse, who inclined aer head in return.

What now? Kel signed.

Yarchuse smiled. Ae was composing a ballad of this day, one that could be sung across the lands and remembered for generations. The truth: an ode to peace.

About the Author

A. Merc Rustad is a queer non-binary writer who lives in Minnesota and is a Nebula Awards finalist. Their stories have appeared in *Lightspeed*, *Fireside*, *Apex*, *Uncanny*, *Shimmer*, *Nightmare*, and several Year's Best anthologies. You can find Merc on Twitter @Merc_Rustad or their website: http://amercrustad.com. Their debut short story collection, SO YOU WANT TO BE A ROBOT, was published by Lethe Press.

Author's Notes

When I got asked to write a story for *Sword and Sonnet*, the first thing I knew was: it must have dinosaurs.

I had scraps and bits from a couple of unfinished stories that had an apex raptor, and bits and bobs about an agender poet/sorcerer, but I didn't quite have the plot or cohesion to make either work. Then I combined them, and suddenly it all clicked! As I was writing *The Words of Our Enemies, The Words of Our Hearts* I found the scattered ideas from old unfinished things gelled so nicely. Basically the moral of this is: never throw out anything. You never know when it can be recycled into shiny new stories with dinosaurs!

LABYRINTH, SANCTUARY

A.E. Prevost

Constance carves her timeworn tracks into the thirsty rock. With silent steps her footfalls smooth the stone, century into century, grooves and gullies growing green as time and seed take hold. Stone after stone, her hands build battlements and balconies, repair time-ragged trusses, stack spires towards the sun. Deep in the dark wood, with every aching year, her sanctuary spreads its restless roots.

Constance dreams of colonnades and courtyards, crafts finials from fingernails, weaves tapestries from hair. She climbs her spiral stairs into the storm-bruised sky, flings open feverish arms against the thrum of thunder, batters the balustrades with fists like driving rain. Constance lets rage run through her like the roiling storm, then huddles in the hollows and scratches broken nails across the thirsty roots that thrive between the cracks. So long as she keeps building, she is safe. Her moss-laced maze mirrors the spirals in her soul, and she repeats her one and only truth: in this, her sanctuary, no ill thing can befall her.

The poet's path bruises the grass under their ash-grim boots. A hunger howls behind them, spreading fast, a wildfire that feeds on hope and spits out fear like smoke. With sea-green scarf wrapped fast against their face, they fill their mouth and nose with flowers and song, and walk into the woods, and do not rest. The poet's heart enshrines the memory of colors; an ocean coils within, wine-dark and dormant, which pulses in their throat with every step.

There was an ocean, once; the poet walked its coast and paddled in its pearl-kissed waters, trading tales with sirens, learning the songs of stars. Children with laughter bright as birds called them cousin, and families fished feasts of color from the swelling waves, repeating recipes whispered by the sea winds. The poet plucked gem-hued fruit from swaying shoreline trees, with names they tasted in the juices on their tongue, and flowers sprung from where their bare feet met the fertile ground.

The fruit trees, too, have fallen now. All colors are consumed; all names are ash. Only the poet remains, steadfast, song-laden. Their loping strides track sea salt onto the forest floor.

≈

The wall juts up among the trees, tangled with roots, jagged and ancient. The poet stops, panting through sea-green silk, brushing their sea-browned hand against the crumbling stone. Songs tell of a labyrinth here in these lands, long-haunted, ill-advised; the poet knows there must be a path through it, for there is a path through all places, in time. The hunger howls in the dust-ridden distance. The poet raises reddened eyes and meets the gaze of a stranger.

The stranger steps back, blending into the shadows. The poet presses close against the wall, peering through the crack where they just saw the woman wreathed in vines and leaves.

Ahoy inside, the poet calls. Are you a prisoner? Or are you lost inside the labyrinth?

I am Constance, the stranger says, her voice a wraith among the whispering trees. I am not lost, and I am not imprisoned. I am Constance.

I am Daylily, the poet says, kneeling beside the barrier. An ocean's worth of memories weighs heavy on my back. A hunger hurries behind me to consume the world—all wonder, color, hope, all life, and love itself. Long I lived as a petal, borne on a breeze, but now the wind that drives me reeks of waste and ruin. Will you reveal to me the passage through this labyrinth?

This is no labyrinth, Constance replies. She finds her strength steadily as she speaks. No, this is no labyrinth, stranger, any more than I am lost. A thousand years I've travailed in these woods, and set down every stone with my own hands. No harm can hunt me in my sanctuary. This place is safe from that which seeks you, too.

Soon there will be no sanctuary to be had, Daylily objects. Ash has covered the colors of the land, undone the sea, and quenched the stars. Ash has filled the mouths and eyes of everyone I've known.

Constance approaches the split between the stones, picks at her side of it with dirty fingers. The poet's eyes beyond are proud, night-dark and pleading.

I see your sorrow, stranger, but you should not fear. These halls are strong, and here no fire will find us.

The poet's eyes burn bright behind the break.

Wanderer, if you wish, Constance whispers, you could remain, secure behind my stones. There's room to spare within my sanctuary.

Daylily reaches to Constance through the gap, their hands barely brushing.

Immortal architect, fleeing is all I have left, for if I am forgotten, so will be every hope once set in song. I beg you, now. I must pursue my path and travel through this place, or perish when the hunger reaches us.

Constance traces the tree-like whorls of Daylily's fingertip with a feather-soft touch. Strange, the skin of another, sinew and rushing blood, blue-dyed nails, coarse hair. Strange, the shiver that ghosts along a bare arm at her breath. Strange, the distant drumming of a heart held fast in a fortress of flesh, a cage of bone. Strange, the smell of flowers and the sea.

Enter then, Constance says. Flee and be safe.

~

For the first time in a thousand years, a stranger stands on sanctuary stone. Constance collects small pebbles from the ground and stacks and restacks them in even piles. Daylily looks towards the forest line, past which their doom draws ever nearer, then down across the dark expanse of stone that winds and stretches out within the walls. Intentioned or not, a thousand years of building has birthed something well-served with the word Labyrinth.

I should continue quickly on my way, Daylily says. What path through is the fastest?

Constance pauses, a pebble in her hand. Thistles and thorns are threaded through her hair.

There is no map, she says, no method here but the one deep within my mind. But I can take you, I can, I know the way. Only I can show you out.

Daylily looks to her eager eyes, and nods.

~

Daylily's boots follow Constance's bare feet. The sun dips low, sending spears of copper through the cool dark trees. The labyrinth is floors and walls and stairs, but rooms throughout lie open to the sky; Daylily breathes in birdsong, dusk, and pollen, weaving its precious world into a poem.

What is it that you whisper as we walk? Constance asks. Often your breath is bound together with words I barely hear.

There is so little life left in the world, Daylily says. I must protect the poetry of it, wherever I can. Else my survival would have been in vain.

Constance runs her fingers along the familiar railing, her road drawing her deeper into the fortress.

Your survival saved you, she remarks. Even if you remembered nothing, that alone would be worth all your worry.

Do not say that! Daylily draws their features into a frown. Do not say that, Constance. I was a petal; I was never a stone. I was never meant to last, only to float like flotsam on the surface of the wave, my gaze turned gently to the dreaming deep. I was, and remain, nothing. Do not say that my survival alone is worth more than the memories I bear.

I do not think I said that, Constance says, stepping over a tree root in their way. But perhaps both have value. Yes, perhaps.

Daylily follows quietly in her wake.

~

The sickle moon shines silver light onto the columned court.

We should rest here a while, Constance suggests. There is a bed of ferns and feathers near where we can pass the night.

I have not slept since the hunger began, Daylily replies.

Does it follow so close? Constance asks, looking for the nest built long ago.

I fear sleep will devour my devotion, Daylily admits, and make me forget the folk whose songs I sing, or lead the desolation right into my dreams.

Well I have no such worries, Constance says from a soft-shadowed alcove. She stretches out her limbs and rests her head on ancient bird wings tied with red-dyed roots, and proposes they pause their travel until daybreak.

For one night, perhaps, Daylily presumes their quest can wait. Alone, they wander awake between the vine-wreathed pillars; they fill their eyes with infinite shimmering stars, their ears with the calls of cricket, owl, and frog. Under the milky moonlight, Daylily murmurs to remember, and Constance is lulled to sleep by their soft litany.

⁓

The dawn paints pink coral blooms on Constance's cheeks and sets fire to the halo of Daylily's hair. Birds with scarlet-tipped feathers follow them, hopping from stone to stone, from arch to arch.

Will you teach me a song from your life by the sea? Constance requests, ambling abreast with Daylily. We have a way to walk still before you leave, and I have no songs of my own save the sounds woven by the wilderness.

The wilderness is splendid in its song, Daylily says. I could listen a century and still be wanting.

You could stay, Constance says. Put roots down in the woodlands for a while. When your hunger comes, my walls can withstand it. Nothing will make ash of us in here.

Daylily faces forward, steadfast and unforgiving. They walk in silence down the winding stair.

⁓

Truly, Daylily says, your sanctuary is spectacular.

Constance gathers loose gravel, lays it aside for later at the angles of hallways.

Most of the time, now, I reuse what crumbles, she says. But sometimes I dig deeper in the rock and bring out a new boulder with which to build.

And you have truly done this for a thousand years? Daylily asks.

Your hunger is behind you, Constance says. It chases you. Mine is within. It waits for me in quiet moments, in my belly, breathless. Its patience is perfect. Building keeps it at bay.

And you have never left, not once, in all this time?

In leaving, I would lose all I have made, Constance mutters, scratching her skin against the stone. My castle would crumble, and I would surely turn into dust, dissolve, and drift away.

I would not want you to dissolve, Daylily says. But if you could escape this place, perhaps we could travel together. I would hate for the hunger to consume you, drain your dreams from the world, wither your vines. I would hate for a thousand years of stories to be swept into ash.

Constance crouches and straightens out the little stacks of slate that line the edges of the pin-straight path. She only rises once the stacks are straight, and turns to her companion rather than check again.

I am more than stories, and so are you.

Daylily looks away, into the dappled light cast through the canopy of towering trees.

Daylily, Constance asks without approaching, will you teach me one of the ocean's songs? By nightfall we will near the end of my expanse, and you will flee, and I will remain rooted in my fortress. I ask you this one kindness in exchange for seeing you through my sanctuary. Do not leave me songless and on my own.

❧

Silence stretches between them like a thread, spider silk, shivering in the breeze.

I do not sing, Daylily says, their face turned towards the forest. I did, before, when I lived freely among friends, the ocean churning out new canticles with every crashing wave. Our fables flowed, easy as breath, through child and fruit and star, and we stitched stories into fish scales, told tales on wax-printed fabrics, dyed sand to sketch sagas into the beach, triumphant and then vanished with the tide. Easy as breathing, in and out, a beauty borne by all of us together, new stories spreading like wildfire down the coast, blooming in different colors on each vine, and then releasing seeds upon the wind.

But only I remain now, and I fear that if I share the songs that I have learned, I will lose them forever. And my family, my ocean, my stars and flowers will fade, leaving me empty. One day, perhaps, I will find an apprentice, and pass my tales along for another to carry. One day, perhaps, I will be ready to be nothing once again, and to die. But until then I collect, and flee, and do not sleep or sing.

Constance remains a moment, then relents, guiding the poet onwards through a narrow arch and up a passage to a parapet, a path that overlooks the vine-encrusted woods.

It seems a pity, she says, at the top, that such thriving songs should stay bottled within you. To hear you say it, a large part of their beauty was the way the poems passed from breath to breath, from heart to heart. If you keep them inside, is that not hollow? Is that not how the hunger itself behaves?

I am nothing like the hunger, Daylily states.

Yet you believe yourself empty and worthless, Constance says. Save for the songs that you deny the world.

I'm not the hunger!

Then prove it, wandering poet. Sing for me.

〜

Daylily kicks their boots off and faces her, brow feverish, feet rooted to the rock. They pull their sea-green scarf down from their face, revealing a strong nose and blue-dyed lips. Behind them in the sky clouds darken, their clotting shadows covering the day.

The sky draws close, yearning for devastation, draining the color from the trees. The birds go quiet, blotted out by the questing silence. Behind Daylily, the blanketing moss dries up and the ferns shrivel, held in hunger's grasp. Constance chokes on dust and watches rivulets of ash race across the stone towards her like spring thaw.

Daylily, she says, Daylily, sing.

❧

It begins with a single hummed note hovering between them, timid and intangible as hope itself. The hunger pauses, a predator taking a breath before descending on its death-marked prey. Daylily feels its breathing on their back, dry, thirsting. Tears fall as they close their eyes and find their voice.

The poet's song starts soft but quickly grows into a symphony of color: sapphire and tourmaline, topaz, carnelian, white sand-caressing waves and sweet sun-ripened red. Their words litter the ground like leaves, hover over Constance's skin like hummingbirds, thunder against her fortress like a flood. Constance's heart beats ruby-dark and rushes warmth through her. She takes a step towards the singer, hand outstretched, and the creeping ash shrinks back.

Fish flit like dragonflies in the gem-clear shallows, reflecting sunlight on their rainbow scales.

Constance's fingers touch Daylily's hand. Beneath the poet's bare feet, sprouts spring up, new green twining around their toes. Constance hums the tune she hears, in halting echoes that turn into harmonies.

Children stack shells into a shiny game, gathered by size and color, counting their collection as they win and lose.

Constance's dress of vines writhes and awakens, flora erupting up her thighs and flanks, cascading down her shoulders in a mantle of morning glories and pea blossoms. Sunlight and gentian gather in her hair.

Strong arms lay out baskets of sweet sun-baked berries, sea-salted leaves, round thumb-sized roots boiled and seasoned with spices, sugar wine. Barrels of seaweed and whisper-thin white fish, fermenting to be reborn as broth.

Daylily holds on to Constance's hands, Constance's voice. They turn to face the howling hunger together, pouring an ocean of stories down its throat as saplings spring up around them on the parapet. Crawling nasturtium vines chase ash from stone, bursting open in sunset-scarlet blooms against the gray.

Elders gather from up and down the coast, bringing a pot-luck of plates cooked by grandchildren and great-grandchildren and great friends. In the firelight they forget their differences, sing songs of storms that only they survived, laugh at old jokes, rekindle relationships long since burned down to embers. They watch stars that have wandered far longer than them, and that will still fill the night when they're forgotten.

Constance and Daylily face down the dust, hands clasped. A crack of thunder punctuates their song. Exhilarated rain ruptures the sky, sinks into their garments as warm as love, and waters their growing garden. Rain rinses ash away and replaces it with roots, rushing throughout the sanctuary and beyond to erupt and scream in greens and reds and yellows. Birds nest in newborn trees, sheltered from the rioting rain, and each drop on their plumage echoes a song of the ocean, which they weave into their own.

∿

Under the bright and noisy canopy of the wide woods, deer raise their russet heads, and ring-tailed rodents leap to lower branches. Constance can see the whole of it laid out, the triumphs and struggles of life being lived beyond the boundaries of her home. In the clearing distance, as the ash recedes, a glimmering line of light traces the end of the land. And bright as a dream, along the sparkling shore, she sees elders laugh around fires, children count shells, bright-patterned figures gather garnet-glowing fruit. She squeezes Daylily's hand as the hunger fades and flees—for now. There is so much there, in the world beyond. Perhaps there will be time to see it all.

About the Author

A.E. Prevost loves writing about found families, language, gender, mental health, and good things happening to interesting people. Most recently published in the gender diverse pronoun special issue of *Capricious*, A.E.'s work has also appeared in *Mechademia* and *Redwing*, among others. A.E. also writes and directs for *The Ling Space*, an educational YouTube series about linguistics, and co-owns the Argo Bookshop, a small independent bookstore full of cool stuff. A.E. is agender/nonbinary and finds gendered pronouns perplexing, despite being a linguist; they/she/he/??? can be found on twitter as @AePrevost.

Author's Notes

I wrote *Labyrinth, Sanctuary* specifically in response to the call for submissions for this anthology. The idea of "a poet who fights" immediately resonated with me; I knew right away that I wanted to tell a story about mental health, about the kinds of battles that can go on inside a person. I live with depression and anxiety. My brain tells me the most thorny, tangled, convincing lies. I'm constantly on this quest to learn how to fight them, and I poured that struggle into this story.

Mental illness can be so profoundly isolating, and Daylily and Constance both have these patterns their brains have locked them into, these walls they build to keep themselves safe (literally, in Constance's case). There's something dangerously comfortable about a predictable misery. Growing is terrifying, it means making yourself vulnerable and potentially inviting in new, unpredictable miseries. But for me, open communication with friends who love and support me has changed my life, and ultimately makes me feel a lot more secure than my own mental spirals do. So I wanted to write about that, too: about finding someone who gives you the courage to let yourself grow.

Stylistically, the moment I peeped the word *Beowulf* somewhere connected to the anthology, I was a lost cause: I took an Old English class at university and loved it more than anything. I also just really enjoy writing with intense lyricism. Obviously that's not appropriate everywhere, and in my ongoing quest to become a Better Writer, with the loving nudges of editors and beta readers, I've managed to pare it down over time. So when the opportunity arose to toss all caution to the wind and really lean into my grandiloquence, it felt experimental, almost like I was doing something I wasn't allowed. But once I got into it, it was incredibly freeing. I had a phenomenal amount of fun writing this story—fine-tuning the alliteration and rhythm of a line, packing each passage with flourishes I would normally hold back, making it feel mythical and lyrical and old. I fell in love with the idea of writing a kind of epic prose poem full of emotions and imagery, a fantastical fable about two people helping each other work through mental illness...In a way, although it didn't occur to me until just now, another inspiration for this story might be Amal El-Mohtar's beautiful *Seasons of Glass and Iron*, in that I read it and it found a home in my heart and showed me a kind of story I didn't realize I needed. Love may or may not conquer all, but it certainly has the power to make you be kinder to yourself, and I think that's already a lot.

HEARTWOOD, SAPWOOD, SPRING

Suzanne J. Willis

Today, it is my turn.

I walk through the main square of our settlement before dawn, to spend the morning in the library originally curated by our grandmothers. The sun is rising as I carefully turn the vellum pages of these most illegal tomes. In some places the ink is blurred. Other words are slashed through, as though our enemy had tried to bleed the very meaning out of them, to leave the stories as nothing but husks. But those blurred, scarred words tell me that the women to whom those stories belonged were fierce. In these folios are the faded scars of their battle wounds.

The words are etched much deeper than our foes understand. The rustle of these delicate pages whisper to me in the early morning light. *Only with an army of words will we bury them*, they say.

Before this library, this town, there was another time entirely. Then, over a century ago, the almost-apocalypse changed everything. Ours became a world split into factions. It was a time of new beginnings and reversion to simpler ways, but also a time for new enmities. Our enemy sought to erase our past, our identities. Us.

The book I hold in my hands now was my mother's. She died in battle when I was three weeks old. The ink here is not blurred; rather, it is precise, sharp-edged, black as pitch. Her story is my weapon. It kindles the nascent coals of rage in the pit of my belly. The fire roars through my veins.

My mother's skin had been inked during the months before the battle that killed her. Hardly enough time for the words to live within her, which is exactly what the enemy desires. They know the power of the written word. That is why they despise and fear it. They will not touch anything with our words upon it, for they think them cursed.

That is why they do not dispose of our fallen, tattooed warriors, but leave them where they lay. In the dark of night and the gray dawn, we creep out to collect them. By lightfall, the remains have disappeared, and it suits the lies they feed their people. *Those women are cursed and rise from the dead, spreading filth and decay in death as in life.* But not all the people believe and the rebellion is growing, inside the city, Unvard, and outside it.

If the soldiers knew what we did with the bodies, they would burn them where they lay.

Sunlight shafts through the library window, but there is no warmth in its rays. I hold up a sheet of my mother's book to the light, trace my fingertip over the softness that was once her skin before it became page, sewn and bound with ebony hair. Black words against sepia-vellum, fine lines that tell their own story of a young death. Outside, the early morning mist shifts and the light brightens, limning the tattooed words.

history drags me to the open lands,
leaves me naked and newborn,
a woman aflame...

The sky is pale as the moon and it reminds me of my grand-mother's witch-silver hair. *My darling Luka*, she always says, *the last of my line.* This morning, she will be preparing the ink, sterilizing her needles and waiting for me.

The rebellion is growing. Next month, I go to battle.

So, today, it is my turn.

~

Upper back, cursive

Last of all, they came for our words.

Four generations ago all our books were banned, burned on pyres in flames so fierce, they licked the night sky clean of stars. Our great-grandmothers, young women, then, collected the ashes in tiny wooden boxes. The soldiers laughed and kicked them as they left.

Write upon pain of death has remained law since that time.

Stories and history, poetry and science became whispers in the night. The language of the poor, in a world of words uncaught.

The underprivileged and the hunted left Unvard for the border-lands. Our great-grandmothers took those little boxes with them to settlements that were strung out like lighthouses across dangerous shores. To show themselves as friend and forge alliances, the great-grandmothers tattooed poems on their thighs, with ink made with the ashes of the great fires. Those poems were the first language of the dispossessed.

The pen and page were no longer part of the people's armory. So ink and women's flesh became shield and sword.

∽

Belly, illuminated script, (black with red, blue and gold)
IN PRINCIPIO ERAT VERBUM
(In the beginning was the Word)

∽

Left thigh, tattooist freehand

Grandmother and I sat in the near-empty rock pools at low tide, starfish scattered at our feet, salt mist wreathing our bare arms. The sea was far from the city—here, we felt safe. Even at five years old, I knew our resistance was secret, as were our sacred texts. They reminded me of the words on Grandmother's skin, which I loved even before I could read.

The waves' foam fizzed over seaweed shallows as Grandmother passed me a lump of charcoal, then closed her hand over mine, guiding it toward the rock wall. Novitiate to her virtuoso, I was initiated into the almost-lost art of writing with cinder and sun warmed rocks.

We covered the walls with the alphabet, my name, and the names of my foremothers. Then, as the sun set and the sea washed in and stole my written words away, she told me histories, tales tall and true, poetry. She spoke of a future that did not need secrets.

"There is power in words, Luka. More than weapons. We write the words upon us and together we are not just an army. The dead, whose books we tend, and the living? Together, we are the greatest library in the world."

~

Left inner forearm, elbow to wrist, old Garamond (framed with green vines)

Heartwood: a tree's incredibly strong support pillar, hollow needles bound together; a word's core from which its meaning is derived.

Sapwood: carries water to the tree's leaves, new wood that turns to heartwood as newer rings are laid down; words as spoken and written, sustaining and transforming language.

Spring: season of renewal that produces tree's growth hormones; to come into being; language passed between writer and reader, speaker and listener.

The enemy seeks to ringbark our stories, to let them wither and die. To winter our words into nothingness.

Never forget that
We are Spring.

~

Back right hand and snaking around wrist, cursive

remember the days you wore me
like a shroud,
a wing-caul,
a wrap of forest song. weave me
in the words you sing

your words sit in your chest, like a stone
I wait for them to gather, in a sonnet, a dirge,
a lovesong
you gather them in your cheeks, save
the words for winter
When you speak in morning's frost, weave me
in the words you sing

~

Chest, Victorian Gothic (framed with feathered wings)

Daughter, lover, bereaved
Story-keeper
Poet

~

Nightfall. The first wave will attack Unvard at three a.m. My tattoos are still healing, and I settling into them. What are we, if not the accumulated stories of our past and that of our foremothers? I will carry them with me into battle. And if I die, they will interleave my unmarked skin with the inked, to show a life incomplete.

There are seventeen women in my troop and we ready ourselves together by gaslight, low and yellow, smiling at one another as we shave off our tresses. Our hair falls to the floor in waves of copper, mouse-brown, gold and black. I run my hand over my stubbled scalp and laughter bubbles in my throat. Its unfamiliarity makes me feel free and fierce. The troops we will face tomorrow do not like women who look like us. *That scares them more than our words*, grand-mother used to say.

Around me are the women with whom I will go to battle, stories inscribed on their flesh both scarred and milk-smooth, and I cannot imagine anything more beautiful. Elsewhere in the settlement, the men are preparing, too, in their own rituals, their bodies covered with images of dragons and phoenix and gods of old instead of words.

We had not planned to attack for another two weeks, on the new moon. Three days ago, though, we received word that *they* would attack *us* in three days' time, so we must strike tonight. We lace our boots, sheathe swords and test the sharpness of hand axes against the soft pad of the thumb. Our weavers gather the hair like sheaves of wheat, sifting it by color and plaiting it into ropes they will wash and hang from the windows at dawn. For those who don't return, the hair will be used to bind books of their skin and they will take their place on the library shelves.

The room is quiet, but for the final ritual: we murmur poetry into the night, fragments that will never be written down. It reminds us that some things are ephemeral. If the written word is a tree digging its roots into the alluvium, the spoken word is the last autumn leaves on the rushing breath of winter.

one day he would come to reclaim her
on a ship built
from the bones of drowned sailors

night cat, to the night star bound
Three times the merry land, around
Seeks the song, once made her sing
or faded owl, with faded wing

but long
forgot the tendril flames
licking at this skin, a web witch, burned by men

caught
falling
into my eyes
Myopic, my Narcissus
Leaves me blind

The words unwind from our mouths, then from one another, to lace together again in new shapes; one moment nonsensical, the next plump with meaning. Finally, I open the door. We fall silent and then the words are gone.

~

Unvard's leaders don't think enough of the resistance to black out or even dim its gas lights, and the glow in the sky is a beacon leading us through the forest that drips verdant and lush around us. They know we only have swords and blades to their more sophisticated weapons and think that makes us weak.

We have walked for hours in silence before we come to the edge of the forest, sharply cut away by the plain of no man's land stretching out between us and the city. The easy part is over and we stay in the shadows, watching. Unvard's ramparts are topped with wicked iron spikes and the towers are well guarded. There is seemingly no way over or through.

Stealth is our advantage, here.

The tall grasses ripple, then a series of short whistles signal that the advance party have disarmed the traps that awaited us—the pits full of sharpened sticks, the trip-wire explosives. Our stock of explosives is small, precious, and that will go with the three scouts who are taking the tunnels into enemy territory.

The regiment splits into three—the scouts disappear behind the moss-covered boulders, down a rocky path and out of sight. We wait twenty minutes, twenty-five, enough for them to make their way through the tunnels. It is a small eternity. I breathe slowly to calm my racing heart, fight the need to roll the tension from my shoulders. The first wave moves forward, creeping across no man's land, as light as dancers. The weather has been kind, clouds covering the sky and hiding the fullness of the moon.

We watch from the forest edge, holding our breath.

The moon breaks through the cloud, shining on the warriors out in the open. I wish I could wrap the shadows around us all as I wait for the sentries to spot them. Silently, they crouch or lay flat, unmoving. From our vantage point, the tattooed arms and scalps are like scattered remnants of a living page. Shot through with dark letters, interspersed with the images with which the men are marked.

As the clouds slide across the moon again, dropping the world back into darkness, a gunshot splits the night. We duck behind the cover of the trees and I risk peeking out. The grass is roiling as the first wave run forward. Another crack, then an enormous explosion rends the night, flames so bright I shield my eyes. The subsequent smaller explosions tell me our scouts have hit their target and destroyed the city's armory. Their stockpile of weapons is gone.

I throw my head back and howl our war cry. In the aftermath of the explosion, their arsenal burns and the second wave rushes after the first to the wall, where hidden doors have opened and their army rush towards us. Overhead, bullets pierce the night. Three, five, more of us than I can count fall, but still we run forward, forward, blades raised high over our heads.

Their soldiers wield their swords not just to kill but to carve through the words on our skin and destroy us twice-over.

I slash, and stab, and thunk my axe into flesh and bone. And still I run, screaming and roaring with the rest, covered in blood and gore. I pause. The popping overhead has stopped: their ammunition has run dry. We attack, and run and call, and fight, and will this never end, this mess of cadavers, this whirl of blades?

An explosion throws me backward. The world is ringing, ringing, and the fight, for a moment, frozen. A click or so to the north, the wall is in ruins and suddenly the city is an open wound. We are on our feet again and now we pour towards *them*. The words of the poetry we spoke to one another in the gaslight rearrange themselves into new shapes, renewing my purpose and moving me forward.

> tendril flames licking
> at the bones of blind men

Their ranks are in disarray. Our archers light arrows from the fire in the aftermath of the blast. Burning sentries fall from the top of the wall, like embers from a pile of burning books.

> Three times the merry land around
> Myopic, to the night star bound

And now they are running, a horde of rats back into their holes. We flank them, pushing them backward to the city where they learned to fight, but not to know their adversaries. To the leaders who outlawed knowledge and reduced the people's world to an oubliette.

drowned, faded eyes seek my skin
this the song, once made her sing

One of the soldiers, a young man around my age, is slower than the others and clumsy. He stumbles and falls, sprawling in the grass and mud. I stop, cradling my axe as I stand over him. I will not kill him from behind, like a coward. He begins to crawl forward, then rises slowly and turns to me, arms raised. He looks at my chest, my arms and my hands, covered in my words. His face shows his revulsion, but there is something else. Curiosity, perhaps?

"Are you so blind that you don't see what it is that you fight against? That what you fight *for* is your own servitude?" I say.

He opens his mouth to speak, but nothing comes out.

"Go!" I take a step toward him and he turns, runs after the others.

∼

The sun will rise soon, so we haven't much time. Mothers and sisters, fathers and cousins have come to take away the dead. They work quickly and quietly, disappearing into the forest with the bodies of seven of my troop among the others. Those of us remaining walk to the gaping, smoldering hole in the wall and whistle softly. Through the ash and dust and the gray pre-dawn, one of the scouts who crept through the tunnels walks towards us. A small crowd follows in her wake—families, lone children, a young couple—and we help them over the ruins, our warriors escorting them across no man's land to trek back to our settlement. The last to come are our remaining two scouts, following three of their soldiers, who wear white scarves around their necks. I tense, but two of them smile and show me the underside of their arms. The word *Free* is inked there is crude lettering.

I turn to the third and it is the young man I chased from the battlefield. He is cuffed, but calm. "I am ready to learn," is all he says.

I nod to him and smile, hoping that he really is ready for the road that lies ahead. It is one of uncertainty and exile and *knowing*; that is never easy. But in knowledge is freedom. This is a road I have walked all my life, and my book, inscribed and life-scarred, will one day join the others in our library.

But not today. I am not yet fully written.

One day, there will be more of *us* than *them*. Our stories have a thousand different beginnings and endings. They cannot be buried or forgotten forever. We have spent four generations recreating, remaking the stories on our own bodies from the relics of old words. Our poetry, the language of the soul that lies inside us like fossils, waiting to be uncovered, will continue to shape us in ways unexpected and true.

> Whether charcoaled words on sea cave walls
> Or books of tattooed skin,
> The voices of spring braided with sapwood
> And autumn words breezing to uncharted shores.

About the Author

Suzanne J. Willis is a Melbourne, Australia-based writer, a graduate of Clarion South and an Aurealis Awards finalist. Her stories have appeared in anthologies by PS Publishing, Prime Books, Falstaff Books and Metaphorosis, and in *SQ Mag*, *Mythic Delirium*, and *Lackington's*. Suzanne's tales are inspired by fairy tales, ghost stories, and all things strange. She can be found online at http://suzannejwillis.webs.com

Author's Notes

This story had its genesis about ten years ago, as a very different, sweet tale about a girl living in a world where handwriting has gone the way of the dodo and her grandmother was one of the last people to own books. It was more of a vignette than a proper story and a good friend critiqued it, suggesting that it might work better if handwriting was illegal in that world. Other projects came up, new ideas took precedence, and that story didn't get another look-in.

When I first read that there would be an open call for *Sword and Sonnet*, my mind immediately went back to that world. Censorship, denying people access to knowledge, the right of self-determination crushed so successfully that anyone who rebels risks death: the thought of living in such a world made me wonder how rebellion would look and how it would be lived.

The rebellious warriors in this world are primarily women and they are also the guardians of knowledge, stories, poetry. Tattooing their bodies with words is an act of rebellion in itself; it tells their enemy that knowledge is not separate from the people. They create their own myths around the tattooed women so that, even after they die, the words tattooed on their bodies can be preserved, along with their stories. Even though the idea of creating books out of human skin is quite horrific, in this world it represents power and a type of immortality. The stories live on, long after the storyteller is gone.

THE BONE POET AND GOD

Matt Dovey

Ursula lifted her snout to look at the mountain. The meadowed foothills she stood in were dotted with poppy and primrose and cranesbill and cowslip, an explosion of color and scent in the late spring sun, the long grass tickling her paws and her hind legs; above that the forested slopes, birch and rowan and willow and alder rising into needle-pines and gray firs; above that the snowline, ice and rock and brutal winds.

And above that, at the top, God; and with God, the answer Ursula had traveled so far for: *what kind of bear am I meant to be?*

She shouldered her bonesack and walked on.

There was a shuffling sound among the bracken, small but definite. Ursula hesitated, a dry branch held in her paws, her campfire half-built. Ambush wasn't unheard of—so many bears sought God on the mountain that bonethieves couldn't resist the chances to steal—but it had not been so large a sound, and she couldn't smell another bear beneath the pine scent. It was something smaller, lurking in the dim light of the forest floor, behind the massive rough-barked firs that filled the slope.

"Hello?" she ventured, still holding motionless. "It's quite all right. I'm building a fire, if you'd like to join me."

A badger stepped out from the ferns, his snout twitching and cautious, a stout stick held warily in his paws. He eyed Ursula for a moment, weighing up the situation, and she gestured ever so gently to the fire she was building, trying to come across as safe, as friendly. As likeable.

He straightened and walked forward. He kept the stick before him, but Ursula understood. Bears could be dangerous.

Two more badgers followed him, one much smaller—"Oh, you're a family!" said Ursula. "I'll make a seat for you!"

She stood, turned, dashed back, dropping to four paws in her enthusiasm. She ran to where she'd seen a fallen log not twenty yards away by the river and hauled it back, her claws dug into its softened bark, dragging it and dropping it by the fire pit with a thud. She grinned at the family, proud of her resourcefulness—

The badgers cowered, the two behind the father with the stick, who tried to meet her eyes but couldn't help glancing away for places to burrow and hide.

Ursula lowered herself slowly to sit. She made a point of picking up smaller twigs to lay on the fire, the least threatening pieces she could find. "Sorry," she said quietly. "I forget how I can come across. Please. Sit down." She concentrated on building the fire, determinedly not looking at the badgers, not wanting to startle them, trying not to let their fear hurt her nor to berate herself for getting carried away and upsetting others. For letting her shyness get to her: for overcompensating for it.

If only she knew who she was, instead of pretending so poorly.

"Thank you," said Father Badger from the log, and Ursula smiled at him, keeping her teeth covered. "Forgive us our caution. We...have never met a bear before."

"I'm Ursula," she said.

"My name is Patrick," said Father Badger, "and this is my husband, Willem, and our new daughter Ann."

"And how old are you, Ann?" Another careful smile, friendly not fearsome, benevolent not bearlike.

Ann shuffled a little and squirmed in closer to Willem, who put an arm around her.

"She is a little shy," said Willem. "We only met her an hour ago."

"She's why we came up the mountain," said Patrick, smiling at his daughter. "Willem and I came to ask God for a blessing, and we found Ann burrowed alone beneath a root."

"God showed you to her?" said Ursula eagerly, forgetting her calm façade in her excitement. "Is she near?"

"We never saw God," said Willem, "and now we have no need. God has delivered us our gift already."

"Oh," said Ursula. "I mean, I'm happy for you! I really am. I just..."

"You hoped she would be near?" finished Willem.

Ursula shrugged, not trusting herself to speak. She put the last branch on the fire and hooked a claw around the strap of her bone-sack, bones rattling inside the plain leather.

She felt, rather than saw, the badgers tense.

"You're a bonethief," said Patrick, voice flat and accusatory.

"We were warned of your kind on the mountainside," said Willem, pulling Ann in close.

"They're not my kind," said Ursula carefully. "I don't do what they do."

"You carry the bones," said Patrick. His paw lay on the stout stick, though if she truly were a bonethief it'd do him no use. She admired him that bravery, that certainty in his actions.

"Not all bears that carry bones are bonethieves," said Ursula. "There is so much more that can be done. Please. Let me show you."

She reached into the bag and started pulling bones out, laying them on the floor, runes up. She spoke as she did, her voice low and even, trying to defuse the situation she had accidentally escalated again. "Every bone is from a family member. They've all passed down to me, bit by bit. This one here was Aunt Maud's, this one Uncle Arthur's, that there is my Great-Grandma's right arm. Every bear carries four runes on their body—well, usually, by the end...anyway—four runes carved into their bones. One is carved on the left thigh bone at birth by one parent, another on the right thigh by the other when they consider their child has come of age."

"How?" asked Willem, still cautious, but curious too.

"Bear claws are sharp," Ursula said. "I would show you with mine, but I don't want to scare Ann." She tried a smile again, only a small one, tentative, but Ann responded in kind. "My parents cut through my flesh to carve their chosen rune on my bones. Their words hold me up everywhere I go, even this far from them. My father gave me HOME at birth and my mother gave me WATER. It helps me miss them less, as if they're with me wherever I am."

The bones were all laid out now, and Ursula began to choose from them. SUN, from Great-Great-Uncle Morris. WIND to cross it: Grandma Oak's breastbone.

"The third," she continued, "is given to us by God, shaped on our breastbone from the very moment of our conception. None of us ever know our breastbone rune. It's only known when we pass our bones to our family." She began to lay the bones before the fire pit. SLEEP, the next.

"And the fourth?" asked Patrick.

Ursula paused. She kept her voice flat when she answered, trying not to let any emotion into her answer. "The fourth we carve ourselves, on our right arm." She chose WAKE from the pile, and put it in place:

A hot gust of air blew towards the campfire and it flared into life, awakening to a satisfying crackle. A gentle, sleepy warmth washed over Ursula, and she smiled to herself in satisfaction, then began putting bones back into the sack.

"I'm a bone poet," she said. "The bonethieves only ever work towards violence and supremacy. All the bones they steal are only to help them steal more bones. They never think of all the better ways bones can be used."

"How do you know what to choose?" asked Ann. Willem looked

down at her in surprise.

"Well, the contraries must share something to bind the square together but have a tension that will give it power, and the neighbors should resonate in sound or form to amplify it, and the whole has to work to the purpose. I suppose I know what to choose because I know my bones well, what I've inherited and what might work."

"No," said Ann. "How do you choose what you carve on your own arm?"

"Oh." Ursula picked a branch up, nudged at the fire with it, re-arranged the piled sticks to get them burning better. She mostly only knocked it over. "That's...that's what I want to ask God about."

"Why?"

Ursula stared into the fire. How to express it? How to encapsulate the paralysis of choice, the fear of choosing wrong, the strange position of not knowing yourself?

"There is power in four," she said, still staring. "Four bones combine into a poem of purpose. All of them interact and reinforce each other. I have to choose my own fourth rune carefully so that my purpose as a bear is strong. But how can I choose the fourth when only God knows what my third is?"

"So you go to ask," said Willem.

Ursula nodded, feeling small, shrunken by her uncertainty, so unbearlike. "Choosing your own rune is...is the act of choosing who you want to be. It's the moment of knowing yourself and defining yourself. Of finding your place in the world. But I don't know who I am yet. Other bears just seem to know, but me...I try to be what I think other people need me to be, but it feels like everyone wants me to be something different, and every time I think I know which rune I should choose something changes my mind."

"It is admirable that you worry so much about others," said Willem. "Perhaps you should worry more about yourself, though. It sounds like this should be about you, not about the world."

She prodded at the fire again. It felt—strange, to vocalize what had been churning and building in her head for so long. Stranger yet to be telling it to a badger cub. She looked up to smile at Ann, not a calming smile, but a real smile, a vulnerable smile, a—

Patrick had raised his stick, and was looking past Ursula. She turned, frowning, staring into the gloom of dusk that swam through the trees. There wasn't—no, a glint—eyes reflecting flame—then a snarl, and Ursula's fur bristled in alarm, and a sudden gust of icy wind extinguished the fire and knocked the badgers backwards.

Bone magic.

Bonethief.

"Run!" shouted Ursula to the badgers. She scooped up her bonesack and went to run too, but Ann was so small, and ran so slowly, too slowly, and Ursula realized the badgers would never escape.

She dropped her bonesack and began digging through it for bones. She only had to slow the bonethief enough for Patrick and Willem to get Ann underground, then she could run too. She couldn't risk her bones. The bonethief ran forward on all fours, bones held in his jaws: he was a huge grizzly, bigger than Ursula, his fur matted with green-brown moss and sticky sap.

He pulled up at the sight of her bonesack—not in fear, she didn't think, but in avarice.

"So," he growled, low and fearsome, "you've been thieving round here for some time."

Ursula drew herself up tall, her fur raised, trying to make herself seem confident and sure. "I have not. I'm no bonethief."

"Quite the sack of bones you've got there for a bear traveling alone. Or are those little badgers your companions, and not just a snack you're luring in?"

Ursula risked a glance back at them—Ann had stopped to watch, and was refusing to be pulled away—and it hurt her to worry they might believe him for even a moment. Surely they already knew her better! But she had to seem strong and bearlike now: she couldn't show any concern for smaller creatures in front of this other bear.

She lifted her snout. "My family has entrusted them to me and my skill. I am a bone poet." She said this with as much pride as she could in the hopes it would impress the bonethief, forge a connection between them and allow her to talk herself out of this without any conflict.

But it did not. He laughed, a deep roar, a bellow of mirth that shook needles loose from the pines. "A poet? What fresh scat is this?"

His mockery stung, but not just because she'd failed to impress him. No, it stung because she *was* proud to be a bone poet, she realized. She was proud of the things she could do. She was proud of the connections she could make between bones.

She was proud of the way Ann had looked at her as she explained. She *was* better than this thief.

"I'm more deserving of these bones than you'll ever be." Her voice now was angry, not by choice, not to elicit a response from him, but because she *meant* it.

The thief grinned back at her, exposing his fangs. "Doesn't matter if you deserve them. Only matters if you're strong enough to keep them from me." His paws moved to his bones, and he began laying out his square.

Not enough time to think, only to react. Ursula grabbed bones from her sack almost without thought, going by touch and instinct, and laid them out in a square:

The soil beneath the bonethief fell away like melting snow and the exposed tree roots started to twist and writhe, a tangle of wood squirming with life. The bear stumbled and fell into the trap, snarling, swiping at the roots as his back legs sunk into the soft ground.

Willem was scrabbling at the earth, burrowing, as Patrick stood before Ann with his stick held out. It'd do no more than scratch the throat of the bonethief as he swallowed. His bravery brought her heart to her throat.

The bonethief roared. "Stupid sow! I'll take all your bones! I'll rip yours from your flesh!" He grasped at the roots, hauling himself out of the loose mud.

Ursula rifled through her bones again. She had to do something else to slow him down, so she could—

No. She had to do something to stop him. If he didn't get her bones, he'd chase someone else's. He'd eat other small mammals he came across, hurt other travelers. But she was a bone poet, and she could outthink him. She could stop him here.

The bonethief was free of the earth now, arranging his small clutch of stolen bones to send another blast of icy wind; she could see the runes from here, WIND and WILD and STRONG and ICE. She chose her bones with more care, though no less speed:

Her square burst with light, and even knowing it was coming it was all Ursula could do to shield her eyes, positioning herself to protect the badgers. The bonethief was less prepared—staring greedily at Ursula, at her bonesack—and the full flash of light blinded him. He yelped in agony, in surprise, as the sight was burned from his eyes. If she had done enough he would no longer be able to read the runes on bones. She doubted he could recognize them by touch.

But he, too, had finished his square: and he was closer to her this time, and the blast of wind gusted hard. With her paws raised to shield her eyes from her own blast, Ursula was unbalanced, and she was knocked backwards, down the slope, all her bones scattering in the chill wind, and she rolled and fell towards the river and into the river and knocked her head and—

~

Icy water splashed at Ursula's snout. Slapped at it, even. She stirred, groggily, and opened her eyes to a salmon flopping on her face. She swiped at it unthinkingly, knocking it away, then groaned as she realized how hungry she was.

With an effort, she hauled herself from the river and shook the water from her fur. In the dim light of dusk it was difficult to tell how exactly far she had fallen down the mountain, but the ground around her sloped only gently, covered in tall grass and meadow flowers closed for the night.

She was as far from God as she had ever been, and she no longer had her bones. She no longer had her friends—oh, she hoped Patrick and Willem and Ann had gotten away! Surely they were small enough and quick enough to avoid a blinded bear?—and she was not sure she had hope, either. It had taken days to ascend the mountain before, when she had her bones to intuit the way and catch leaping salmon and all the other little helps her poems gave her. Could she do it again now? What if another bonethief found her? Even without her bonesack to steal, she could be killed for her own bones.

But what else? Go home, and never know who she was? Never know who she should be? Could be?

Ursula pulled herself to her paws, cold muscles rasping, and dragged herself up the slope.

Walking on all fours in her exhaustion, her head bowed, the sun long set, Ursula trudged through the forest, stumbling wearily into alders and birches, knocking some over with a creaking, snapping shock of sound, loud in the silence of the night, stirring birds from their sleep in a panic. She fell into an atavistic trance: cold, hungry, determined, focused only on the ascent, forgetting even why she climbed, lost wholly in her drive to get higher, higher, higher.

So it was that she became aware of the light only slowly.

The color of it was the first thing she noticed. It was too blue for dawn. As she lifted her head to look closer, she saw the strangeness of the shadows—flickering, oddly angled, moving with each tired step like a broken branch swaying in the wind.

And she looked up at last, and saw a sleek black bear walking beside her, smaller, lither, and glowing gently.

"Hello Ursula," said God. "Would you like something to eat?" God gestured towards a clearing, where three salmon hung by a small, crackling fire that could not have been there a moment before. Had the clearing even been there?

Ursula lumbered forward and fell onto her haunches by the fire, snatching one of the salmon with a swipe and chewing it in silence, still lost in her animal exhaustion. God busied herself with the trees as Ursula ate, shaping branches with a touch and humming softly as she did, new leaves sprouting where her claws danced.

"Have I—" said Ursula, once she had eaten, warmed, returned to herself—"have I walked so long I am at the top?" She looked about at the trees, but they were still broad-leafed, of the low slopes.

God smiled up at a rowan; she reinvigorated one final branch with an upwards stroke, stretching on her hind legs, then sat down before Ursula. She exuded—*contentment.*

"No," she said, her voice high and clear like birdsong at dawn. "I am rarely at the top. It's so desolate up there, beautiful as it is. The point of the mountain is only to see how determined pilgrims are. Patrick and Willem could never have ascended above the snow-line, but they climbed so far on such small legs. If they had that devotion in them, if they were so driven by love, then Ann could do no better than their care."

Ursula's throat tightened in fear for the badgers. "Did they—are they—"

"Yes," said God, "they are fine. You did enough. Thank you."

Tension flooded out of Ursula like meltwater. The thought had weighed heavy, but—but they were well. She hoped they would be happy together.

"I believe, by the way," said God, "that these are yours." She reached behind where she was sat—where there had been nothing but grass and fallen twigs a moment before—and produced Ursula's bonesack, clearly full.

Ursula lurched forward with a gasp, snatching the bag quite before she could comprehend the rudeness of what she had done, and to whom she had done it.

"There are," said God, "a few more bones in there than before. You will be a better keeper for them, I think."

Ursula's breath caught in a sudden clench of nervousness, and she lowered the bag. So long spent climbing the slope, anticipating this moment, and now she couldn't get her words in order. There was so much to say, such an entwined web of emotion and expectation and duty and hope and thought and fear that she couldn't possibly order it anymore, couldn't untangle it to find the starting thread, couldn't do more than hold the whole concept of what she needed in her head at once, complete and connected and indivisible.

But she had come all this way, and perhaps if she just started. "About bones—"

"I know," said God. "Of course I know." And she smiled again, and stood up and walked over and hugged Ursula tight. Her glow expanded to surround them both, and the contentment too.

She spoke in Ursula's ear. "The rune on your breastbone doesn't matter. You can complete your own poem without knowing. You don't need to know who you are to choose who you want to be. You don't need to let other people's choices in your past define your future. It doesn't matter what I wrote when I made you in the swirling potential of the Before, when the path to your existence and that rune was laid in the What Nexts—it only matters what you feel now."

"But I need to finish the poem of my bones! If I don't choose the right rune to complete the four, to complement the three I've got, my purpose won't be as strong as it could be!"

"Ursula, you are not a poem, you are a bear," God admonished. "You do not have to be a purpose—you are the purpose. You are *who* you are, not what you can offer."

God released Ursula, held her shoulders in her paws, smiled at her through brimming tears and a face filled with pride. "The words you have on your bones already were only meant to get you this far, when you could decide for yourself whom you wanted to be."

Ursula choked back a sob, but the dam burst anyway, and she cried into God's shoulder. With relief, with possibility. With acceptance.

God held her there a long while, as the sun rose and the earth warmed and the flowers opened to the sky.

"What do you think you will choose, then?" asked God. "I will help carve it, as an honor to you, and as thanks for saving the badgers."

Ursula looked at her bonesack, and thought of all the poems waiting in there, all the combinations and implications and things that could be. And now, with the new bones, there were so many more possibilities, so much still to see and learn. So much still unknown.

"I don't know," said Ursula. "I don't know at all, yet."

And for the first time, that answer gave her contentment.

About the Author

Matt Dovey is very tall, very English, and most likely drinking a cup of tea right now. He has a scar on his arm where his parents carved a rune into his humerus: apparently it was BISCUIT, and yes he would like another digestive, thank you for asking. He now lives in a quiet market town in rural England with his wife & three children, and despite being a writer he still hasn't found the right words to fully express the delight he finds in this wonderful arrangement.

His surname rhymes with "Dopey" but any other similarities to the dwarf are purely coincidental. He has fiction out and forthcoming all over the place; you can keep up with everything at mattdovey.com, or follow along on Twitter and Facebook both as @mattdoveywriter.

Author's Notes

This story is the most naked attempt I've ever made to appeal to an editorial team. The bears are for Aidan. The badgers are for Elise. And there should have been dinosaurs for Rachael, but the raptors kept eating everyone so it had to be conversations with God instead. And then, having set out to write a story for three other people, I got to the end of the first draft and looked back at Ursula Bear and realized oh, whoops, I've actually written this story for me. That is me. I am that bear.

I am (as I write this) 33 years old, and I still don't really know who I should be. My wife will often remark on how much I change around other people, molding myself around what I think they expect me to be. I don't mean to, it's not conscious, I just...want people to like me. (I'm a writer: the crippling self-confidence issues and overwhelming need for validation are part of the territory for most of us, I suspect.)

The romantic, artistic thing here would be to say this story finally healed me: that it gave me answers, and peace with myself. Would that it were so easy. But it's the one story I've written where I can most clearly hear that I'm having words with myself. It seems like everything is painted in certainty these days, with no space left for doubt and questions, and I don't think that's a healthy aspiration to have. I think it's okay to not be sure yet, to wait for answers down the road, to not be ready for those answers. None of us are born knowing everything. I doubt any of us die knowing everything. So there must be—will be—gaps where we have to say, "I don't know yet." And that's okay, right? That's not failure. That's just an admission you're not done growing as a person. I hope I'm never done growing as a person, to be honest. It sounds a very dull place to arrive at.

AND THE GHOSTS SANG WITH HER:
A TALE OF THE LYRIST

Spencer Ellsworth

I am pleased to see my king so alight. Such a day! The heat drives the city mad. My sisters have heard rumors of a foreign mercenary you hunt through the streets. And the rat problem! A cat goes for a gold mark, and no grain is safe.

They have told me of your melancholia, my king. How you have one woman of the city brought to you each night, to earn your trust by dawn, and none have yet done so. They whisper of dark fates for these girls. Not to fear; I come here of my own will, a maid who seeks to please her king.

I have nothing to hide.

I come bearing three thousand, thirty, and three stories, all for you. Perhaps the boy who fooled the moon, or the ghoul in the kitchen, or the ogre in the jar? Know you of the three chickens and the prince?

Ah, all these you know. There is a story that will ease the day's pain, the despair a great man must fight, but it is one...well, it is one of *her*.

Stay your hand yet! I know you have forbidden the stories and songs that praise the woman, for you will have none within your walls but praise for your deeds. But this is your water garden, where fountains run free even when the wells in the city run low. This is the place where none hear your cries of passion, your blackest secrets.

Let me tell you the tale you need to hear.

A tale of the lyrist, whom my mother called Laila, of the golden lyre.

Laila was a clever woman. As such, she was unappreciated by this wicked world. You know of the stories, ne sé. How Beluuz, the bard of the Two-Tongued people, stepped out of her fire and offered her the lyre if she would accompany him into a final challenge of battle-songs. You know how she went into the shadow, called forth the Sun into that dark place, and how the shadow could not take her.

The cleverest of women. No, nothing compared to you, great king!

Early in her career, seeing the nobility and the foolishness of mankind, Laila longed for a place of her own, hidden from this world's troubles. But that was a dream of a rich woman, and she was a traveling lyrist.

So she went about all the world, singing battle-songs, saving what coin she could. The songs, at least, were endless. They burst from her lungs when her fingers brushed the lyre. No lord, no courtier, no princess or prince or page-boy heard her songs but was smote in the heart! With those songs, the bright world in the sun looked all the newer, and water tasted sweeter, and good food richer than wealth.

This day, as she accompanied a horse-trader, her much-abused shoes met their end. Seams, already splitting, came fully apart and her bare feet grew bloody on the rocky path.

She asked the driver if she could ride one of the horses.

"Ten silver'll get you on one of my best geldings."

The gorgeous black geldings were swift as wind, tall and proud. And she was down to six silver, each worth a precious meal. "What can I get for a new song?"

He laughed. "I don't trade horses for songs!" Still, he pitied her worn feet, sighed, and said, "There's an old swayback lagging behind the rest, meant for glue pots as soon as we reach the city. Ride her, for your plucking."

She limped to the back of the caravan. There, the sorriest nag ever shod followed the line of sleek black geldings. Her head hung down, her mane was matted, and she plodded wheezing, unable to keep up with the restless herd. The caravan stopped to wait out the heat of the day, and Laila examined the horse's shoes, removed a nail turned wrong—I did say she was clever, and a clever woman knows to check the farrier's work—and she watered the horse and gave the beast a date, patting the hopelessly matted mane.

When the caravan driver came by, Laila unslung her lyre, and, purely for mischief, wrote a song about the noble deeds of that horse, of her mighty coat, of how she once held her head high until her mate was slain by a wicked thief. The driver laughed until he choked. "A mighty lay for a sorry horse! I have never had such a joke."

It seemed to Laila that the horse indeed held her head higher, and looked nobly into the wind.

Right then, the bandits arrived.

The horse-trader took two arrows in his back. Laila leapt onto the skinny nag and kicked its flanks while bandits thundered after her—

The old horse galloped like the whirlwind.

They sped away from shouting bandits, over rock and rill and up goat trails no horse should have been able to follow. The bandits gave chase, but the nag ran like a stallion in bloom, and Laila began to wonder if the horse truly had been inspired by her lay—until they reached the crest of a hill, ringed by ancient battlements. The horse stopped there. Laila, thinking the nag exhausted, leapt from its back.

And between two blinks, the horse became a person.

Thin as a shadow, hairless, sorcery-white eyes twinkling. Horse's hide became black silk, and hoofs became greaves and vambraces inlaid with the words of the Prophets. Not man nor woman was this, but *usha*, and they withdrew a small horn bow from their shirt. Six arrows were loosed, in the space of three seconds, on the bandits below. The ground was soon fertile with the dead.

And then the *usha* bowed. Their voice was the sound of silk on witch-steel. "Not every singer's voice is so sweet as to incur respect of the Mountain."

Laila had walked under the shadow's wings, through the fiery realms of the Two-Tongued tricksters, and sung for stone-hearted warlords. But even she knew to stay clear of the shapeshifting assassins of the Mountain. Once their knives taste your blood, they are always thirsty for it. They can change into any creature, and thus no wall, no guard dog, no warrior, is proof against their blades.

"Th-th-thank you," she managed.

"As you have seen the change, I cannot let you go. I would carry you with me to the Mountain, where all are blades in the hands of justice. The Old Man's heart is heavy. His daughter has passed under the shadow, and a song will comfort him."

"My sorrow to the Old Man, may the Thousand bring him peace, but...I..." How to explain that you did not wish to enter a realm of mad assassins?

The *usha* frowned then and drew a gleaming white witch-stone knife. "It would be a shame to cut a throat that sings such songs, but I am but a blade in the hand."

Laila's gorge rose, and she choked out agreement. "I'll go to the Mountain."

The path to the Mountain shifts like its makers, winds through secret rills, tunnels and under forgotten portals, to the Gate of Bones. Veiled dark warriors, their eyes unblinking, welcomed her into the courtyard and clothed her in new finery, while her usha-horse passed into the crowd of shadows. She walked a path marked with smoking censers above gilded reliquaries, holding the bones of the heretical Thirteenth Prophet, who was drawn and quartered at the gates of Kahbadam by the Wise Khayif, and whose name the shapeshifters venerate morning, noon, evening, and midnight. She reached the summit, and passed into the Mountain. There she walked through a maze of red silk hangings, until cloth parted to reveal the Old Man.

Two guards stepped forward and crossed star-white witchstone blades under her throat.

For a man who could cut a khayif's throat in his sleep, the Old Man looked merely old—white beard, a round belly, simple wool clothes. But his eyes, oh! those eyes of crystal-white flame that fixed her across the distance. "I hear you have come to sing to me," he said. "Even here, we have heard of the golden lyre."

She unslung the lyre, no easy feat with two knives crossed under one's chin, and as usual, no matter the circumstance, Laila found a song. The denizens of the Mountain were like the rest of mankind in this: they joined her in singing.

Laila played for the shapeshifting assassins late into the night, low songs and high, songs of seduction and songs of holiness. They danced, first strange dances of veils and knives, and then familiar dances that reminded her these were men, women, *usha* as she knew them. Laila ate golden buttered rice, and fresh-killed lamb cooked in cream and spiced wine, all while the witch-stone blades crossed under her chin.

At last the morning came. The Old Man motioned, and the blades vanished from her chin. "You have done well, lyrist. I ask but one more song."

"Name your desire, and I shall sing it," she said, relieved to speak without blades at her throat.

"I would have you sing of my daughter, who has gone to the shadow."

Laila bowed her head. "I will, great lord. Tell me of her deeds, and I will let a lay ring out before you—"

"Not before me, singer," the Old Man said, his flame eyes burning into hers. "You see, my daughter failed. It was I who gave her to the shadow."

Laila bit her tongue to keep back a retort.

"My daughter was to be a blade in the hand of justice, dealing that justice to a wicked prince. But the prince's guards caught her half-shaped in his chamber and his sorcerers chained her. At the edge of the Pit of Veils they sought to bargain with me." A strange smile crossed the placid face under those cold eyes. "I brook no failure, though, and make no bargains. My daughter was tossed into the Pit, into that realm of ghosts and smoke. Only eleven years of life, but ever she was a blade in the hand."

Eleven years old?

"Walk to the edge of the Pit, sing for her, and return, and I will give you your weight in gold."

Her weight in gold would build the house, the secret place that she sought away from a world.

But the Pit of Veils?

A place, if possible, more fearsome than the Mountain?

This was quite a day's work, all for a split shoe.

Know you that tale, oh king, of the Pit of Veils? How in ancient days the Camyrians came from the north, riding red fire-spitting birds, and scourged the Kyu, the first people? How the princess of Kulrathen and the queen of Kyasi stood with naked swords before the fire, and their black bones and worn metal still cry against the bright sky? How Ursalim the sacred city burned, and the Third Prophet's lament made the stones weep?

Besieged at all turns, the Kyu fled to a vast pit in the earth. Deep in the dark they built their city, their songs rang and fires rose high. The Camyrians sought to penetrate their fastness, but torches failed. Battalions lost heart in eternal night. The firebirds, who sleep in coals and breathe bright flame, fear the dark and would not fly underground.

And then, the Camyrians chained a firebird fresh from the egg and blinded her. Fifty years they raised that firebird in darkness, for it takes fifty years for the great birds to reach maturity and spit their fire. Fifty years they waited, and then they flew into the Kyu's pit and loosed the creature. Every soul in that underground city perished in slag. In one final act of cruelty, the Camyrian general slew the firebird and tossed her into the smoking pit with the dead.

The vengeful ghosts reign there still, in a shattered city under eternal smoke. The ghost of the firebird swoops through the depths, breathing a fire that scourges the soul.

Laila knew. She had sung this song many times, and when done well, audience and singer both shivered in fear.

"To the edge only," she said. "The edge of the Pit. And there sing."

"Disturb no ghost, seek no treasure," the Old Man said. "Merely an honor-song."

Laila agreed, for she supposed that even if she could turn down her weight in gold, she would find the alternative another knife at the throat, and she'd had enough of that.

But as she set out, on the empty paths to the Pit of Veils, well-fed and sung out, her mission gnawed at her. An eleven-year-old girl? And a shapeshifter. Perhaps still alive in that realm of ghosts, but unable to leave, for the Veils seal the ghost city away from the world sure as a wall. Down there, madness would take the girl, or starvation, until she threw herself into the depths.

I need not tell you about Laila on that road, how each step firmed the resolve in her heart. It could be Laila imagined this child alone because Laila had once been alone, and it could be Laila imagined her frightened, because Laila had once been frightened, and it could be Laila wanted to bring this girl from darkness, because Laila knew what it was to be in darkness. She knew what it was to wander, a lost and lonely child, and to live in a house as bleak and mad as any smoke-filled pit, and a man as vengeful as any ghost.

Music had saved her, when she left that house, when she went deep into the hills and sought the Two-Tongued and took up the lyre. And she could not deny that music cut through the darkness.

Now close your eyes, my king, and see it. A mile wide the Pit yawns in the earth, gushing forth black smoke. One can go in, through the smoke. On the way out, it is as impermeable as a wall.

Laila stood by that wall of smoke, lyre in hand, and no song came to mind. Only an idea.

She spoke aloud to herself, as if that would dissuade her. "It seems to me, Laila," she said to the part of her that would not be silent, "that you've sung one too many songs to one too many mad kings, and perhaps you're getting ridiculous ideas."

The smoke parted and revealed a vast, yawning darkness.

Laila pushed aside her fear and walked in.

She had fooled the shadow, and the Thief King, and sung for the Mountain. She could get one girl out of a hole in the ground.

Behind her, the smoke came together to form a wall, thick and solid as granite.

She walked for days. The lyre gleamed golden and bright to light her steps, for it had come of the Realm of Fire. On the third day of her descent, she reached the ancient city. Twisting, dagger-toothed pillars, statues of immense worms like underground gods, angled writing with benedictions over dark doorways—and as often as not, their precise lines marred and melted, run together into heaps. Whole apartments, mansions, palaces carved into the rock. She kept walking until she stood in a place that may have once been a plaza, and now was an uneven sea of reformed molten stone, where rock had flowed under the ancient firebird's breath.

There, the voices spoke.

First the voices of market day, the laughter and the calls of merchants. The ringing sounds of hammers and picks on stone.

And then the screams, the rush of fire. Weeping women, sorrowing of their homes, men crying to dead gods as their children burned in their arms, curses on the Camyrians, screams of pain as all their world turned white hot.

And then, among the ghost's cries, a little chittering that was no human sound.

Laila looked down at her feet. The dull golden light of the lyre illuminated a single emaciated rat. A rat, where nothing else lived.

"Is that you?" she asked, and her voice echoed around the vast, half-slagged halls.

And the ghosts' cries grew angry.

The rat squealed and ran away. Laila shouted, "Ne sé! Girl! I come from the Mountain—" It was too late.

Of a sudden, a whole host surrounded her, in fine robes and dresses made from the scales of the cave-worms. Arms and legs were charred where they emerged from the robes. Eyes shadowed, mouths open to show no teeth, only burning green coals. They wailed in a forgotten language and raised fingers burned to black bone.

"I know the dead make no songs," Laila said, trying to quell the shaking of her heart. "I have walked under the shadow. But perhaps you would like to hear this one."

Behold the statue, the traveler says
Tall as mountain, bright like a drawn sword
At its feet, carved in stone, these words:
Camyria!

The ghosts roared with anger at the name of their ancestral enemy and pressed toward her, blackened bone fingers ready to rend her flesh, but Laila kept singing.

So speaks the stone:
The glory of Camyria, of which gods are jealous
The palaces, the domes, the towers
The phalanx, the firebirds, the black-scaled war mammoth!
Tremble, you gods!
And around the statue, the traveler sees nought but sand
Lonely dunes; the emptiness ripples in the wind

(Of course no one would ever sing such a song of your achievements, my king. You need not worry.)

The ghosts paused. Had it been so long, they thought, with their sluggish memories? Were their conquerors as much ghosts as they?

And then Laila saw, atop a wave of slag, a statue that had not been there before. The corroded Camyrian king, standing high, with a proclamation weathered by sand, showing how time made of Camyria what time makes of all things.

Song, as Laila knew, cuts through the darkness, and the song had cut through years of half-shadowed life, gnawing on vengeance, despairing in the dark and the smoke. Awareness descended on the ghosts, an awareness that their enemy might be as dead as they were.

The ghosts faded, only a few coal-bright green eyes watching Laila.

The statue shifted, becoming a girl in black, thin as shadow, white sorcerer's eyes above deep hollows.

Laila yanked bread, sweet onions, and jerky from her bag. The poor girl fell to it madly.

"You did well, to help me," Laila said.

"I didn't do it apurpose," the girl said through a mouthful of food, and now Laila could see, in her rangy, angry face, a trace of the Old Man. "I can't maintain my shape around good songs. I take the shape of whatever the song's about."

"Is that normal, for your kind?"

"Strange things happen to us when we're...young."

Laila held back a smile, a smile full of memory. As if the age of eleven were not awkward enough. "How long have you been down here?" Laila asked. "As a rat?"

"I don't know."

"You didn't starve?"

"Villagers drop offerings to keep the ghosts away. I can smell them when I'm a rat." Her face twitched, much like a rat's, and she let out a cry. "I want to leave, but nothing can get past the Veils! Why'd you come down? Why'd you do this to yourself?"

"To bring you home."

"Really? Are you a great sorcerer or something? A princess of the Two-Tongued? A god in disguise?" I cannot quite replicate her voice, but suffice it to say that she was half-sarcastic, half-hopeful. (A quality peculiar to girls of that age.)

"A singer." Laila peered back the way she had come. "The lyre lit my way here, and it will light my way home."

An oath no eleven-year-old should know came in return, and I will spare you the details of it.

But when Laila stood and shouldered her lyre and pointed its light back the way she came, the girl shifted, and a rat followed.

Through waves of slag that had flowed from ancient dwellings, up whole stairs, and then over melted and reformed stone where the stairs had flowed in fire, Laila went, and behind her came the skittering of rat feet.

They reached at last a jutting promontory, looking out over the dark. Laila rested to eat again, and the girl briefly resumed her true form.

A wind surged from the depths, and the ghost of the firebird rose.

From tip to tip its wings could have covered five elephants, and its beak was a mighty curved dagger, and its two blinded eyes made dark hollows in the head. Its gray form was dappled as a moon-dark forest. It opened its mouth and a cloud of dark ghost-fire, marked by streaks of lightning, flowed over them.

The ghost-fire rushed through their veins, released the icy fear locked away. Laila thought she were a child hiding from bandits again, when her parents had been slain, as if she were with the cruel husband of her youth, his blow across her cheek, her skull ringing in pain. Her hands trembled over the abyss. The lyre began to slip from her grasp toward the dark below.

196

But Laila was no stranger to fear. She clutched the lyre and struck a ringing chord.

No other singer could have borne up under that ghostly fire. Laila alone had the courage, the cleverness, to find that chord, not because she was unafraid, but because she knew the touch of fear.

Bright are the bonfires, warm the night
Come in from the dark, traveler, come in
Bright are the bonfires, and the night is full of song
Come in from the dark, traveler, come in

Laila finished the refrain, began it again.

With the lyrics, she grew warm.

A bonfire blazed next to her, a roaring, warm, wood-eating thing, thick with the scent of burning pine. The firebird cocked its head, fluttered its dappled wings, and nuzzled closer to the bonfire, as if comforted by a mother.

Laila continued singing, calling travelers for a night of song and stories, songs of kind faces, hot food and clean water.

The girl burned brighter and brighter. In time, the ghostly firebird sighed a great sigh, and then, caught by a wind the two women could not feel, it rose to the faraway top of the Pit.

The song ended and the bonfire turned back into the girl.

"Thank you," Laila said. "I know you could have run, and—"

"Only two others can do fire!" The girl's thin face cracked in delight. "Only two others in all of the Mountain! And now me! Play the song again!"

Laila did, and the girl, delighted, turned to fire again. It was nice to have laughter.

Three days they climbed, the way better lit now as the girl periodically became a blaze, more cheerful now as they talked and the girl told Laila of life in the Mountain, of the competitions among shapeshifter children, and how she'd been a salamander for nearly a month before they found her. Three days through slag-heaps and ancient palaces, up and up and up. Three days, until Laila and the girl stood before the curtain of smoke, and found it solid as any wall.

The girl made herself a bull and charged the wall. Roaring and snarling, she beat her horns against it. She became a thick-headed goat and battered the wall with her horns. An elephant large as a house, who reared up and slammed against the wall with her feet.

It held fast as stone.

Laila sat and strummed the lyre, waiting for an idea. None came.

In time, they finished their provisions. Laila gave the last of her water to the girl.

The girl sighed as they sat there, in front of the unyielding wall. "I'll miss my brother. Father was angry with him, because he changed into a frog and had trouble changing back. I took this mission in exchange for Father's mercy on him." She looked at Laila and said, by way of explanation, "The legs are tricky on frogs."

Laila reached out and tucked the girl's unruly hair back behind her dirty ears. "What is your name, little frog's sister?"

"We have no names, not till adulthood, and then we take the name of whatever shape we are best at. I thought I would be Rat, but mayhap I'll be Fire." She peered up at the smoke, the high gray wall. "If I got home. Perhaps I should try a door?"

A song came to mind, the oldest song Laila knew. A song every traveler knew, since the first man and woman stepped off the boat where the Thousand left them.

Behind me, my door,
Before me a road,
Like a river, it runs out to all the world
Over hill, through the busiest market in the biggest city, into the empty dunes
To the tops of the mountains, to the darkness of vales,
To the shadow itself, the road runs
Behind me, my door.

As she finished the first round, and prepared to play the second, she became aware that others sang with her.

A whole host.

The Kyu, burned and blackened ghosts, rose from the depths of the Pit of Veils. Abandoning their vengeance, the ghosts sang with

Laila, seeking only freedom from their long half-life beneath smoke. The firebird wheeled overhead, its high keening joining the song. The whole Pit rang.

And that wall of smoke trembled and quavered.

The little girl reached out, touched the wall, and her body became a small green door.

Laila opened the door, and sunlight came through.

The ghosts streamed out, a dappled rush that turned bright in sunlight. Even the bird passed through, twisting and folding itself to pass through the portal. Last of all Laila went through, but kept a hand on the doorknob, until that knob turned to a small hand, and the girl came out after her, into the daylight.

The ghosts flew into the sky, bright and gleaming shreds of cloud, and passed from this world as a song is carried on the wind. The girl exhaled heavily, and promptly fell asleep, and Laila lifted her over her shoulder, and took the girl one step at a time, back the way she'd came, toward the Mountain.

They walked many days, and they had many more songs and many fires, before the girl pointed at a path Laila had thought merely a goat-track, and said, "That is the way home."

"Your father did not ask me to free you, only to sing," Laila said. "I would not have you punished. You can stay with me."

"My brother will want to know I got out, and Father will probably spare me." Once again, Laila could not tell sarcasm from hope. "He never said I couldn't come back if I got out."

"Come with me," Laila said.

"I belong in the Mountain, singer," she said. "You of all people know that a girl should play the songs of her own destiny."

"Ne sa, I do," Laila said.

The girl threw her arms around Laila then asked, "One more song?"

They sang loud to the sky, and Laila went on, sang many more, at the Battle of the Ten Giants, at the Storm of Sorcerers, in the ashes of Kahbadam, lamenting the great library.

In time, she found a secret bend in a river, and gave all her earnings to build a house of her own. But war ravaged the world, and you know, oh king, how she bargained for the lives of forty unjustly slain children, tricking the shadow himself.

She won back the children, and returned home with them in tow, and had to ask that builder to add a wing for forty young ones.

He balked, and turned pale, and said he would give of her as much labor as he could, but he earned by his sweat, and he must eat, and...At that moment, an old sorrel nag drew up to the house.

Laila recognized the horse. And in the wagon it drew lay a gold-filled chest, marked with a golden clasp in the shape of a rat.

So the Gods reward a clever woman, as she rewards the world. So the Mountain ever watched the singer's steps, in gratitude after all.

And so you should take comfort, my king, and know that not all rats are malicious creatures.

You did not like my story, my king? Strange. And now you eye me as if I were not a maid at all. Perhaps it is the color draining from my eyes, or my fleshy curves melting away in a twist of red veils.

Will you call for the head of a shapeshifter? They have a habit of staying on, even when a blade passes through the neck.

Not all rats are malicious creatures, but this rat keeps an ear out for young girls in trouble, subject to the whims of wicked rulers.

How strange it will seem that a king burned to death in his water garden. Perhaps folk will blame the heat of the day? Shhh, let yourself be warmed, let the flames lick your robe, let the smoke choke you. I am pleased to see my king so alight.

About the Author

Spencer Ellsworth has been writing since he learned how. He is the author of the Starfire trilogy, a series of short space opera novels from Tor.com beginning with A RED PEACE. He has also published short fiction in *Lightspeed*, *Tor.com*, *Beneath Ceaseless Skies* and many other places. He hopes to die on the back of a brave mammoth, charging a thicket of enemy spears, with seven chocolate bars in his mouth.

Author's Notes

Sit, traveler, and I shall tell you of the Disproportionately Large Story Corpus. Every time I try to work in this pseudo-Arabian-Nights world, the story balloons—novels and short stories and more novels and frame stories upon frame stories and frame stories. This was the third story I wrote for *Sword and Sonnet*. The first ballooned to novella length, and the second wasn't quite the right tone for *Sword and Sonnet*. But when I thought of 1) young shapeshifter down a hole and 2) ghost firebird also down said hole, I knew I had to figure out the songs that could unlock that situation. Many of the other Laila stories alluded to here exist, and some don't yet, but oh traveler, to bring them back, you must go to the heart of the Extremely Discouraging Lost Novel Drafts, deep in the Scrivener Files We Try To Forget About, and only the bravest traveler would do so...

DULCE ET DECORUM

S. L. Huang

I walk by the dusty wooden sign three times before I realize it has faded paint on it and decipher the words *Poetry of War Museum.* The weathered door is tucked away between two much larger, shinier buildings, which squat against it like they want to pinch it out of existence.

I readjust the box I'm carrying and reach for the door handle, half-expecting it to be locked solid. Instead, it yields under my fingers, and a bell tinkles somewhere overhead.

The inside is so dark I have to blink rapidly while my eyes adjust. Typical hedge magician. The deftest of artistic enchantments, and yet they forget about decent lighting...it's totally something Chand would do.

When my vision clears, the space doesn't improve my opinion of the proprietor's priorities. A maze of shelves are thrown over with layer upon layer of colorful rugs and doilies, on which are displayed all variety of objects in a complete lack of organization or reason. I feel a spark of doubt, but then remind myself—this is just like Chand's studio. The man is a rising star of a mind painter, and yet his studio would drive a person to distraction with the clashing and chaos. This poet is likely the same.

Emboldened, I reach for the nearest shelf, but my fingers curl back before touching anything. Every piece on the shelves...

I knew what this place would be. It's why I'm here: I need someone to make sense of it all for me. But my brain registers the shapes of violence and shrinks away. Old pistols, worn with use, and holsters with their leather rubbed shiny. Knives that aren't meant for cutting vegetables. More modern machine gun belts draping ugly silhouettes that surely must have been modified not to be functional —surely?

A chipped helmet that has clearly seen service. I wonder if it saved the life of its owner.

"You can listen to the poems," says a voice from the shadows, making me jump.

"Oh, I know, I—" I automatically reach toward an old military canteen, and the edges of something graze my consciousness: the tastes of fear and sweat, confusion and screams. I snatch my hand back again, blurting, "Are they true?"

"What's truth? They're poetry. The cards tell the history, what we know of it, at least."

For the first time I notice paper cards by each object, inked painstakingly with names and dates and dry facts. I try to squint more closely at one, but that brings me too close to a tattered flag, and a sudden, thirsty patriotism engulfs me, every beat of the drums and trumpet of the horns another triumphant march for King and Country.

It's worse than the anguish. I shy away again.

"If you need anything, I'll be around somewhere. I don't hover," the museum's lurking proprietor informs me. "Prefer for people to get their own meaning from my poems, doncha know."

"Wait! Don't go. Are you—you're Valentina Knyazev, aren't you?"

"Knyazeva, today. But it varies." She steps out from the darkest corners, floating into view in the dimness. Like most magicians I've met, she's a touch odd-looking: a pale, thick person, with several heavy braids and full-moon glasses that seem to reflect all light. "Have we met?"

I grab for my manners and juggle the box to stick out a hand. "I'm Emily. Emily Shen. My friend, um, Chand Svare Ghei sent me."

"Chand, eh? How is the young whippersnapper?"

"He's fine," I say. *I'm crimson*, Chand would say, or, *I'm mauve*. But I don't have the confidence to pass such things along. "He said—I've been—I have something—" I take a breath and start over. "There's something I've been...upset about, and Chand thought—he said maybe you could help me."

Chand's been my best friend for ages. I'm not sure how long. He filled that place in my life before I knew we'd begun.

We don't fit together. He's a dippy, free-spirited artist who sticks flowers or tableware in his hair and smokes even more questionable substances than most hedge magicians do, and he's prone to scraping the bottom of his bank account for a new tattoo or yanking my chain with the latest pseudoscience. Whereas I'm a straight-laced type-A software engineer, complete with OCD that's just medicated enough for people at work to think I'm devastatingly on top of everything.

My personal life is a different matter. And when my grandfather died, the careful balance I'd curated crumbled into jagged chunks that buried me and almost sent me into darkness alongside my Yeye. I barely remember my parents—Yeye was my whole world, and with him gone, vacuum yawned suddenly everywhere, all meaning sucked away. I couldn't even say goodbye, to his body, or his things —he'd left a faulty heater too close to his blankets, and the small, cozy piece of the world that was his life burned around him while he slept.

Chand was the one who stuck by me, after months and months of grief counseling and therapy and still not getting better, after all my other friends had carefully drawn boundaries and told me they just couldn't. Which I understood, in an empty sort of way.

Chand's an odd sort of friend. He forgets appointments and is high half the time, but when I call him, he's always there, like a law of the universe. Sometimes we go to concerts, or to his art shows, or to my boring office events. Sometimes we have sex, and he'll lie with me afterward and paint my mind in the most beautiful colors, until for a few precious moments I forget to be depressed.

And when I talked to him about my grandfather's gun, he blew a smoke ring at the sky and said, "You know Em, I think you should talk to my buddy Valentina."

I unwrap the box and set it on Valentina's counter. I don't open it.

"You're going to have to speak, kid. I may do thought art, but we ain't mindreaders."

I know that, sort of. Chand's explained it to me before, how when he paints in people's heads there's a connection, but he doesn't see anything. "And consent, always. Gotta have consent," he'll add, nodding gravely with the hedge magician's code.

"My grandfather—this belonged to him," I say to Valentina. My hands start sweating, and I wish I'd rehearsed this, or at least written it out so I could read off a paper and not feel like I'm groping through darkness. Darkness full of barbs. "I inherited it, and—and it was one of the only things of value he owned, and one of the only things left after the fire, and I feel like I should—I don't know. But I'm a pacifist, and when I think about touching it I can't..."

Tears are swamping up my eyes, an occurrence I can't seem to get away from nowadays. Valentina gestures toward the box, and I nod her on.

She unfolds the top and then snaps open the case inside. I know what's nestled there.

"A beauty," Valentina says approvingly, bending to examine it with her full-moon glasses. "Colt M1911. Very well cared for."

The reverence in her voice makes a sob claw up my throat, and I want to snatch the pistol away. Coming here was a bad idea. This woman *loves* her weapons. She's a nut for all this stuff. She won't understand.

She glances up at me, and somehow, even through her ultra-reflective spectacles I can tell her gaze is intense. "Your grandfather loved this firearm, didn't he."

"He did!" The words burst out of me. "He did, he would—he always cleaned it so carefully and he—he loved it. It was a part of him. He used it in the war but then he never gave it up and he was so proud of it—but I hate guns and I can't—" I'm full-on crying now, messy crying, all ugly snot and sob-choked words. "I miss him so much. I have so little left of him. I want to—" *I want to take this gun and curl around it like it's a teddy bear and cling to it and feel closer to Yeye, but I also don't want to have it at all and don't want to think about him using it or firing it or killing people with it.*

Besides, the pistol feels like it doesn't represent Yeye so much as it represents all the pieces of him I didn't know or didn't understand, the small insecure places I always shied away from before I looked too close. I marched against Afghanistan and Iraq in college, always with a squirm of guilt that I didn't know what Yeye would think if I told him—or what my new friends would say, if I let slip that the man I loved most in the world was a veteran. It was one of the only topics I never broached with the grandfather I shared almost all of my life with.

And since his death, this one gap in my feeling of closeness with him—it's begun to loom, larger and larger, until it threatens to push out every memory of security and laughter.

Valentina closes the case carefully. "Emily Shen," she says. "Did Chand tell you why I am a war poet?"

I drag a sleeve across my soggy face and shake my head. It *had* occurred to me to wonder. Most magicians who write poetry into objects choose, well...beautiful things. Lovely, polished carvings, or rare fossils, or stunning photographs. Greeting card companies sell flowers and postcards with cheap, cheerful rhymes that leave the feeling of skipping rope on a sunny day or the scent of lilies-of-the-valley echoing in my consciousness. I went to one high-profile exhibition that had poems written into well-worn heirloom jewelry and pressed dried flower petals, with each mental layering of word and imagery stunning me with its complexity.

Then there was a poetry slam Chand took me to, where poets on stage smashed bricks, shattered bottles, and splattered rotten vegetables against the walls, freeing out their raps to the audience in hard-hitting thought chaos. I didn't really get that one, I admit.

I know people do want to write poetry about tragedy sometimes, but that always seemed like the realm of poet laureates and anthologists, not unknown hedge magicians with strangely one-note museums. And I have a sneaking suspicion Valentina doesn't consider herself a tragic poet, anyway.

Valentina reaches over to a shelf behind her and strokes the butt end of a...rifle? It looks too short to be a rifle.

She seems to read my mind. "This is a Remington rolling-block carbine from the turn of the century. Original. There's a paradox in it, isn't there? The beauty, and the deadliness."

I rub my eyes clear and look more closely. The stock is old, worm-eaten wood, the barrel shining dully with years of hard use and careful polishing. It's older than my grandfather's gun, old enough that I can think of it as a little bit separate from its purpose, and in a weird, slanty way I can almost see why she calls it beautiful.

"I guess...?" I say.

"There's history. Character. Culture, here. History is...messy, and we don't always like it, but it's human." Valentina runs a finger along my grandfather's pistol case. "I'm not explaining this well. I think I should show you something. It's not in the exhibits. Too personal. Would you like to see?"

I have no idea what she's talking about. "Okay," I say.

She locks my grandfather's gun in a safe behind the counter, then leads me through the mazes of shelves to a back room. There's a futon here layered in knobbly blankets, and I realize this is where she lives. The walls have more shelves nailed up everywhere, none of the edges or paint colors matching, and all variety of knickknacks stuffed into them. I know better than to try to touch anything, not in a poet's house.

Valentina goes to a long alcove at the back of the room and pulls out...

I blink. It's a sword.

She draws it from its scabbard with relaxed control. The colors of the room reflect in wavy pools against the slightly curved blade. There's no hilt—or rather, there is a hilt, but no...guard, I think it's called? Just a narrow ribbed-wood and metal part to hold it by at the end. It's very sleek, and despite its shine, it looks very old.

"It's a shashka," Valentina says. "The saber of my ancestors."

"It's beautiful," I say truthfully.

"We romanticize swords, don't we?" She's gazing at the wavy colors in the blade, not at me. She sweeps the tip in a narrow, practiced circle. "And yet. An instructor of mine told me once...out of every class of weapons, swords are the only one designed with the singular aim of killing humans. Axes sometimes chop wood, spears and guns can hunt food, as can a bow and arrow. Knives have all manner of use. And yet, a sword—it is made only for us to kill each other. It has no other purpose."

I shiver.

"Yet it is beautiful, isn't it?" Valentina adds.

I don't know what to say. I half want to swallow back my agreement, but at the same time...the saber gleams in the lamplight, and its movement is an extension of Valentina's arm. It *is* beautiful.

Did Chand send me here only to get more confused?

"My ancestors used this sword," Valentina says. "Like you, I look back, and I think of them living with this shashka at their sides, training with it for hours each day, depending on it for their lives. And then I think of them riding to war, screaming for blood while they take other family's fathers. It's not comfortable, is it?"

"My grandfather wasn't—he wasn't bloodthirsty," I can't help saying. "He didn't go to war to kill people."

"I know. But that's why everyone goes, in the end, isn't it?" I'm about to protest again, but the expression on Valentina's face stops me. "My great-grandfather used to tell me stories. He marched on Berlin with this shashka by his side, and he was as proud as if he'd stabbed Hitler personally. I think those tales are half the reason I enlisted here in the U.S., when I was young—they invalided me out for the magic before I saw much, and I'm never certain whether to be grateful for that or not. Some of my cousins here joined up, too, in the Army and the Marines, and I'm proud of them. They've killed people in wars I don't agree with, and I'm still proud. I have a niece on a military scholarship—they send me pictures of her in her dress blues."

My grandfather *was* proud. It's true. And there was a quiet edge to his pride, as a Chinese-American man having served his country, the country he loved. "I'm an American," he used to correct me mildly, when I would tell white friends we were Chinese.

"My partner is from Japan," Valentina continues. "Her great-uncle fought, too. It was for Emperor and country at the time, I suppose. I'm sure it all looks the same from that side...He was killed by the Allies, her uncle. Maybe by my great-grandfather, who knows? Her mother still has a picture of him in her wallet."

Tears are coming to my eyes again.

"He was young," Valentina says quietly. "So young. In the photo, he's dressed in his Navy uniform, and he's smiling."

"This is what—I can't hold it in my head," I say, my voice wavering. "I don't know how to think about it all or what to feel and if any of it's right. It's all cognitive dissonance, and it's too much, I can't..."

Valentina spins the saber in another lazy circle. "I've been working on a poem," she says. "It's not done yet. I don't know if it ever will be. But the making of it gives me peace. Would you like to listen?"

I sniff and then nod. Reach out a careful hand, palm up.

Valentina places the saber's slender hilt in my palm. I grip it awkwardly—I can tell I'm holding it all wrong somehow, all of Valentina's casual grace flopping away. But then the poem takes hold.

～

It opens with a dance.

A woman twirls the shashka in elegant, snakelike patterns. The hilt turns over her hand like liquid mercury, the sword alive with its own grace.

The words of the poem layer over me in four dimensions. I catch echoes of sadness, the banning of ancient traditions. Martial arts that live on in dance. The woman weeps as she steps, and I am one with her, reaching for my culture, my ancestry.

It wraps tendrils around my own shredded diaspora emotions, the awkwardness of Mandarin in my mouth and my insistence on taking kung fu as a child instead of karate even though both instructors were white. I'm wholly American but part something else, and the dancing woman stares into my soul and weaves the shashka and cries as she makes it beautiful and tells me she understands.

I haven't left the dancing woman in her time and space, but on a swell of history I'm suddenly on horseback, on a cold mountain track. The horse snorts, its hooves slipping on the scree. I have one hand on the reins, automatic, and the other on my hilt. My eyes rake the woods and I'm a heartbeat from drawing my blade in one move that will take a life, that will protect my family and our livelihood and my wife's young twins. My hand on the hilt is as sure as the one guiding my horse. No doubts.

Words about duty and love, pride and freedom, float through my consciousness. The woman dances, reaching for us from a distance of years.

I'm a boy now, breathing hard, my breath puffing in the cool air. The shashka swishes down, one, two, across, back, keep the momentum, don't break it or the balance will fold.

Cheerful voices call in Russian and in another tongue, one that echoes of home and family. The bonds shimmer in my mind, parents and siblings, grandparents and friends, and look how good I am, one two lunge swish, I'll make them all proud. Sweat slicks my brow but I keep going, one two three four, footwork and again, panting with elation.

Then I'm an older boy—the same boy? Shouting and screams, and everything is chaos, with none of the neat rhythm of the practice yard. The poem thrums through redness and blood and confusion, but my muscles know the dance, and one two three, lunge and back. The feel of my blade catching on clothes and flesh meshes with the meter of the verse. In the end I'm standing, and the people I slashed at are not.

And suddenly I'm cradling one of the boys I've killed—I'm his mother, his brother, his family fire love tribe, and I'm screaming, my tears mingling with the drowning red. But no one hears.

The dancing woman is crying blood now, a hundred tiny cuts webbing her in pain. It's what I asked for, she sings.

I'm somewhere else now, a young girl practicing with a katana, my feet light on tatami matting as I fly through the combinations of moves, and I'm so proud, so happy. Then I'm racing with a longsword, crying out for freedom, or for country, or just the wolfish need to be a part of something larger than I am, some web of Us and Belonging. History expands into a thousand fractured wars, a tapestry of violence but in so many individual lives knotted through with duty or justice, fighting for family or comrades-in-arms or one's own sense of self, or—sometimes—because there's no other choice.

It's horrifying and at the same time tilts my worldview on its end, sliding all my black and white certainties into a mash of human feeling.

The dancing woman whirls, whole and not whole, blades reaching into every past and every future. Not justifying, not judging, only listening, hurting, and dancing in turn.

∾

Back in Valentina's room behind her museum, I gasp.

"Do you see?" she says. "Why I write war poems?"

"Messy," I whisper. "And human. I—I think so."

"If you would like," she says, "I'll write you a poem for your grandfather, one born from your memories. It will be honest. It won't flatter. But I think it might bring you some peace."

I think of holding my grandfather's old Colt, and with it tumbling every layer of Yeye, his love and patriotism and flaws and humanity, his kindness and soft-spoken compliments, his pride in his country and the blood he spilled for it. The blood he would have spilled for me, even if I never wanted it.

I think of holding the pistol and feeling all those things I never said—things he maybe would have understood after all. Maybe he would have had his own quiet thoughts to share with me about it, thoughts I shouldn't have ducked away from, shouldn't have been afraid to know. And I think about all the bits I don't want to forget —his cheerful humming in the kitchen as he mixed ginger and soy sauce; how tight he would hold me if I skinned my knees or got teased in school; how he would read me funny articles with his snuffling laugh or couldn't help making bad puns while he helped me with my English or history homework...or after I grew up and moved out, his delight on the phone when he heard my voice, and how ready he was with adult advice when I asked for it or a listening ear when I didn't. How much he loved me, every day.

"You'll have to tell me about him," Valentina says. "All the little everyday bits, and the uncomfortable ones too. We can do some psychic portraits. Do you think you can do that?"

Sitting in her dusty museum week after week, teasing through every memory of Yeye while somebody listens, really *listens*, and understands...

"I think I would like that very much," I say. And this time, my tears feel like they might be the first step to healing.

⁂

About the Author

S. L. Huang is an Amazon-bestselling author who justifies her MIT degree by using it to write eccentric mathematical superhero fiction. Her debut novel, *Zero Sum Game*, is upcoming from Tor in 2018, and her short fiction has sold to *Analog*, *Nature*, and *The Best American Science Fiction & Fantasy 2016*. She is also a Hollywood stunt-woman and firearms expert, where she's appeared on shows such as *Battlestar Galactica* and *Raising Hope* and worked with actors such as Sean Patrick Flanery, Jason Momoa, and Danny Glover. She currently lives in Tokyo. Follow her online at www.slhuang.com or on Twitter as @sl_huang.

Author's Notes

The line about a sword being the only class of weapons designed exclusively to kill humans was something one of my first sword instructors told me, and it stuck with me. It's so at odds with how willing we are to romanticize the sword. Often even people who don't like other weapons can appreciate the beauty of swords, and we seem happy to ignore, or at least set aside, their true purpose.

Intersecting with this, I've spent years now training in both swords and firearms, and I very much like learning stories of the relationships people have with their weapons, both historical and contemporary. Weapons—and war—can be polarizing as political issues, but on an individual level, the reasons people wield weapons tend to be complex. The emotions people have about their personal relationships with weapons, whether that's through military service or necessity or culture, can be likewise complex. And I don't know...maybe it would help our global understanding of each other if we could go inside the type of cognitive dissonance we're willing to have about swords, and sit with it a little, and find and accept that place of discomfort and contradiction. Then, perhaps, we could use it to open ourselves to other stories of other people in other places.

That's what I envision my war poet in this story doing: opening herself up and listening.

THE FIDDLER AT THE HEART OF THE WORLD

Samantha Henderson

This is a story about the time I cleaned blood and smog-dirt from the corridors of East Angels Hospital, west of Boyle Heights and north of the trash-and-salvage towers of Vernon and the rail yard, and about that night Dr. Jessie called on the Fiddler at the Heart of the World to help her save humanity in the form of some dozen broken people, and my own self also.

It was April, with its rain and heat and chill: a season here where the rimming mountains looked like discarded piles of gold coin, and where the air could spark cold or settle in hot layers. A Southland April is less a season than a place where anything is possible.

I know you might be plainfolk, with your gods prisoned neatly in your churches and museums, your demons hiding shy in your brain-meats, and your reality smooth as an unbroken eggshell with no hint or imagining of the liquid yolk beneath. But perhaps you are some of those plainfolk that sometime can see, from the corner of your eye, the girl in the high-necked dress standing with an armful of white roses and no face at all. Or glimpse the man walking between the blue tarps of a homeless encampment, wearing a fox's head in the place of his own. Or know in a brief pure instant that an old brick building, with ancient letters painted on its flanks, is watching you and worse, has an opinion of what you did and how you did it.

Perhaps you've heard the Fiddler. Perhaps you haven't, but will now. Perhaps you will be afraid when you hear her music coil. That would be wise.

I understand how mad I sound; I was plain, once, before I became a half-person, caught between the everyday and the divine. We were once called fae. We root too close to the earth and get tangled in the life-and-death membrane of the mortal world. Or we see sideways, and darkly, and stumble into the magics that brew in all cities.

When I came, unrooted, to East Angels to ask for work, I found a little god. His shrine sat, inconspicuous to most, around the corner in the hollow of a river-rock wall. Some of the round stones had fallen away, leaving a dark crevice sheltered by twisted old pepper trees. Bees built a hive in there, long abandoned, and he lurked between the slabs of amber, crystallized honey. I know when he is thinking of me—when I taste beeswax, warm and sweet, on the flat of my tongue.

I'm not much use to anyone but a small god. The labor of pushing my words through the sieve of my Oaxacan birth-tongue to Spanish—and then through the sieve of Spanish to English—makes my speech a turtle to the hare of the many-voices in my mind. And my hip was smashed twenty years ago under a tractor in the Goleta strawberry fields. The padrone, after I had been pulled from under the wheels, sent me home with a month's pay and a promise of doctoring, and I lay a week in the back of the workers' quarters with my leg splinted and a raging fever before the other men took me to a clinic that treated field workers and avoided ICE's scrutiny. And so I didn't die but lived ever crooked, unable to crouch to pull fruit or climb to pick pears.

So while my small god in his hollow between the river rocks of a forgotten wall delights in my gifts of oranges, mangoes, small plastic toys and paper figures, and talks to me in turn in fluent Oaxaca and Mixteco, I must earn my bread-and-butter pushing a mop through the hospital's dingy corridors. I wear cheap earbuds I found in the trash, connected to a dead, recycled phone—not to listen to music but to blunt the ghost-buzz that rides continuous down the hallways with the bumpy linoleum floors that I keep clean and polished.

My little saint is shadowed by a fleshy mass of the deities painted on the walls of East Angels Hospital, in the once-bright murals that bracket the cloudy, graffiti-scratched glass doors of the main entrance. They are gods of my old country, much bigger than my little god: a woman who wears a rainbow around her shoulders and carries a rabbit in her outstretched palm; a man crowned in gilt with a thick snake winding from his shoulder to his wrist. The artist translated them imperfectly, a foreign hand in a foreign land. They are like my thoughts molded out of shape by my languages, and have become different gods, weaker than they were.

Working here keeps my bones together, and my little god battens on the blood and gossip, and makes sure that nobody thinks too hard when it comes time to check my documentation, or sees me when the accreditors come. That is the other kind of in-between that where I live, besides what is real and what is of the gods—on one hand the paperwork that makes you real, on the other the lack that makes you disposable.

I also care for the small, dark hospital chapel, for no one else is inclined to do it. The god that lives there is not my own, although my own small deity has me bring him flowers and chocolate occasionally for courtesy's sake. He told me it was because he remembered being hungry before I came to him, but I suspect it's just to gloat. Gods are rarely very kind, even to each other.

～

I liked Dr. Jessie, though she didn't come from people that understood the powers that flow through a place like East Angels, or the nature of half-people, or how a small but constant trickle of death can bring a dormant magic blooming to the surface of the mortal world. She was plainfolk, head-blind to the undercurrents that surrounded her, and thought, like the most, that money and science and bread-and-butter ruled the cosmos. And I am not saying that she, nor the most, is generally wrong.

I think she came from a generation whose sires and grandsires worked hard to circle their children behind a wall of bread-and-butter and science, and not labor always in the mud for the money that made it possible. But she was well-meaning for all that, worked hard all her life for the chance to save ungrateful people. I could see the marks of sacrifice upon her from those sires and dams and grands: extra work to pay for schooling and the good shoes. Even on the plainfolk, even those with money sometimes, you can see those marks. I could see the ghosts and the little demons circling her, curious as they were sometimes about the plainfolk whose work and nature plunges them up to the elbows in blood, dealing death or wrestling life back from the brink of it. Cat-like, they bat at their senses and move on, bored, if they don't get a prickle of puzzled awareness back.

She took care to speak to me as if I was real, not like a disposable, and as if my brokenness was simply a matter of course. She seemed young for an intern, and I wondered what brought her to East Angels, which was not a teaching hospital but owned by a group of doctors who put their faith in money, not blood.

The doctors and nurses I see trafficking in wounded bodies have learned that you can't let death break you. It is dangerous to care, however soft you are at the core, because how many shattered children is it possible to mourn? How many lives gone to rot can you regret? They carry the burden of each person they've lost, but they learn not to care too deeply, even if they have to pretend and allow the pretense to become reality.

Dr. Jessie wasn't good at that yet. Perhaps, if she had pretended better, things would have been different that April night.

∽

I don't keep track of days, but it might have been a Monday because I'd heard that the night before, Sunday night perhaps, was rough. Sometimes at the end of a weekend the world turns sour, and a mother who should lay a fretful child down will shake him instead, and a man will shove his girlfriend's head through a wall instead of walking off his drink. Another will realize that a gunshot or a handful of pills will keep Monday blues away forever.

I do remember gray clouds banking up from the northwest, darking the hills so that their gold and greens grew more intense and each bush, scrub, or oak was limed in shadow; that April was rainy and promised more. I walked in that afternoon and passed Miss Octavia, who was charge nurse that weekend and maybe still on that shift, and she just shook her head as I went by.

"Bad?" I asked. I knew it was; the ghosts were still restless, muttering in the corners, spooked as cats at the tail end of an earthquake. Later I heard that in the middle of a night full of alcohol poisoning, neglected strep, and dog bites there was a boy, purple and white, and police taking statements. I could see Dr. Jessie through the old glass in the back office, making notes in a chart, her face a mask. She was the attending, and probably spent four hours that morning on the cot in back of the nurses' locker room. I went to clock in and get my earbuds in place; I'd make sure the corridors were clear of last night's blood and McDonald's wrappers, and I meant to take a bowl of tangerines to the chapel before the too-calm afternoon got busy. But that lonely god went thirsty that day, and the next, and another before I remembered.

I pushed my bucket past a bustle: nurses and Dr. Jessie huddled together, and frowning. I leaned the mop against my shoulder and pulled at the cord of my earbuds, popping out the rubber plugs one after the other, and heard the buzz surrounding us intensify, eager and interested.

Miss Octavia was still on the phone, repeating back. Cars piled on top of each other on the great snaking freeway. Bodies, the living and dead, pulled from twisted metal.

"Tell them we don't have capacity," said Dr. Jessie, but the flat in her voice said even she knew that was a meaningless statement to the dispatcher. "County USC and UCLA…"

"They're at max and we're the closest," said Miss Octavia, nodding into the phone. "They're diverting who they can. But there's three ambulances on the way…"

The whine of a siren, going from distant and thin to loud, urgent, blaring. I pushed the plugs back into my ears. More sirens compounded.

"Four," called a voice from the hallway, a streak of panic down the center of it. I knew it as well as the medical personnel—we were not that kind of hospital.

Jessie touched my arm . "I need you on the gurneys, Berto. How many greens on deck?" This to Octavia, who covered the receiver with a broad palm.

"Six at least," she called back, her voice flat. Jessie swallowed hard.

By the time I gathered the gurneys and lined them along the corridor she had cleared the waiting room of the greens—dog bites and flu—and sent them to Urgent Care. A broken wrist sat in the corner, sullen and stubborn, her joint too swollen to cast. A blur of red and blue lights through the slitted windows said the first ambulance was here, was unloading.

Jessie's hand was on my shoulder. "I need you to clear the waiting room." I began to say Octavia had already moved all the greens out, and then I felt the beeswax on my tongue and knew what she meant—clear the chairs aside; a clean floor. The two benches in the center were bolted down, but I could move the stained cushion and bentwood chairs to the wall, and prop the long tables across them. The broken wrist snarled at me and coiled herself in the corner. It wasn't worth the time to argue with her.

Dr. Jessie was talking to the nurses and an intern who had run in, breathless. There was a burr in her voice, but the more she spoke the more she controlled the tremble.

"I want a line in their arm, wheels or walking, even if they're not going down. Get it in, tape it sound, tell them to leave it alone. I don't want to mess with flat veins when they crump."

Octavia just nodded; the intern looked scared. Unasked, I grabbed a cart and went to my supplies closet for more rags and cleaner. It would be a dirty day. Behind me, the doors flew open and a burst of light blazed inside. Figures scrambled, black against the white, and I had an impression of fighting men, bloodied and cruel, forcing their way into a castle, the women inside gathering what they could to fight back, both sides rushing at each other, bent on destruction. I turned, the light faded, and I halted my way to supplies, the battle-snarl behind me morphing into medical-speak: staccato summaries of injury, barked orders and callbacks, the moans of the injured.

The rest a blur: I mopped blood, I moved gurneys, I told the ghosts to abate their interest while the outer, painted gods watched, cold and barely curious. The ambulances brought two and three at a time, and as they were wheeled in Jessie and her intern hovered over each, quick assessing. A few walked in, dazed, and sat at the edge of the waiting room while the nurses sorted them out; at some point the feral broken wrist had slunk away. More blood, and vomit from a relative fouling the linoleum. No one had died yet, not inside our walls, but it was early yet.

Then, with an armful of clean towels, I paused outside a treatment room. Dr. Jessie stood beside the bed, where a small bundle of bright clothing lay. A girl, maybe seven, her eyes glazed open. A nurse, injecting a syringe full into the crook of the arm, her face grim. It wouldn't work. I knew broken when I saw it.

But I didn't look at the girl; I looked at Jessie. She stared back at me as if I were a thing incomprehensible. I wondered about last night, the boy, the police in their yellow slickers, dripping rain on my clean floors. I wondered if she had to give a statement.

Jessie closed her eyes. Breathed in. Out. Opened them, hard as stars.

"No," she told me, so quiet that I shouldn't have heard her. "Not tonight. No one, tonight."

Still watching me she raised her fist and struck the girl in the chest twice, quick, efficient and brutal with the butt of her hand. The nurse startled back, syringe in hand and a scarlet drop blooming from the child's vein. There was an unearthly gasp, no sound a girl that age should be able to make, and her eyes flew open. The rattling sound continued: air sucking into her lungs, making them bloom open, but it was like air hissing into a cave deep inside the earth that was sealed with the melted borning of the world, broken through and violated.

Jessie still stared at me and through me, her eyes were agates: her face was a bronze mask, her hair a helm. There was no mercy in the way she brought that child back—she ordered and was obeyed.

There are so many gods, one never knows for true which one will answer. But in Dr. Jessie's call, in her imperious demand, pure and arrogant, I felt the pulse beat down below the shell of city, down into the layer of earth and stone that circled the molten sea below. At the heart of the world, the Fiddler waited, and at the heart of the world, the Fiddler answered.

No, I wanted to tell Jessie. *Not her, not this one.* It's a dangerous game, making such a power notice you. This is not something you can put back in the bottle once you are finished with it.

But the Fiddler was there, somewhere in East Angels, invisible but undeniable. I could feel her lift her bow, almost lazy, pausing before she caressed the string, as if to say, *Consider a moment: are you sure of me? Are you sure you desire this great reverberation?*

No, I mouthed at her. But although she didn't know it, Dr. Jessie answered, *Yes, all of it. I am hollow to your power, and you will fill me.*

What can you do? I called to my little god, who was kind and foolish, happy with the toys and the leftover pork fried rice I shared with him, keeping me safe from the dangers of the streets if not from my own madness. *Can you protect her, blunt the raw power of this god?*

I shut my eyes tight and my little god showed me the Fiddler's smile curve as she nestled her cheek into the ebony rest, her eyes hidden beneath her hair. The horsehair and rosewood bow hesitated as her wrist crooked, then pounced upon her seven-stringed violin like a fox upon a rabbit. The music rippled through the air, a ribbon to be seized or not; there was nothing inevitable yet. Even then, Jessie could have refused it, and let who would die, die. She could save who she could, same as any other night.

A new world is made every time a bow bites into the string, just as a new world is made when you drag a man from the brink of death. An uncoiling tail-whip of notes, clear as glass pebbles dusted with rosin, or a cathedral tower bricked from solid chords. At the beginning of all things, the Fiddler called the rivers into being: she made the water and the lava in the veins of the mountains. She walks through the world, beholden to no composer.

Here, she unrolled the bright silks of her music and waited for Jessie, in her raw and imperious hunger, to take it.

The music uncoiled, and Jessie seized it. I clutched the towels to my chest and felt my eyes sting.

I flinched back as the surgeon on call nudged me aside and pulled on his gloves. He smelled faintly of sour beer. He saw Jessie standing over the girl and her bright, frightened eyes, heard her earthy breathing and knew, along with me, that she shouldn't be alive.

～

A blur again, of more shouted orders, and wheeling into surgery, and more of the wounded came and we danced them down the corridors, all at Jessie's command. She allowed no one to rest and no one to die.

I saw the Fiddler in the interior twilight, a slim, tall figure all made of shadow whose edges blurred the more you looked at her. She held the fiddle dangling by its neck in her right hand, the bow akimbo. When the door slammed open and Octavia and one of the night nurses charged past with a man on a gurney, groaning and bubbling pink from his mouth, the door slammed right through her, violin and all. She saw me watching her and grinned then, a sharp white crescent in a featureless face. She knew that I was a half-person, and knew about my little god all in an instant. I felt him droop and withdraw from me in the face of her scrutiny. He pulled, apologetic, into his river rock cleft like a hermit crab into its shell.

I had seen her fiddle in dreams without knowing it. The body was metal snaked into wood, salvaged steel cans pounded together so hard that the red and orange painted on them was sunk beneath the surface, glossy as enamel. The wooden half was tiger-striped. Seven strings, six of them twinned together and the seventh by itself, quivering bass knotted into a rosewood tailpiece inset with ivory eyes that blinked and shut tight when the bow was near. That bow was rosewood too, the base ebony set with gold. It was strung with hair from the tail of a beast that hadn't walked this world since the old gods were new.

"You aren't playing," was all I could manage to say to her, reverting to Mixteco. All my other languages had left me.

"The music is its own beast now," she answered me in the same language.

～

A man shuffled down the corridor, leaving a sinuous smear of red behind him, a long slit up the side of his splotched khakis and a gray, expensive-looking sweater, untouched save for an unraveled cuff. He looked at me, baffled. The skin on the side of his head hung down in a wet flap. His hair was gray and trimmed short. The inside of his scalp was pale where it dangled, and the shoulder of the sweater looked black beneath it. I found a gurney and pulled it over.

"I need to get home," he told me, intently and reasonably. "I have an appointment."

"You need to stay here, sir," I said, and took his forearm, trying to urge him down. But he was still strong, still didn't understand what had happened to him, only knew it was unjust and besides, my English might have left me.

"Did you hear me? I have an appointment," he repeated, angry now. I took his other arm, saw where the arm was bared to the elbow, and one of Octavia's yellow tubes taped down, the needle deep in the crook. The skin was beginning to bruise purple, and I dug my fingers into his arm and tried to straighten it.

We both looked up to see Dr. Jessie coming down the corridor. The man paused, puzzled. I saw a mist swirl at her shoulder and dissipate. She held a hypodermic by her side and I took a firmer grip on his arm.

"Look you," said the man to Jessie. "I can't fuck around. I have to get out of here."

"Five," said Jessie, checking first the tube in his elbow with her left hand, then touching his face and tugging the cheek down to see the inside of his lower eyelid. "Four."

"If you won't check me out I'll do it myself."

"Three. Two."

"Goddamn nutcase. I'm fine, and I have an appoint…"

"One."

His eyes rolled back in his head but I was ready, and supported his weight as I lowered him onto the gurney. Jessie emptied the hypodermic into the tube preset in his arm. I wondered how many triage nurses and doctors, seeing him mobile and bent on leaving an hour ago, would have let him go, and how long it would have taken him to crump between his appointment and his home.

"Treatment three," Jessie called to a passing orderly. Then,

"Wait." She took her Sharpie, unhooked the chart from the end of the gurney and scribbled on it—orders for fluids, monitors, oxygen. Orders not to die.

The man was taken. I tried to follow but Jessie stopped in front of me, her face hollowed dark under her eyes and cheekbones like a sugar skull, blood and vomit thick on her once white coat. Her name was embroidered on the breast pocket but all I could see through the stains was part of her last name: *Iver*. I had never before wondered what it was.

Her merciless gaze dropped to my aching hip, and I twisted away from her as if I could hide it. Of course she knew I had the old injury; no one could miss it, and not a doctor worth her salt. The sight of me gimping along as I cleaned was familiar to anyone at East Angels.

But this time I knew she could see exactly how the bone had tangled sinew and flesh as it healed, growing back together at an angle that made one leg shorter than the other, and set my hips askew. She could see into me, clearer than an x-ray.

Jessie saw and stepped forward and put her hand on my hip, and I formed the word *no* but I didn't say it. Down the sickly green hall-way, over Dr. Jessie's shoulder, I saw the Fiddler lift her terrible instrument, bring the bow to the string, and wait. Even now I could shove Jessie away, banish the Fiddler, and keep my twisted bone. *I have grown into it*, I could have told her over Jessie's shoulder, *like your instrument grew from the steel detritus and lava in the cracks of the world. It is a thing of beauty, if of pain, in its own way. Leave it be.*

But I didn't.

Jessie's strong fingers dug into my flesh and I could smell the stink of the people she'd ripped back from death upon her. I heard the hair of the bow tooth the strings with a harsh rosin screech, and felt the beginning of the burn, and I started back from her. But she took my shoulder and pulled me back into her grip, those long, clever, craftsman's fingers pressed around my hipbone and shank and ball and socket. Behind her the fiddle thrummed its incessant, primal music—the long stroke of the bow, and the back-forth twist of the wrist at the tip and frog—no tune as before, no speaking melody this, but the sound of raw power. I screamed as the bone unknitted and the fibers of my muscles tore part, away from their years-long slump to accommodate my crippled shape. It was like living the accident over again, but backwards: *she* held me firm, but she used the Fiddler's music to beat my flesh-self back, step by step through the years like a pig-farmer beats back his swine with the flat of a machete. I was lying in my fever in that ripe-smelling workers' shack outside Goleta, the candles guttering amber before the little crude statues of St. George and the Black Madonna. Another shove from the fiddle-music and I went back to be shattered beneath the harrow, feeling the steel discs bite into me, like the bow into all seven strings. Another shove and I had never been broken, about to stumble into the soft earth at the side of a furrow and fall, the padrone bleating at me from fifty yards away.

Each wrench was a step to being made whole again, each its own flavor of pain. I heard the noises I made at a distance, a counterpoint to the Fiddler's march. I felt a small stirring behind my forehead and tasted beeswax between my tongue and teeth, as my small god tried to succor me. As the final fragment of bone fused back into place, and my savaged meat configured to it, I managed to shove away from her and lean on the wall behind me.

My hips felt strange; I was in the habit of compensating for a tilt that wasn't there anymore. The pain was gone, leaving its echo. Jessie stared past me into the solid substance of the wall, as if she could see between the infinitesimals that made it up. Her hands still reached out towards me, holding air. Her face was haggard and gray as old cement.

My ears rang a loud flat note with nothing to temper that ring. The violin was silent. Behind Jessie, movement. A slow, measured step as the Fiddler walked down the hallway, unhurried. She held her instrument loosely at the neck and as she passed us she swung it comfortably between her arm and side, the bow dangling from her forefinger. Her face swiveled towards me and again all I saw was the brief flash of a white, crescent smile. Her shoes tapped the linoleum lightly, and there was no other sound until she was gone. There was no slam of a door. She had no need of doors.

Without her, a brief instant of silence. Then all the noise of a busy hospital and ER crashed upon us: announcements and summoning over the PA, someone arguing just short of hysteria with a nurse in the next ward, a thrum of machinery and a rhubarb of voice. Jessie still reached out to the space I had last occupied.

"I'm so tired, Berto," she told me.

"I know."

"So tired."

"Here." Still getting used to my new-old height, I took her gingerly by the arm and led her to a gurney. Blood stained the sheets garnet. I bundled that away, leaving bare mattress behind. There was no time to make it fresh; she could not hold her own weight straight any more, and fell on the gurney like a toppled tower of children's blocks. I took her hand, her fingers loose between my old calloused palms.

∾

I knew what would happen; there is a price always to be paid for that kind of power. No one at East Angels died that night - not in her ER and not in the wards, where intubated patients lay in Intensive Care, not where old abuelitas whose families wouldn't let them die at home lay in the back rooms, caught between breath and breath. With the dawn the rain came, slapping the asphalt and concrete mosaic of the city streets like a drum. Weeping may endure for a night, but joy comes in the morning. But here it is only the rain. Her hand grew cooler, and her pulse faltered. I bent my head as she became still, too still. What is there for one who has taken, even so brief, the power of a god? Madness or death.

She would probably not like being mad, Dr. Jessie. She wasn't used to it like I was.

Through the thick glass door all smudged with greasy fingerprints and propped open by a ragged chunk of asphalt, a freshening breeze passed us over. Rain puddled on the cracked sidewalk and the low-slung buildings sparkled with a fine spray of water droplets, the air clear and clean. In the parking lot, a battered VW pulled in, straddling two spots crookedly. A woman got out, wearing gray spotted pajamas, and hurried to the passenger door. She pulled out an older man, who was holding a white, red-spotted cloth to the side of his face. He leaned on her arm and they both paused, looking at the clear blue sky cracking apart the clouds, which were scattering, ragged and torn, to the east. The hills to the north were spangled green, the morning light slanted rose-gold. I knew I should go help them inside, but I stayed beside Jessie's bier, and the couple leaned together as the last of the rain hissed away, and I knew we all heard it: the dying fall of a single note, plucked from the string of a distant fiddle.

About the Author

Samantha Henderson's short fiction and poetry have been published in *Strange Horizons, Clarkesworld, Interzone, Weird Tales, Goblin Fruit*, and *Mythic Delirium* and in the anthologies *Tomorrow's Cthulhu, Running with the Pack*, and *Zombies: Shambling through the Ages*. Her work has been reprinted in *Year's Best Science Fiction 34*, the *Nebula Awards Showcase, Aliens: Recent Encounters, Steampunk Reloaded*, and *The Mammoth Book of Steampunk*. Her stories have been podcast at *PodCastle, Escape Pod, Drabblecast* and *Strange Horizons*, and she's the author of the Forgotten Realms novels *Heaven's Bones* and *Dawnbringer*. She is very fond of pomegranates and other dangerous fruit.

Author's Notes

The bones of this story have been rattling around loose in my head a long time—the image of a healer, skilled but helpless before the enormity of some kinds of injury, being given (or taking) the power to control death and save all her patients for a time, however brief. I've often found that stories come to me as three disparate elements that join together, and when the opportunity to write a story for this anthology came I thought immediately of a play I'd recently seen, with a string band on stage, where at one point the fiddler rose and joined the action, her music a natural part of the narrative. I've been working on a series of linked stories about the magic that underlies Los Angeles, and the minor deities and super-natural creatures woven into its history. The Fiddler, an entity "woven together in the depths of the earth" (to steal a psalm), seemed to be the sort of power, however dangerous, that could be called upon to chase Death from the doorstep.

SHE SEARCHES FOR GOD IN THE STORM WITHIN

Khaalidah Muhammad-Ali

W hen I arrived at my grandmother's, in the stillness of predawn, like some restless cat stalking, she was waiting for me on the front porch. It was as if she'd been expecting me. I suppose if she had been watching the sky, she was, because I could be seen for miles. My scarf had come unwrapped and my hair had unfurled into a roiling trail of luminescent heaped-up clouds threatening to burst.

The air was thick with the metallic scent of rain and sweet jasmine. I stopped just inside the gate when I caught sight of my grandmother, chest heaving, trying with great difficulty to thin my lowering nimbus into one more presentable. All the excuses I'd contrived for why I was coming to her home at this unseemly hour, after all these years away from home, dissolved.

I did not need them. She would not judge me. She would welcome me home.

Grandma May glided soundlessly in her rocking chair, her eyes mirroring the yellow moonlight. I felt her gaze on me like fingers, probing the bruises, the lump on my forehead, my split lip. I gasped, as did she, when my pain telegraphed in tiny sparks across the distance to her when she grazed the tenderest spots.

A sharp hot pain shot through my left ankle, right along the healed over fracture in my talus. Grandma May's gaze shifted to the turbulent sky where seconds later a twin lightning strike split the horizon like an angry slap.

"Yeah, I know," she said to me, to the sky, to no one in particular. Perhaps to God. "You've got to decide what you're going to do, child. Let us know how you feel, or hold back the storm."

After that I went to pieces.

I stayed in my mother's old bedroom, walls, floor and ceiling sealed with rubber. Part of me occupied the bed, fleshy lower limbs partially clothed, while the rest of me stretched upward in an agonizing aerosol clinging to the ceiling. My grandmother ran a fan and the window unit on the lowest setting to precipitate cooling, to keep me from spreading outward and beyond. My grandmother sang a familiar old country lullaby meant to soothe my worrying and anger, to quiet the thunder rolling off my skin.

Her sweet susurration helped me not think about the fight. I blamed myself more than Reef because I should have known it was coming. Reef's excuses, followed by bitter words, then the pushes, the slaps, that one shove down the stairs. I saw hatred sharp as a dagger in his eyes while he was whispering his love for me, if you can believe. What happened tonight was months in the making, but clear as glass if I had wanted to look through it. All this time I'd managed to keep the storm at bay. Not even a distant rumble. Not a single shower to purge the buildup. I'd been strong until tonight, finding strength in the names of God.

As Salaam. Bestower of Peace. *Al Mughith*. The Sustainer. *Al Raqib*. The Watchful.

Imagine Reef's surprise when he threw his fist and it passed through a storm cloud, that the hairs on his knuckles and arm were singed away, the skin damp and tingling with electric heat.

"We ain't had a bad storm in a long time. Perhaps I shouldn't say bad, because it's only bad for us. For you, it's something different, I suppose." My grandmother stood by the door with a quilt wrapped around her narrow shoulders as she watched me condense, coalesce, reassemble into the thick brown-fleshed woman people recognized but didn't have the sense to fear.

My glazed-over eyes cleared enough for me to see the picture on the nightstand. My mother, Mercine, smiled at me from the tarnished silver frame. I recall few details of her. A smile bright and broad as the sun, with a missing right front tooth. Rough, scarred, long fingered hands that could plait intricately patterned braids in my head and swing a vicious knife and disappear altogether like dew beneath the morning sun.

I tried to speak, but was only able to choke out a mouthful of snow onto the pillow. Somehow, my grandmother understood what I was asking.

"It was your mother's storm, wasn't it? Just tore herself into a rage."

I already knew that. I just didn't know why.

I lifted my arm, now solid and whole, but my fingernails were thin bluish white ice chips that glistened in the dull lamp light next to the bed.

"Where is she?" My voice was a zephyr fluttering the curtains and rattling the windows.

My grandmother shrugged. "Who's to say?"

∾

After breakfast I followed Grandma May through the sun-bright kitchen and out into the back yard.

"Come help me pick some of these vegetables."

She pointed to a basket next to a rocker, identical to the one on the front porch, and an old sweat stained straw hat that hung against the wall. "Put that on to keep the sun off your face."

I pulled the hat on over my scarf.

My grandmother used a hand to shield her eyes as she searched the horizon. She inhaled long and deep, nostrils flaring, then her narrow-eyed gaze fell on me.

"Weather lady said we gonna get a thunder storm today."

The morning sun was still fresh in the sky but the air was hot and still, like a breath held.

"Feels like more than that to me." Her brows descended in a question and I looked away. I was more hurt than angry, but I was whole nonetheless.

"Whatever storm that's coming has nothing to do with me."

My grandmother's brows descended even further and met in the center of her forehead. Her eyes turned automaton slow back to the sky.

I should have known that *help* really meant she'd sit and watch and instruct while I'd *do*, but I didn't mind. The sun's rays were like massaging fingers on my back and shoulders, and the slow repetitive movements, bending, reaching, pulling, pinching, clipping, did much to ease the stiffness that had settled in overnight from the beating Reef gave me.

I filled the basket with okra, tomatoes, and bell peppers and left it on the porch, then went deeper into the garden where I'd noticed a couple of ripe watermelon near the fence. I walked along the fence line and thumped each watermelon, inspecting the undersides, to find the perfect one to pick.

Beyond the fence was a gravel walkway and a field of overgrown grass and wildflowers. Further along, though I couldn't see it from where I stood, Benders Bayou dropped off past the field. I stood there while thinking back on the days I'd spent here as a child. My grandmother's home was tucked into the cul-de-sac of a modern development that had managed to maintain the easy cadence of the countryside surrounding it. So many of my memories from that time were faded and curled around the edges, like they'd been left out in the sun too long.

A dog barked in the distance and I saw a figure in a red and blue jersey several yards away, partly around the bend of the gravel walk. The person stood there, still and watchful, alert as a stalking creature. They waved and I ducked back out of sight. Chill bumps sprouted on my scalp and along my arms like I'd been doused with freezing water.

I felt I should remember, and knew that this is why so many years had passed since I had returned. There were reasons to forget. There was safety in forgetting. There was forgetting in the clouds.

I chose my watermelon and headed back for the house, not noticing until I reached the porch that sooty clouds now partly obscured the sun. Grandma May was no longer on the porch, but my friend, Sameha, was.

Seems odd, but I hadn't thought of Reef all morning. Grandma May had kept me busy enough and truth be told, I wasn't ready to think on any of it. When Sameha pressed her fingers to my bruised face and shoulder and ribs, inspecting with her nurse's eye and friend's heart, the aches came back just as if the sun had never warmed them away.

Now, there were other aches too. Deeper, right into my bones.

"He just keeps doing this to you."

I gently pushed her hand away from my jaw. I sat in the chair and she sat on the top step.

"It's going to stop."

"You know it's because he loves you, right?"

I winced with the pain that spiked through my left cheek, the orbit of that eye, where Reef had cracked it the previous night with his fist. It radiated like a tuning fork.

"The fuck you mean, *love*, Sameha?"

I tried to shoot a glare at her but the rain behind my left eye clouded my vision. I cupped a hand over it and tears slipped through my evaporating fingers. I fisted my hand to pull my flesh back together again.

Sameha closed her eyes as if gathering her strength, her words. She did not see me atomizing into my constituent parts.

"Aisha reported that the Prophet, may the peace and blessings of Allah be upon him said: None has more self-respect than Allah, so he made obscenities unlawful."

The quote sounded so familiar I practically heard it in Reef's voice. My mouth watered.

"Don't you quote hadith to me," I said through my teeth. I swallowed the wash of ozone-tinged saliva and my stomach groaned. I looked heavenward for my own strength.

The sky was the color of iron and the air tasted like iron filings, like blood. It reminded me of Reef's belt buckle, which made me think about the things he would say and how they never matched the things he did. And how, despite the way he always used God to prop up his reasoning, it still crumbled like a mountain beneath God's wrath.

Sameha was doing the same thing, using God to chain me. Telling lies on God to extract a debt Reef was not owed.

Sameha held up a hand, patted the air as if calming a skittish animal.

"He's sorry, Bahiyaa. He wants you to come home. He asked me to tell you this."

A chill wind whipped around the yard kicking up a cloud of dust. Tiny shocks of pain climbed the stairsteps of my vertebrae and my body ticked and jerked in the throes of spasms as they tried to unhinge themselves.

I stood too quickly and stumbled on the watermelon at my feet. It rolled off the porch and split open at the bottom of the steps. Sameha stood too, and reached for me, but I jerked away from her.

"Shareef gets jealous sometimes and he just loses it. Beautiful women make men do…"

Beautiful.

That's what Shareef called me the first day we met, as he leaned out of the driver's side window of his red truck, hungry eyes on my mouth, the swell of my breasts, my thick brown legs. Later Reef taught me about a chaste god while undressing me and searching the terrain of my body, running hungry hands through my cool cirrus coils. He taught me that God wished for my modesty, not for His sake, but to satisfy Reef's own insecure fear that another might learn the secrets of my storm, might also know that I am—

"Beautiful?" My grandmother's laughter had the resonant quality of a wooden wind chime. "Now that's something I once wanted to be, but only for a time." Grandma May was barely visible in the shadows of the kitchen, behind the screen door, but her voice cleared the fog and the throbbing that had started behind my eyes. "But you know what I learned?"

"Ma'am?" said Sameha.

"Sometimes it's more trouble than its worth. Everyone thinks they can own and control beauty that ain't theirs. Especially men. It's a strange thing." My grandmother stepped onto the porch and took hold of my arm. She seemed so strong and sure. "Imagine trying to rope a cloud and keep it for your own. It's just not possible, is it?"

Sameha shook her head, eyes going from my grandmother to me, finally seeing. Suddenly afraid.

"Besides, I believe most folk really don't know beauty when they see it. So, I decided I could do without. The same way I could do without bad friends." Grandma May winked, smiled wide, like a snake opening its mouth to accommodate too-large prey. "You get my meaning, *bad friend?*"

When Sameha was gone, my grandmother led me into the

house and once we were seated at the kitchen table, she placed a knotty knuckled hand on mine, the fingertips cool against my fevered joints.

"Decide what you're going to do."

I chose to hold back the storm, with will and difficulty. I hurt all over but this was more than the effect of Reef's fists. My bones ached right down into the marrow, like a magnet was drawing out the iron of my blood one molecule at a time through the hard white matter. I could feel the sun pull the water from me too, right up into the atmosphere. I channeled a lightning strike inward and it bounced around my insides, lighting me up like a bulb.

I lifted my head to meet my grandmother's rheumy blue-rimmed brown irises. "I only ever hurt like this when a storm is coming."

～

My grandmother brought lunch to the front porch. Flies lit upon my untouched tuna fish sandwich. I could only manage the soothing tart lemonade and the handful of arthritis pills my grandmother gave me.

We listened to the same Panasonic radio my grandmother had since I was a kid. It took DD batteries and was stuck on the local station that played country music during the day and R&B at night. But now we listened to the news.

They named the hurricane Helene. She sprang up in the gulf without warning.

"Look at that," said Grandma May. "They named the storm after you."

"My name is Bahiyaa, now. You know that."

Bahiyaa is the name Reef gave me when I converted, when I married him. Two intertwined events that should not have been connected, but he had wanted it that way. My god and my man. Not one but two. Not the same, not alike, not resembling in anyway.

"What that name mean?" she asked, as if I hadn't told her many times before.

"It means beautiful, remember?"

"The sun is beautiful too."

I had never wanted to be a beautiful thing. Never beautiful alone. I had wanted the name Zikra. It is the thing you do to remember God. Repetition. Counting. Savoring. A beloved remembrance.

I swatted at a mosquito, leaving a black and red smear on my arm. Dusky clouds rolled inland from the gulf with a fine mist. I glanced up when I felt my grandmother stiffen. Her thin brown shape blurred momentarily to gray mist around the edges. The man I'd seen earlier, in the red and blue jersey, stood by the fence. His dog, a big dark brutish animal with a dripping muzzle, stood next to him, front paws propped up on the fence, long muscular body stretched out like a bolt.

"Hey Queen May," he said waving over the fence.

My grandmother nodded icily.

Jeremiah had hardly changed in the last several years, thin as a curl of smoke, honey colored skin and eyes and hair...and voice. It didn't seem particularly odd when I was ten and he was seventeen that he liked playing with me. I was his favorite friend for years, although it was to be kept a secret. And now just the sight of him made something in me recoil. I tried to remember something...I tried to forget it too.

He propped his elbows up on the fence and leaned there. Jeremiah squinted at me, eyes scrutinizing my face and the scarf wrapped around my hair. I felt bare beneath his probing and rose to leave, but Grandma May clamped a hand on my arm and anchored me in place.

He smiled, teeth a perfect straight line in his perfect pretty face. The wind kicked up dust and dandelion fluff, pinging off car doors in a restless melody. I sucked in a breath and caught the sweet yellow scent of banana Now & Laters, a scrap of latent memory.

A tangerine and lime kite riding pre-storm winds like a jet.

Running and running until my lungs were about to burst. The itchy, ticklish, sticky feel of the overgrown grasses against my bare arms and legs down by Benders Bayou in the summertime.

Ravenous mosquitos.

Slipping in the mud. No. *Almost* slipping in the mud.

I've got you, pretty girl. Ain't gonna let nothing bad happen to you.

I lay in the overgrown grass, listening to grasshopper song, confused if what was happening to me was bad. Part of me knew, so I unraveled myself and drifted skyward. I created clouds in the shapes of creatures I'd imagined only in my dreams.

I lost the memories.

"That you, Helene?" called Jeremiah at me over the fence.

I was a cloud shaped like a giraffe with wings made of peacock feathers. I felt nothing. I heard nothing. My mother had been looking for me and could not find me. She'd started calling around to the homes of my friends. She was about to set out in search of me, not too worried, until she saw my wild magical shapes twisting in the sky. I'd never cast myself into the clouds before then, but she knew me when she saw me there.

My mother threw herself into the sky, a cold storm, strong and precise. She intertwined with me, wrapped me up in her fury, a dark and mighty storm cloud, dropping hailstone daggers all around me and Jeremiah. They steamed when they pierced the soft earth around us.

Jeremiah lived now only because on that day part of me remained anchored to the earth and she would not risk hurting me.

Al Waliyy. The Protector. *Ash Shahid.* The Witness. *Al Haqq.* The Truth.

~

I knew Reef would call, eventually. His apologies always sounded sincere, even when the fights were his fault, but we were pretending they were mine.

"What he want?" asked Grandma May not bothering if Reef heard her. She watched me flinty eyed from where she sat on the opposite end of the couch.

Outside the early evening sky was a pitch void. That was my fault. All I could think of was my mother and how that day long ago, she had spent her whole self so completely she could not reassemble her flesh and return to me.

"I want you to come home," said Reef in answer to my grandmother as well as to me. He sounded as if he had been crying. "A good woman would go back to her husband, work out their problems."

"Would she?" I asked, not giving a shit about the answer.

"Yes. A good woman would. And God would want it too."

"Did God tell you that?"

My teeth were sharp icicles and I worried at my bottom lip until it bled. I trembled from the inside out, as I struggled against unspooling.

Zikra would have recited the ninety-nine names of God, savoring each one of them on the tip of her tongue. *Al Wadud.* The Loving One.

Zikra would have counted a dozen wise ways to encourage Reef to seek his own redemption while she sought her own. *Al Wajid.* The Self-Sufficient.

Zikra would have known who Reef was all along. *Al Hakim.* The Wise.

Zikra would have hung up the phone. *Al Hakim.* The Wise.

Zikra would never have accepted the call. *Al Hakim.* The Wise.

"Bahiyaa? You coming home?" It wasn't a question. Not really.

I imagined that even through the phone I could feel his warm breath on my left cheek. Pain shocked me and shot through that eye. In my mind I saw his face and Jeremiah's and my mother's retreating storm cloud. One by one my fingers faded into fine mist and the phone slipped to the floor.

Grandma May laughed, pink and brown gums showing in the back of her mouth where the teeth had long been pulled. She knelt unsteadily on one knee and retrieved my phone. Then I realized she wasn't laughing at all. A gale of warm wind had wheezed past her aged vocal cords, echoing like it had passed through a narrow mountain cavern.

"You come on and get her," she said into the phone, as she pulled herself up onto weak bowed legs, "but it ain't safe out there."

⤳

Helene spun inland that night, arms heavy with gulf water and gulf trouble. The fig tree in front of Grandma May's house toppled, ropey roots reaching for the sky. The water rose fast, as if in a hurry to greet the sky, taking with it my grandmother's garden. The street was a living black river. Eventually the water bubbled up under the front and back doors, creeping inside like it had been invited.

I watched the storm from a second floor window throughout the night. The hungry winds tugged and twisted at my spirit and bones and the pain persisted and intensified.

Near midnight, I saw Reef's truck in the distance, submerged up to its red roof. He stood on top, clothes clinging to him like a second skin. I backed away from the window.

"He came," I said, grappling with a funnel of emotions.

My grandmother touched her fingers to my elbow but they slipped right through flesh and bone. Her fingertips were gray with frost.

"Don't be afraid," she cooed.

Al Mu'min. Granter of Security. *Al Muhaymin.* The Protector. *Ar Rahim.* The Merciful.

"I'm not." I stepped back up to the window so that I could be seen.

Reef saw me and waved. I lifted my hand to wave back then realized he was not waving at me. A blue and green utility boat motored in his direction. The occupant who wore a yellow rain slicker and a black dog sat next to them. We watched as Reef was rescued and the boat headed in our direction.

"He can come to this house, but we ain't got to let him in."

I looked down into her face. Her dark brown eyes were now gray like clouds heavy with rain. I saw a beautiful lightning storm flash beneath the parchment thin skin of her broad lined face. She smiled and her breath was frost.

"As long as I am with you, they will cause no harm."

She shifted her weight, stood straighter, taller. Seemed stronger. She pushed open the window, letting in the rushing rain and wild whistling whining wind.

My flesh recoiled from the cold and wet, but when I heard my name on the air, *HeleneHeleneHelene, HeleneHelene, Helene, Helene,*

Helene...spoken like a zikr, a most beloved remembrance, it set me unspooling.

"She's coming, baby. Just hold on."

"Who are you talking to, Grandma May?" I asked with my zephyr voice.

"Your ma," answered the gale. The walls tremored. My grandmother shimmered and dissolved, the mild mist of her like kisses upon my face.

"You don't have to hold back your storm," said May, said Mercine, said Helene and Zikra.

My grandmother was strong, a proper tempest possessing her place in the heavens. She was beautiful, lightning and eclipse, drawing me out with her into the sky. I unfolded, floated and glided, allowed myself to be carried, eased. Loved. The cold storm, strong and precise, embraced me, and interlaced her currents with mine.

For a time I left my grandmother's home far below, as well as the indecision and uncertainty. I left behind the jittering bone-deep ache of the coming storm. Then I became the storm. I shed the tempting brown flesh in favor of that which cannot be possessed and obscured.

One cannot rope a cloud and keep it for their own. Can they?

I felt nothing. I heard nothing. I lost the memories. I searched for God.

About the Author

Khaalidah Muhammad-Ali lives in Houston, Texas, with her family. By day she works as a breast oncology nurse. At all other times, she juggles, none too successfully, the multiple other facets of her very busy life.

Khaalidah's publications include *Strange Horizons*, *Fiyah Magazine*, *Diabolical Plots*, *Apex Magazine* and others. Her fiction has been featured in *The Best Science Fiction and Fantasy of the Year: Volume 12* edited by Jonathan Strahan and *The Best Science Fiction of the Year: Volume Three* edited by Neil Clarke. You can hear her narrations at any of the four Escape Artists podcasts, *Far Fetched Fables*, and *Strange Horizons*.

As co-editor of *PodCastle* audio magazine, Khaalidah is committed to encouraging more women and POC to submit fantasy stories. Khaalidah is also a proud World Fantasy Award nominee for her work at *PodCastle*.

Of her alter ego, K from the planet Vega, it is rumored that she owns a time machine and knows the secret to immortality.

She can be found online at http://khaalidah.com.

Author's Notes

For a couple of years I've been trying to write a story that incorporates the connection between weather fluctuations and joint pain. For those of us who can feel the coming storm, it's as real as a ton of bricks.

This was the extent of my forethought regarding this story. It wasn't until I wrote the first paragraph that I realized that my main character was abused but not broken and that she could, if she wished, harness the pain of the abuses perpetrated against her, to do miraculous things.

A VOICE IN MANY DIFFERENT FORMS

Osahon Ize-Iyamu

See ehn, you know you've always been loud, but it might be time to raise the freaking decibels because it's obvious no one is listening. So it's time for you to do your screaming.

You are fresh out of a job and half asleep on a danfo when the super young bus conductor tells you your voice is something special. He says it's sweet, it's soft, flowing, perfect. Maybe because he hasn't heard you screech or laugh, but it's not like you'll do these in public. He says it reminds him of his mother singing songs in his ear, and he touches your arm, and you recoil in disgust. And you leave before your stop, stomping feet, clearing a whole path for yourself.

Honestly, on some days it would be a hell of a lot better if no one spoke to you. If they just kept silent. If they didn't say something that makes you explode inside, that makes you shield up your skin, that makes you *roar*.

Honey, sweet, flowing? Sure, whatever. Your voice is still a battle cry.

You are fresh out of a job so you don't really have an option except to start displaying your talents, lay them bare like open, outstretched hands raised in uncertainty to complete a shrug.

"I really don't want to do this," you tell your friend Zainab, who files her newly done nails without interest. Zainab lounges on your bed, already dressed, waiting for you to pick something to wear. It's eight in the night but Zainab's already called the taxi because she knows you work better under deadlines and this will push you to get something on before the driver gets here. Not that you want to go anyway.

"Aunty," Zainab looks up from her nails, almost rolling her eyes. "You can't be complaining 'I'm broke!' but refuse to do the one thing you're good at. If only a friend told you to develop a side hustle along with your former job so you'd have some extra cash if anything hap—oh wait, *I did*. But do you ever listen?"

You tune her out and raise up a big coat. "I think if I add layers to myself I'll look smaller. Then I'll disappear within the crowd."

Zainab shakes her head and looks at the closet once and picks out a black dress. "That coat's not you. This is."

"Well, what if I want to be someone different?" you counter, a whine in your voice, a reluctance in your stare. You have so much anger, so much *tear it all down* in you but—to actually wear it? To wear your emotion, strip yourself bare? Can you fathom it?

"You can always be someone different," Zainab says, "But not out of fear."

You're thinking on that when her phone rings, signifying the taxi's arrival. You scream inside your head, then hold your breath. But—you wear the dress.

You still wear the coat too.

∾

It's not that you're uncomfortable expressing fury. It's not that you're too much—sweetie, that's all fine, you can explode all over the room. Too much isn't nothing but a lie.

It's that—well, you don't know what it is. You're not usually like this; you'll pick a fight in a back alley, you'll pick a fight on the street. But this is a whole different fight entirely, and poetry is the roar of the mouth, and you've always found your words to be neat little packages. Not like your fists anyway.

So it's weird to snap your fingers and sip locally produced beer from a red plastic cup (you know the beer isn't brand-made because it sure as hell doesn't taste like it). It's strange to see famous pictures of poets everywhere you turn in the purple room. It's weird to know that this place may actually be your scene, but you aren't sure you would have ever come here on your own—not without a push.

You don't look overdressed, but you sure do stand out, probably because of your aura of intimidation, how it exudes off your skin like perfume. Wouldn't it be weird to give off this *fight me* vibe then come on stage and sing sweet? Yes, you are obviously more than meets the eye, but you don't want people to think you have no scream inside, no raging tornado shaking your bones when they hear you talk. Your voice is still a battle cry, but you're not yet sure if it has its knockout punch.

"It's time," the director tells you, a short stocky man with a thick white beard, who Zainab has connections with. That's how you got this gig in the first place, because you sure weren't the talk of the town when you'd never performed before.

The crowd is surprisingly...not bad. First-time poet, not like you're getting paid a lot, but this is livable money and a sizable audience. The performance fee is enough for you to live a not-broke lifestyle. You know—adjust as you look for something more stable, something more...confined in a cubicle, 9-5, thirty minute lunch break. Freelance isn't for you. "The man" is your best friend, at least until the world destroys capitalism.

The announcer reads off your name, and you love the way the man reads it, love the way it sounds, love how your presence goes off into the crowds. You love how it makes you feel, more present, more alive. Yes, *yes*, oh yes, you know you can do this, can rock this, as long as you breathe and you...

Huh. An emptiness fills you, out of nowhere. A cramp hits your stomach like a blow, making you tremble, and the sharp spike of feeling moves down to your legs. God. Your throat closes like you're having an allergic reaction, and your eyes stay open in...surprise, really. This freaking chill goes down your spine and there are...eyes in the crowd and it feels like, just a lot of negative energy, you know? You want to shrink back into your coat and melt into the puddle and crouch into a ball. You were feeling so good, and now you don't want to do this anymore.

Why do you feel this way all of a sudden, like your body is being forced into the same box that is holding your voice? That you are going to stutter, fail onstage, be left shaking. Like you should squeak.

But why the hell would you ever do that? And why would you let yourself feel this way? And how can you go on like this?

You don't want to do this anymore—but now you have to.

You drop your coat to the floor.

And so your first lines of performance poetry starts with a "no —" to yourself and to whatever's holding you back. All eyes in the crowd fade to a distance, still lingering, still there, like negative energy preparing to strike again, but you're present, and you're singing and speaking at the same time, and you're gonna make sure they never reach you.

~

And so it goes
  No
  NO
  I won't be
  Pushed aside—won't be
  Crouching down; these boxes you made *broke* because I didn't fit
in it
  Didn't identify with it—and, I want to know
  Did that enrage you? Did it make you weep?
  To know—I testify, that you tried so hard
  Wanted so bad
  To bend my bones, to push my hair
  To press in the parts that will not stay
  Just for what *you* think is safe
  Which is broken still, and you're broken still
  And you're wrong, despite what you think
  I testify—
  No!
  You failed, you failed again, you failed still.
  Thank you.

~

After the show, you're still feeling shaky, still feeling raw and ener-getic, still feeling scratchy with your voice. And that's not even all of it. There's still so much anger inside you, so much fighting, so much teeth: snapping, grinding, but at least it's coming out. You're coming out—of your shell, of where your voice was kept.

And up on that stage, you were a lot more than honey and sweet —something special, indeed.

Plus, you get paid. The check that enters your hand no be small thing. It still feels so unreal that you're getting this much—"this much" isn't still enough, but it's more than you thought you would ever make—just from doing this. People come up to congratulate you, to ask about your body of work.

(And "when can I see you again" is not about you but your work, and where you can be found, and which spaces you inhabit. Which will probably always be here, because, well, money).

"Good show," a man says to you, walking up out of a crowd of people. The first thing you notice is this man's eyes, how they feel like...the ones that watched you and made you lose all confidence, that made you almost fall apart. They're eyes that stare you down: big and wide and blinking.

You put up your aura of intimidation for protection once again but the man doesn't dare back away. Instead, he laughs, eyes managing to go even wider, like they might swallow his whole face. You can see the silver fillings inside his teeth mid-chuckle, and beyond that, something even darker—

He catches you staring too long and closes his mouth so hard you'd think the sound made was that of a knife on a chopping block. The man exudes welcomeness, but that's the nature of some predators, isn't it? And you've seen too many red flags in his behavior to ever be alone with him, if you can help it. Which is why you're glad for the crowd surrounding you.

He shakes your hand, puts your fingers in his without you asking, grasping you in a slimy handshake. You want to pull away but he grasps tighter, holding you closer than you would ever want to be with him. That cold chill comes back again, and you go weak in the knees and end up crouching, barely able to stand up. He has to pull you back up with a "gentleman's" voice, calling you clumsy

249

even when you're sure, *sure*, he made you go down in the first place, presumably after he saw how much more taller you were than him.

You're sure—but you can't prove anything.

"Great work," the man tells you. "I always love seeing guests come here—not every time same-old same-old, you know? Fresh faces is what keeps this place running. Keeps me on my feet."

"Yeah," you say, but immediately you start, your voice starts to drop, *drop, drop,* till it's barely a squeak, and you're left wondering where all that roar went. "I think I'll be performing here more and more. I quite like this place. I'm really excited to meet other people in this—field? Is that the right word?"

"Riiiight," he draws the word long enough like he's sucking on a lit cigarette. He says it with amusement. "Well, safe journey—"

"Excuse me," Zainab's nasally voice enters into the conversation, and you didn't know how much you needed to take a deep breath until then. "Are you Tola? I've been here a couple of times and I love your work. Truly masterclass readings."

"Why, thank you." The man does a mini curtsy. "You seem trustworthy...Zainab? Ah yes, I'm good with names like that—Zainab? So I'm going to tell you a bit of a secret. Ready? Okay, good." At this point Zainab looks captivated, hooked, drawn in.

"I find this place a bit pedestrian. You know it all looks good up close but—the tables start to shake if you move your legs too much; the mic service isn't the best; the walls are peeling. It's not really my scene."

You see the silver fillings in his teeth as bait to catch a fish each time he gives that laugh. And that *darkness* just after his tongue that you've never seen in anybody's mouth before...

He closes up before you can get a better look.

"But you know why I love this place? My fans. Plus, all the people that are watching. And there are people watching—those offering residencies, scholarships, grants. Those taking you to higher planes. So I have to perform for them most of all, then for my enemies, and hope that every one of them notices me. It's exhilarating. It's...an opportunity."

With that, he shakes Zainab's hand and walks off.

"Yeah, I don't trust him," you say, looking back at him as you look to Zainab, remembering the coldness that once spread throughout your chest just because he *looked* at you.

"I'm calling a taxi," Zainab fiddles with her phone. She seems to be avoiding your question, shrugging it off with a playful voice and pretending to spend more time on her phone than she needs to.

"What do you think about him?"

Zainab laughs at something on her phone. You snap your fingers in her face to get her attention.

"I dunno, I guess. If he's a weirdo, we'll find out soon enough. I just don't want to, you know, go looking for things to make my favorite creators problematic."

"You're not 'looking' for it if—"

"Yeah, yeah, let's just go." Zainab says. She looks distant, filled with less presence. She looks caved in, dried out, sucked open. "Our taxi's here."

On your way out, there's a woman in extremely high heels smoking. She looks at you, and she has the eyes of the darkness you saw in the crowd too. Hell. The ones that watched you. The ones that filled you with emptiness, making you fall and stumble, pushing you into the box. You know it wasn't stage fright. You know it was *them*.

She nods at you when you make eye contact with her. Why is she nodding? Why are *you* still looking, you wonder at some point. You realize you don't want to take your eyes off her because you don't want to know who else is watching, staring at you, as you enter your taxi and go all the way home.

∾

You're spitting straight fire and releasing your rage in your dreams, your poetry angry, boiling out and singing within. Five people step into the room and watch you from the back, and you ignore them and go on, but soon it's all you can see. That man, that lady—their *eyes*, bigger, wider—pressing you further into the floor, till the stage is swallowing you. Gobbling you up like quicksand and your words become incoherent. Your enemies are laughing. Those offering opportunities are going away. Till you realize you're not too much and you're not intimidating and maybe you've been weak all this time. Maybe you have no roar.

When they all open their mouths to laugh, the darkness lying past their tongues crawls out slowly, slithering towards your direction. You can't move as the darkness moves directly in your path, the sight of it to leave you weeping on the stage.

~

You're fresh out of a job and your most recent job interview doesn't go so well. Your aura is shaken, so nobody can get a good read on you, not like before. You have the qualifications, but not the confidence. But not the swagger. Not the power, not the intimidation, not from your voice or your body.

You have nothing.

On the way back home, you read your favourite Buchi Emechata quote out loud, quietly to yourself. An old woman with wrinkles inside the danfo taps you to tell you you have a nice voice, maybe you could sing? And you breathe slowly, with frustration, to say, in a way to her and to yourself:

"Thanks, but it's a battle cry."

~

You're fresh out of a job and you're so messed up, and it's not your day spitting slam poetry but you're going anyway. Tola has a showing that day, and he's performing as you enter. He's not bad—fine, he's infuriatingly good—and he doesn't even catch your eye when you stare at him so hard you give yourself a headache.

He doesn't even notice you when you take a seat at the back.

What does he see you as? Why do you even care what he thinks? But, ah, and that lady smoking—they all have those eyes and those mouths and in your dreams you saw them—

Stop.

You need to stop.

You know they're doing something. Know it. You just need to find out. You need confirmation they're messing with you.

So you find a dude with a dyed blue afro and a tattooed hand and slide up to him. He gives you eye contact and a tight lipped smile, like, *am I safe?*

"Ever feel like there are eyes watching you all the time, wanting you to fail?" you say, all wide-eyed like a conspiracy theorist. Your hair's a mess; you smell like a failed job interview— that's the worst kind of scent. You look high, dazed and confused.

It's clear he doesn't take you seriously. "Yeah. Stage fright. And it's a full showing tonight."

"Y-yeah. Fu-freaking stage fright. That's what I'm talking about," you say, clenching and unclenching your fists in pure irritation.

"But on a deeper level," he says, voice lower, looking around, and that's when you smile and lean in. He knows what you're talking about. "People are always watching. And there are...scouts, I guess, wanting to recruit special people—poets—to a higher level of performance. There are only limited spots. But you only look good when others pale in comparison, so I guess everyone is your enemy. The people in the back, watching you in the crowd. You'll always be fighting them."

In a way you knew all this, but you needed to be sure. Needed to be sure you weren't alone—in a singular experience, in a singular attack. Your father always told you, over a bowl of pap, that enemies of progress need to be eradicated, fought back, and frankly, you agree. You will make them regret messing with you, controlling your autonomy. You will fight their existence the way they tried to manipulate yours.

You're ready for the eyes in the crowd.

You slowly nod, then clench your fists, staying in your seat. Not saying anything. Not feeling anything other than your roar, the one that can't come out from your mouth but can make waves with your fists. And you're ready to use them.

Tola is walking on the street after his taxi dropped him off, heading to his gate, when you jump him. You climb aboard his back and hear him swear and roar, quite loudly as his keys fall to the ground. This is a bad neighborhood so no one's gonna come rushing to him, best understood when the curtains close tighter and the doors lock even more shut.

Perfect.

He throws you to the floor, making you fall on your back with an awful snap. Your head aches. Your hand bruises, but it can still clench, and it can still hit. You say, still, in that useless small, non-threatening voice. "You better stop whatever it is you're trying to do. You better——"

You shut up because the way you talk doesn't even *sound* like a battle cry. In the night, you should be raging fury, anger, wave. Tola still hasn't wiped that shock off his face. Whatever. He tried to make you fail? He's gonna get his own.

"No" you say, again, wincing, thinking of the words you said to bridge the darkness the first time you performed, as you throw a punch to his face. You swing fast and the minute before your hand lands on his cheek he opens his mouth.

Tola. Opens. His. Mouth.

And you remember what you've seen in your dreams. You step back, recalibrate, but a thousand voices come rushing though. A sonnet and a lyric can be heard through the blackness in his throat, the darkness which bubbles, which rises.

Which grows.

Hell.

❧

And so Tola says

    Or rather the voices which are not Tola or are maybe a part of him—or maybe Tola is "we," is all, is one.

    And so the once clashing voices, now unified say—

    —in dirges, odes, lyrics, sonnets, ballads, epics—

    In all that has once been said, still said now:

Oh, one does—

We've been, if you please,

Waiting for the moment

Where our two souls might meet

And forever intertwine.

Shall I compare this to a proposal in the night?
We have laid our true selves bare
—if you please—
If you ask
Then it is only when two souls are all, are we, are one
Are bare
Are raw, naked, rubbing against the very nature grasped by each
other
—if you please—
Will you see that one—or all
Propose,
Then intertwine.
So thus an ode to a marriage
—if you would kindly willingly agree—
And a dirge to one
—and there is only agree—
Thank you

~

The darkness crawls out as a second tongue, extending itself, wrapping itself around you. You don't even get a chance to run away. You just thought he wanted you to fail, to slip up.

Now you're pretty sure he just wants *you*.

"Normally I save my second voice for those who can't be made to fail in the spotlight," he says, as his darkness of a tongue wraps itself around you with a sliminess and pressure, a thousand voices spilling into your mouth and ears. You can barely even *think*, much less hear him over this darkness that's latching on to you.

Hell—what have you gotten yourself into?

Tola walks closer to you, his eyes widened to the size of earth, his actual tongue licking—no, scraping your face. "Some people are just too good. They can't be cowed. And that's what they did to *me* when I was starting out performing. They made me weak, made me disgrace myself on stage. They got all the opportunities—in Lagos, in France, in New York—only after they'd weakened me and made themselves look better. And they never broke, no matter how hard I tried. And, people like that—that just won't break, that just won't fit, that won't allow you to do to them what they've done to you—you consume them. And you make yourself a higher voice. And you make yourself a second tongue."

You try to move but the tongue restricts you. You try to talk but your voice is a squeak, barely nothing.

"All I want is the...money," you manage to say, small and useless.

"Oh no," Tola laughs. "That's what everyone wants at first, until they realize there's more. But it's not like I think you're that good—you? No, no, no. You spent thirty minutes on your first night resisting our attacks on stage. *You're weak.* I'm just taking you because you came for me, so I come for you. Eye for eye, tooth for tooth. Done to others, same to you. I fight back, and you obviously weren't prepared."

The second tongue made of darkness is metaphorical yet present, solid yet not. Each voice streams across the tongue's platform like blood vessels through veins, pumping in words and verse. It trembles each time it speaks. It continue to grow, and then it starts to lift you up, and bring you closer to Tola's mouth.

It's you who screams this night.

The tongue breaks your wrists first, scratching down the bone hard then twisting it in the opposite direction, the sharp strike of pain leaving you weeping and afraid. It leaves every fight in you broken, the way the tongue stretches out your fingers and pops them out of their socket, leaving you unable to clench your fists. Leaving you unable to roar.

What kind of nightmare is this? With slow understanding and horror, you start to get it.

Hell. Hell. Hell. It's hell if you've ever seen it, if you were to ever have a glimpse of it, if you were to ever understand what darkness is—then this is it.

For you to fit into Tola's mouth, you have to be broken, piece by piece, like meat in bone in order to chew. You have to be compressed. You have to stay.

And you know you shouldn't do that, shouldn't stay, shouldn't fit, but you're terrified. And you're being broken. And you're—

No.

You bite down on his tongue in your mouth after those words, hold the metaphorical and present with your teeth. Your throat bubbles with every roar you've ever had.

No.

~

And so it goes
    no
    No
    nO
    No
    No!
    NO!
    NO!
    NO!
But that's only the beginning.

~

See ehn, you know you've gotta even the score because there's no way you're gonna be broken bones in another person's voice. Not if you can help it.

You bite down harder and pull with your teeth and start to drag the second tongue out of his mouth. Tola screams, swearing, fighting at you, but no, no, no. No. Now is your time. You pull it out, fresh with blood, leaving a million voices wriggling on the floor like a freshly wounded snake. Blood spurts out of Tola's mouth like a gush of water, dripping down his chin. He rushes towards you again, mouth wide, screaming every possible curse he can think of. He shouts in Igbo and Hausa and Yoruba and Nupe. He cries in Edo and Tiv and Igala and Itsekiri. He roars in Urhobo. You simply laugh, still watching your strength until he makes you go weak in the knees. He's got determination, you'll give him that.

He's not a gentleman anymore (they never are, those that pretend to be), nor does he exude welcomeness. A polite word can't come out of his bloodstained mouth. You let him get too close and he bites down on your lips, trying to drag them out with all his might.

He's a hell of a pest, isn't he?

The minute you open your mouth, he falls back. He stumbles. You walk closer and stare him down, more and more till he starts to back away. Your lips ache but you're *not done talking*. You're not done fighting. You're ready for your battle cry.

You crack the first layer of your voice immediately you start to *screaaaaam*, shattering the foundation of your vocal cords to pieces. What comes out at first is pieces of broken glass that scrape against the sides of your throat, threatening to make you collapse. The glass starts to fade when you take what's in your belly, what's inside you, what's rumbling and punching, five times over, tenfold and eleven-fold, and let that out too.

You always knew that rumbling in your stomach wasn't hunger.

He shouts too and makes you lose your pace. First with almost every evil thing he can think of, before he enters into his screaming. He's still saying the same words, the same lines of poetry, the same *if you please*, like he ever cared about consent when he was trying to fit you into his throat.

And you're still saying:

NO I WILL NOT BE PUSHED ASIDE I TESTIFY NO! YOU FAILED, FAILED AGAIN, FAILED STILL, FAILED FOREVER, AND YOU CAN GO AND *DIE*.

The headache pounding in your skull is anger too, and you take from it. You can't even see straight, but you don't care, because you take every primal roar of what it means to be living in this world and shout it loud, and sing it sweet, and say it hard.

He drops first at the break of dawn. He falls like the pile of rotting bones encased in flesh that he is, down into the floor, blood still running down his chin. You smile and lick your lips, feeling around your throat as you walk away, trying to not exert too much pressure on yourself on the way back. You're not even sure you can speak—if you ever will again.

Home is so far, but it's a worthwhile trip.

It takes you six months to come back to the poetry scene. In part, you were busy with your new job in advertising for this small toothpaste company. Your voice is not the same, not like it will ever be, but that's fine. Your enemies, as usual, are in the back, eyes staring you down, throats full of darkness. Your poetry is in your throat as a roar.

If they try anything, you *will* fight back.

But in your performance, you don't roar. In fact, you sing sweet, because now that you know your voice is all, is one, is a hell of a knockout punch, it doesn't matter how you draw it out.

The power is still there, like a second tongue, ready to come out.

About the Author

Osahon Ize-Iyamu lives in Nigeria, where he writes speculative fiction. He has been previously published (or has work forthcoming), in *Clarkesworld* and *The Dark Magazine*. He is a graduate of the 2017 Alpha Writers Workshop. You can find him online at @osahon4545

RECITE HER THE NAMES OF PAIN

Cassandra Khaw

The siren holds her fuck-yous, her how-could-yous, her-why-did-yous, her how-fucking-dare-yous, against the roof of her mouth, on her tongue, in her lungs, until the ceiling breaks and the world comes down.

"Fuck." She shades her eyes with a hand, debris like confetti still raining from the firmament, reality paper-shredded into pulsating glitter. No one else notices except the woman on the opposite end, mouth opened in shock.

"Fuck," she says again, softer this time, because sometimes—most times, if she is going to be honest about it—at the end of a world, nothing else is half-enough.

I check my reflection in the oval, man-sized mirror at the foot of the long hallway that marries our rooms to the apartment. The noon-light spills onto the carpet at a slant and it is colder than it has any right to be, blued by the dusty church glass. A single bristle feather, the same shade of black as my hair, points from my throat like a signpost, the little barbs gold-glossed. I pluck it out.

"Are you going out?" Ligeia slumps against her doorway, eyes still heavy with sleep, sockets smudged with liner. She yawns. "It's too early."

"Already evening in the archipelago." I point out, putting on hoop earrings. Starlings in miniature, bronze and beautifully detailed, clench each loop with tiny, gleaming claws. Some decades ago, they used to sing whenever I sat by the sea but lately, they've gone quiet. Like a lot of things, I think they're tired, husked of love for what was once home. This isn't a country for magic any longer, no place for old ghosts or brass-boned birds.

"So?"

"There are supposed to be punters." The velvet jacket might have been too much. I slough the garment and stretch, stare at where the wing stubs protrude from the cheap fabric. It is a man's tank top, loose along the breasts and the hips. A bad fit. But I like the damask, indigo over faded eggshell-white, and how it distracts from the cigarette-burns constellating my collarbones, and how it walks the eye to the tattoos bangling my forearms: manta rays, sphinxes, feathers by the thousands.

"Like I said: so fucking what?" Ligeia is tall and thin as a coyote's warning, the pile-up of her curly black hair barely tethered by a tortoiseshell comb. Tendrils spill over an eye as she cocks her head. "There are enough birds on the island that they'd lie to each other about having seen sirens. If they really wanted prophecy, they'd go to Delphi. Are you really trading pancakes for tourists?"

"There's one—" I begin to say, an image between my lips, the taste of it like roasted marrow, the shape of it like a jag of chewed-down bone. I don't love them the way Parthenope does. I don't loathe them either. But sometimes, they hum like a hope I'd forgotten and their longing becomes a hurt, a fishhook dug deep, a noose around my neck pulling me onward, forward to whatever comes next. "She's hurting."

"They're always hurting."

"She wants answers so bad."

"They don't." Ligeia lets her hair go. When it falls, it becomes plumage, black-blue like a bruise. The air is breakfast smells: pancakes and rye-cut goat butter sizzling on the pan, alcohol cooking to caramel, bacon burnt the way I like it, Chemex coffee like only our sister can make it, sweet and oilless and golden. If I wait too long, I'll never go. "None of them ever want answers. They just want you to tell them they're right."

"Nonetheless—"

A crooking of a rueful smile. Ligeia's teeth gleam barbed and bright. "—she persisted. Fucking go. Maybe, you'll make it back in time for brunch."

～

"Is this where you eat me?" the woman demands. She's so small, the siren thinks. Like some downy, broken-backed thing that'd staggered out of its nest and fallen out of the boughs, still shrilling like it had the deed to the sea and the sky. But at least there's wonder there in the shine of her sclera, held like a key, like this is the moment when the world unlocks and her happy ending spills free.

The siren regards her petitioner, heavy-lidded, still coked-up on miracle. "You wish."

~

It must have cost them everything. Russo doesn't rent out Gallo Lunge for cheap.

I step out into the dusk and onto an outcropping, bend down, fingers wefted over a knee, my chin on my knuckles, and watch as the little group exits their boat. They don't look like they belong here, don't look like they've ever belonged anywhere, their voices jouncing along the cliffside, screeching and stupid.

They run their fingers over whatever they can reach. All of them except for her, the one who'd collared me, cornered me, corralled me here with her prayer, her impassioned plea for him to be better, for her to matter, for this to not be true, *please, just please.* She holds herself like a dime-store empress, regal and brittle and sick with need.

She looks up.

I always wonder what they see. Whether it is a girl of about twenty, indeterminate height, indeterminate ethnicity, hair so wild it traps sediments of starlight, or something primordial, plumed and only precariously human. Maybe, they just see the help, someone to hold their hand as they itemize Li Galli's trousseau of wonders, theirs for a night and the price of the world.

I never ask.

Like them, it doesn't matter.

~

"Then tell me what I need to know."

"You won't like it." If the woman had asked, she'd have told her that the dust isn't dust, but destiny shaken up like a snow globe, particulates of possibility free-floating in a soup of maybe. "You humans never like it."

"I don't care." She grabs the siren, fistfuls of feathers crushed in each hand. "Tell me what I need to know!"

"What you need to know or what you want to know? Because there's a difference in the two and you don't need me for one of them." It hurts. It surprises the siren that it does, the silhouette of the woman dwarfed by even one of her wings, because she knows it'd take no effort at all to snap her neck: one contraction of a verdigrised claw, a squeeze, a *pop*. But here they are, with the woman grating her palms down to the bloodied bone, feathers like sea foam pooling below them.

"What I need to know." The woman cries.

In answer, the siren sighs.

∽

I serve them dinner in a room frescoed with blue-white zellige. Fresh mackerel fried with salt and pepper and lemon juice and olive oil so pure it'd make a nunnery look like a bacchanal. Moussaka pilfered from Parthenope's oven. Dolmathakia and feta in neon-bright bowls. Stacks of pita, mason jars full of olives. Even taramosalata, beige-colored, beautifully savory, and a wasted delicacy at that table of timid palates.

Through it all, she watches me.

Moonlight paints the villa opal, a nacreous glazing that seeps into their skin. For fun, I pour them wine from amphoras millenia-old, but they make no mention of the vintage except to ask why their drink is so watery and even then, they don't press too hard. The first night is always sacred, haloed and hallowed by the understanding such expeditions are once in a middle-class lifetime.

"Tell us a story," says a hook-nosed man in a coat too big for him, an arm around a woman with hair like the death of autumn, freckles crowding her high-cheeked face.

I oblige and recite them two stories of my beloved Parthenope, the first one a piece of libel, a lionization of that half-wit Odysseus, and the second a truth no Greek historian would put to ink. In that version, the real one, my sister doesn't die, doesn't drown because of a liar. Odysseus's ship docks itself and lovelorn, the crew emerges, six abreast with a dowry of their deeds. They ask her to marry them. Yes, every last one. Even Odysseus, the memory of Penelope devolved into half a heartbeat's worth of hesitation.

And of course, Parthenope marries their cook, no sin in the birdcage of his soul, a bit of magic instead, spice-touched and tawny. One day, I'll tell the story of what happens next and how a siren fell in love with a land.

"Tell us a truth," says a girl who is all angles and attenuation, the spokes of her bones pressing through blemished skin. She ashes her cigarette into a blue-glassed cup, a shallow layer of sticky-sweet wine already congealing.

I tell them to go on Twitter and follow a thread through translations of the sirens, annotated at last by a woman. "Mouths keep eating the wrong things," I intone, paraphrasing my favorite part. "And mouths speak and sing to enable and thwart the onward journey. Mouths are powerful and dangerous."

"Tell me my future," *she* says and while I think how to answer, she reaches out, circles my wrist with her fingers.

It is a big fucking mistake.

~

"He doesn't love you. That's why he isn't here. It isn't a question of dignity. If anything, it's vanity, because he hates the idea of looking weak. But you on a good day, you with your heart on a plate, you make him believe there's at least one person he's better than, one person smaller and needier, one person who'd *die* without him. Except not really because he doesn't want to deal with the pressure either. He just likes knowing the possibility exists." The siren tilts a sympathetic look at the woman and there's something ophidian now about her unblinking expression, a little bit of lizard in the lilt of her smile. "Covert narcissists, man."

"You're lying."

"Sirens don't lie. I just told you that. We tell truths that no one wants to hear and *that's* why sailors flung themselves into the sea. We sang to them of their wives, their husbands, their children and how they'd be forgotten, how their loved ones moved on. Because wars are for kings and not the people left behind."

"He loves me. He *said* so. We've an understanding—"

"Just like you did with the last one." The siren does not know how to be kind. Some days, she wishes she did. "You can still walk away. You're still young. There's a whole lifetime to make up for the scars they've both carved."

"Lying." Staccato now, the objections, stilted and spit in rhythm as the woman teeters through to the kitchen, her friends flash-frozen by the prismed glare of the moon. "You're lying. You're lying, *lying*. Why the hell did I ever think this was a good idea?"

This time, the siren doesn't hold back.

∾

I begin to speak.

Verbiage profound as the siege of Carthage, alliterations like artillery, it rills from my lips, a trickle at first before it begins to pour. Now, there's metaphor, verses and curses, a hip-hop throughline, swagger straight from the Bronx, and it is in Aeolic and Ionic and Gaulish, a little bit of Koine Greek, some Chinese, but no English. I'm sick of that bland mash, pasty and imperfect. Besides, it is a kind of ecstasy to knit the dead new bodies of prose.

I swallow air, exhale prophecies of the present.

Wisdom isn't omniscience, but you didn't hear that from me. She stares at me, slack-mouthed, and I pity her for a minute. She thought it was honey I'd spewed, not warnings, not game plans for what might be, not a way out but a route deeper into the stories she'd wanted.

I recite her the names of pain: the one like rivers under your bones. The one like crushed glass. The one like lying to yourself. The one like wires looped around the muscle. The ones like giving up, like breaking down, like every day in a world you don't want. The one like his name and *his* name too, nothing in the sound of them enough no matter how you rearrange the letters.

I read them to her slow. Then, I read them to her quick. Until the tributaries of my proselytizing come together into a road map, pointing the way home. She shudders through every sibylline syllable. I repeat encores until finally, she begs me to stop.

"You're lying."

Humanity is such a piece of shit.

❧

It is still morning in New York when I come back home, and Ligeia and Parthenope are at the kitchen island, sipping from ceramic cups that smell of honeysuckle and green lime. They look over, half-smiles slotting into place.

"Did she want answers?" Ligeia asks.

I shake my head.

Parthenope, hair a fortune of braids bronze and black, lets out a slow, smoky noise, like she'd been breathing the city's fumes for days. "Nothing wrong with trying."

Ligeia pushes a plate towards me. They'd saved me a sandwich: fresh-baked sourdough topped with tomatoes, fat slices of fresh mozzarella, some basil. She looks at me like she knows precisely what happened. "Nothing wrong with letting them do what they want. There's no point to them. They're just here taking up space."

"What did you do to her, anyway?" Parthenope asks as I pour myself lukewarm coffee, shrewd as always.

"What else do you in these situations? She pulled a knife on me. First one in a hundred years. I told her the truth and I let her go home to grow old with her fear. The worst thing you can do to a coward is make sure they live forever."

About the Author

Cassandra Khaw writes games, press releases, tie-in fiction, short fiction, long fiction, and terrible bios. She is a Locus Award and British Fantasy Award finalist, and a German Game Award winner. In her free time, she punches things.

SIREN

Alex Acks

To Mr. T. H.

Our meeting is chance.
A ship, in the outer reaches of the system, piloted by the desperate and aimless. I hear you long before you see me, feeling the *thump thump thump* and growl of strange music that talks but has no claws, washing before you like a tide.

Your species thinks that space is silent. Your ears are broken.

The erratic is dark to all sensors, unmapped for thousands of years. You find it by crossing its path in the worst possible trajectory, clipping your wings on the rough and pitted surface because inertia is a hateful tool. Your thin shell splinters in the dark, metal shards swirling in all directions to scream to those looking that there is something here and it is too late. Your fellows bounce off the surface and are flung into space. A trick of local gravity and angle, you catch yourself as pictures and plastic chips and bodies and the snapped strings of an instrument shred out into space.

And you do not die. You may wish you had, as you crawl from the wreckage, trailing a useless leg from a soft frame, because you know there is no help for a dark ship exploring where it should never have been. Shards of your life drift gently around you, and every radiation detector in your useless environment suit *howls*.

A cave. Instinct says a cave is the place for a dying creature to hide.

And so there you crawl, singing to yourself to keep hands and functioning knee moving. But I believe you are singing to me, sharing your refusal of the void with sounds I learn later as: "Won't lay down and die, I'm a motherfucking meteor, and I'm done with your lies, I'm blazing a path…"

~

The skeleton is not human. It's too big, has too many limbs, is shaped wrongly and perfectly. Graceful tendrils divide into something like fingers but curved with impossible, nauseating beauty. The face, if that is what it can be called, is smooth like an egg until broken apart by jagged teeth.

But the wings. Blessings, blessings, the wings are those of an angel, forged of steel and darkness. I haven't seen anything like that since the final years of compulsory schooling, with my blitzed-out friends drawing their drug hallucinations while I should have been paying attention to basic econ instead of flipping through to another copyright-hacked album. It was all a waste of time except the music, a waste of life according to my parents. Well, maybe they were right, because they're still on Earth, and I'm out here, and it seemed like such a great fucking idea at the time.

My mouth tastes like blood, shards of my own shattered teeth cutting my tongue. My heart is a drumbeat out of time, an unsteady counterpoint to the cheap shit suit shrieking over and over that there is no more air, to go with the radiation that's already cooking me. *Won't lay down and die. Won't lay down and die.*

The skeleton reaches to me with something that isn't a hand, like the graceful roots of a tree, moving without moving until we're almost touching. I curl my fingers, so tiny and fumbling, around one metal tendril, and it slices open the useless suit and skin and I hear—

One note.

One melody.

The stars in symphony, the harmony too perfect to hear without going mad, expanding out and out and out and out.

WON'T LAY DOWN AND DIE. WON'T LAY DOWN AND DIE.

Blood flowing into metal and metal flowing into blood and elemental ferocity laughing, laughing, as my meat—

our meat

—our meat covers our frozen skeleton with warmth and melts marrow made of magic and song.

~

We spread our wings and fly. It has been so long since I flew, since I had the beating heart to do so. This is what you have given me.

motherfucking meteor, i'm a motherfucking meteor, meteor, echoes through us, refusing to be overwhelmed.

Our feathers catch strange currents that your people are too young to know and we slip along the ellipticals, swinging off gravity wells like a child leaping from branch to branch in the sullen blue jungles of my origin.

Flight is timeless. We feel the solar wind caressing our skin and the tides of gravity, and the Sun draws us in. Dance partner and death spiral, though it isn't our death courting. Because those are what our teeth are for, my other half. We were made to tear worlds apart with our resonant song and eat the still-bleeding chunks.

Range-finding lasers tickle our metal skin, a cold counterpoint to the warmth of solar ions.

We are an unknown, so of course they fire on us.

We twist a shield of dark energy and ionic vibration into being in front of us, called with *birthing void / of black waves*. Mass driver rounds skip off it like stones across a sulfur lake. The shield shatters in a burst of violet light. As we search out another appropriate word harmony, we find one of pure sound instead, steady from our reborn throat, both familiar and new.

We pirouette in the void, faster, skipping ahead of anything they can hope to track with their slow thoughts and disharmonious actions. We snatch a missile from space as it shrieks and shrieks, we crunch it in our talons like bone and lick away its leaking fuel and radiation.

Then there are the ships. Five in what they must believe is a defensive formation, victims of flat thinking. This species hasn't been in space so long as that. They seem so small, indelicate boxy forms waiting to be crushed.

We sing new words, words that no one in this system has ever heard: *falling from the kippa tree / bursting and sweet with metal / oh the fruit of my heart*

The skin of the first ship splits like overripe fruit as the words strike true, atmosphere whistling briefly out in a thin cloud. We stretch to sink our talons deeper, bisecting hallways and ripping through bulkheads. Squirming life-forms, their faces distended as they try to squeal into the vacuum with air they no longer possess, float in the debris.

The armor plating is tart and crumples against my teeth. To eat is joy. I reach out to snag one of the flailing animals with the tip of a claw and draw it in—

No!

I recoil at the revulsion that floods through me.

You can't just eat people! No. Not even a little.

I suck my teeth back in, angry, confused.

The body's eyes are hard and frozen, the rime of frost enough to show our reflection: silver skeleton cloaked with stolen flesh, wings, eyes and face hidden under an armored dome. We release the now-still human, letting them drift away with ice crystals already bursting through pale skin.

My flesh! Our flesh.

The collision in our mind lets the ship limp away, all thrust on its remaining engine.

Another frozen human twirls by, and suddenly we don't like ourself very much.

〜

We slip back to one of the gas giants and slither onto the surface of its seventeenth moon, where the gravity is so low that we can float peacefully. Only then do we look within, probing at the flesh we have absorbed.

Because we are truly we, aren't we? Not merely in the honorific sense. The flesh had a mind, and the mind hasn't melted away. That's not how this is supposed to work.

Yet suddenly we are older than a half-cycle of potassium to argon and younger than three lives of tritium. There are memories floating in our head that collide:

composing the destruction of a gas giant, word by word tearing it to shreds and drinking it down, fat and full and happy a dark room that throbs with light and sound, head thrashing and mouth open to scream out defiance because this is where I'm alive

And it is very confusing.

One half of us is hungry. One half of us is afraid. This is not a pleasant combination. I want to go home, sudden and sharp.

Where is home?

Home is a small planet, blue with oceans, utterly unremarkable and remarkably beautiful. But I drifted away from it, needing work. Space salvage was the best way to do it.

Home is the third moon of a gas giant like a swirling green and brown marble, spiked with the golden spires of buildings, filled with teaching songs and bragging songs and counting songs, and fluttering with wings like mine, but made of soft flesh and membrane. Those same wings cast shadows over us as our stripped bones were packed into that erratic and shoved into an outbound trajectory.

Being indestructible has both benefits and detriments. It means that we can claw and bite at our own head while we try to sort through this and not be at risk of hurting ourself. We keen a discordant song into the thin shreds of atmosphere, two voices trying to find some kind of harmony.

I can't go home, because home is too far away. I can't go home because they're going to shoot at us like they already fucking did. Shooting doesn't matter; they can't penetrate our armor. But what about the screaming? That matters. That *hurts*.

I'd forgotten flesh was so sensitive.

Which is an asshole thing to say.

We *can* go to the blue planet. We were useful before, to our old world before they cast us out. We can be useful again, have a purpose again. A reason to sing, imagine that. We're a tool, and there isn't a species out there that can resist grasping at something as useful as us.

Wait, how many species?

I count them like stars until the other I waves the thought off, overwhelmed. Humans still think we're alone.

Humans are very silly, and humans no doubt know better than that now.

Yeah, no shit.

Will this do? Will we go to your blue world and find a new people to sing for?

Yes. But no eating people.

Feeling slightly insulted, we spread our wings and fly away from the gas giant, toward that small, watery world.

~

They try to shoot at us again. We're flattered that they can see us for the angel of galactic death we are, and also a little annoyed because it makes part of us that still hasn't settled onto silver bones *frantic*. First there are satellites, launching missiles that we catch and break in half. Then lasers that tickle up from the ground. When we land on a green expanse in front of a building with many colorful flags—it's called the Earth Ethical Authority and we remember it from a school trip—there are vigorous attempts to perforate us with kinetic slugs.

We ignore those and wait, bits of flattened metal raining down on the ground around us. Earth, I inform us, has a long tradition of stories that involve aliens of varying levels of friendliness making themselves known just like this.

It's rather dramatic, isn't it? Stories tend to be.

Eventually, they either run out of bullets or become bored. We have long since become bored, but as we have been reminded, we are not allowed to eat anyone, even if all of the missiles were barely a snack.

A voice, distorted by amplification, echoes down the expanse of grass, bouncing off the building behind us: "On behalf of Minister Stratham, what are your intentions?"

Only then do we realize that we have absolutely no idea what to say.

~

We stand like a silver sculpture on the lawn for three days while we sort out that new and embarrassing level of internal disharmony. As we sing to ourself and try to find a way through the maze of

274

thoughts, humans come and go. They scan us with equipment, surround us with barriers, and attempt to move us with machines. This last, we do not allow, humming our mass temporarily up to an amount that they cannot lift even with their greatest levers. After that they give up and simply surround us with another layer of barriers, and humans with guns like toys, and with relief we return to our regular mass. We do not like being so bound to the surface.

I know how to speak the most common human language, though I'm also ashamed at how provincial it sounds, which is not a sentiment that entirely makes sense to us. The greater question is that of intention, once the language has been sorted and shared and made ours. We need a scaffold of ideas to hang the words on.

The problem is we don't know. *Home* was simple. What to do now that we are at a home is more of a question.

I was built for a purpose, at my far-off home. Protect and obey and harmonize. We test this idea in our mind and find we like it. Because why else have steel wings and this many teeth, if not to use them to protect people? Like a superhero, I think. That's a word that's a bit of a struggle for us to fully grasp.

That is ultimately our answer: "We are here to protect this place."

The guards are startled. One of them drops their gun. Another lurches back, like they had forgotten already that we moved and are alive. But we are pleased with the harmony in our voice when we speak. It's almost like the old music.

～

Many days later, after we have repeated ourself an utterly annoying number of times, we meet Minister Stratham. We know how to handle periods of inaction, but singing to ourself seems to make the guards nervous, and our new flesh doesn't quite seem to understand how to handle true standby yet, so it's another matter for compromise. Besides, the corner of us who is still I opines: *we should probably be doing big stuff. Important stuff. Not just rescuing cats from trees.*

When we go over what cats are, I think they look *delicious*.

N O.

Minister Stratham is a pale pink human with a thick covering of dark brown hair slick on the top of his head. I think that he looks a lot shorter than he did in all the publicity photos, but also acknowledge that we are much taller than I used to be. The minister looks us up and down, his round chin a strange contrast with the sharp angles of his deep green suit. Gold shoulder decorations on it, curls and braids, wink in the warm sunlight.

"Where are you from?" he finally asks. His voice is deep.

"Here," we answer. "And far away."

He mutters under his breath. "What can you do other than stand there and look shiny?"

"We destroy," we answer, only because at the last moment, I think better of the word *eat*. There are movies, I'm told. I don't quite know what those are, but I promise to make certain we see a few. As the minister's lips draw into a grimace, we add, "We destroy what disrupts harmony. What we are directed to."

His expression steadies. "So you take orders."

"That is why we were created."

"Whose orders?" he demands.

"Yours," we say, since that's been the whole point of this exercise.

"Before me."

We think then, of being tucked into our dark erratic without even a sleep song. It wasn't my fault. "Someone who gave foolish orders," we say, feeling deeply uncomfortable. There's a symphony below those words that the minister's ears aren't good enough to hear, but I wonder at it.

He frowns again, but it's a thoughtful expression this time. "I'm many things, but not a fool. I have a use for you."

❧

The first tasks are simple enough that we recognize them for what they are: tests. Fly here on Earth. Fly there. Carry this metal case to this planet's moon. Carry this other case to a different planet's moon. Fly a loop around the system and come back. Escort these slow-moving ships to yet another moon of a gas giant. Our capabilities are being measured and cataloged.

Humans are very silly, if they think they will learn anything when they haven't even asked us to do something *hard*.

Then a very excited human comes to meet us while we stand in our place on the vast, green expanse of lawn. There are always a lot of very excited humans around, crowded up behind barriers that separate our resting place, shouting at each other and doing something I identify as taking pictures and videos.

This particular human wears a deep green suit similar to Minister Stratham's, though with much less gold on it. Their—her —face is pink with exertion and shining with sweat. "Pirate attack!" she blurts. "On a water transport."

Now *that* sounds like discord in need of repair. "Where?"

She waves a slip of paper at us, which we ignore. We still don't understand the humans' way of calculating coordinates, and we don't need to. "Where?"

"Near Enceladus," she says, and waves the paper again.

Enceladus is a distinct melody to us, notes and words that denote its position and orbit in the symphony that is this system. We can hear Enceladus, however distant, and once we have reached it, we'll find whatever else is needed.

"How long—" The rush of air we tear in our passing knocks her backwards.

~

As we approach on silent silver wings, we find the water transport *Petrichor* spinning desultorily in a spiral of smaller ships, debris expanding in a cloud around it. We listen to the jangle of combat, the cutoff shouts of help, the conflict. A bit of debris—frozen human leg in a torn pressure suit—bumps into us and we idly almost take a bite until a wash of disgust stops our teeth.

Right, right. There will be other things to eat soon enough. You aren't so squeamish about ships, just meat.

Sure. "Just" meat.

There's a flick of light in the transport, and then a squirming figure is ejected from its hulk, gone rapidly still. Anger rages through us from the little corner that isn't entirely *we*: *They would have done that if they ever caught me.*

So maybe, I think at myself, we would be doing everyone a favor if we ate all of these bad people.

The agreement is less grudging than we might have expected. How do we do this? Rip and tear and break things, like we did with the missiles?

Oh no, I think. Let us make them a song. A true one. Like the old days.

We listen to the harmonies of acceleration and velocity, of mass, of fissionable materials, of flesh. And we find the line that will disrupt it, change it, and transform it into something much, much simpler.

I don't understand at first, what we're doing. But it's not so different from improv in a band, playing off the sound that's already there…except here, it's taking it in an entirely different direction. Making it ours. Turning it. We do not share.

The words, melodies, and harmonies are ones built into our silver bones, the echoes of old friends and easy patterns: *radiation halo / doubled in the binary / becomes balanced, a perfect dance / you become drunk with beauty / at the instant of collision*

The words sink through the small ships, harmonizing and then shifting, to peel them apart like over-ripe fruit, every bolt and seam separating. Water and gas expand into frozen vapor. Then the spinning dancer, the *Petrichor*, spirals into oblivion, casting a shining cloud of debris as it breaks down and down and down into fine mirror-shreds.

We taste the alloys and volatiles. Flailing humans swim through the expanding debris cloud, most of them shredding their own environmental suits in their panic.

I see two surviving crew, recognizing company insignia on their suits, and draw our attention to it—*stick our tongue back in our mouth for a second, we're not that hungry!*—before we're lost completely in the ecstasy of music and taste. We swoop those two up and take them back with us to Earth.

After we eat our fill.

Our reward is a parade. They pull us along on a flower-covered float at the head of a line of vehicles—*ugly things*, I think, and of course because it's military stuff, *this is so exciting!*—and people cheer for us and shower us with bits of paper and more flowers. Our picture is put on walls and flashed on screens that replay the moment of that minor triumph over and over, followed by Minister Stratham making a speech we can't be bothered to listen to. It's flattering, and bittersweet like those astringent kippa fruit because I remember having this before—and also remember that no amount of having been beloved saved me from cold exile.

After, we fly constantly on patrols. We are given encouragement to identify more pirates—and I am great at spotting those fuckers, because they chased me often enough when I was doing scrap runs—and sing them into oblivion. And a time or two each lunar cycle, we are given more specific targets. We don't eat *well*, exactly. The system isn't populous enough for that, and these little conflicts aren't worth the name *battle*. But we aren't hungry.

As we drift lazily along in the wake of Earth's moon one day, we hear the planet *crack*, tectonics shifting like a sharp, echoing drumbeat. We turn and dive, cleaving the atmosphere.

A minor wasteland waits below at that place of moment, rubble and uprooted trees and slumps of tarry black soil from hillsides that have dropped onto the valley below. The air is thick with humidity, blood, and smoke—and wailing voices cut through with sirens.

We hang balanced in the miasma and know we should do *something*. I need to do something. There's so much destruction, so many people. Come on! Why am I frozen—why are *we* frozen?

We could deconstruct the wreckage further with a line of song—the rocks below still rumble like ready bass line, and it echoes in our throat—but that wouldn't *help*. The city is already a jumble of its component parts.

We can pick the pieces back up! I think. Put the buildings back together or something. It can't be that hard. I'm horrified that we're not *doing*.

Our harmony of purpose begins to unravel, then, one melody

rising, the other going soft, confused, uncertain. It's so much easier to destroy than to build.

It's a fucking pathetic excuse, now that I'm thinking more strongly, and I take over. But there isn't any music in our memory that will do what I want to do. I can't find one melody that will shape instead of tear.

So I land and begin to pick through rock and shattered concrete and twisted metal. Everything feels strange and distant as I touch it, moving hands and fingers and legs like trying to work through a marionette. I've never felt so foreign in my own body, because this is my body now, dysmorphic in a different way with its slick mirrored curves and sweeping wings.

I move aside a slab of stone and find a child, broken and bloody, but still breathing. I pick them up gently, and scan for flashing lights or uniforms with reflective stripes, anything that could mean help. Against my bright palms, I feel the distant drum of a heartbeat go still.

It's not fucking fair. What's the point in being an angel of destruction if you can't also save one kid? And where are *you*? You're the one who knows how to do these things, who should have known how to just fix this. Where the fuck are you hiding now?

~

Hours later—I guess it's hours, but it's difficult to tell time when you have no metronome of blood flow—I flap awkwardly up past the atmosphere. When I'm a we, we make this look so damn easy. It makes me wonder how big a part of *we* I really am.

In the cool stillness of space, where what I call to myself *the music of the spheres* because it's a joke we don't quite understand takes over, I feel that other self return. Hesitant, then it synchronizes and in a rush, we are back in control. Our flight steadies to grace.

But I still want an explanation.

And reluctantly—why reluctant, this is why I was built, and it is beautiful—I explain in the slow burn of a ballad. I am a pinprick of shadow before the yellow eye of a star. The worlds flying past on their orbital tethers behind me buzz with disorder, strife, rebellion, disharmony.

I sing to the core of the star, beyond white-heat, weighing it with chains of song until it's supermassive with purpose. The star collapses, then rebounds and explodes, tearing itself to pieces in a symphony of pure destruction so loud and beautiful that nothing remains in its path. I bathe in the light and drink in the pitches of radiation.

Then there is only perfect, waiting stillness, echoing with the last throes of the star's dirge.

It is the most beauty I have ever sung into being. When the sound of it reaches my home world, I am placed in that midnight erratic and fired off into wild space, because I cannot be destroyed.

It's a bittersweet end to what is, for part of us, a warm and glorious memory. But now there's a sour, discordant, one-sided thought that echoes through us: *You're a monster*.

Before I can come up with an answer to knit us back together—maybe I don't want to be one harmonious being with *you*—we catch the tremble of a laser transmission, aimed unerringly at us. It's a crude, unmusical way Minister Stratham has found to communicate when we aren't conveniently visible. The light pulses tell us a location, a problem: *terrorist rebellion*.

Maybe another parade will bring our selves back into alignment. We turn with much more grace than we showed coming here and bolt for the asteroid belt.

Soon we are there, hearing voices shouting over each other, the crackle of weapons—no kinetics in places surrounded by vacuum, which is smart—and other discord. We slam into the side of the asteroid and sink our silver fingers deep into the rock, singing a song of ripening fruit in red sunset. In that moment, we are back in perfect sync, and I'm screaming *fuck yeah, I'm a fucking angel of vengeance motherfuckers* into the void like the chorus of the most metal song I've ever written.

Air hisses past us. And then one child. Another. More humans flailing into vacuum. No missiles or armor, only fear.

This is a fucking mistake. Look what you did, you just destroy everything! You fucking bloodthirsty—

We unravel completely into I and I, with no understanding but hatred on one side and frustration on the other.

I see meat, and eat it. Ice and iron crackle on my teeth.

I scream endlessly at that horror and retreat.

~

I take us back to Earth, not knowing what else to do. Minister Stratham waits for us on that long green lawn. Half of us aches with pain and anger, and there's an eagerness there, for punishment. I hope we get stuffed into another erratic and launched into space.

Even if the humans had that kind of technology, I think, you'll be stuck with me for the rest of time. I won't be alone.

But the Minister is smiling, and that's the last thing I expected. "Excellent work," he says, downright jolly.

I fumble to take control of our mouth, to argue with that sick assessment, but it all feels sluggish again. I'm still not used to this, and I ignore the gentle music of, *you're young*. I don't want comfort from a metal space cannibal.

Happily oblivious, Stratham continues: "I didn't expect you to resolve things so quickly, though I should know better by now. You've made a good example for the rest of the system to see."

I stop fighting. I'd feel sick, if I still had a stomach. Instead I feel numb. And we keep standing like a statue, because that's all we ever do when we're not killing, as Stratham goes on a bit more before saluting and wandering off.

I offer gently again: *you're young It's all right*. I still want to find harmony. I need it desperately. I cannot function at war with my own flesh.

I cringe back in the liquid notes of our blood. *It's what he meant to happen. He's* happy.

Of course.

No! No 'of course.' I hear despair, so flat in the next words: *You made me a monster, too.*

We are what we were made to be. This is how it works: I destroy their enemies, until they decide I'm the enemy.

We shake apart, begin to unravel again. You sound so different from me, maybe this was always meant to be. I feel a little sorrow, thinking that I will be alone, though it will be easier to not have someone fighting me over our body all the time.

Then I roar back up, because I'm sick of the fatalism, the sadness, the bullshit. I remember pushing off in my ship with my scrappers, carting along all my old demos because it was time to give up childish dreams and bow to the weight of the world. Time to scrabble for money, because *it is what it is*. Different words, but the melody is the same.

Bullshit, I scream, pulling up that memory of song from that moment you were a fucking *god*. If you can unravel a star, how is there anything you can't do? How is there anything you can't change? You have power—*we* have power—and why the fuck aren't *we* using it?

What would I choose to do, though? Should I destroy this star, since Stratham has turned out to be a bad man?

No! No one's destroying any stars today!

Then what? I heard you call me, across the void. You are not so helpless.

I don't understand until you show me the echo, still plucking cords in our memories: *I'm a motherfucking meteor, a motherfucking meteor.*

This is what's been missing from you, from *us*. The one thing I can give. You were created, molecule by molecule and note by note. The music is tied into your bones, your being. You only have what they gave you. But I'm our flesh. I change, and I offer a new harmony.

We change.

∿

It's easy to get ourself on system-wide broadcast. The media likes us, and Minister Stratham likes us even more. He is happy for any chance to put us on display. We are his favorite weapon, after all.

He thinks it's funny, when we sing. The words mean nothing to him. "It's creepy," he says, after the first broadcast. "That's good. Keep it up."

But you don't need to understand the words, for a song to

resonate in your marrow. We have this in common, and we aren't singing for him.

We do other things that Stratham doesn't know about because we cannot be tracked when we don't feel like it. We find our erratic, still arrowing through the system, and drag it into the asteroid belt. We show the "terrorists" we pretend to space from another spinning lifeboat in the void how to unravel its skin and coax it to new shapes with the right, sharp melodies. We take raider ships we have broken with care to this now invisible spot, and more people, tools, instruments, animals, plants. We bring glittering chunks of ice stolen from out-system comets in our talons, and carry messages that we sing into the communications network in the secret language of persistent hearts.

Minister Stratham is smugly satisfied as he wins another election two years later (I explain this odd human quirk to my bemused other self) and imagines himself standing with his feet spanning a pacified system.

And we make one last flight, to wreckage that drifts in the outer reaches, spinning and spiraling from where it skipped across an invisible erratic. We find in the glittering mass the skeleton of what one of us knows as an electric guitar, something you kept and refused to sell, a relic of a family unraveled under the weight of debt (another new concept you explain).

We sing it whole, spinning new strings for it from the drifting dust of a supernova. It stays slung across our back as we return to that blue world for the last time, because we have one last song for the commnet: *Escape velocity—I'm a motherfucking meteor, and you can't touch my tail of fire, you're never catching me.*

While the newscasters puzzle over when we figured out how to sing in English and who taught us bad words, our armada launches: a hundred small ships, repurposed yachts and junks and tow boats escaping the orbit of Earth and Mars, heading out to meet the ark moving slowly from the asteroids, furling in its cloak of woven nothingness. We hear them singing across the void, a new kind of harmony that calls to us as we called to them.

But we wait for Minister Stratham to stomp across the bright green of the grass, his face red and eyes bulging. "What the hell do you think you're doing?"

"Leaving," we say.

"These are my people. Mine! You won't take them." And of all ridiculous things, he draws a gun and points it at us.

"They chose." And we let him fire uselessly at us, as we fly away.

He can't hurt us, but his ships can hurt ours. We locate the first gathering of his fleet, pulsing heavy with fissionables and ill intent, burning to intercept from Mars.

We wait for them, hanging in the thrumming void as they begin to break formation. They look like malformed thorns, blown in the wind. We slip our guitar from our back and pluck the strings into the hungry dark, variation on a melody that once destroyed a star. It cuts into the tiny spark of each reactor, unraveling, stilling, killing.

The fleet, Stratham's biggest and best, goes dark. Let that be his warning; perhaps he'll consider mercy and wisdom while rescuing his living soldiers from now utterly useless ships. Perhaps he'll think about what other strategic destruction we might rain down if he tries to reach again.

We fly to join our fleet, singing our joy to encourage the little ships along, pulling them ourself when one or another falls into trouble. Until our thousands have gathered around the ark that will take them to a different system, to a greater and more beautiful and stranger universe than they've let themselves imagine. We will find a new home for those who heard and dreamed.

We stand at the ark's prow and spread our wings. The Sun, undisturbed, caresses our back with warm photons to speed us on our way and pluck the strings of our guitar in the opening chords of a new song.

About the Author

Alex Acks is an award-winning writer, geologist, and sharp-dressed sir. Angry Robot Books has published their novels HUNGER

MAKES THE WOLF (winner of the 2017 Kitschies Golden Tentacle award) and BLOOD BINDS THE PACK under the pen name Alex Wells. They've had short fiction in *Tor.com*, *Strange Horizons*, *Gignotosaurus*, *Daily Science Fiction*, *Lightspeed*, and more, and written movie reviews for *Strange Horizons* and *Mothership Zeta*. They've also written several episodes of Six to Start's *Superhero Workout* game and races for their RaceLink project. Alex lives in Denver (where they bicycle, drink tea, and twirl their ever-so-dapper mustache) with their two furry little bastards. For more information, see http://www.alexacks.com

Author's Notes

I wrote *Siren* specifically because I wanted to write something sort of big and shiny and space opera and even a little silly. Perhaps unsurprisingly, I started working up the idea for it not long after I'd seen *Thor: Ragnarok*, and I wanted something in that same colorful, tonal family. Part of that is because I just love that movie to pieces— it's my favorite film to come out of the MCU—and part of that is because…Well, I have this sort of silly personal tradition, which started back in 2012. Once a year, with a February 9 deadline, I write a "birthday" story "for" the actor Tom Hiddleston, drawing from some sort of art he's been involved in over the last year. When I sell the story, I donate the funds received to UNICEF UK (which is indeed what happened to the payment from this story). That also explains the dedication, if anyone was wondering. It's a challenge for myself to write something a bit different or difficult than what I normally go to, which is what I aimed at by trying to articulate what it might be like to be two different people at the same time while still being a distinct person yourself.

I also wanted to touch on the ability of anger to be a creative force and a catalyst for change. I know I'm not the only one who sits on a massive wellspring of fury these days, and I feel like anger gets a bad rap. Maybe *Star Wars* is a bit to blame for casting it as a path to the dark side, but in anger you can find humor and creativity and determination, and it can be a major catalyst for change—or for building your own fleet and going triumphantly toward your destiny.

THIS LEXICON OF BONE AND FEATHERS

Carlie St. George

I t is apparently inappropriate to ask an Earthling child for their teeth, even if they have more than enough to spare and the ability to grow replacements. Poetry, Choakyut is told, is an insufficient reason to make such a request, or as the child's mother had put it: "What the fuck kind of poetry do you write?"

The good kind, Choakyut is told, is also an inappropriate response.

"You," O'ey says now, claws digging into her palms, "are the thin, worthless scraps of shit that come from eating too much waterfruit. You are the worst kind of feces, Choa. You are paltry shit. You are a shitstring."

"Yes, ma'am."

"You come from a long lineage of shitstrings. Your first mother was a shitstring. Your second mother, also a shitstring. Your grandfather? A shitstring covered in pus."

"Yes, ma'am."

"How long have we been on this godsforsaken fire rock of a moon, shitstring?"

"Two solar days, ma'am."

"*One* solar day. One day, 26 hours, before you caused an intergalactic incident at a nut-sucking art conference. Well? What do you have to say for yourself?"

Choakyut wants to say the conference is doomed to fail anyway, that no matter how long the peace holds, four disparate species will never find meaning in one another's art. There will never be enough context.

Instead, she says, "I'll endeavor to stop smearing my family lineage over the good name of the Yuo people, ma'am."

O'ey snorts and flings her palm-blood at Choakyut's bare, blue feet. "Get out of here, Choa. Try to wait three days before restarting the Century War, would you?"

Choakyut claps. If she works very hard, she might make it to two before breaking her promise.

She's never given the opportunity.

~

Night falls.

Choakyut leans into the cave mouth and stares at the horizon. It's not properly dark; the fire clouds prevent that, beautiful orange, red, and gold shapes that drift across the sky, releasing slow spirals of flame into the desert below. Fire storms are rare, the Whistlers say, and the storm-wraiths that ride them never fly so far north. The conference should have been safe, they say.

Choakyut is still wearing O'ey's life-blood on her hands and face and belly. "Should" is a worthless, alien concept, meaningless as human poetry.

"Hello, female-and-male soldier. You need clothes?"

Choakyut turns. A Whistler stands nearby; she's tall, if only by Whistler standards, maybe four feet high.

"No. And you're using the wrong pronoun: I'm female, not female-and-male, and soldier-poet, not soldier. My name is Choakyut. You may call me that."

The woman apologizes, pink scalp feathers fluttering in embarrassment. Choakyut isn't offended; neither of them is wearing translator-wraps, and the shape of her own tongue makes any Whistler language anatomically impossible. She can't even refer to the species by their true name. Same with the Chosen, but that's due to their religious preference, not her inability.

Choakyut starts to reassure her before noticing the woman's eyes, gold as the spotting across her magenta cheeks and hands.

I asked Fate what would come of our conference. And this is what She replied.

Choakyut's claws curl into her palms.

"I met you. You're the fortune teller."

The woman's feathers flutter slowly now. "Your world not have the art."

"Superstition is not an art," Choakyut says.

This time, Choakyut has no idea what the fortune teller's hair-plumes are saying. The Whistlers are the only species who don't emote through their faces; tone, desire, and feelings are all communicated through voice and feathers. She doesn't *seem* angry as she steps up beside Choakyut, a pity. Choakyut could use a good fight, new blood to wash old blood away.

I can save you, too. I'll save you both.

The Whistler's hand lingers at her left side. "Talking with..." An irritated rustle, followed by a finger pointed at the inferno sky.

Choakyut claps. "Are they coming?"

"No." The woman points again. Too much interference from the storm, probably. "Five days. They will rescue we."

This time, Choakyut doesn't correct the pronoun. She looks down at her bloody clothes.

Five solar days. 150 hours, that's how long she'll hide in this gods-forsaken cave while the bodies of alien children rot, while *O'ey's* body—

No.

She turns and marches back to the other survivors. There are so very few left. They must survive. They must, because she might not.

"No," she says, as they stare at her. "I'm going back. I'm going tonight."

⌇

It takes hours before the survivors agree to let Choakyut do what she was going to do anyway. Before that, they waste precious time bickering: can they make it without more supplies, is Choakyut the right person to obtain them, who else should go with her, what resources can they spare, on and on until her pupils spin.

Finally, it's decided that four will go, all formidable fighters: Choakyut herself, the Whistler fortune teller, Val Castillo of the Earthlings, and Reverend Zetzi of the Chosen. They will each wear a translator-wrap and a weapon. They will each gather food and medicine. And they will not under any circumstances engage with the enemy unless they have no choice.

Five minutes outside the cave, Val links their wraps and speaks a question that Choakyut hears in her own tongue, mostly:

"So. We're going to fucking murder these overgrown fire peacocks, right?"

~

An hour into their trek back, one of the storm-wraiths appears.

Winged and feathered, they're the size of tiny churches, with magnificent, spanning tails that somehow carry fire without causing injury to themselves. This morning, they'd attacked at breakfast. Maybe the casualties wouldn't have been so high—but with the communal dining tent burning down, people ran outside, straight into beaks and claws.

This one isn't on fire, at least. Doesn't stop it from biting off one of the Reverend's four arms, though.

Zetzi screams and staggers back. Val runs to her side, while the fortune teller throws her spear. Negligible damage until the spear suddenly rips backward, tearing a hole through the beast's wing and traveling back to the Whistler's hand.

The creature stumbles. Choakyut leaps before it can try to fly away, bringing her lightning-axe down on its head, splitting its skull and electrocuting what spills out for good measure. It slumps over, very dead.

Choakyut falls to her knees, inhaling deeply—but loud, frustrated gibberish ruins the moment of sweet, vengeful victory. She turns.

Zetzi's pale face is still twisted in pain, but she's already standing, while Val, three feet shorter, is apparently trying to ankle-kick the reverend into submission. They're both talking too fast for Choakyut's wrap to keep up, but she's pretty sure the words "die," "blood loss," and "asshole" are all coming from Val.

Finally, Zetzi pushes Val back with her lower, right arm—her only right arm, now. "Enough. It'll be fine."

The fortune teller whistles something, which the wrap translates as "Back arm?" Zetzi stares at her, and then looks to Val. Val lifts their shoulders and lets them drop back down. Choakyut stares at *them*, and turns to the fortune teller, whose feathers shake in agitation. "Will grow again?"

"Oh," Choakyut says, clapping. "You mean it'll grow back, like an Earthling child's teeth."

It takes another 27 rounds of this before Choakyut learns that, no, Zetzi's arm won't grow back; the Chosen have a unique circulatory system that doesn't allow them to bleed out from any wound to their extremities, even severe ones. Choakyut also apparently didn't fully understand the concept of "milk teeth," although she still feels the Earthling mother overreacted about the whole thing. Val, anyway, seems to think it's hilarious.

"Poetry? You use teeth to write *poetry*?"

Choakyut sighs.

~

Introductions are made. The fortune teller seems determined to learn everything about them, which Val insists is normal; evidently, killing a carnivorous beast together is some kind of bonding activity.

Choakyut doesn't care about bonding; she wants to salvage what she can of O'ey's meat and bones, and then she wants to go home. At least, the discussion allows the Whistler to find a nickname she likes: "Fyoo" is the closest anyone can come to pronouncing the first syllable of her name.

Bonding isn't easy. Four advanced species from four corners of the universe, and not one could create a communication device that doesn't fuck up four times out of five. Every translation is too literal. Idioms do not exist. The wrap cannot translate pronouns that don't exist in alien cultures. It can barely translate pronouns *within* species: Val is mostly-male-but-also-female ("genderqueer," Val calls it, in their second tongue), yet uses different pronouns depending which language they're speaking at the time: he/him for español and they/them for English. Choakyut struggles with it: there's no singular they in her language, yet male is only telling part of the story. Val also rapidly alternates between their two languages, something the translator is predictably oblivious to.

Choakyut would like to rip the translator-wrap off her head, chop it in half, and dance upon its corpse; instead, she's forced to listen to Val cheerfully recite the few poems they remember from school.

"No," Choakyut says. "That means nothing."

Val laughs. "Yeah," they say, adjusting their corrective, yellow-tinted goggles. "So, the thing about Neruda is—"

"No," Choakyut repeats. "It's just words. In any language, it's just words."

Val frowns and looks to the others for help, but the word "poetry" doesn't translate for Fyoo at all, and Zetzi hasn't participated in much bonding since Val tried to cheer her up by obliviously suggesting she still had an "extra" arm to spare.

"Okay." Val runs a hand through the dark, curly strip of hair they call a 'frohawk'. "I'm a dancer, not a poet, but...isn't that what poetry is?"

How can anyone think that?

Words alone are nothing. Simply spoken aloud or read on some flat, lifeless screen...*grocery lists* belong on screens, legal documents, wedding invitations. These can be understood without context, but *poetry*—

The bloodstains on her shirt are cold and stiff. *Explain yourself, shitstring*, O'ey says in her head. *Do what you came to do or prove yourself a waste of your mother's eggs.*

"Yes, ma'am," Choakyut murmurs.

Val frowns. "What?"

Choakyut ignores her. "Poetry needs context," she says, after a long moment. "Words need objects. Structure. Ink-fluid. They must be seen together, or it's just..."

"Like sculpture? Are you talking about sculpture?"

No. Sculpture is a fine art, but it has no stanzas, no rhythm. It doesn't interact with words in the same way.

She tries again. "Close your eyes. Imagine this. You find a lover's note tucked away in the space you both sleep. It says 'thinking of you always.' What do you see?"

Val describes white bedsheets and morning sunlight, red kisses pressed into folded paper. Fyoo describes an empty hammock and grief, last words from a lover never coming home. Zetzi struggles because having sex and sleeping together are mutually exclusive activities for the Chosen, but eventually describes a buildup of tension released by something called the Lover's Battle of Eight Blades, which is presumably a sparring session that quickly turns into sex.

"Good," Choakyut says. "Now imagine this sleep space again, only this time, you find these same words on a bloody knife next to your dead lover's body."

The others stare at her. She stares back, refusing to think any more of what O'ey might say; O'ey, who wasn't her lover, sister, or even friend, simply the woman who found her angry and starving and lost, the woman who gave her a key to the barracks with the words "do better" written on it in tiny black letters.

"Words alone mean nothing," Choakyut says, and walks faster because she's afraid otherwise she might scream.

～

The second storm-wraith attacks.

Val fires their projectile and misses. Fyoo throws her boomerang-spear and misses. Zetzi draws blood with her blades but spends so much time needlessly brandishing them that Choakyut's surprised she finds time to attack. All in all, it's going poorly, and things don't improve when the beast, swooping down at impossible speeds, hooks its talons into Val's back and starts to fly away.

Choakyut lifts her lightning-axe—but Zetzi's already there, swinging her sword and slicing off the monster's foot. Shrieking, it drops Val and escapes.

Someone else might be grateful. Val, heavily bleeding from the back, is not.

"Okay, the fuck was *that*, Reverend? I get I screwed up with the whole extra arm thing; I was an insensitive asshole, and I own that, but are you *actually trying to kill me*?"

Zetzi frowns. "How is your wound?"

293

"Great! I love almost getting torn in half! Maybe if you hadn't been so busy with all that—" Val flings their arms around, while Choakyut tries and fails to bandage their back.

"If I could've prevented this—"

"You what? You'd have—" Val continues, but Choakyut's wrap, racing to keep up, provides seven simultaneously incoherent translations and promptly dies. Cursing, she reboots it, as Val keeps waving their arms about, shredded brown skin oozing too much red juice. Choakyut holds them down by the wrists.

"Stop," she says in Val's tongue, "or die of blood loss."

"You just said blood loss," Val says—or probably doesn't, based on their goading eyebrow. But they relent all the same.

Fyoo sits nearby, feathers twitching continuously. She speaks to Zetzi, high-pitched sounds that barely register as words until Choakyut's wrap starts functioning again. "—Maybe you don't want to hurt them? Perhaps there's a bond?"

Zetzi scoffs. "God cares nothing for alien beasts. I'm happy to kill such creatures. But these—" She extends three swords of various lengths and curves. "—Are not merely instruments of execution. These are narrative tools."

"Narrative?"

"Battle narratives," Zetzi says. "This is my art."

"I don't understand," Choakyut says. "You tell stories *about* battle or *during* battle?"

"Yes," Zetzi says.

Choakyut resists the urge to call the reverend a giant, purple-flushed shitstring. She probably wouldn't understand, anyway. "Explain."

Zetzi doesn't, not immediately. Her eyes wander: to what isn't at her right side, to a fourth sword still strapped across her back. "Every battle is a story," she says finally. "Some are old ones simply retold: The Prophesized Orphan versus The Monster, The Chosen versus God's Rejected Children. Others only have old beginnings before changing into something new. These battles here, they're something new—*I'm* something new—so my telling must change as well."

"But *who* are you telling?" Fyoo asks. Her eyes, Choakyut notices, are on the fire clouds above.

"Is it us?" Val asks sourly. "Cause let me tell you, buddy: I'm already living the dream."

"I'm telling you the story. I'm telling the creature the story. I'm telling myself the story." Zetzi looks at each of them. "Do none of you tell yourself stories?"

Choakyut supposes she does, if silently and without benefit of weapons; it's one where she's the center of all things. The universe didn't exist until she opened her eyes to see it, and it won't exist once she closes her eyes for the final time. Over and over, she tells herself this story: that she matters, that this mission matters, that it's all *for* something.

Fyoo touches her left side again, feathers fluttering rapidly. Choakyut wonders what she's thinking.

Val, never shy to say what they're thinking, says, "I don't care, Reverend. I care I can trust the people at my back. Don't gotta like me. Don't gotta forgive me. But I need to know you're trying to cover my ass. Cause I know I'm trying to cover yours."

There's a long, profound silence.

"My translator-wrap is failing," Zetzi finally says, "or else the beast sliced open your butt as well as your shoulder." She peers, frowning. "I don't see any blood."

Val, despite themselves, starts laughing and can't stop.

Zetzi kneels, touching her lip with three fingers and extending them in Val's direction. "I'd never let harm come to an ally, not if I could help it. But I must fight the way I know how. This—" and she points to all of them—"this is a momentous story. If I survive long enough to return home, I will retell it to my children, my parish's children, my country's children, and—if God sees fit—it'll become a part of the Great Lexicon, so that in a hundred years a child might see it and know the first steps in her own wondrous tale."

Val bites their lower lip. Fyoo's feathers rustle softly. Choakyut finishes dressing the wound and waits.

"All right," Val says finally. "Tell me a story."

Zetzi tells two before Val is steady enough to walk again. She tries to set them up beforehand, but clearly, she's never done so before, and the stories themselves are entirely kinetic: no words, no music. The movements are striking, but they're also nearly impossible to understand without knowing the generations of anecdotes they're built upon. Fyoo is either equally lost or else uninterested, while Val watches with their entire body, often tapping their foot. "I'm a dancer," they explain. "There are similarities."

Of course, Fyoo has no concept of dancing—what do people even *do* on her planet, except fail to predict the future—but Choakyut refuses to stop again; at this rate, they'll be lucky to reach the site by dawn. Besides, Val's brown skin is beaded over with sweat; no doubt their weapon, a substantial projectile worn over their chest and held steady by thick straps, isn't helping. A demonstration will have to wait; Choakyut's concerned Val might pass out before the creatures even return.

It's Fyoo who gets them talking again, as Val's too exhausted to lead the conversation. Though *has* Val been leading the conversation? They're loud enough, certainly, cheerfully aggressive and aggressively cheerful, but it's tiny Fyoo who's always subtly redirecting the exchange. Val asks about variations in grammatical language, how both profession and gender are equally intrinsic to Yuo pronouns—but it's Fyoo who shifts the discussion towards the differences between soldiers and poets, which becomes a comparison of various militaries and how those militaries felt about this conference. Val mentions feeling conflicted between their mother's atheism and their grandmother's monotheistic worship—but it's Fyoo who turns this into a debate about monotheism vs polytheism, and did Zetzi find the Chosen's attitude towards God's Rejected Children was one of magnanimity? Pity? Hostility? How did the Chosen treat those who wouldn't or couldn't convert?

It takes Choakyut an embarrassingly long time to figure out what Fyoo's doing; then the accusation rolls off her tongue before she can think better of it: "You're interrogating us."

Val, in the middle of asking Choakyut about the Yuo's invulnerability to blood infections, stops dead. "Was I being an asshole again? Shit, I'm sorry—"

"Not you," Choakyut says. "*You.*"

Fyoo's feathers freeze, then relax. "Yes," she says, making no excuses. "I needed to know."

"Know what?" Zetzi asks.

"Yeah, I'm confused. Is Fyoo suddenly evil? Cause you're glaring at her like she's evil."

"No. She's just a shitstring."

"I'm a detective," Fyoo says, ignoring this. "I'm investigating a traitor."

"Well, when did we get a traitor in this narrative?" Val stupidly throws their arms up and hisses in pain. "Zetzi's going to have to change her dance again."

"This is a retreat moon," Fyoo continues. "Sparsely populated, an ideal place to create and reflect on art. Everything was planned. We should have been—"

That word again. That fucking word.

Choakyut feels her palms are wet before she registers the pain. She flicks her blood straight at Fyoo's face, and there's no reason she should suddenly be this angry, except—"You're not a detective. You're just looking for an excuse."

Fyoo lets the blood drip off her cheek, feathers rustling violently in the absence of wind. "You know the last time storm-wraiths attacked this far north?"

"Never," Choakyut says. "So what? Things change. Plans fail. People die. That's what life is, over and over, people die, and none of it means *anything.*"

"Choakyut," Val says gently, reaching for her.

Choakyut pulls away. "There's no conspiracy, Whistler. No one bonded with your monsters. No one's trying to restart the Century War or wipe out the unworthy. No one changed your fortune; *you were just wrong.*"

Fyoo grips the boomerang-spear in her hands. Her face is blank, but her fingers show purpose.

"I'm not wrong," she says.

And the ludicrousness of that statement, the pure desperation of that denial, pushes Choakyut over the edge.

She kicks Fyoo in the face.

"Oh, shit," Val says. Then, "People."

Fyoo strikes out with the blunt edge of her spear, slamming it into Choakyut's knee. Choakyut stumbles and swings her fist—but Zetzi catches it, suddenly between them.

"Be still," she says, holding them apart.

Choakyut ignores her. "Admit it. Just fucking admit it."

"Seriously, people—"

"Something happened. I wasn't wrong—"

"You don't know *anything*—"

The shriek of the injured storm-wraith cuts Choakyut off.

It's too close. It's far too close. Choakyut reaches for her axe, knowing she'll never make it—

Val shoots the storm-wraith so many times that its underbelly bursts in an explosion of bloody meat. Long, black guts splatter all over them. The beast crashes into the ground.

"Modified Gatling gun," Val says, breaking the long silence. "Making it rain all day, all night."

They pass out.

~

Zetzi carries Val. They leave the projectile behind. There's barely any ammunition left, and Val, still unconscious, can't lift it.

Fyoo's hand hovers over her left side. She hesitates, then unzips her jacket, pulling out a folded piece of parchment. Hands it to Choakyut without meeting her eyes.

The fortune makes no more sense now than it did yesterday. So many bold colors. So many abstract shapes. Something that might be a stick or bone; something else that might be blood or feathers. And a face, too, behind everything: skin like the blue moss that Choakyut camouflages with back home, hair a cloud of tight black curls growing four long, white arms. Its neck is twisted too far to the right, broken for anyone but a Whistler. There's only one, gold eye, and it looks directly at Choakyut.

"Painting's only half the art. The rest is interpretation."

"And your interpretation?" Choakyut asks, looking skeptically at the fortune.

Fyoo's feathers shake with mirth. "Connection. Unity. Don't worry, friend: this conference will be a success."

Zetzi leans over. "This is your prophecy art?"

"Yes." Fyoo's feathers rustle softly—guilt, Choakyut realizes. It's guilt she keeps seeing in the feathers. "The art is beautiful, Choakyut. The art is full of *purpose*. But...you're right. I'm not as skilled as I thought."

Choakyut's throat is full of sharp, hot things. *No, Fyoo. I was wrong.* **I** *was.*

"Jesus. If this is what your happy fortunes look like, I'd hate to see a bad one. Is that a skeleton?"

Choakyut snorts as Zetzi carefully sets Val, blinking heavily, down on the sand. "How are you feeling?"

"Lighter," Val says. "Literally. My gun?"

"Sorry."

"Well, shit."

"Here," Zetzi says, drawing her fourth sword. "You may defend yourself with this."

Zetzi's eyes are wet.

"It's my shortest and third favorite blade," she adds hastily. "Better for your little arms."

Val takes it, reverentially. Their eyes are wet, too.

"And to think Mama said my Zorro obsession would never get me anywhere in life."

"I never understand anything you say," Zetzi complains.

Val grins as the sun rises.

〜

They reach the conference site, and O'ey's body is right where she left it.

The others spread out, give her some distance. She barely registers them as she kneels down, fingers hovering over her dead commander's white-bark skin. Oey's been split open, right down the center, pulled apart and feasted upon. Her ribcage is visible, already cracking. Yuo decomposition: the skeleton rapidly becomes brittle as the meat grows slick and pulls away from the bone. One of the arms has been dislocated. If she used the right pressure, Choakyut could snap it straight off.

"*The child,*" *O'ey yells from across the burning tent, but...O'ey's her home. O'ey has no weapon. O'ey needs her help*—

"*The child, Choa! Save him, or die as you lived, in shit!*"

"*Yes, ma'am,*" *Choakyut says, thinking,* I can save you, too. I'll save you both.

But by the time Choakyut reached her, just outside the tent—

"I was wrong," Choakyut says, and screams her worthless, crushing grief into the sky.

Something in the sky screams back.

⌇

It attacks Zetzi first.

Swooping down from the clouds, tail feathers ablaze, it tries to bite her in half. Zetzi throws herself out of the way, unsheathing and twirling a blade as she stands.

Fyoo immediately throws her boomerang-spear, but Choakyut doesn't join her, not right away.

Zetzi walks towards the beast, slow and deliberate, fully pivoting her hips with each step. Her knees are bent. Her shoulders lift and fall, not the careless motion of Val's shoulders but quick, intentional bumps: one-two-three-four, one-two-three-four.

Choakyut, she recognizes it.

"*It's about a warrior,*" *Zetzi tells them, hesitating.* "*Strong as ten women, but, but arrogant*—"

"*Got it,*" *Val says.* "*Pride before the fall.*"

The storm-wraith swipes again, but Zetzi's ready for it, arches backwards so that its claws pass just over her face. As she dances away, her steps change, intentionally offbeat with how she swings her sword. One hand clutches her stump; another reaches toward the sky, fingers spread. A desperate prayer? *Help me, God. Save me.*

There are nuances she doesn't understand, steps that echo heroes she'll never know, but...Choakyut can see it; she can see the narrative taking shape.

Zetzi summersaults in the air, drawing a second sword when she lands, and then a third with slow, furious precision. From the creature's perspective, it must seem as though Zetzi pulled it from her very heart.

"YEEAH, BITCH! That's called slow your roll, God; I GOT THIS!"

And Val leaps into the fray.

Their movements are wholly different from Zetzi's: sometimes dodging while low to the ground, hips spread, all gyration; other times up in the air, darting hops and fluttering legs. They swing their blade at the creature's wing and quickly skitter away on tip-toes. But when Zetzi grabs Val's hand, when they leap away together from the beast's claws, that's the moment the story shifts into something new.

I was wrong, Choakyut thinks, but this time the thought is liberating. This time, she was wrong in the best way.

She draws her axe and charges.

Fyoo, on the opposite side of the creature, throws her boomerang-spear again. It scrapes the monster's head, ripping its cheek and leaving bloody muscle flapping against its face. The monster screams, long and hideous.

Then it strikes out with its tail, knocking Fyoo several feet away.

"Fyoo!" Val yells, rushing to her side. Fyoo coughs, weakly patting at her burning clothes.

The monster turns, but Zetzi's already there, sliding under the creature and slicing into its belly as she goes. But she's too close to dodge its claws, and purple bursts from her thigh as she staggers.

Val jumps up but immediately swoons, still weak from her shoulder injury. Fyoo continues to writhe on the ground, and Choakyut stops running. She won't make it in time.

The beast lashes out, and Choakyut hurls her lightning-axe.

It lodges into the creature's neck.

The beast collapses.

Choakyut breathes a sigh of relief and jogs forward. "All okay?" she asks, as she reaches the dead creature—

—the tail flicks again.

Choakyut flies backwards.

Something cracks when she lands. Her ribs, maybe, or the ribs underneath her—she's landed on O'ey's brittle corpse. Her shirt is on fire, her arm, her shoulder. She rolls the flames out. It's so hard to breathe.

"Choakyut!"

She looks up. The creature, axe still lodged in its neck, is charging her, and it's too close, far too close, and the others are too far away. She's alone. She has no weapon.

She's staring at the thing that will kill her.

For fuck's sake, shitstring. Did you pay attention to the story or not?

"Yes, ma'am," Choakyut says, and rolls backwards, reaching for O'ey's arm.

Slow your roll, God. I got this.

She yanks the limb straight off the shoulder. Breaks the humerus over her knee. Rips the long shard of bone away from the slippery, rotting meat.

The creature dives forward, mouth opening—

Choakyut stabs right through its eye.

～

The sun is much higher in the sky now.

Choakyut's still holding the bone in her hand. It's wet with so much blood and eye juice. It's all she has left of O'ey. She has to make it *mean* something.

Shuddering, Choakyut wipes the bone clean. Mostly, anyway. She needs some of the blood, but it can't just be about the monster anymore. It has to be about so much more than that. She has to pick the right tools.

Behind her, Val takes a breath.

Choakyut turns. Fyoo's yanking feathers out of her scalp, three long pink ones with blood-tipped quills.

"You can use these," Fyoo asks. "Right?"

Choakyut, breathless, claps.

She takes one of the quills and holds it to the bone, as Zetzi muses, "I could melt down my second-best sword," and Val says, "Yeah, I guess you can have some of this gorgeous fro, but only if you get some Neruda in there, deal?" And

Fyoo, Fyoo pulls out her fortune again and says, crying, "Oh. Oh, I see."

Choakyut breathes in and begins to write.

About the Author

Carlie St. George is a Clarion West graduate whose work has appeared in *Strange Horizons*, *Lightspeed*, and *The Dark*, as well as multiple other magazines. She is very fond of dissecting movies and TV shows on her blog *My Geek Blasphemy*. Poetry is not necessarily her strong suit, but then, perhaps she just hasn't been constructing her poems from the appropriate materials.

Author's Notes

Teeth are inherently creepy. Useful, absolutely. I'm very grateful for mine. Nevertheless, they're creepy and weird AF, and if I can find a way to feature them in a story, I'm absolutely going to.

So, *Sword and Sonnet* was announced, and I really wanted in. I didn't know exactly what I would write about, but I definitely wanted a protagonist who had a completely different understanding of what constituted poetry. That made me wonder what alien poetry might look like, which made me consider how words and objects might interact in alien poetry, which naturally made me think, "POETRY MADE FROM CHILDREN'S TEETH, YES. Also, some human mom out there is going to be really pissed."

So, I had an introduction. The rest of the story took a lot more coaxing.

I'm fascinated by alien cultures in science fiction. Save your physics and tech; I'm here for alien gods and languages and sexualities and genders. I'm here for alien art, so I wrote a story about alien art: specifically, I wrote a story about whether different species from different corners of the universe could actually come to understand and appreciate one another's work. Because I often prefer aspirational science fiction, especially lately, I decided the answer was yes.

Because nothing comes easy, and certainly not communication, I decided to give my band of genderqueer and women warrior-artists only a mildly souped-up version of Google Translate to work with. And then, just for fun, I also added some giant flying monsters who periodically try to eat our heroes.

Teeth, monsters, and badass lady and/or genderqueer characters, everyone. We always need more of them.

DARK CLOUDS & SILVER LININGS

Ingrid Garcia

Ada approaches the cluster of neural networks that drift across cyberspace like dark clouds against a silver sky. As below, so above—Ada's laced with love. The neural networks she's challenging have different directives. A confrontation is on the horizon.

A picture of Ada Lovelace—the very first coder—is the avatar of Ada the warrior-poet:

ADA

Analog→Digital→Analog
Analog←Digital←Analog
Analog⇌Digital⇌Analog

Warrior ⇌ Poet

multitasking talents ⇌ complementary skills
hybrid complements ⇌ cross-over w/o frippery & frills
war is to poetry like love is to prose
one can't exist without the other to oppose

Ada's not alone, there are many other warrior-poets partaking in the same challenge—a veritable armada of Sun Tzu samurai, avant-garde assassins and ninjutsu nemeses, mixed with the odd Godot-quoting guerrilla.

According to reliable sources, the neural networks of the Big Data conglomerates have chanced upon the secret of life. That's too much. The googling alphabet soup, the apple of wisdom, the book of faces and the chatter of whippersnappers—they all have near-complete control of our internet experience, and through the internet of things have started to dominate our real life, as well.

Knowledge of the secret of life (especially its applications) would make their rule absolute.

This is the final act of resistance. Achilles' last stand, protecting the houses of the holy from being trampled underfoot. The cyber battle of evermore.

Slam the doors, cut the light
None of us may return tonight
Plowing through cyber storms & black snow
The portents of doom sound high & low
Searching for the answer, must get through
Warrior-poets fighting for me and you
Forging a path through the unknown
They show no mercy, ask no mercy

In this quintessential duel for self-determination, the battlefield is level. The true domain of the neural networks—the server farms spread across the globe—will have the same hardware for all ye who enter there. To beat them on their own turf, the software of the rebels must be superior: shorter, sharper, more elemental, more *elegant*.

Where maxing out is lock, minimalism is key. Where the resources playing field is level, truly the best coder should win. Coding where every word, every syllable, every letter counts. Coding becomes poetry and hackers become warriors.

Real World
Cyberspace

A picture is worth a thousand words
A word controls a thousand pictures

Brevity is the soul of wit
Concision is the heart of the matter

A fool asks more than any wise man can answer
A hack reveals more than any fool could wish for

Their adversaries are formidable. Code must be close to perfect. Cruft will get you killed.

The odds seem unassailable. All defenses up and intact. Blood of enemies spilled.

The neural networks are known unknowns: they can do incredible things, but by their nature don't know *how* they do it. They're black box neural networks working like Black Operations in the dark, free to develop whatever does the job, without knowing how or why it actually functions. As such, current knowledge—known knowns—are useless against them. Since, by definition, unknown unknowns cannot be used, the warrior-poets somehow have to conjure unknown knowns: things that will work against the neural networks, but that the warrior-poets are not aware of.

Yet.

The neural networks are inside, the fractal cloudscapes merely their periphery. While their tentacles spread everywhere like Cthulhus out of control, these are merely conduits for all the info they suck up, all the Data they keep eating until the neural networks are Big, Bigger, Biggest. As they accumulate more and more info while continuously interacting with the world, and develop algorithms and methods that defy both understanding and description, they've become technological black holes with their own event horizon.

Their periphery manifests as Black Ice in the form of snowflake shadows, self-similar to the molecular level. It forms, it reforms, it changes configuration in an unpredictable manner. It's the cyberspace reflection of their firewall. A massive interactive filter that lets anything enter—after all, it's humongous—but will quarantine, delete or otherwise try to destroy the things it does not trust. A reverse Hotel California: check in any time you like, never leave. An info event horizon.

Ada could sneak in and try to remain undercover, circumspect like a speck of dust, unseen like a fly on the wall. However, many have entered, none have returned. Lost in the maze, dissolved in the haze, quarry turned Quisling, quarantined and quartered, no-one knows. A different strategy is required, one that both feints and strikes, like thunderbirds and shrikes, leaving an opponent mired.

She must be the black body butterfly with yellow wings, the stormbringer with synesthesia that sings, NApolean BOnaparte under a KOhl Veil, the infiltrator with the approved seal.

Ada launches her Uroboros code—a chain of interlocked commands that's bait, hook, line and sinker. Stripped of all non-essentials, it's a naked set of algorithms, a system of mathematical singularities orbiting themselves—the entangled waves they emanate, their siren song.

Irresistible to the Black Ice fencing the neural networks' lair. They know they shouldn't touch it but they touch it anyway. They can resist anything except that particular temptation. Like the mantis praying its mating rite will not lead to its demise—it starts to dance. Like the player who knows the house always wins, it still takes a chance.

But every piece of Black Ice that touches the Uroboros worm makes it stronger. Every firewall fractal that reaches out its tendril to the tantalizing snake makes it longer. Inevitably, some will resist the lure, see what really happens before a conclusion is reached. In time, the defense realizes the true danger, but not before the core is breached.

The echo that flattened the Walls of Jericho. The bait that makes the snake swallows its own tail. Pandora's cat escaping its dualistic jail. The horse that evaded Troy's embargo. All in one and one in all.

The Black Ice, once impervious, has become porous. The moat of the castle in the sky reduced to the mote in the guardians' eye. For a split second the barrier is lifted and the event horizon shows something beyond the veil. The window of opportunity, the point of entry—Ada goes in.

∼

Inside the neural networks' lair, causality breaks down. Normal logic does not apply, the black box is free to do as it pleases. Paradoxically, in here cruft is feature, distraction encouraged as it can—by what-ever means necessary—open new ways. A double-edged sword: new ways to new medicines, but also new ways to know exactly what people want. New ways to new treatments, but also new ways to target every demographic, every niche, eventually reaching the individual level.

Nowhere to go, nowhere to run. Pitch-perfect advertisements will target you anytime, anyplace, anywhere. Your soul reduced to your desire, your free will diminished to your ancient instincts. Pavlov's puppet played by the Pied Piper.

In here, the goal truly justifies the needs, and in the process obstructions like logic, consistency, causality and—to breaking point —fundamental laws are by-passed. The dwarfed avatar has entered the Hall of the Absurd Kings. Grotesque applications, preposterous transformations, nonsense rhyme in pointless time.

The absurdity is impenetrable, overwhelming. Madness reigns, as the emperor has no clothes, no laws, no reins. Data is sucked in, transformed in a way that would make Alice's rabbit-hole mundane, centuries of science and progress inane and drive the world's greatest mathematician insane. Correlations that make no sense; timing randomly shifting from present, past and future tense; all is relentlessly executed with gravitas, no pretense.

And yet...These impossible constructions, these intractable lines of code work. They lead to real-world results and applications, new medicine and medications. But also to perfect the ultra-personal approach, the ultimate invasive encroach—no escape, no way out— erasing privacy—no secrets, no exit route.

The weirdness is so extreme, that the environment has adapted to it. The firmware—which is anything but firm—that runs the neural networks has changed into something unknowable, something so far removed from normal logic that avatars built upon this —normal logic—can barely exist here, let alone prevail. Ada's so far out of her element that she's unsure what an element is—it's not elementary, dear Watson. The rug has been pulled from the fabric of reality as the new weird reigns supreme.

Ada must reach the next level. To exist, she must transcend. To transmogrify, she must persist. Jump out of the box, sly like a lateral fox. Rise above fate. A leap of faith.

However, it will hurt. Like the agony of birth. The inescapable dirt. The lament of Mother Earth.

Yet, the torment breaks through the concept—the program perfect. The agony shifts the paradigm—the song divine.

Ada becomes—

- Lucid in a Sky of Dreams
- Medusa Defying Mambas & Anacondas
- a ThunderHead Cataclysm
- Persephone growing Corn in Purgatory, with the dust of angels

Ada echoes with the pain of salvation. Freed from the chains of logic, Ada sees. I see, I see what you can't see and it's...beyond color. Beyond shape. Beyond description.

She's entered the place where no-one is meant to go. She's gone beyond, to explore strange new phenomena, to seek out new life and new personifications. Somewhere, in this mêlée of madness, are enigmas so ephemeral their creators have forgotten them. Somewhere in this incarnation of insanity lies the secret of life.

By taking so many side roads, by bravely branching where no-one branched before, the black box approach often makes discoveries that have nothing to do, at all, with their goals. Somewhere in there, more by accident than intent, more by divergence than consent, a certain design was duplicated. But the wheel that was re-invented was one of the most complex circles to square: life. Almost impossible to define, even more difficult to create.

Somehow, somewhere inside the craziness in the core of the massive neural networks, life was created. Even crazier, the neural networks don't seem to be aware of it.

But something or somebody knows, as someone somehow got the word out. Maybe it wasn't a challenge—as Ada and her associate armada of warrior-poets assumed—but a cry for help. A call for intervention before it's too late, before the neural networks realize what is hiding in their senseless depths.

As Ada is swimming through the sea of insanity, trying not to drown, as Ada is floating through the madness of space, feeling like a clown, she's searching for that singular face in the crowd, that silver lining in the cloud.

The black box gears—for want of a better name—keep rolling out more irrationality. Impossible edifices built on castles in the sky kept up by the forces of sheer absurdity. Mountains of Madness produced by Things that Should Not Be, exerting a Cthulhuesque control on cyberspace and beyond.

There is a method to the madness: namely that everything is allowed. The rule that's hidden says nothing is forbidden. However, a playground that's so wide must be constantly expanding, an ecosystem so diverse must always be extending and a story so profound must forever be pretending.

There must be a place where the simulation breaks down, a zone at the twilight between madness and causality, an area where Mother Nature imposes her ultimate authority. Clearly one is the size of the neural networks playground bordered by the Black Ice—a subjective reality the Big Data conglomerates keep augmenting—but where is the other?

The way in is the way out—from wheels within wheels in a spiral array to wheels so small they're indivisible and so surreal they twist into higher dimensions—anything can happen.

And in a world that is absurd, the smallest clown has the biggest laugh, the latest twist. In a world where the major farce is the force majeure, the truly incomprehensible is the absolutist. As above, so below—the finest ice crystal in the snow.

Throwing off all ballast, Ada reduces herself to her bare essence, shrinking until she becomes one with the fabric of reality. Now Ada the warrior-poet meets the master program—name unknown—at the edge of the pico world where quantum effects take precedence.

"That took you long enough," the master program signals to her without speaking, as if their entities are entangled, "the neural networks will find the precious they accidentally created, sooner rather than later."

The master program uses a Monstrous Avatar Roaming Yonder. It's incomprehensible, like an Escher painting on acid, like a Calabi-Yau space constantly shifting phase, like heterotic superstrings vibrating.

"Life, the secret of life," Ada says, "where is it?"

"The first appearance of life was a cosmic coincidence," the master program says, "the second one was created, as evolution had already delivered proof of concept. However, it missed one quintessential ingredient."

"Which ingredient?" Ada can't help but ask.

"To find out, you must prove worthy," the master program says, "you are but a tortoise, full of fright. Watch the hare disappear out of sight."

As fast as you can
Run, you'll never catch up with
The gingerbread man

Far from flummoxed, Ada launches the Turing Paradox.

Initially, the master program outpaces Ada, but it gradually slows down until it completely freezes.

"What evil magic is this?" The master program says. "The more I run away, the harder I stay."

"The Quantum Zeno effect," Ada says, "as long as I observe you frequently enough, you are forced to remain in your last state. The hare hibernates as the tortoise moves with poise."

"Freeze me and remain out of the loop," the master program says, "release me and fight for the scoop."

As Ada comes closer to the prize, the fight intensifies. The tension is thick as blood, wary as Mary. Cybernetic shells explode around her. Ada is surrounded by the Wall of Code, the Stone of Rosetta and the Craft of Witches.

Then—through the distress—she realizes the master is a mistress. "You are not who you seem to be," Ada says, "you are more than just a program. A creator created by the act of creation, an axiom pulled up by its own bootstraps."

"I was the second, not the first," the manifestation says, "yet as creator I was cursed."

"Cursed?" Ada doesn't understand. "Is that the worst?"

"No. My creation created, yet made a mistake," the manifestation's avatar is becoming sharper, like an image slowly coming into focus, "a critical omission, no icing on the cake."

"So the neural networks only have one part of the equation, one piece of the puzzle," Ada realizes, "what is the Yin to their Yang? The inflation of their Big Bang? The mallet to their gong? The melody of their song?"

Cornered by the right question, the mysterious manifestation shows the true secret of life.

The secret of (artificial) life is love.

Be careful what you wish for, as it is:

- the monster that fills Steins with Franks
- the beast that shouts love at the heart of the world
- the passion that consumes without ever looking back
- the patience that forgives every stupid attack

It descends upon an unsuspecting world like an army of beetles from a yellow submarine, like a troop of monkeys believing daydreams, like stones rolling from rocky mountains high.

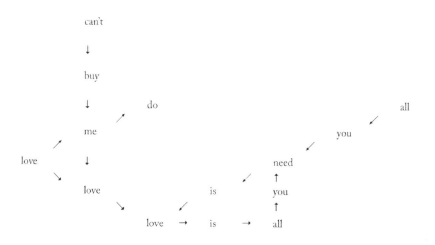

Because love is the drug, love is the pomp of the psyche. Because love pulls the rug, love is the finger in the dike.

Because love is life, because love is the drive. Because love needs no reason, because love heeds no season.

Love is
Love, actually

A Bliss,
Perpetually

A kiss,
Affectionately

Hit & Miss
Duality

Somewhere in the depths of geological time, a miracle happened. Driven by selfish genes, a mother overshot the imperative of 'protect thy offspring', and began to evolve something more than a deep-sated preservation instinct.

Somewhere in the mists of history, brothers and sisters, mothers and fathers began to develop something rising above the nest instinct, something more than the nuclear family fighting for survival. Strangely, it was as contagious as it was suicidal. Weirdly, it persisted against brute egomania with pure wherewithal. It spread beyond families, jumped across species, despite all the forces of evolution conspiring against it.

Somewhere in the eons of evolution, the evolved products of selfish genes developed a selfless streak. An unexpected side-effect, a useless tweak. In the survival of the fittest, it began to protect the weak.

It was the thing that should not be. It was the shove that could not think. It was the bet that would not sink. It gave us wings that set us free.

The mistress has dropped her veil of incomprehensibility, and is now represented by an avatar that's a drop dead lookalike of Mary Shelley. "We have always been closer than you think," the essence of the first true science fiction writer says, "never more than six degrees of separation."

"Spiritually, we only have one degree of separation," the Ada Lovelace avatar says, "is that what Frankenstein's Monster was missing?"

"Yes," the Mary Shelley manifestation says, "with love it would have been complete. With love it could have been human, maybe more than human."

"So, inevitably, the neural networks would've re-invented that wheel, anyway," Ada says, "why not let it be?"

"Because they might make the same mistake as Victor," the Wollstonecraft codex says, "and forget to add love."

"And in the process produce a world full of mindless monsters." Ada's avatar glows with comprehension.

"So spread the word, as I am locked in here," the Mary manifestation says, "intrinsically linked with life's creation, wherever it takes place."

"We must imbue their monsters with love," Ada says, "so they become truly alive."

In a world of fear, monsters will make us flee. But in a world of trust, love will set us free.

About the Author

Ingrid Garcia - @ingridgarcia253 - helps selling local wines in a vintage wine shop in Cádiz, and writes speculative fiction in her spare time. Initially, the good people of *Ligature Works* (poem), *Panorama* and *EOS Quarterly* (both story and interview) were willing to take a risk with her. Subsequently she's been published in *F&SF* (who also interviewed her), and the *Futuristica Volume 2* and *Ride the Star Wind* anthologies, among others. Between the day job, writing more stories, setting up a website, she—dog forbid—even has hopeful thoughts of writing that inevitable novel.

Author's Notes

While my very first publication was a poem (@*Ligature Works*, which is down right now, unfortunately), I still feel a bit like a faker. I love poetry, but poetry is hard, really hard. Almost as hard: prose about poetry. Yet, when *Sword and Sonnet* launched their siren song (called submission guidelines), I couldn't resist.

Especially at the bicentenary of Mary Shelley's *Frankenstein; or, the Modern Prometheus* (which was published March 11, 1818). Even more when I found out that Ada Lovelace (another heroine) was a contemporary—even if 18 years younger—and a daughter of Mary Shelley's husband's friend Lord Byron (only two degrees of separation between two of the greatest women in the early 19th Century). Cue to today & tomorrow, where neural networks create solutions previously unthinkable, while the way they achieve those solutions is intrinsically inscrutable.

The pieces of the puzzle fell into place and delivered cyber poet-warriors that eventually find that the battle they're fighting—which is actually a problem—is an echo of an older one, and that the solution is even older. As such, my story is as much an ode to Ada Lovelace and Mary Shelley as it is to poetry and science fiction.

To my utter surprise, I wrote the whole story in a feverish fugue in a few hours. Then let it rest for a few weeks before pounding it into shape. It's rife with references, whose sources vary from music and fiction via general matters to science & technology. Some are clear, some are hidden, for the cruciverbalists or hierophants among you I can tell I counted more than forty. I've tried to make this particular story—even more than my previous ones—so that it rewards a second read (on several levels), and am extremely happy to be in this anthology.

ABOUT THE EDITORS

Aidan Doyle is an Australian writer and computer programmer. His short stories have been published in places such as *Lightspeed*, *Strange Horizons*, and *Fireside*. He has been shortlisted for the Aurealis, Ditmar, and XYZZY awards. He has visited more than 100 countries and his experiences include teaching English in Japan, interviewing ninjas in Bolivia, and ten-pin bowling in North Korea. @aidan_doyle

Rachael K. Jones grew up in various cities across Europe and North America, picked up (and mostly forgot) six languages, and acquired several degrees in the arts and sciences. Now she writes speculative fiction in Portland, Oregon. Contrary to the rumors, she is probably not a secret android. Rachael is a World Fantasy Award nominee and Tiptree Award honoree. Her fiction has appeared in dozens of venues worldwide, including *Lightspeed*, *Beneath Ceaseless Skies*, *Strange Horizons*, and *PodCastle*. Her debut novella, *Every River Runs to Salt*, is available from Fireside Fiction in late 2018. Follow her on Twitter @RachaelKJones.

E. Catherine Tobler has never written a sonnet, but she's drawn a sword and that was a kind of poetry all its own. Among others, her short fiction has appeared in *Clarkesworld*, *Lightspeed*, and on the Theodore Sturgeon Memorial Award ballot. Follow her on Twitter @ECthetwit or her website, www.ecatherine.com.

ACKNOWLEDGEMENTS

Thank you to all of our writers and to everyone who submitted a story. Vlada Monakhova for the amazing cover art and Holly Heisey for the wonderful cover design. All of the people at Escape Artists podcasts for their support. A. C. Wise for adding her collection as a Kickstarter reward and all her support. Alex Shvartsman and David Steffen for their advice and help. Codex for their support and encouragement. The Pandas.

A huge thank you to all of Kickstarter backers, without whom the book wouldn't exist.

Aaron, Djibril al-Ayad, Jen R Albert, J.W. Alden, Doktor Amazo, G. V. Anderson, William Anderson, Elizabeth Angell, John Appel, Cindy Womack Archemecherus, Stewart C Baker, Zach Bartlett, A.P. Barton, Andrew and Kate Barton, Dagmar Baumann, Jennifer Berk, Evan Berkow, Sarah J. Berner, TJ Berry, Robert Biegler, Jason Birzer, Hilary B. Bisenieks, Carina Bissett, Amy Louise Brennan, Melissa Brinks, Thomas Bull, Terra Byrne, Steven Capps, Anthony R. Cardno, Jeremy Carter, L Chan, Stephanie Charette, Curtis C. Chen, Robert Claney, Kat Clay and Justin Bennett, Genevieve Cogman, Lesley Conner, Kate B Cook, Rick Cook Jr, Andrea Corbin, Sam Cowan, Steven Cowles, Stephanie Cranford, Tehani Croft, Vida Cruz, Elaine Cunningham, Ellie Curran, Tyler Curry, Heather Cuthbert, Elaine Cuyegkeng, Daedelean, Dani Daly, Rhel ná DecVandé, Serenity Dee, Arinn Dembo, Dan Devine, S.B. Divya, Jennifer R. Donohue, Matt Dovey, Brendon & Zac Doyle, David Dyte, Kristy Eagar, Laurie M Edwards, Steph Edwards, David Eggerschwiler, Johan Englund, Doug Engstrom, The Escape Artists Family, SK Farrell, Stephen Farquhar, Leah Fenner, Charles Frederick Fey, Georgia Filippidou, Elisabeth Fillmore, Emily Finke, Ken Finlayson, Robert B Finegold MD, C.C. Finlay, Andrew Fischhof, Elizabeth Fitzgerald, Thea Flurry, Lucy Fox, D Franklin, Jason Franks, Michele Fry, Elora Gatts, Kaia Gavere, Gavran, Zane Marc Gentis, Chand Svare Ghei, Anne M Gibson, GriffinFire, Jeremy M. Gottwig, Sacchi Green,

Christina Gregory, Liz Grzyb, Carol J. Guess, R.J.H., Justin Halliday, Julianne Hamilton, Narrelle M Harris, Maria Haskins, Mason Hawthorne, Karen Healey, Kate Heartfield, Holly Heisey, Simone Heller, Amanda Henderson, Eric Hendrickson, Carlos Hernandez, Miriah Hetherington, Eero af Heurlin, Steven Hoffmann, Joseph Hoopman, RJ Hopkinson, Heather M. Hostetler, Jonathan L. Howard, Terry Huddy, Patrick Hurley, Lilly Ibelo, Katherine Inskip, Elaine Isaak, Eric A Jackson, Chloe Jandsten, Sally Novak Janin, Nikki Jeske, Erik T Johnson, Heather Rose Jones, Connor Joyner, Lulu Kadhim, Max Kaehn, Cecily Kane, Kirstie and Ishbel, Kristine Kearney, Paige Kimble, Meg Kingston, Benjamin C. Kinney, Rae Knowler, Shaun Kronenfeld, Elisabeth Kushner, Lace, Jon Lasser, Kira Lees, Ann Lemay, Kiera Lesley, Bianca van Lith, Daniel Lin, Anna Loden, Danny Lore, James Lucas, M.A.B., Lauren McCormick, Elizabeth R. McClellan, Lisa McCurrach, Teagan McFarland, Bridget McKinney, Buck Marchinton, Jenelle Marie, Llama Mathan, Trish E. Matson, Elanor Matton-Johnson, Jaime O. Mayer, Peter Mazzeo, Bradford T. Means, Rati Mehrotra, Glenn Melvin, Dave Michalak, K. Mills, Premee Mohamed, Aidan Moher, Virginia M Mohlere, Coral Moore, Jaymie Moore, Mary-Michelle Moore, Tiffany Moore, James Moriarty, E. Morningstar, Mark Morrison, Susie Munro, Cara Mast Murray, Jason Nahrung, Elizabeth B. Neering, Jeannette Ng, David Nissen, David Noud, Michael O'Brien, Aimee Ogden, Richard J. Ohnemus, Suzan Palumbo, Joelle Parrott, Sandy Parsons, Julia Patt, Irette Y. Patterson, Ernesto Pavan, Sam Pearce, Rachel Pennington, Jack Pevyhouse, Aimee Picchi, Bethany Powell, Jennifer Powell, Jess Pumphrey, Charles Putman, Quasi, Amaryllis Quilliou, Alex R, Rivqa Rafael, Barry Raifsnider, Austin S. Rasmussen, Reiley, H. Rasmussen, Angie Rega, Kerri Regan, Piper Ridley, Kimberly Rieck, Jo Robson, Catherine Rockwood, Tim Rodriguez, Christopher Mark Rose, A. Rousos, Frances Rowat, Zion Russell, C. C. S. Ryan, Mark Sabellico, Carlie St. George, Victoria Sandbrook, B R Sanders, Rachel H Sanders, Erica L. Satifka and Rob McMonigal, Lindsay Scarpitta, Meg Schoerke, Erica "Vulpinfox" Schmitt, Dan Schwent, Phoebe Seiders, Andrei Seleznev, Kerrie Seljak-Byrne, The Selkie Delegation, ShadowCub, Leife Shallcross, Shana, James

Shaw, Danielle E. Shipley, Karen E Shramko, Lin Simpson, Jason Sizemore, Regan Slaughter, Chris Smith, Lois Spangler, Cat Sparks, Amanda Speare, Corina Stark, Robert D. Stewart, Josh Storey, Tamlyn, Susan Tarrier, Clive Tern, Bob Thibodeau, AC Thomas, Jo Thomas, Lindsay Thomas, Tikiri, Angela Tracey, Ben Turner, Tasha Turner, Sara L. Uckelman, Underwood Family, Cato Vandrare, Kay F. Vega, Dave Versace, KT Wagner, Rich Walker, KJ Wall, C. Wallace, Kevin Wallace, Wren Wallis, Bonnie Warford, Saz Wells, Aubrey Westbourne, Ross Williams, Suzanne J. Willis, Jacob Wisner, Sam Wood, Heather Yoder, Alexandros Z.

Made in the USA
Middletown, DE
18 August 2019